THI

They waited, and minutes seemed to crawl by. Then, activity within the fortress startled the commandos and thunder rumbled within the base.

Bolan and the other veterans of Vietnam immediately recognized the sound of helicopter rotor blades. The whirlybirds rose from the base. Two craft headed south. Another pair rose as soon as the first cleared the area. Although small, the choppers were equipped with machine-gun mounts and aerial rockets.

"They must have picked up McCarter and Grimaldi on radar," Bolan whispered as he watched the copters vanish beyond the treetops. "Those four have been sent to take out our friends' gunships."

"Can we warn them with the radio?" Manning asked tensely.

"They'll know in a matter of seconds, anyway," the Executioner declared. "Our guys in the sky are on their own—and so are we if they can't get past those four flying killers."

Other titles available in this series:

STONY MAN II
STONY MAN III
STONY MAN IV
STONY MAN V

DON PENDLETON'S
MACK BOLAN®
STONY MAN VI

A GOLD EAGLE BOOK FROM
WORLDWIDE®

TORONTO • NEW YORK • LONDON
AMSTERDAM • PARIS • SYDNEY • HAMBURG
STOCKHOLM • ATHENS • TOKYO • MILAN
MADRID • WARSAW • BUDAPEST • AUCKLAND

If you purchased this book without a cover you should be aware that this book is stolen property. It was reported as "unsold and destroyed" to the publisher, and neither the author nor the publisher has received any payment for this "stripped book."

First edition March 1993

ISBN 0-373-61890-5

Special thanks and acknowledgment to William Fieldhouse for his contribution to this work.

STONY MAN VI

Copyright © 1993 by Worldwide Library.
Philippine copyright 1993. Australian copyright 1993.

All rights reserved. Except for use in any review, the reproduction or utilization of this work in whole or in part in any form by any electronic, mechanical or other means, now known or hereafter invented, including xerography, photocopying and recording, or in any information storage or retrieval system, is forbidden without the permission of the publisher, Worldwide Library, 225 Duncan Mill Road, Don Mills, Ontario, Canada M3B 3K9.

All the characters in this book have no existence outside the imagination of the author and have no relation whatsoever to anyone bearing the same name or names. They are not even distantly inspired by any individual known or unknown to the author, and all the incidents are pure invention.

® are Trademarks registered in the United States Patent and Trademark Office and in other countries. TM are Trademarks of the publisher.

Printed in U.S.A.

CHAPTER ONE

Fog drifted across the oil derricks from the North Sea. Ramon Cazazo smiled as he looked at the dark, blurred shapes of the iron towers. Most would view these ghostly images, shrouded in the gray mist, as sinister. Cazazo regarded the scene as ideal conditions for success. If the fog clouded his view of the oil derricks, it would also help conceal his approach.

Cazazo tugged on the hood to make certain his ears were covered. He had to be able to hear clearly, but he wanted his ears shielded from the cold, damp wind. His gloved hands held a Czech-made Skorpion machine pistol, the weapon feeling as familiar in his grasp as the handshake of a close friend.

Five other hard men accompanied the Venezuelan across the rocky surface of the Scottish coastline. All wore dark field jackets with hoods. They carried automatic weapons, pistols and knives. Cazazo was also known as "El Cuchillo," the Knife, and his weapon was a special instrument of death. A trench knife, based on a World War I design, was sheathed on his belt. The double-edged blade was ten inches long. The handguard to the bronze handle could serve as brass knuckle-dusters, and a steel stud at the butt could also be used at close quarters. It was Cazazo's favorite weapon. He'd never shoot an opponent if he could use the knife instead.

A man known as Roger Nielson led the group. He was familiar with the area and the oil rigs. Cazazo followed and the others tailed behind him. Their rubber-soled boots moved silently across the rugged terrain. No one spoke. Lights at the windows of the shacks and bulbs strung along the derricks cut through the fog around the rigs. A tall wire fence protected the British petroleum operation, but it wasn't electrified or equipped with an alarm system. The security guards weren't patrolling the property. They remained in their shacks, huddled by heaters to combat the bone-numbing cold.

The security at the oil rigs had formerly been a greater concern. Radical elements of the Scottish Nationalist Party had threatened to attack the wells in the 1970s when English engineers were put to work at the derricks instead of hiring Scots who needed the jobs. There had also been fear that the Irish Republican Army might target the wells. However, the site had been unmolested for years, and security was no longer a vital concern.

Cazazo was about to show the British what a serious mistake they had made. Nielson led the group to a section of the fence concealed from view of the security guards by rows of barrels. He removed a pair of clippers from his web belt and cut the wire on a portion of the fence. The others stood watch, weapons held ready, until the hole in the fence was complete. They filed through the gap and headed for their designated positions within the base.

The guards had to be taken out. They carried only clubs, but a shotgun was kept in each shack. Cazazo moved to one guard station while a Frenchman named Gounod headed for the other. The Venezuelan saw the door to the shack open as he approached his quarry, and dropped into a crouch by the side of the little structure. He pressed the Skorpion to his chest with one hand to prevent it rustling against cloth while his other hand gripped the handle of the trench knife.

A figure emerged from the shack. Bundled in a long coat, the guard was still identified by a badge on his saucer cap. His head was bowed as he marched forward, flashlight in hand. He didn't notice Cazazo until the terrorist suddenly rose in front of him.

Cazazo lashed out with his knife. The greatcoat presented a problem because the thick fabric could prevent the blade from piercing flesh deeply enough to be effective. He used the knuckle-dusters instead and punched the guard in the face. The bronze fist smashed the man's nose, crushing cartilage, blood splurting from the mashed nose as the guard staggered backward, stunned by the vicious blow.

The terrorist stepped in and rammed a knee into the man's groin and swung the trench knife again. The metal knuckles crashed into the side of the guard's face. Bone cracked and the man's jaw broke.

The guard dropped to the plank walk. Cazazo knelt beside his fallen opponent and adroitly slit his throat. When the man's death throes had stilled, Cazazo released the body and wiped the blade on the dead man's coat before returning it to the sheath on his belt.

Gounod dealt with the other guard. He simply kicked in the door to the shack while the man was still seated at his desk. The Frenchman pointed a silenced MAB pistol at the startled guard's chest and calmly shot him twice through the heart.

The terrorists approached the derricks in a horseshoe pattern. Engineers and riggers were busy on the platforms at the base of the derricks. Clad in yellow slicker coats and hard hats, the workers watched the steady churning motion of the drills. No one saw Cazazo and three other terrorists creep along the pier to the platforms.

An engineer, with a pair of laborers, turned his head and saw Nielson and another armed figure. The terrorists opened fire and sprayed the workers with 7.65 mm rounds. The barrage of gunfire hurtled the engineer backward into the iron frame of a derrick. One rigger toppled over a handrail to plunge into the freezing sea below. The third man fell back onto the platform, his chest riddled with bullet holes.

Cazazo and a second gunner reached the other platform. The Venezuelan triggered his Skorpion and slashed a stream of bullets across a pair of riggers. They crumpled as another rigger desperately threw a large wrench at the terrorists. Cazazo glimpsed the tool and ducked. It whirled above his head and sailed into the chilly waters beyond.

The other terrorist responded with a French MAT-49 submachine gun, 9 mm slugs sparking against iron girders and ricocheting near the fleeing oil rigger, who dashed for cover by a generator. The terrorist anticipated the move and nailed the man before he could reach shelter. Struck by three parabellum rounds, the man collapsed to the platform and slipped across the slick surface to a large coil of thick chains.

More employees of the petroleum company heard the gunshots and emerged from shacks on the shore. Gounod and a fellow terrorist were ready for them. The pair opened fire with automatic weapons to bring down three unlucky oil workers and drive the others back into the buildings. The French terrorist took a grenade from his belt, yanked the pin and tossed the bomb at the shacks. The explosion blasted windows with shrapnel and tore loose part of a roof.

"*¡Mantener a distancia!*" Cazazo declared with approval. He realized none of his companions understood Spanish and repeated the statement in English and French. "Keep at bay! *¡Se tenir à distance!*"

He headed for the base of the derrick at the center of the platform. Cazazo opened his jacket to remove a canvas pack hooked to his web belt. He unzipped the bag, removed three kilo blocks of plastique and set the charges next to the pumping drill.

His companion joined him and unloaded another trio of blocks from a pack. They prepared the charges and linked them together in a semicircle around the drill. Cazazo set the timer to a detonator for one minute.

Nielson and another terrorist carried out the same procedure at the other derrick. All four saboteurs ran from the platforms to join their companions. The combined group fired their weapons at the shacks to keep the petroleum personnel inside as they jogged to the gate.

A tossed grenade blasted the gate off its tracks. The hit team kicked through the broken barrier and kept moving. They heard the explosions and glanced back at the derricks. The iron towers toppled into the sea, and oil splurted from the funnels. Black ooze poured into the water.

The platform burst into flame. The plank walks burned, and the fire spread to the barrels and storage tanks. Metal containers burst, spilling more crude oil into the North Sea. Cazazo smiled as the clouds of dense black smoke rose above the wreckage.

It had begun.

YUMI NAKADAI WAS frustrated with his job as security officer at the Hagiwara Chemical Company. The pay was better than most security guards made, but Nakadai's income was still less than that of virtually any other employee at the plant, with the exception of fellow guards who had worked there for a shorter period of time. There was little chance he'd get another promotion, and he had probably risen as high in the ranks as he could hope to at the job.

Like everywhere else, in Japan everyone wanted a job that would include a high salary and prestige. Nakadai had neither as a security officer. The Hagiwara plant was also a boring assignment. He usually just walked around the place, rattling doorknobs and checking for fires. If it didn't cost the company less to hire guards than to pay the insurance costs without security personnel, Nakadai wouldn't even be there.

The technicians studied gages and worked control panels. Nakadai didn't understand what they were doing as he passed the huge silos and a maze of pipes connecting machinery with chemical storage sections. Perhaps, he thought bitterly, he wouldn't be working as an underpaid security officer if he knew about such things.

The best jobs in Japan were given to those with the best qualifications. Those individuals did well in school, and their families could afford to send them to colleges and trade schools. Nakadai had been a less than average student, and his education was adequate only for low-level employment. He could look forward to a future that might well be worse, but would almost certainly be no better.

Those unpleasant thoughts haunted Nakadai as he walked along the tile floor of the chemical-processing center. He moved into the corridor, still brooding about his cruel fate. Suddenly a figure appeared before him. Nakadai gasped and his eyes opened wide in fear. A tall man dressed in a gray *gi* jacket and trousers confronted the security guard. Nakadai recognized the stern, angular face and fierce almond eyes; he'd seen this face in a recent magazine article about terrorism. Photographs of ten of the most notorious international terrorists in the world accompanied the article. The face of Arashi had been among them.

Known as "the Storm," Arashi was a former member of the Japanese Red Army. Reported to be disillusioned with the extremist politics of this organization, Arashi was said to be a free-lance assassin, willing to work for anyone with enough money to hire him. He was considered to be one of the most dangerous men in the world and was believed to have personally killed at least fifty people.

"Watch out!" Nakadai exclaimed as he raised his flashlight as a club.

Arashi's gloved hand grabbed the handle of the *katana* thrust in his belt. The samurai sword slid from the scabbard as the terrorist stepped forward. He delivered a cross-body slash with a single fluid motion, the blade striking Nakadai before he could move. Razor-sharp steel cut the security officer under his raised arm.

The pain and shock to the body was so great that Nakadai was paralyzed. The flashlight fell from his trembling fingers as blood gushed from the terrible wound. Arashi slammed a kick to Nakadai's torso and knocked the dying man to the floor.

Knowing that the guard would never get up again, Arashi headed toward the technicians. The men in white had heard Nakadai's shouted warning and turned to see the guard's body sprawled on the floor, surrounded by a growing pool of blood. Arashi held the sword in one fist as he drew a Nambu pistol from shoulder leather. He pointed it at the startled employees.

"Good afternoon," the terrorist greeted with a curt nod. "Stay where you are and don't move."

The technicians froze in place and slowly raised their hands in docile surrender. The killer's voice was calm, and he spoke in a conversational manner. Yet the blood on his sword and the corpse of Nakadai left no doubt the threat was genuine. Two other men dressed in gray appeared from the archway. Like their leader, they carried weapons.

Arashi barely glanced at his comrades. Without a word he shot the closest technician through the heart. The others followed his example and opened fire. Bullets and buckshot tore into the workers and sent their bodies hurtling into the machinery and pipes.

"Enough!" Arashi told his men. "You know what to do now. Get to work!"

His comrades moved quickly. They'd been chosen for the mission because they had experience working in chemical plants and knew how to operate the equipment. Arashi didn't understand such things. His knowledge of technology was limited to fundamental use of firearms and explosives. The terrorist didn't favor such instruments of destruction. He preferred to kill with a sword or his bare hands.

He believed he absorbed strength and spiritual power from each opponent he killed. The energy of their lives was gone, and Arashi thought he claimed it. Energy, like vibrations or electricity, was best absorbed through solid contact.

The others would consider his belief absurd superstition, but Arashi didn't care what they thought. He had trained them in martial arts and urban guerrilla combat, yet they didn't have the hearts of true warriors. The pair understood Western technology. They believed in machines and hardware. They were Japanese, but they had been tainted by the Occidental influences Arashi blamed for crushing the fighting spirit of Japan.

In his opinion Japan had become a nation of spineless merchants. His countrymen were no better than prostitutes who sold worthless factory-made merchandise to a world as corrupt and greedy as Japan. Arashi believed his country deserved to suffer for these moral failings. Indeed, some misery and hardship might show Japan the error of its ways and force the people to reconsider the path that threatened to transform them into a contemptible imitation of the Americans.

He had welcomed the opportunity to personally command the terrorist forces for this "edification." The fact the despised nations of the West would also be punished pleased him even more.

"We have finished," one of the henchmen announced proudly as the pair approached. "The chemicals have been rerouted to fill the silos outside the building. We need only set the charges and blow up the silos to pour the contents into the ocean and the air itself."

"The others have certainly put the explosives in place," Arashi declared, and checked his wristwatch. The operation was proceeding on schedule. "We must go. Time is running out, and we don't want to be here when the bombs go off."

THERE WERE PROBABLY worse jobs than being the captain of the largest garbage scow on the East Coast, but Marty Lampert didn't know what they might be. It sure seemed as if he'd been assigned the shittiest duty in the history of New York City trash disposal. There was some pretty stiff competition for that number-one slot. Not that anyone would deliberately set out to achieve it.

Lampert was a native New Yorker and had spent almost all of his fifty-one years in the Big Apple. Every year the city seemed to get worse. The crime rate continued to escalate, the population kept getting bigger and the cost of living got higher. Every year he figured things had gotten as bad as possible, but events proved him wrong.

He figured the problem was all the outsiders who kept moving into the city. Immigrants still headed for New York like moths drawn to the flame. Half-wits from all over the United States swarmed into New York. Aspiring writers, would-be actors and ambitious young stockbrokers all thought they could hit it big in the Big Apple. Add to that the regular wave of tourists and traveling indigents, and it guaranteed the city would always be overcrowded with people Lampert figured didn't belong there.

One thing was for sure—the people of New York produced tons of garbage. Every other corner on the streets of Manhattan seemed to be marked by a stack of overstuffed plastic trash bags and cardboard boxes loaded with rubbish. The city had a major problem with garbage, and getting rid of it wasn't easy.

Which was why Lampert was hauling a huge flatboat loaded with garbage down the Hudson. Sea gulls swooped over the piles of stinking cargo. The birds were welcome to anything edible they could find in that mess, Lampert figured. At least the gulls had some idea of what to do with some of the garbage, which was more than could be said for the city officials who had ordered the trash loaded onto the scow.

They had done something similar to this a few years earlier, Lampert recalled. Just dump all the garbage onto a boat and send it down the river. Eventually somebody would let you dump the crap somewhere. Brilliant, Lampert thought sourly.

Still, it was a job. Lampert planned to retire in another year or two. He could use the cash to add to his savings. He glanced at rows of skyscrapers along the east tip of Manhattan. The only structures he recognized were the Empire State Building, the World Trade Center and the South Street Seaport Museum. Odd that he had lived in the city all his life and still knew relatively little about the buildings and history of New York.

Big deal, Lampert decided. He knew about people and hard work. He knew how to survive in the dog-eat-dog city. Lampert also knew how to get the hell out of New York and set up a new life somewhere that wouldn't be a lunatic asylum disguised as a metropolis. One of these days he'd leave the city and never come back. One of these days...

The explosion blasted the bow of Lampert's tugboat. The bridge collapsed beneath him, and glass shattered all around him. Lampert was cut to ribbons as he plunged through the gap. The water rushed into his open mouth, silencing his screams. A second explosion erupted, and the water became a churning whirlpool. Garbage and other debris were spewed across the river.

JOÃO SILVA WATCHED the scene of destruction with satisfaction. The Brazilian peered through the eyepiece of a periscope as he sat in the pilot's chair of a diminutive submarine. He had carried out the attack personally because there could be no mistakes. He trusted no one but himself to handle the assignment.

Silva had helped to design and to build the minisub. He knew the exact range of the torpedoes used to destroy the tugboat and smash the hull of the flatboat attached to it. The mountains of garbage had been blown from the giant scow and into the water. The trash mingled with the wreckage and seemed to transform the entire bay into a giant cesspool.

"Very good," Silva murmured, congratulating himself.

He worked the controls with ease, and the submarine dived deeper. Silva turned the nose to face the open sea and accelerated the speed of the sub to maximum level. He had to move quickly, but was confident he'd be far from the scene of destruction.

And he was confident that the others would also be successful. Cazazo and Arashi were experts in sabotage, assassination and terrorism. Their targets would be as unprepared as the garbage scow had been. The attacks would certainly baffle, alarm and confuse the nations where the incidents took place.

The world would soon know the reason for these terrorists attacks. Then they would truly know the meaning of fear.

CHAPTER TWO

Mack Bolan held the Beretta 93-R in a Weaver combat grip, left hand cupped under the butt of the weapon in his other fist. He walked along the row of plywood shops and houses, frames of building fronts with windows and doorways cut in the flimsy wood.

A shape popped into view at an archway. Bolan glimpsed the masked face above a painted gun in a cardboard fist. He snap-aimed the Beretta and fired two shots, bullet holes appearing in the wide forehead of the target. The figure fell from view, and Bolan continued to walk the combat practice range.

It was a Hogan's Alley-style setup. Police and the FBI had used similar ranges for training personnel in the use of firearms in a simulated combat situation. Of course, Bolan had plenty of genuine experience in combat. The warrior known as the Executioner had learned his skills in the U.S. Army and had seen his first battlefields in the jungles of Southeast Asia.

Bolan was already a superbly trained fighting man, but he realized it was important to maintain his skills and keep that warrior edge well-honed between missions. Hogan's Alley was little challenge for the Executioner. Yet he took the exercise seriously because he knew he couldn't afford to take anything for granted. His marksmanship had to remain at peak level, and his reflexes needed to stay sharp and ready for any emergency.

A horn bleated a signal to cease fire. Red flags suddenly appeared on every building to make certain the shooter knew to hold his fire. Bolan obliged and shoved the Beretta into its holster.

"You got a perfect score, Striker," the voice of John "Cowboy" Kissinger called out from a bullhorn. "But you'll have to wrap it up for the day."

"Somebody else want to use the range?" Bolan inquired as he approached Kissinger. "We might try some competition. Speed up the targets. Maybe see who can score the most head shots."

"Nobody wants to use the range," Cowboy replied. "The big guy is calling a meeting. Something has come down from the White House."

Bolan nodded. The "big guy" Kissinger referred to was Hal Brognola, the director of Stony Man operations and the liaison with the White House.

"Good luck, Mack," the weapons expert said as he headed for his regular station. "Watch your ass out there."

"I always try to."

The warrior reached the main house and punched in the numbers to the coded access door. The steel portal opened, and Bolan entered the building to be met by Carl Lyons at the threshold. The big, blond captain of the Able Team commando unit nodded in a silent greeting. He and Bolan went back a long way.

"You heard?" Lyons inquired, already sure of the answer.

"Yeah, but I don't know what it's about."

Both men walked to the steel door to the computer rooms, which opened before they could punch in the access code. Aaron Kurtzman met them at the door. The Stony Man computer expert looked at the pair as he rolled back his wheelchair. A terrorist bullet had paralyzed Kurtzman, yet he still seemed like a giant even in the chair. His old nickname, "the Bear," was still appropriate.

"Hal is waiting for you guys downstairs," he announced. "Better move it. Katz is already at the table."

"Hello to you, too," Lyons said dryly, but he realized the situation must be serious for Kurtzman to skip all social niceties.

"I already got my work to do," Kurtzman replied gruffly. "Go find out what you got to handle and then come see me. I should have something useful for you by then."

Bolan and Lyons made their way through the maze of computer equipment to the elevator in a corner of the room and rode the car to the basement level.

The elevator doors opened. Hal Brognola looked at the pair as they stepped from the car. The number-one federal officer in the country chewed an unlit cigar as if trying to grind it out of existence. Brognola's shirtsleeves were rolled up, and his necktie was at half-mast. He waved Bolan and Lyons to the conference table.

Yakov Katzenelenbogen was already seated at the table. The middle-aged one-armed Israeli was the unit commander of Phoenix Force. Katz used the steel hooks of the prosthesis attached to the stump of his right arm to tear open a pack of Camel cigarettes. The Israeli's expression remained tranquil as he turned to face his fellow warriors. Bolan and Lyons knew that Katz's nonchalant appearance didn't mean that he was unconcerned about the reason they'd been called to the War Room.

"Okay, guys," Brognola began as he moved to his seat at the head of the table. "We've got one hell of a mess to deal with. You might have already guessed what part of it is about."

"Afraid not," Bolan answered. "I've been out of circulation the past couple of days."

"Figured you might have caught the news on TV or the radio," Brognola explained. "Somebody sabotaged a tugboat and garbage scow in the Hudson only a mile or so from Manhattan."

"Are you kidding?" Lyons asked. "A garbage scow is supposed to be a vital concern to America and national security?"

"You know me well enough to know I don't call an emergency conference for a joke," the big Fed said gruffly. "That boat was an enormous vessel. Tons of garbage were dumped into the bay when the scow was hit. It caused serious pollution in the waters. Environmental experts claim it will take weeks if not months to clean up the mess. It will also cost several million dollars. That's the most optimistic and conservative estimate they've been able to come up with so far."

"You said it was hit," the Executioner commented. He figured Brognola wouldn't have used the term unless it was specific and important to the incident.

"Damn right," Brognola confirmed with a nod. "Hit by two torpedoes. Believe it or not, eyewitnesses say the garbage scow was attacked by a submarine."

"A submarine?" Lyons echoed, startled. "Are they sure? That's not typical hardware even for the biggest and best-armed terrorist outfits."

"I know. The evidence that's been put together so far indicates the scow really was attacked by torpedoes. FBI, Justice, NSA and the Organization of Naval Intelligence are all looking into it. Leo was already contacted, and I sent him to New York to get us inside the investigations."

Leo Turrin was another Stony Man member. A former wiseguy in the Mob, Turrin had become one of Bolan's allies back in the bad old days of the war against the Mafia. The Executioner had nearly taken him out before discovering that Leo was deep under cover.

"But it's more than just the incident in New York," Katz stated. The Phoenix commander had already received a partial briefing before the others arrived.

"That's a fact," Brognola said. "Two other similar attacks occurred, at a chemical plant in Japan and an oil well off the coast of Scotland."

"You think these are all connected?" Bolan asked, frowning. "Were all these attacks carried out by submarine?"

"To answer the first question, yes," the big Fed replied. "The second gets a no, but the targets and the results of the terrorism were almost identical."

"So all the attacks caused extreme levels of pollution, as well as general destruction and loss of lives," the Executioner guessed.

"You got it. They have an oil spill in the North Sea that's almost as bad as the *Exxon Valdez* disaster in 1989. All the chemicals from the attack in Japan have caused even worse problems there. A lot of that stuff is toxic. People can't get close to it due to poison fumes. All these incidents occurred within the past two hours."

"Somebody is deliberately attacking the environment?" Lyons asked. "Sort of similar to the way Saddam Hussein had oil wells and tankers bombed during the Gulf War. Dumped millions of tons of oil into the Persian Gulf."

"That's what the President thinks," Brognola stated. "So far, nobody has taken credit for the terrorist attacks, but we figure we'll hear from them pretty soon."

"Yeah," Lyons commented. "You'll hear from every chicken-shit extremist group and crackpot, as well."

"It shouldn't be too hard to weed out the majority of the false claims," Katz told them. "These attacks are the work of a large international network of professionals. If they make contact, they'll include details that will make it clear they're responsible."

"You said 'if they make contact,'" Brognola said. "Does that mean you don't think they will?"

"It just means I don't know enough about the enemy to try to guess what they'll do," the Israeli explained. "These incidents don't sound like the sort of sabotage generally conducted by espionage agents working for an Intelligence agency. They'll probably make contact and give the governments of the United States, Japan and Great Britain a list of demands. Most likely they'll want political prisoners released, troops pulled out of some country or something like that."

"Japan doesn't have troops stationed in other countries," Bolan reminded him. "Not much point in conjecture when we don't have enough information to work with. The President must want us in the field or he wouldn't have called."

"And that's where you're going," Brognola confirmed.

Barbara Price entered the War Room from the coded access door. The lovely lady member of the Stony Man outfit was the primary mission controller. She carried a clipboard and scanned attached sheets as she approached the table.

"I contacted Schwarz and Blancanales," she announced. "They're on their way to New York."

"So I'd better get up there to join my guys," Lyons commented. "Is Leo working with the Justice Department or FBI on this one?"

"He's still using the Justice cover, but he's got White House authority so the other Feds and local cops will have to cooperate with him," Brognola answered. "You, Gadgets and Pol will have the same sanctions from the President. Anybody gives you a hard time, tell Leo and he'll contact me. If I can't take care of it, the man in the Oval Office will."

"Sure hope so," Lyons replied. "Isn't Gary Manning in Canada? Thought he was on a camping trip near Lake Winnipeg."

"Winnipegosis," Price corrected, checking her notes. "That's another lake in the province of Manitoba. The Bear is trying to contact him on a shortwave radio frequency."

"Manning is our best explosives expert," Lyons explained. "I could use him to evaluate the alleged torpedoes used to sink that garbage scow."

"Explosives were used at all the terrorist attacks," Price told him. "Manning is Phoenix Force, and they'll need all their people for their assignment in Scotland."

"Does that mean I'm going to Japan?" Bolan inquired.

"You've done missions there in the past," Price answered, "but so has Phoenix Force. I had to decide who was best qualified for all the assignments. Phoenix has an advantage in Scotland because they've worked a mission there recently and David McCarter is part Scot. According to his file, he spent some time in Scotland before he joined Stony Man."

"Hopefully that will be an advantage," Katz said with a sigh. He was aware that McCarter wasn't the most agreeable person, and anyone he knew in Scotland might not be eager to help him.

"Now," Price continued, "I almost decided Phoenix would be better for the assignment to Japan, but I noticed on the last mission to the Land of the Rising Sun they were assisted by an individual outside Stony Man. A guy who worked on a couple other missions, although he isn't a member of any government agency."

"You mean Trent?" Brognola inquired.

Price nodded. "John Trent. He's an expert in martial arts, speaks Japanese fluently and he's probably spent as much time in Japan as in the United States."

"I never worked with Trent, but I've heard good things about him from Yakov and the other members of Phoenix," Bolan commented. "The guy is a civilian. He doesn't do this sort of thing as a profession, and he doesn't have a security clearance."

"Trent is a good man and you can trust him," Katz assured the Executioner.

"I also thought Grimaldi ought to accompany Striker and Trent," Price added. "Calvin James would be another logical choice. He's a chemist, as well as a warrior. You might need his expertise in Japan. The target there was a chemical plant."

"Makes sense," Brognola said, approving of Price's choices. "Of course, James is one of your men, Yakov. Phoenix would be short one man, but I have to agree Calvin's skills may be put to best use in Japan."

"All right," Katz agreed, although he preferred keeping his teammates together on a mission. "Have the others been contacted?"

"Yeah," Brognola answered. "They'll be arriving here in another hour or two. We'll have their individual assignments ready when they get here."

"Okay," Lyons remarked as he got up from his chair. "I guess I might as well pack my bags for New York."

"Grimaldi is getting the chopper ready to fly you out," Brognola assured him. "Now, I know you guys are pros, but I want to remind you whoever the enemy is they seem to be a well-organized, well-armed outfit and big enough to hit three sites in three countries almost simultaneously. So far, they've killed more than two dozen people and caused millions of dollars in damages. The harm to the environment may prove to be even worse than the experts figure. These sons of bitches are obviously ruthless and don't give a damn about how many lives they ruin. They have to be stopped, gentlemen."

CHAPTER THREE

John Trent faced three opponents. He wore a black cotton *gi,* and a *bokken*—wooden sword—was thrust in a belt knotted around his lean waist. His opponents were dressed in white and also armed with *bokkens*. They all stood on the mat, facing one another, and formally bowed.

"Now!" Trent ordered as he grabbed the handle of his sword.

All four men drew their weapons. The men in white charged, swords raised in attack. Trent suddenly stepped backward, taking a long stride to the right. His closest opponent swung his sword too soon, the wooden blade missing Trent when he executed the quick evasive move.

Trent struck. His *bokken* delivered a cut as he stepped forward, the rock maple slashing air near the first opponent's right ear. Trent stepped past the man as his second adversary closed in and attempted a sword stroke.

Wood clashed as Trent blocked the attack. The blow shoved his opponent's blade away from Trent. He turned sharply and slashed the *bokken* across the opponent's jacket at chest level. Trent continued to move, body and sword in harmony as he smoothly stepped from the second opponent to face the third.

The last guy had been unable to attack because Trent had been too close to the other attackers during the battle. He swung a diagonal cut. Trent slammed his sword into his opponent's blade forcibly to bat it aside. He pivoted with the motion and whirled in a complete revolution. The sword rose as he spun and descended as he finished the move. He faced the man and slashed the *bokken* at the guy's neck. The wood blade stopped less than an inch from the flesh.

"Jesus, *sensei!*" the opponent rasped, his eyes wide as he glanced at the rock maple shaft that had come so close to the side of his neck.

"Control," Trent explained. "It's important to remain in control. Mind, body and spirit must be one for the techniques to be successful."

He stepped back and lowered his weapon. The three opponents followed his example. They bowed once again as the match was finished. Trent told them to join the other students seated on the floor at the edge of the mat, smiling at the attentive faces of his class. They were advanced students, but they still had much to learn.

"You see why footwork is important," Trent continued. "Evading a direct attack can give you an advantage in combat. It can also allow you to avoid being attacked on all sides by multiple opponents. You don't want to face them head-on or at the center. Try to strike at the opponent at the end of the group, either right or left."

Movement at the entrance to the dojo caught Trent's attention, and he turned to see a tall slender black man at the doorway. He immediately recognized Calvin James. Trent had first met the tough African-American warrior when James was a member of the San Francisco SWAT team. They'd been reunited several times in recent years, and a visit from James usually meant that Trent was needed to participate in a dangerous and covert mission for the supersecret organization James now belonged to.

A man Trent didn't know stood behind James. He was a big guy, tall and athletic. The stranger's face was hard, but Trent saw the strength of a true warrior in the man's eyes and firm jaw.

"*Sensei?*" a student inquired, wondering why his teacher had suddenly stopped the lesson when the newcomers arrived.

"Yes," Trent replied as he turned to his class. "Of course, in a real fight you can't always anticipate what your opponent or opponents will do. That's why a fighting style must be flexible to deal with any unexpected tactics from an opponent."

"But how can we prepare to fight if we don't know what to expect from an attacker we might meet on the street?"

"Learn the techniques and practice them again and again," Trent explained. "You have to imprint them into your reflexes so you can use them without thinking. There's no time to think in a life-and-death struggle. There's only time to act and react."

Trent gestured for the class to rise to their feet as he concluded the lesson. He was eager to find out why James and the stranger had come to his dojo.

"Of course," he reminded his students, "it's important to remain physically fit, alert and spiritually focused. You are all aware that the martial arts aren't merely for self-defense. Use the discipline, patience, concentration and self-control you learn here to help you in everything you do."

He dismissed the class and told them to call before coming to the next session because he might have to close the dojo for a few days. After the students left the building, he locked the doors and pulled down the shades.

"Glad to see you didn't decide to quit the school and move out of 'Frisco, John," James remarked as he shook Trent's hand.

"We call the city San Francisco, not 'Frisco," Trent replied, grinning.

"I never did get used to that when I was living here," James said with a shrug. He turned to Mack Bolan. "Mike Belasko, meet John Trent."

"A pleasure to meet you," the Executioner said as he took the hand of the martial-arts instructor. "I've heard some good things about you from Cal and four of his co-workers."

Trent nodded. Bolan studied the man's face. Despite his Anglo name, Trent was half-Japanese. The Asian cast of his dark eyes, oval face and straight black hair had been inherited from his mother. His handshake was firm, the fingers strong. Yet he didn't try to impress Bolan by squeezing his hand with painful force. So far so good.

"I guess you figure this isn't a social call," James commented, glancing about the dojo. "We need your help again."

"All right," Trent replied as calmly as if James had asked to borrow five dollars. "Where will we be going?"

He headed to his office next door, Bolan and James following. The room was small, with a large metal desk and two chairs. A cork bulletin board was mounted on the wall, covered with dozens of notes and messages.

"Japan," Bolan replied. "You still have connections there?"

"I have some friends who have connections," the man answered as he stepped to one end of the desk. "When do we leave?"

"I feel it's only right to warn you that this could be very dangerous," Bolan explained. "I know you've risked your life on previous missions that concerned the safety of the United States, but you're under no obligation to do it again. You can help us by giving us some names and addresses of people we can contact in Japan."

Trent smiled. "I'm afraid most of my friends in Japan would not cooperate with strangers. Especially foreigners. The only way I can help you is by going with you to Japan. I accept whatever danger might be involved."

He shoved the desk with both hands and pushed it across the room. He knelt by the exposed floorboards and reached inside his *gi* jacket. Trent drew a knife with a short, thick blade and inserted the tip into a crack between boards.

"We don't know what the risks might be," Bolan said truthfully. "Information is still being gathered, but I can tell you that the mission concerns threats to Japan, as well as the United States."

"I see," Trent replied with a slight smile. "You realize that Japan is the country of my birth, but America is the nation I belong to. You're right. I have a sense of loyalty to both the United States and Japan. Anything that threatens both is certainly something I will fight against."

He pried a loose board from the floor and used the knife blade to unhook a latch hidden beneath other boards. Trent opened a trapdoor to reveal a secret compartment. Inside lay two black canvas duffle bags and a sword with a black scabbard.

"You don't want to know anything about the mission?" James asked.

"All I need to know is which bag to bring," Trent replied. "One contains a .45-caliber pistol and a disassembled pump shotgun. If you'll supply me with firearms, I won't need to bring my own."

"We've already got that covered," Bolan assured him. "We've also got a passport, other identification papers and cards printed for your cover name."

"See, we were pretty sure you'd decide to come," James commented as he watched Trent select a bag and gather up his sword.

"Of course," the man said with a nod. "I am ninja. A ninja who teaches and doesn't actually use his skills for what he's been trained to do is a ninja unfulfilled. When do we leave?"

"There's a plane waiting for us," Bolan replied.

JACK GRIMALDI CHECKED his wristwatch. The others weren't late, but he was getting anxious. The Stony Man pilot had heard police sirens and had seen flashing lights on speeding squad cars headed to the heart of the city along Highway 101.

Japantown was located in that general area, Grimaldi thought, the section of San Francisco where Trent had his martial-arts school. He wondered if something had gone wrong with Bolan's meeting with the guy. Grimaldi told himself he was getting paranoid. Hell, the cops could be headed for Chinatown, the Presidio, Candlestick Park or Jackson Square. There could be trouble anywhere in the city.

Moments later he sighed in relief as he spotted the blue Toyota on the dirt road near the airstrip. Bolan and James sat in the front seat, but Grimaldi could barely see the blurred shape of the guy in the back. The car rolled through the open gate and slowed as it approached the pilot and the C-130 transport plane.

The Toyota came to a halt. Doors opened and Bolan emerged from the passenger side. James stepped from behind the wheel. Grimaldi had never met Trent, but the man getting out of the backseat fit the description of the guy.

"I got her all fueled up and ready to taxi," Grimaldi announced. "Climb aboard and we'll be on our way. The meter's running."

CHAPTER FOUR

"How's it going?" Rico Gomez asked as João Silva entered the room.

"Well," the Brazilian replied, not bothering to add the usual polite thank-you.

Silva wasn't concerned about appearing rude. He didn't like Gomez. The Colombian was cocky and crude. A produce of the streets of Bogotá, Gomez was a slum kid who had clawed his way to a high-ranking position in the second-largest cocaine cartel in Colombia. Silva figured that made him just another savage with more money and power than he had the ability to use with wisdom.

"You've traveled far," Gomez stated, trying to sound more concerned than he felt. "You should rest."

"I got some sleep on the plane," the Brazilian assured him. "Has Cazazo returned yet?"

"Yes," Gomez confirmed. "He arrived at the airport an hour ago. Some of your men went out to meet him."

"Good," Silva said with a nod. "Is Aguilar here?"

"I think he's in the den," Gomez replied. "Aguilar has been trying to follow the news on as many different international radio broadcasts as possible. Everything seems to be going according to plan."

Silva figured it was too soon to claim any major victories, yet he was pleased by his own successful attack in New York.

The news did sound encouraging from the assignments in Scotland and Japan. He was feeling a bit uneasy. Perhaps annoyed was a better term. Gomez and Aguilar were his allies, but he didn't care for the company of either man.

He found himself getting annoyed that he had to address them in Spanish. This was foolish, because he spoke their language and they didn't understand Portuguese. However, they were guests in Brazil and he felt they should make an effort to at least learn a few expressions in his language.

Silva realized it was an illogical resentment. The language difference was minor and just contributed to the main problems. Silva didn't like the business Gomez and Aguilar were in. Narcotics was a trade he regarded with loathing. Not that Silva was a candidate for sainthood, but he thought selling cocaine was beneath any man with a shred of honor.

Fatigue also might have contributed to Silva's sour mood. Although he'd told the Colombian he'd slept on the plane, Silva had gotten little rest since the mission began. He was forty-nine years old and no longer had the strength and vigor of his youth. There would be time to rest later, he thought as they headed for the den.

The building was designed for practical functions, but Silva had included a few concessions to aesthetics. He had to spend a great deal of time at the base and had no intention of living in a grim, ugly mausoleum. The walls were painted bright yellow and blue. The terrazzo floors consisted of ornately painted granite, and oil paintings decorated every room.

Guillermo Aguilar sat in a leather armchair next to a universal radio receiver unit. A balloon glass containing some brandy rested on the edge of the table beneath the radio. Aguilar gently puffed a cigar as he listened to a news broadcast in Spanish. He looked up as Silva and Gomez entered the room.

"The whole world seems to have taken notice of our attacks in the United States, Japan and Scotland," he announced, rising from his chair.

"Little doubt that would happen," Gomez commented with a shrug. "That doesn't mean they'll agree to our demands. We'll be very upset if we've spent so much money and contributed such efforts to this operation and it doesn't pay off."

Silva glared at the Colombian. "We've all invested a great deal into this operation. Some of us have been putting our lives at risk, as well as our money. Need I remind you that I personally carried out the attack in New York?"

"And we admire your courage," Aguilar assured him. "But Rico has a point. His organization in Colombia and my people in Bolivia have invested millions into this project. We are financing the bulk of the operation costs."

"I've put my entire fortune on the line," Silva declared. "My business is in jeopardy. Everything I've worked for my entire life will be lost if this fails."

"Life is risk," a familiar voice announced from the doorway. "Your life is not what you own. It is what you do."

The others turned to see Cazazo. The master terrorist entered the room with a silent, catlike stride. Clad in jungle fatigues and beret, he appeared ready for combat at any moment. Cazazo wore a gun belt with a holstered pistol on one hip and his ever-present trench knife at the other.

"If you do not put yourself at risk, your life is controlled by others," the terrorist continued as he approached. "We are trying to force the hand of the entire world to do our bidding. That requires enormous risk by all of us."

Silva nodded his agreement. Gomez and Aguilar didn't acknowledge the Venezuelan's comments. They didn't find the idea of risking everything, including their lives, appealing. The cocaine syndicates were involved with the project to increase their power, to create a safer environment for conducting their trade and to protect their money and personnel.

It was a bold and very dangerous venture, but the cartels wanted to stay in the shadows. If anything went wrong, they didn't intend to be directly linked with the conspiracy. Gomez and Aguilar were at the secret base in Brazil because the syndicates wanted representatives at the site to make certain their investments were being used for the purposes agreed to.

Cazazo's attitude was different from that of the others. He had no fortune to lose or family to care for. The terrorist was already a wanted man, hunted by Interpol and a dozen other law-enforcement agencies around the world. He seemed to live for killing and destruction. Whatever political ideals had once justified his violence had been discarded long ago. Cazazo was a killer who enjoyed his work, and he was very good at his job.

"Welcome back," Silva greeted the Venezuelan. "The reports we've heard about the missions in Scotland and Japan sound like everything went well. Are they leaving anything out that we should know about?"

"Nothing that could jeopardize our operation," Cazazo assured him. "I can't say for certain about Arashi's mission in Japan, but he is a very good operative and not apt to make mistakes. The media probably omitted some information about what type of explosives were used, how the sabotage was carried out. I killed one man with my knife and finished off a wounded opponent with the brass knuckles. I doubt the authorities shared those details with the press."

"Good," Silva said with a smile. "That will give us the sort of information we'll need to convince the authorities we're serious when we contact them with our demands."

"What did you do with the submarine?" Gomez inquired. "You didn't bring it back on the plane, did you?"

"Unfortunately I had to abandon it. A very expensive piece of equipment, but we'll make more. When this is over, we'll be able to afford to build an entire navy of submarines, battleships and aircraft carriers."

"And you'll make the profits on the manufacture of such hardware," Aguilar said, resentment in his tone.

"I am a military arms manufacturer and merchant," Silva said with a shrug. "Of course, I intend to make a profit by continuing in my business after the takeover."

"We'll all make a profit," Gomez declared with an unctuous smile. "An enormous profit. The rewards from this venture could make our current fortunes from the cocaine trade look like a pittance by comparison."

The idea that twenty billion dollars a year could be regarded as a pittance seemed incredible. Yet, if their plans were successful, they would achieve wealth and power of staggering dimensions. They would be impervious to their enemies and virtually allowed to do anything they wished. There would be no reason to fear the police, the military or the government. They would literally own and control these factions.

If everything went according to plan.

"You all realize they're looking for us," Aguilar remarked, glancing down at the floor as he spoke. The

Bolivian didn't want the others to see the fear in his eyes. "The CIA, British Intelligence and God only knows who else will be hunting the people responsible for these attacks on the environment throughout the world."

Silva grunted with disgust. He glanced at Gomez and noticed the Colombian shake his head. Gomez appeared to be amused by Aguilar's concern. No wonder, Silva thought. He was aware the Colombian cocaine cartels dominated the narcotics trade because they had always been willing to take more chances than their counterparts in Bolivia.

Although Bolivia produced more coca plants than Colombia, the Bolivian cartels relied on others to handle the distribution. The Colombians not only sold their own locally produced cocaine, but they also purchased most of the Bolivian-made drugs at what was considered relatively low prices when compared to the stunning profits made by selling the white poison to the legions of users in the United States.

Bolivia is a landlocked country and has no direct ports to the oceans. It is also located farther south than Colombia or even Peru. These geographical conditions presented problems for the Bolivian coke syndicates' ability to sell to the United States. They could manage if they were willing to accept the risks involved in moving large shipments of cocaine over long distances. However, the Bolivian cartels preferred to sell to others who came to their country rather than export the illegal products.

This same unwillingness to take risks was expressed in Aguilar's apprehension about their current operations. Silva had some difficulty getting the Bolivian outfit to back their scheme, but now it was too late for Aguilar and his people to pull out. The mission was already in progress, and there was no turning back for any of them.

"Guillermo," Gomez began with a chuckle, "you know how effective the DEA has been against our operations in the past. They send some helicopters to fly around the jungles and try to convince the public this is supposed to be successful in their so-called war against drugs. Who cares about the CIA or the British or whatever the Japanese might have for their national police? They won't be able to do anything to us unless we get careless."

"Then we can't afford to get careless," Silva declared. He looked at Cazazo and added, "You're an expert at evading the authorities. They've been hunting 'the Knife' for years without getting close to capturing you."

"On two occasions they got close," the terrorist said with a smile. "That limited success cost them their lives."

"I thought we agreed that we don't want any more killing than necessary," Aguilar said with a frown. "I know there's no way to avoid some deaths, but mindless slaughter is apt to cause the governments to respond with more vigor than any wise person would encourage."

"No one is trying to kill any more people than we need to in order to strike at the environmental targets," Silva insisted. "The greatest threat is the dangers to the air and water. That's what will force them to agree to our demands."

"They haven't agreed to them so far," Gomez commented. "In fact, we haven't even announced our demands yet."

"Don't worry. We will. First, we have to make certain the world realizes they are powerless to stop us and no place will be safe from us."

CHAPTER FIVE

Lieutenant Randall Perry popped some aspirin into his mouth and washed it down with orange soda. His current case was a royal pain in the ass, and it seemed to be getting worse by the minute. Perry had been with the NYPD for eighteen years, but he'd never been involved with a case like this one.

Whoever had blown up the garbage scow had stirred up a hornet's nest of trouble. Since the boat was attacked in the bay, no one could even agree on the jurisdiction. Perry's precinct was in the financial district of Manhattan at the east end near the river. The department was still trying to figure out who was best suited for the assignment and had dumped the case in Perry's lap until they could decide what else to do.

The Feds couldn't make up their minds, either. FBI, Justice Department, National Security Agency and the Coast Guard were all involved in the investigations. Perry wasn't impressed by most of these federal hotshots. The snotty bastards seemed to get in one another's way and didn't even try to cooperate. The Feds treated New York police as if they were a collection of uniformed morons who couldn't be trusted with more than a few fragments of information.

There was one exception among the big-shot government dudes, though. The guy called himself Leonard Justice. It was fake, of course, the cop realized. Too far-fetched to think an agent in the Justice Department would really have "Justice" for a name. But the little Fed knew his business, and he seemed to be the only one who could get everyone else to work together on this thing.

"Hey, Lieutenant," the Fed called from the doorway to Perry's office. "Got some guys here I want you to meet."

Perry nodded and gulped down the rest of his soda.

Leo Turrin knew the cop was tired and handling a truckload of stress, but he needed the insider knowledge and connections of the NYPD and Perry was the best available source at the moment. Turrin figured the lieutenant was a good cop. He'd read a file on him and knew the guy had risen through the ranks the hard way. He knew the men in his precinct and he knew the streets. He'd also know things that couldn't be obtained from police records, computer memory banks or official information centers.

"They with Justice or one of the other outfits?" Perry asked in a weary tone. He was about as eager to meet another federal agent as Custer would have been to find extra Indians at Little Big Horn.

"We handle all sorts of work for various agencies," Rosario Blancanales announced as he entered the room. "And sometimes they're working with us and don't even know it."

The compact, dark stranger smiled as he extended a hand. His expression seemed genuine, but Perry sensed the guy was a hardass. The cop had encountered enough tough Hispanics in the Big Apple to recognize Blancanales as one of that breed.

He didn't know how right he was. Blancanales was even tougher than Perry suspected. The Able Team warrior had survived the killing fields of Southeast Asia and dozens of deadly campaigns with Stony Man. Yet he could seem quite amiable and diplomatic. Blancanales had been nicknamed the "Politician" or "Pol" because he was adept at dealing with people.

"You sound mysterious, Mr....?" Perry began as he shook hands with the stranger.

"Garcia," Blancanales replied with a nod. "At least that's the name I'm using today. We are a bit mysterious, Lieutenant. It's necessary to do our kind of work effectively."

"Like Mr. 'Justice' here?" the cop commented, tilting his head toward Turrin. "Okay. I can live with that as long as you guys help solve this mess."

"That's why we're here," Turrin assured him. "We have authority directly from the White House. Doesn't get much higher than that."

"I'm impressed," Perry replied. "I'll be even more impressed if you guys can find out who the hell blew up that garbage scow. I'm just a plain cop who deals with run-of-the-mill killers, muggers, rapists and drug pushers. This stuff is out of my league."

"Hell, we're after criminals," Carl Lyons announced as he entered the office. "They might use some fancy hardware, they might spew political crap and their motives might be weird and twisted. But when all's said and done, terrorists are just another brand of criminal."

Perry looked at the big blond man. Lyons sounded like a cop, the sort of man the lieutenant could relate to. Somebody who spoke his language instead of the tight-lipped, arrogant and high-handed vocabulary of most of the Feds he'd encountered.

"Any idea who 'they' are?" Perry asked with a raised eyebrow.

"Sort of hoped you could help us with that," Lyons explained as he leaned against a wall. His jacket was open, and Perry saw the butt of a big revolver in shoulder leather. "Most of the Feds here are trying to get information about political extremists, foreign agents, all that shit."

"But that's not what you're doing?" Perry inquired with interest.

"We figure some locals had to be involved to know the precise route the boat would take," Blancanales told him. "Probably somebody who worked the docks or used to be with the crew of the tugboats that hauled garbage along the river."

"Makes sense to me," Perry agreed.

Hermann "Gadgets" Schwarz appeared at the doorway. Slender and a few years older than the other two members of Able Team, Schwarz didn't look like a commando. As his nickname suggested, "Gadgets" Schwarz was an electronics expert and a mechanical wizard.

Yet Schwarz was also tough and highly skilled in combat. Like Pol, he was a veteran of Vietnam. In fact, Schwarz and Blancanales had served together in Southeast Asia. They also worked together after leaving the service before becoming part of Stony Man. The ex-soldiers were teamed with Lyons, and they had operated as a professional unit ever since.

"Oh, man," Lyons groaned. "Will you lock the door? Anybody could walk in here and listen to this conversation."

"Hey, I just got here. Don't blame me," Schwarz said with a shrug as he closed the door.

"I just came from the FBI lab," he went on. "The explosives used in the torpedo were a pentolite compound. Pretty standard for military-shaped charges. The ONI is looking into it and trying to identify the type of torpedo used and what sort of submarine could have been involved."

"They might never be able to figure that out," Turrin said, unimpressed by the efforts. "We already know it had to be a small sub. Probably no bigger than a one or two vessel. Anything bigger would have been easy to track by sonar and probably wouldn't have been able to escape unnoticed."

"You were saying about an inside job?" Perry prompted, wanting the conversation to shift back to more familiar ground.

"Yeah," Lyons said with a nod. "Now, your investigation included questioning people at the docks. Standard stuff. You were checking on who was working for the tugboat company, who might be the enemies of Captain Lampert and his crew."

"I was looking at the case as a murder investigation," Perry replied. "The Feds pretty much laughed that theory out of the running. They said it was obvious the attack was environmental terrorism and had nothing to do with Lampert or any of his crew as targets."

"So you discontinued that line of questioning?" Blancanales inquired.

"The brass said I wasn't to buck the Feds. They don't want trouble with the FBI or NSA. Some guys with Justice are even members of the American branch of Interpol and came in here acting like they owned the precinct. My captain basically told me to give these people whatever they want and just let them run the show."

"We're in charge now," Lyons told him. "And we want your cooperation, Lieutenant. What we need is a variation of the investigation you already started."

"Okay," Perry replied. "So you don't rule out the possibility this was an elaborate murder plot?"

"Murder was committed," Schwarz commented, "but that was just because Lampert and his crew were in the way. The people we're after don't give a damn about human life."

"But we still need to know as much about the personnel working at the docks and those who worked there recently enough to know details about the garbage scow," Lyons added quickly.

"I've already got names collected," the lieutenant stated. "FBI didn't seem interested in running checks for me."

"They will now," Turrin assured him. "If I find those guys from the Interpol branch of Justice, I'll have them run a records check, too. Especially if we have any reason to suspect any of the dock workers might have international records."

"You think the terrorists might be foreign agents?"

"We don't know enough to make any guesses one way or the other," Blancanales stated.

"So what are we looking for?"

"Anything that might be suspicious," Lyons answered. "We'll have a better idea when we find something."

LAMPERT'S TUGBOAT and the giant garbage scow had departed from the piers along the west end of Manhattan, which had limited the number of potential suspects to be screened.

Not surprisingly, a fair number of men working the docks had been in trouble with the law at one time or another. A lot of tough characters could be found at the piers, and many had served time to prove it.

However, one name interested the Stony Man operatives more than any other researched by the FBI computer banks. A former employee at the harbor, who had briefly served as a crew member with Lampert, called himself Greg Harris. This wasn't his real name, and his social security card, references and background information listed on his job application were also false.

Unfortunately for "Harris," he had accidentally left a very clear fingerprint on his application form. The FBI was able to match the print along with the guy's physical description and came up with another name. "Harris" was really Greg Harrimon. He had a history of criminal behavior in Ohio that ranged from shoplifting to armed robbery and attempted murder.

Harrimon was supposed to stand trial for the latter charges, but he'd jumped bail in Cleveland and fled the state in 1990. He had disappeared without a trace.

He hadn't gone to work at the docks on the day of the attack on the scow and hadn't returned to the harbor to collect his paycheck the following day.

Perhaps Harrimon had decided not to return to the job because he'd guessed the police would be crawling all over the place and the fugitive feared he might be found out. Still, it looked like the closest thing to a lead Stony Man team had thus far.

Able Team learned that Harrimon was staying at a rundown boarding house in the Lower East Side. The Stony Man warriors arrived at the building as twilight claimed the sky.

Able Team mounted the wooden steps that led to Harrimon's third-floor room. The cracked and splintered boards creaked under their weight. The handrail was broken at the staircase to the third landing. The stench of garbage and urine was heavy as they climbed the stairs.

"Nice place," Schwarz muttered.

"The guy could afford something better than this on the salary he made at the docks," Blancanales commented.

"Yeah," Lyons agreed, "but this is the sort of place a person can disappear in. Nobody asks too many questions, and none of the neighbors wants to know what the others are doing."

"I just hope Harrimon hasn't already fled the coop," Pol said. "This is also the sort of place where a person can pack up and leave without attracting much attention."

"Let's find out," Lyons replied as he approached a door with the numerals 33 on the top panel.

The big ex-cop rapped a fist on the door. He heard footsteps inside the room and the sound of something striking the floor. He knocked again, but stood to the side of the doorway in case the guy inside panicked and started shooting through the door. The other two Able pros took care to stay clear of the door, as well.

"Mr. Harris?" Lyons called out. "My name's Larson. You don't know me, but I was told you work at the piers up on the west end."

There was no answer.

"I just want to ask you about getting work at the docks," Lyons continued. "See, I'm new in town and I need a job."

"I don't work there no more," a voice replied from the room. "Fuck off, buddy. I ain't the unemployment office."

"So just tell me what sort of work you used to do," Lyons insisted. "Maybe your old job is still open. It ain't gonna kill you to give me a little information."

"Go to the pier and bother them, asshole."

"I'd rather bother you. You're too chicken-shit to even open the door. I figure you'll tell me what I want to know eventually. I got all night, fella."

"I'll give you somethin' else!" the voice growled.

The door suddenly swung open, and a burly figure appeared at the threshold. His round face was framed by long, unwashed hair, and his expression was filled with anger. Although his belly suggested he was too fond of beer, the guy's arms and shoulders were thickly muscled. He had obviously been lifting more than beer mugs. A baseball bat in his fists added to the threat.

Lyons immediately stepped back and thrust a hand inside his jacket. Harrimon swung a wild stroke, but the bat missed Lyons as the commando moved out of range. Wood smashed a hole in the plaster as the Able Team leader drew his Colt Python from shoulder leather.

"Strike one," the warrior announced, and pointed the big revolver at his opponent. "You don't get three. Try again and you're out."

"Forever," Schwarz added as he aimed his own Colt at the attacker's head.

Harrimon looked at the muzzles of the .357s. His eyes opened wide with fear, and he dropped the bat. Lyons nodded and returned the Python to the holster under his arm.

"That's more like it. Let's talk, Harrimon."

"Harris," the guy replied as he raised his hands. "The name is Harris. Who the hell are you? Cops?"

"Who we are isn't important," Blancanales said. "And spare us the masquerade. You've been made, Harrimon."

"I want a lawyer. You're messing with my rights, man."

"Maybe we don't care," Lyons replied as he shoved a hand to the center of Harrimon's chest.

The push sent the guy across the threshold back into the room. Lyons entered, Schwarz right behind him. Pol remained in the hallway to stand guard. They left the door open.

"If you're gonna arrest me..." Harrimon began.

Lyons cut him off. "Shut up and listen. We know about Cleveland. We have enough to put you away for at least five years, and the courts in Ohio will probably convict you for the charges you ran from when we ship you back to them. That means you could be looking at fifteen to twenty behind bars."

"Not to mention another charge of assault with a deadly weapon," Gadgets added. "Two witnesses saw you swing that bat at my partner."

"Shit," Harrimon rasped. "What the hell do you want?"

Lyons glanced about the room. The place was a pigsty. A suitcase and a duffel bag were set against one wall. Lyons approached the luggage and opened the suitcase lid. Several adult magazines were stuffed inside, as well as a shaving kit and a toothbrush.

"Planning a trip?" he asked.

"None of your business. You got a search warrant? This ain't legal if you don't."

"All we need is permission from the landlord," Lyons said as he picked up the magazines. He discovered a thick pile of bills beneath them. "Looks like a lot of traveling money."

"There's no law against having money," Harrimon stated.

"You didn't even pick up your last paycheck," Schwarz remarked. "What happened? Win the lottery?"

"I ain't saying shit until I get a lawyer," Harrimon insisted.

"We're not placing you under arrest. We didn't show you a badge or claim to be police, did we? So you'd better think about whether you want to talk to us or if you're ready to die."

Harrimon stared at Lyons. The Able Team commander was sometimes referred to as "Ironman," and for good reason. Lyons was a big, powerful man, but his hardness was based from within. He was a tough character and Harrimon knew it—and also knew that the blond hardass was serious.

He decided to resort to the tactics he had always favored in an emergency: violence. Harrimon started to turn and suddenly whirled to throw a fist at Lyons's face. He had used this sucker punch numerous times in the past, and it usually worked. This time it didn't.

Lyons weaved away from the fist and quickly grabbed Harrimon's arm before the man could launch another attack. He pulled hard and turned to increase his opponent's momentum. Harrimon was thrown face-first into a wall. Lyons punched the guy in a kidney and stomped on the back of his knee. The dockworker groaned and slumped to the floor.

"You want to do this the hard way?" Lyons remarked. "Okay with me, pal."

Harrimon sucked air through clenched teeth and started to get to his feet. He considered trying to lunge at Lyons or Schwarz, but realized the effort would be in vain. He couldn't hope to take all three of them. Hell, he doubted he could even handle the big blond bastard.

"We'll get right to the big questions," Lyons began. "You gave information to the terrorists responsible for the attack on Lampert's boat and the garbage scow out in the bay."

"I don't know nothin' about that..." Harrimon began.

"Like hell you don't," Schwarz snapped. "We can try to wring it out bit by bit. If that doesn't work, we'll turn you over to the cops. You're already wanted by the law, and we'll make sure the Feds know you're involved in the terrorist attacks, too. They can screw you pretty bad. You'll be in jail, and they'll be able to do anything they want with you until you decide to cooperate."

Harrimon glanced at their faces, trying to determine if they intended to carry out their threats. He saw nothing but grim determination.

"Company!" Blancanales called from the hallway.

Schwarz turned to the doorway. Harrimon figured this was the best distraction he could hope for and lunged for Ironman's gun hand. Lyons sidestepped the clumsy attack and hooked his left fist to the side of Harrimon's jaw, then followed through by chopping the butt of his revolver behind the guy's ear.

"Stay put," he muttered to the senseless figure as he headed for the door.

Blancanales had spotted the men on the stairs, two nasty-looking characters dressed in dark clothes and hats, brims pulled low to conceal their faces. One wore a pair of dark glasses despite the gloom, and both carried weapons in gloved hands.

They also saw Blancanales stationed in front of Harrimon's room. Gun muzzles rose abruptly and Pol jumped for the cover of a doorway at the opposite side of the hall. Gunfire erupted from the stairs, bullets tearing into walls and doors.

The fury of the gunfire revealed that at least one opponent was armed with a full-auto weapon. Schwarz realized this as he knelt by the open door to Harrimon's room. He'd have to act quickly, and he couldn't afford to make a mistake or a barrage of slugs could cut him in two.

Schwarz hoped the enemies' attention was still directed toward Blancanales as he leaned around the doorway. He saw the muzzle-flash of a compact machine pistol in the fists of an opponent. He snap-aimed his Python and triggered two shots. The gunman's body jerked from the impact of the 158-grain Magnum messengers. His arms swung wide, and the Ingram subgun flew from his fingers as he fell back into a wall and slid from view.

Gadgets threw himself backward and rolled from cover. Pistol shots responded, and slugs chipped splinters from the door frame. Lyons moved to the doorway and fired his Python in the general direction of the enemy to try to force the gunman to retreat.

The man ducked low as the .357 rounds slammed into the wall above his head. He stayed low, almost sprawled along the top risers to the stairs, and pointed his H&K pistol.

His attention was no longer fixed on Blancanales, and Pol took advantage of this. He aimed his .357 at the gunner and squeezed the trigger. The big revolver roared, and his target's arm suddenly jerked in an unnatural spasm as blood oozed from the entrance and exit wounds caused by the Magnum bullet.

The gunman screamed, and his pistol clattered on the stairs. He slid down the risers to the landing, shattered arm clutched to his chest with his good hand. Footsteps pounded the stairs as another pair of armed men ascended the steps to assist the first hit team.

"These guys are like cockroaches," Lyons muttered as he joined Pol in the hall.

This time Able Team had the advantage. Lyons and Blancanales fired down at the new arrivals as the enemy reached the landing. Both commandos targeted the same opponent and blasted the first man with a double dose of .357 Magnum power. The guy toppled down the stairs, an unfired pump shotgun in his fists.

The second gunner swung a .45 automatic at the Able Team warriors. Lyons rapidly triggered his Python, the .357 round drilling the hardman in the torso. The high-velocity slug missed vital organs, but punched a punishing hole in the gunman's side.

The Magnum missile smashed two ribs, and the impact spun the guy off balance. He fired his pistol, but his aim was thrown off and the second .45 round plowed into the ceiling. The gunman didn't get a chance to try a third shot. He slipped to the edge of the landing, then plunged from the platform and fell down the stairwell.

Lyons and Blancanales saw the man drop two stories before he connected with a railing on the last flight of stairs. Rotted wood snapped and collapsed beneath his weight. He was down and he didn't get up.

"His back must be broken," Pol remarked, shaking his head. "That's an ugly way to go."

"Not too many good ones," Lyons remarked. He glanced at the gunman with a broken arm. The guy had passed out on the landing. "We need an ambulance. I don't want that son of a bitch to bleed to death before he can answer some questions."

"One question has already been answered," Blancanales stated. "We know Harrimon was involved in something bigger than running away from the cops in Ohio. Looks like this lead was the right one."

"Yeah," Lyons agreed without enthusiasm. "But it hasn't paid off yet."

CHAPTER SIX

The bright Caribbean sky was clear and warm. Hal Brognola inhaled the salt-laced air. The Stony Man boss had arrived at Owen Roberts Airport two hours after dawn. He was still on D.C. time and hadn't adjusted his wristwatch.

Brognola had been asked to go to Grand Cayman by the President because an emergency meeting had been set up by the British SIS. The Cayman Islands remained a British dependency, and the Security Intelligence Service had no trouble arranging a top security conference at Georgetown. They had also assembled representatives from Kompei and Sûreté, as well as a case officer with the American Security Agency.

The big Fed knew this meant the crisis was even bigger than it appeared... and it had seemed pretty goddamn big. Although the United States, Great Britain, Japan and France were allies, their governments kept secrets from one another. The Intelligence networks of those countries seldom cooperated. A lot of powerful people had to be very worried for an emergency meeting such as this to be put together on such short notice.

Brognola glanced out the window as the Saab rolled through the Pantonville area. The gingerbread houses surrounding the road were almost a hundred years old. The quaint setting was ironic, considering the reason for the Justice man's trip to Cayman. The driver barely spoke as he steered the car onto a side road and pulled into a parking lot.

"They're waiting for you inside, sir."

"Thanks."

The big Fed walked to a block-shaped brick building. The windows were shielded by thick metal shutters. Two large men, dressed in dark suits and straw hats, were posted by the entrance. They asked to see Brognola's passport. He obliged and they ushered him inside.

A slender, middle-aged man greeted Brognola when he stepped through the entrance. The guy's houndstooth tie and Cambridge accent labeled him as SIS before he verbally confirmed it.

"Hello, Mr. Smith," the Briton said as he shook Brognola's hand. "I'm Geoffrey Whitney, British Intelligence. So glad you made it. The others are waiting for us, including Mr. Garret."

"Garret?" Brognola repeated with a frown. "Is that the guy from NSA?"

"Yes. I thought you knew. I am a bit confused which organization you belong to. CIA? Perhaps Interpol?"

"Something like that."

"I see," Whitney replied, accepting the restriction of information with the ease of a man accustomed to dealing with people who never told him more than he needed to know.

They moved to a thick steel door, and Whitney punched in a series of numbers to a control panel. It was similar to the coded access doors at Stony Man Farm, Brognola noticed. He waited for the door to open, and both men entered a conference room.

Three men were seated at the oval-shaped table. Whitney introduced "Mr. Smith" to the others. They called themselves Moissan, Tanaka and Garret, but Brognola realized every man in the room was using a pseudonym. Whitney escorted him to a chair, then took his own seat at the head of the table. A television set was mounted on a nearby cabinet. A VCR was set atop the TV, and a remote-control unit was near Whitney's right hand.

"You might wonder why an officer with Sûreté is present at this meeting," Moissan began. "Two hours ago my country was also a target of terrorism."

"Yeah," Brognola replied, "I know. We got a report that a bomb exploded at a nuclear power plant in France. Some employees were injured. Not sure if anyone was killed, but at least there didn't seem to be any damage to the silos where the nuclear vessel and radioactive waste are stored. That's about all I know. The report was pretty sketchy."

"I'm surprised you know about it at all," Garret admitted. The NSA man seemed to resent the fact Brognola's sources of information were so efficient. "My agency only contacted me with fundamental details half an hour ago, and I didn't know the rest until Mr. Moissan told me."

"We try to keep up on current events," Brognola stated. "Have there been any leaks from the nuclear power plant?"

"Fortunately, no," the Frenchman answered. "However, two employees did die and another is in the hospital. I do not want to make light of these deaths and the suffering of the wounded man, but we are relieved that there was no radioactive spills or meltdown at the plant."

"Not this time," Garret added grimly.

"That's precisely what worries all of us, Mr. Garret," Whitney announced. "These terrorists are attacking the environment in all of our countries. They seem to be able to strike anywhere and anytime they wish. The bastards don't appear to favor any particular type of target or any set method. Nuclear plants, chemical-processing centers, oil derricks and even boats hauling large loads of garbage have been the targets so far. God knows where they'll hit next."

"I believe Mr. Smith does not know about the videotapes," Tanaka stated. The Japanese hadn't spoken until now. He seemed to be a quiet man who listened and thought carefully before contributing to a conversation.

"I know a videotape was delivered to the White House," the big Fed replied. "My sources also told me tapes were sent to the prime minister of Britain and Japan. I assume one was also received by the French president."

"Your sources are very good indeed," Whitney said with genuine admiration. "Do you know what's on the tape?"

"Not yet. To be honest, I just got the information about the tapes before I hopped on the plane."

"Well, here it is," Whitney said as he reached for the remote unit and jabbed buttons with his thumb.

The television switched on and the VCR began to play. Images appeared on the screen. A figure dressed in a field jacket and black ski mask sat behind a small metal desk. A trench knife was on the ink blotter in front of him. Sheets of paper were tacked to the wall behind him. The masked figure remained silent as whoever worked the camera closed on the signs.

Written on the paper were large black letters, printed with felt tip pen. Whitney read the messages aloud. "We carried out the assault on the North Sea oil derricks. The news did not mention certain facts. The knife on the desk was used to kill a guard at the site. The calibers of the firearms used were 9 mm parabellum and 7.65 mm.

Weapons included Czech-made Skorpion machine pistols and French MAT-49 submachine guns. Soviet-made F-1 hand grenades were employed, and the explosions at the derricks were set close to the drills.

"This should convince you we are genuine. We regret the need to use such extreme and destructive methods, but will not hesitate to do so again if our demands are not met.

"By now you must also know we have carried out similar operations in the United States, Japan and France. The damages caused will cost millions of pounds sterling. Future attacks will be even more costly and will cause permanent harm to the environment.

"We do not want to poison the air and water. We do not want to destroy your natural resources and soil. We do not want to kill thousands, perhaps millions of people and throw your economy into ruin. Yet, we will do this if our demands are not met.

"The government of the United Kingdom will pay us six billion pounds sterling a year. Part of these payments may be delivered in the form of military weaponry, computer equipment and other technical assistance, medical supplies and other methods that will be determined in the future. However, the first installment must be two billion in unmarked pound notes, gold or silver.

"We will give you the location for the delivery of the payment after you assemble at the United Nations to discuss our terms with the other nations contacted in this matter. You must publicly grant us a complete amnesty and immunity from prosecution and an iron-clad guarantee that no efforts will be made to retaliate for our actions or to deny us anything in our terms. Only then will we negotiate the delivery of payments and future arrangements for annual support by Great Britain.

"Failure to agree to this and to do as we demand will result in more attacks on your environment and that of your allies.

"Understand this—if we do not get what we demand, we will not hesitate to take action. We would rather destroy the entire world than fail. We also realize we have gone too far to stop now. Unless your country and the other nations involved agree to all of our demands, we will constantly be hunted by your Intelligence agencies and military forces. Eventually you would find us, but before that could happen we would have crippled your economy and slain most of your people. The rest of the population would have nothing left except a poisoned and polluted land in which to suffer every day until they died.

"Bear this in mind and do not allow pride to cloud your wisdom. The fate of this planet rests on your decision."

Whitney switched off the television. The whirl of rewinding tape was the only sound in the room for a few quiet seconds before Garret turned to Brognola and spoke.

"The President of the United States received a tape almost identical to this one except it included details about the torpedo attack on the garbage scow off New York," the NSA man explained.

"The same is true in my country," Moissan added. "Our president also received such outrageous demands. These terrorists are incredibly arrogant, as well as insane."

"Why do you think they're insane?" Brognola inquired with a shrug. "They have a goal, and they're going after it in a very methodical and premeditated manner. They may be the scum of the earth, but that doesn't make them insane."

"They have to be out of their minds to make those demands," Garret insisted. "There's no way the United States government will give in to blackmail."

"I assure you my government feels the same way, and I think we can assume the same is true about France and Japan," Whitney added.

"France and Japan don't need you to speak for them," Moissan said, obviously annoyed by the Briton. "Mr. Tanaka and I are here to represent our countries."

"Of course," the SIS agent replied with a nod. "I didn't mean to offend you."

"Might I point out," Brognola said, "that the terrorists' demands aren't as outrageous as they might appear at first. Even that crap about wanting amnesty isn't beyond possibility. How many times have we seen our governments decide to ignore state-sponsored terrorism when it became advantageous to have a hostile country for a temporary ally?"

"You think our leaders will agree to the demands of these terrorists?" Tanaka inquired. The Asian folded his hands on the tabletop and looked at Brognola as if sitting in a classroom of a particularly interesting teacher.

"I'm sure none of them want to. But they'll be getting pressure from advisers to cut a deal with these bastards if more terrorist attacks occur and we aren't able to stop them or locate their main base."

"So, what you're saying," Garret stated, "is we've got to move it and find the terrorists PDQ."

"We're already working on that," the big Fed replied. "I'm sure you guys all have people on this. I've already sent my best people to start hunting down the terrorists. The President has been in touch with the other leaders, and we've been assured of cooperation from SIS, Sûreté and Kompei."

"You're not suggesting our departments are incapable of handling this crisis without your help?" Moissan inquired, a veiled challenge in his tone.

"I'm saying we'd all better work together on this. This is the sort of mission my outfit specializes in."

"You really think they're that good?" Garret asked.

"I know they are," Brognola replied. "And for everybody's sake, they'd better be."

CHAPTER SEVEN

David McCarter drove the black BMW along the road to Aberdeen. The Briton's foxlike features displayed a broad grin as he accelerated to pass an Italian sports car. Rafael Encizo sat in the passenger seat. The Cuban commando glanced out a window at the green pastures.

Scotland seemed quiet and peaceful. Indeed, this impression was usually accurate, but Encizo knew that the most halcyon setting could be dangerous. Aberdeen was near the site of the oil derricks that had been a target of terrorism. It was the starting point for Phoenix Force's mission.

Encizo had arrived at Heathrow Airport ahead of Katz, James and Manning. The Cuban had been vacationing in the Mediterranean when he was contacted by Stony Man Farm. He headed directly for Great Britain and found McCarter waiting for him at the airport.

Aberdeen was large by Scot standards, although considerably smaller than Glasgow or Edinburgh. Yet Abderdeen retained a quaint, old-town quality typical of Scotland. Few buildings stood more than two or three stories high. The cobblestoned streets were better designed for horses and wagons than modern vehicles. However, a dark synthetic cloud hung above the city. The smog was evidence the city wasn't immune to the negative effects of twentieth-century industrialization.

McCarter and Encizo noticed that the majority of this pollution came from beyond the city limits. The thick black clouds rose from the sabotaged oil wells. It was a disturbing and sinister display. The sight was a reminder to the Phoenix pair of the importance of their mission.

The commandos located a boarding house at the edge of the city. McCarter parked the BMW, and both men walked to the manager's office.

The manager was a stocky, balding man who didn't seem interested in rising from the chair behind his desk. He remained seated while McCarter asked about a tenant named Brian Locke. The man grunted as if hearing the name suddenly upset his stomach.

"Always feared that one would be trouble," the manager said with a weary shake of his head. "Been at odds with the law in the past, you know. Got himself fired from the job at the oil drills, too. And jobs being so hard to come by these days."

"We know about that, sir," Encizo assured him. "We need to talk to Mr. Locke. What room is he staying in?"

"Number fourteen, but he isn't there now. Left about an hour ago. You can probably find him at the Black Boar. Spends a lot of time at that pub, he does."

McCarter asked directions to the pub. After supplying the required information, the manager turned his attention to a newspaper on his desk. The commandos realized this was a signal that the discussion was over. They thanked the man and left.

The Stony Man warriors were aware of Locke's background. He had previously served seven months of a two-year sentence for assault, and he'd been arrested on less-serious charges, as well. He'd been fired from the oil company because he'd been too difficult to get along with and had picked fistfights with fellow workers on more than one occasion. The company had let him go less than a month before the terrorist attack.

Following logic similar to that used by Able Team for their mission in New York, Phoenix Force checked the backgrounds of current and recent employees at the oil derricks. Locke seemed a promising candidate to be involved with the terrorists. McCarter and Encizo had gone to Scotland to look into this while the rest of the team would meet with SIS and Scotland Yard as soon as they arrived in London.

"Well, let's see if we can find this bloke at the Black Boar," McCarter mused cheerfully as they walked from the boardinghouse.

"Let's try to be diplomatic," Encizo urged, "not physical. We don't have any evidence Locke is a terrorist or connected with the people who attacked the oil rigs."

"I know. We're just going to talk to him. It'll all be as polite as a bloody tea party."

"Uh-huh," Encizo muttered, aware that his British partner wasn't the most subtle person he'd ever met.

The Black Boar was only two blocks from the boardinghouse. They found the place easily. Its sign sported a fierce boar head, with large curved tusks and a wrinkled snout. The Phoenix pair heard voices from the pub as they approached the door, the boisterous sounds laced with numerous obscenities.

They entered the pub and scanned the room. The men who formed a line along the bar and sat at tables were tough-looking characters who appeared to be accustomed to hard manual labor. Their hands were callused, and lines of hardship were etched into their faces.

Eyes turned toward the men in the doorway. The pub was a favored haunt of the locals, who tended to be suspicious of outsiders.

"You lost?" a burly man inquired as he rose from a bar stool and stretched his massive frame to full height.

He stood more than six feet tall, and his chest was as thick as a beer keg.

"I don't reckon we are," McCarter replied with a slight smile. "How'd you blokes like a round on us? Just to show a bit of good will."

"Cockney," a craggy-faced customer muttered when he heard McCarter's accent. He sipped some ale and added, "We ain't got slums here in Aberdeen. Don't imagine you'll feel at home here."

"You're trying hard to make sure of that," the Briton commented with a shrug.

Three men glared at McCarter and Encizo. They appeared to be ready to attack the newcomers at the slightest provocation. The others seemed less apt to join such a contest, but they didn't seem interested in preventing a confrontation. If violence occurred, they'd probably choose to watch.

"What the hell is wrong with you lads?" the bearded bartender demanded. He didn't want a brawl in his place and saw all the signs of trouble taking shape. "You're acting as if you have no more manners than a Welsh lawyer. These fellers come here for a drink. Ain't no law against that."

"Glad to hear it," Encizo said dryly as he approached the bar. "I know this won't increase our popularity here, but we're looking for someone. Anyone here know a man named Brian Locke?"

The men in the tavern became very quiet. Eyes shifted toward the craggy-faced guy, who stared down at his ale as if trying to forecast the future by gazing into the brew. The others looked away from him quickly, but they had already betrayed his identity.

"Well, hello, Mr. Locke," McCarter announced. "We'd like to talk to you for a minute or two."

"I'm busy," Locke replied, not looking at the strangers.

"Yeah," Encizo said, "we can see that. But you can either talk to us now or Scotland Yard later. They'll probably take more of your time than we will."

Locke turned sharply and stared at the Cuban. "Scotland Yard? What the hell does Scotland Yard want with me?"

"You used to work at the North Sea oil rigs. You know what happened there recently?"

"And because I've had some rubs with the law in the past, you figure I'm responsible for that?"

"Nobody is accusing you of anything," Encizo assured him. "We just want to talk."

"Fuck 'em," the big bull-like man declared with a sneer. "They ain't Scotland Yard. Probably ain't even coppers. Let's see a badge if they got any authority here."

"Nobody's talking to you," McCarter said, meeting the big guy's gaze without flinching.

"You ain't coppers?" Locke inquired, climbing from his stool. "Ian is right about that, ain't he?"

"Of course I am," Ian said with a grin. "These two are probably insurance investigators for the oil company. Who else would send a Cockney lowlife and a greasy wog to come lookin' for you here? Coppers know it was terrorists what blew up those derricks, but the company is tryin' to blame it on you, Brian. Save 'em insurance money somehow if they can claim it was the work of a disgruntled ex-employee than organized, professional terrorists."

"That's a pretty stupid comment," McCarter snorted. "Besides, we're not with the oil company or insurance."

"You ain't nothing and I ain't going with you," Locke declared as he slammed his mug of ale on the counter. "Now you just be on your way before things get worse."

"That won't make things any better for you," Encizo warned.

Ian stepped closer to the Cuban as two of his aggressive friends also moved from their bar stools. Locke seemed to linger near his place at the bar, allowing the other three men to form a shield between himself and the two strangers.

"Why, darkie?" Ian inquired with an unpleasant smile. "We ain't goin' to the hospital with a lot of broke bones."

"That's enough!" the bartender shouted as he produced an ax handle from beneath the counter. "I won't have you fightin' in here."

"Don't reckon it to be much of a fight," Ian replied.

"Hope you're right," Encizo said with a sigh.

He suddenly kicked Ian in the crotch. The big man gasped in pain and surprise. He began to double up, his mouth open in an oval shape and eyes bulging as if he were trying to imitate a frog. Encizo didn't give his enemy time to recover from the boot to his manhood. The Cuban quickly rammed his right fist into the larger man's solar plexus and followed with a left hook to his jaw.

The two clods who had elected to back Ian were distracted when their mighty comrade was abruptly knocked into the edge of the bar by the smaller, dark stranger. McCarter took advantage of this. He charged the closer man and thrust his head forward. The tough Briton slammed the hard frontal bone of his skull into the Scot's face, the head-butt stunning the guy. McCarter immediately shoved the bully into the second opponent and turned to thrust a side-kick into the first guy's torso.

Both Scots were driven backward by the kick and crashed into a table and chairs. Men and furniture toppled to the floor. Locke saw his protection was getting taken apart by the two strangers. He quickly grabbed his glass mug and smashed it across the edge of the counter. Locke held the handle in his fist, the sharp edges making it a deadly weapon.

"Put that down!" the bartender shouted as he waved his bat in a frenzied manner that was intended to threaten rather than cause physical injury.

Locke lashed out at Encizo. The Cuban saw the move and jumped back to dodge the vicious swipe of the broken glass. Locke snarled an obscenity and slashed a backhand sweep at Encizo's face.

The Cuban jerked his head clear from the path of the attack, and the jagged glass fist missed his face by scant inches. Encizo plunged his hand inside his jacket. He could have drawn his Walther pistol, but elected to grab another weapon instead. They wanted Locke alive and able to talk. Encizo didn't intend to shoot the surly Scot. He wasn't about to let the son of a bitch slice him to pieces with a broken beer mug, either.

Locke saw the blade in Encizo's fist. Light reflected along the blade of the Cold Steel Tanto. Ten inches long, the sharp steel was a fearsome weapon with a razor edge and a slanted tip. Designed in the manner of a samurai fighting knife, the Tanto was a high-quality weapon Encizo had used many times in the past.

"You don't want to take this any further, pal," the Phoenix commando warned.

Locke punched his glass-studded fist and tried to slash the sharp shards across Encizo's hand and wrist in an attempt to disarm him. The Cuban was a veteran knife fighter and easily avoided the attack. He raised his knife hand to dodge the stroke and swiftly snapped his wrist to bring the blade across the mug before Locke could withdraw his fist. Glass shattered, and the Scot screamed as fragments bit into his fingers.

Encizo hit him with his empty left fist. Locke staggered from the blow and lashed out with a kick. Encizo sidestepped the clumsy attack and slashed the Tanto low. The edge cut Locke at the calf and shin. The man cried out and dropped to his knees, clasping his wounded leg with both hands as blood oozed from the cut.

"Christ!" he exclaimed. "I'm bleedin' to death!"

"It'll take a long time for that to happen," Encizo said with a shrug.

The Cuban turned to see if McCarter needed help with the other opponents. One man the Briton had knocked to the floor started to rise. McCarter hammered the bottom of his fist into the junction of nerves where the shoulder connected with the neck. He then whipped a knee under the guy's jaw to knock him unconscious and sprawling across the floor.

The second opponent lunged from the floor and drove a fist into McCarter's abdomen. The punch caught the commando off guard and sent him two steps backward. The enemy Scot pressed his advantage and swung a ham-sized fist at McCarter's face. The Briton ducked the attack, and his opponent's arm whirled above McCarter's bowed head.

The Phoenix fighter moved in and raised his head swiftly to ram the top of his skull under the Scot's chin. The blow clashed the guy's teeth together hard and dazed him. McCarter hit him under the heart with a short right and swiftly moved his arm high to hook it under the guy's armpit. Then he turned and bent forward to send the Scot hurtling over his hip in an adroit judo throw. The guy crashed to the floor hard.

"Bloody half-wit," McCarter growled.

The bartender stared at the two formidable strangers, shocked by their swift and efficient combat skill. The other customers remained at the bar. None of them wanted to get involved in a fight with McCarter and Encizo after they saw the pair take out four opponents in a matter of seconds.

"Take your belt off," Encizo told the wounded Brian Locke. "I'll tie on a tourniquet to stop the bleeding. Then you're coming with us. Agreed?"

"For God's sake," Locke rasped through clenched teeth. "Anything you say! I didn't have nothin' to do with what happened at the oil derricks anyway."

"Then don't give us any more trouble," McCarter warned.

"Don't worry about that."

CHAPTER EIGHT

The little chrome-plated pistol was disassembled on the table as Guillermo Aguilar inspected the parts and carefully cleaned and oiled them. Although chrome was less susceptible to rust, Aguilar knew it wasn't immune and looked after the little Raven .25 autoloader.

João Silva watched with amusement as the Bolivian ran a cleaning rod through the short barrel. Aguilar inserted the spring under the barrel section and slipped the slide into place. He slid a magazine into the butt well and worked the slide to chamber the first round. Aguilar pressed the selector switch to safety and put the Raven in his shirt pocket.

"That puny little gun doesn't have any stopping power," Silva commented. "You'd be lucky to kill a mouse with such a small-caliber weapon."

"I've killed two men with it," Aguilar stated as he buttoned the pocket. "One must be very close to an opponent and shoot him point-blank in the face. Several bullets are needed to be sure the man will die. Nonetheless, this little .25 will kill."

"Not very efficiently," Silva insisted. "I'd like to show you something. Follow me, Señor Aguilar."

The Bolivian shrugged as he rose from his chair. He didn't really want to see whatever Silva had to show him, but the Brazilian was the host and it would be impolite to refuse this offer. As long as Aguilar was Silva's guest, he was obliged to acquiesce to the arms dealer's whims.

He led Aguilar from the den to a hall that extended to the parade field outside. Several of Silva's men were there. They wore fatigue uniforms and combat boots. The arms dealer had a private army stationed at the base. They were on his payroll as security personnel, but the troops were mercenaries. Aguilar was uncomfortable among these hired gunmen. They didn't speak Spanish and were obviously suspicious of the Bolivian. He also realized they were loyal only to Silva and would take orders only from the Brazilian boss. None of them would hesitate to kill Aguilar or Gomez if Silva told them to do so.

They crossed the square to a row of long wooden billets, the soldiers watching Silva and Aguilar as the two men headed for the motor pool at the opposite side of the billets.

When they reached the line of vehicles, Silva waved a hand at an odd vehicle that resembled an armor-plated golf cart with a Plexiglas bubble at the dome. It was mounted on tractor treads, and twin machine-gun barrels jutted from the steel plates above the nose of the ugly little rig.

"I call this the bear," Silva announced with pride. "It is a miniature tank, operated by a single man. The armor protects him from small-arms fire. Rifle or machine-gun fire will not pierce these steel plates. The turret can revolve to allow the tank man to fire his guns in any direction. The guns are belt-fed ammo operated, and the capacity is more than two hundred rounds for each weapon before reloading."

"Sounds impressive," Aguilar remarked with a frown. "If it works."

"It works," Silva assured him. "This is a prototype, but we'll be able to manufacture hundreds of them after the first few billion in funds are sent to us. Imagine an army equipped with hundreds of these? Each man in one of these tanks will be as efficient and dangerous as a dozen conventional foot soldiers. This is a real weapon, Señor Aguilar. How does your little .25 pistol compare with this?"

"Your tank won't fit in my pocket," the Bolivian replied with a shrug. "And we haven't received any of that blackmail money, so it seems a bit premature to start spending it."

"Not to start planning how it can be spent," Silva insisted. "Besides, it won't be blackmail money after the UN Security Council meets and agrees to grant us amnesty. The payments will simply be assisting a progressive liberating force that will then become the ruling party of a nation. Future payments will then be foreign aid."

"And what country will that be?" a voice inquired in Spanish.

Rico Gomez approached the pair. He glanced at the tank, unimpressed by Silva's most recent war toy. The Brazilian was better at conjuring up dreams than facing the present in a logical and pragmatic manner. Silva's talk of conquest was like his claims of creating a small yet invincible combat force that could defeat armies a hundred times larger.

"What country?" the Colombian repeated. "Assuming we even get the first payment from the countries we've attacked, what nation do we successfully invade and overthrow? That's something we haven't figured out yet."

"That's simply because politics of the three countries most vulnerable to such an invasion tend to be unpredictable," Silva replied mildly. "We discussed this before. Obviously Brazil, Colombia and Bolivia would be too large to be our first targets. The most likely candidate appears to be Paraguay, unless the circumstances in Suriname or Uruguay change drastically in the next month or two."

"Paraguay is a small country," Gomez agreed, "but it has a large military for its size."

"A military that has generally been used to keep its own people in line," Silva stated. "Not a military accustomed to real fighting. There have been some changes since the coup of 1989, but the population in general is still less than satisfied with the government. I don't think we'll find too much resistance."

"We've contributed a great deal of money and effort to this project," Aguilar stated. "The cartels want more than your opinion that this might work."

"Your Bolivian cartel doesn't like to take great risks," Silva stated with a thin smile. "That's why you haven't made as much profits from selling cocaine as Señor Gomez's organization in Colombia."

"We're all working together on this project," Gomez declared. He didn't want any escalation of the rivalry and resentment felt by the Bolivian toward the Colombian cartel. "We all have a lot to gain if it succeeds and a great deal to lose if it doesn't."

"It will succeed," Silva promised. "We can easily take Paraguay after we get the finances to build more military devices such as this tank. We can hire thousands of extra men. Professional mercenaries will flock to us when we offer fantastic wages for their skill in combat."

"More men like Cazazo?" Gomez asked with a frown. "The man is a terrorist, and most of the people he's connected with are cut from the same fanatical cloth."

"Cazazo is no fanatic," Silva insisted. "He's obviously more concerned with financial profits and personal power than extremist politics. Whatever he was in the past, Cazazo has very different goals now. We couldn't hope to accomplish our plan without him."

"And what does he want in return?" Aguilar wondered aloud. "Cazazo doesn't seem to have much interest in money or luxuries. Why would he be interested in our mission when our rewards to him hold so little fascination?"

"You'll probably find that he is more interested in wealth than you seem to believe," Silva replied. "He'll also gain a position of considerable power as the new minister of internal security and Intelligence operations. That post won't wield much power when we only command Paraguay, but Cazazo knows his influence will increase when we're able to seize more territory in the future."

"That will be the difficult part," Aguilar mused. "The idea of conquering all of South America and controlling it under a single government seems almost impossible."

"That's one of the reasons it will work," Silva insisted. "Besides, it won't be necessary to carry out military victories in order to control all the countries. We can put the people we want in power by financing their campaigns and eliminating competition. Enough money and influence can give us a very long reach. The puppet leaders will allow us to run those countries without the rest of the world realizing we're the real power."

"The idea that we could carry out the processing and distribution of cocaine throughout the continent without any interference by the authorities is truly staggering," Gomez admitted. "We'd be able to increase the profits from the trade at least ten times within the first year."

"That's only one advantage and a fairly small one," Silva said. "Don't forget that we'll also run the banks. Think of all the money criminals will send to us for investments. Money that the FBI and Scotland Yard won't be able to touch. Money safe from Interpol and tax collectors. Of course, we'll also be able to collect interest on bank accounts being held for such special clients. We'll be able to offer this service to anyone who can afford it."

"Not to mention the fact we'll be able to offer immunity from extradition to anyone fleeing the authorities," Aguilar added. "We could even set up plastic-surgery centers and have printing operations available to supply them with new faces and new identities complete with passports and papers."

"None of that can compare with the enormous profits we'll acquire from the natural resources of the continent," Silva declared. "Think of the oil, lumber, agriculture, crops, mining products, chemical processing. After we nationalize the corporations and place them under government control, we'll all soon become fabulously wealthy. Then there will be my munitions and arms business. No longer fettered by regulations and restrictions, I'll be able to sell arms at top price to any client in the world."

"These daydreams are intoxicating," Gomez said with a sigh. "Yet that's all they'll be if the countries we're trying to blackmail fail to pay. You must realize they'll try to stop us."

"And they'll fail," Silva said with conviction. "And if they don't pay, we'll deliver such destruction to the environment they won't be able to drink the water or breathe the air. They'll either agree to our terms or watch their children die. They surrender to our demands, or this planet will be turned into a cesspool of pollution and poison."

Gomez stared at the Brazilian and glanced at Aguilar. The Bolivian was visibly alarmed by Silva's fierce determination. The cocaine kingpins had agreed to the operation because it promised to produce incredible wealth and power. The possibility they might actually carry out attacks on the environment on the scale Silva spoke of was more than they had bargained for.

"Aren't you forgetting we have to live on this planet, too?" Aguilar remarked with a forced smile.

"We may have to die on it along with the others," Silva answered. "If we win, we win everything. If we lose, we lose everything, including our lives. But we won't die alone. We'll take as many of them with us as possible."

"Dying wasn't part of the plan," Gomez reminded him.

Silva seemed amused as he said, "That's something we all have to do eventually. I'd just as soon die if we fail. At least we'll be remembered in the history books if more than a million also die because the world was too stubborn to agree to our demands."

"If there is anyone left to write history books," Aguilar said grimly.

CHAPTER NINE

Hatsumi Shojin's face remained stoic as he examined the documents handed to him by the four men from the United States. The Kompei officer knew the Americans had sent some special operatives to assist in their investigation of the Hagiwara Chemical Company sabotage. These four weren't what Hatsumi expected. He had encountered CIA and NSA agents before. They tended to be neatly dressed, well-educated men in single-breasted suits with expertise in electronic eavesdropping.

The visitors were different. They were tough-looking men, especially the big hard-faced character who called himself Belasko. One man was black. Few African-American CIA or NSA worked in Japan. Another was Euro-Asian or an Amer-Asian. The fourth was a pilot who appeared to be anxious to examine the American-made Bell helicopter arranged for their use while in Japan.

"This is very unusual," Hatsumi remarked. "You have authorization to carry firearms. Even automatic weapons. We have very strict laws concerning guns in Japan."

"That's how those terrorists at the plant shot so many people," Calvin James said dryly. "Like you said, man. We've got the authorization. It comes directly from the prime minister and your own boss in Kompei."

"I doubt you will need guns here," Hatsumi replied as he pushed the documents across his desk, closer to the visitors.

"Maybe we're just a little insecure," Grimaldi commented, and took his ID from the pile. "What about the chopper?"

"It is ready for you at a military base one hundred miles from here," Hatsumi answered. "You are aware that there is a definite link between the terrorist attacks in the United States, England and France and the incident here in Japan?"

"We got a coded message on a computer unit on the plane," Bolan stated. "Apparently the terrorists are trying to blackmail at least four countries with threats of further environmental terrorism."

"Correct," Hatsumi confirmed with a curt nod. "Unfortunately this makes our investigation more difficult. The police have been looking into a few suspects. Political radicals, mostly Communists. However, since this is an international conspiracy, those efforts may be sheer folly. Do you have any idea who these terrorists are?"

"None," Bolan admitted. "Any details you can give us that were left out of the reports we've already seen?"

"Autopsy reports state that two murder victims at the plant were killed by a *katana* wielded by an expert swordsman," The Kompei man explained. "Do you know what a *katana* is?"

"I believe it's a samurai long sword," John Trent replied.

Hatsumi glanced at the long, sleek object wrapped in a cloth case among Trent's gear. He recalled that the Amer-Asian had a special permit to carry a ninja *ken*. In Japan a license was required to legally own a sword that had a sharp edge. Hatsumi knew there were some Americans who had "ninjamania." They were fascinated with the mythology and romantic notions of the ninja of ancient Japan.

However, he suspected Trent hadn't brought the ninja *ken* because he was an overzealous fanatic. The man spoke Japanese fluently, and his hands were callused by regular use of a *makawara* striking board. They were an intriguing group of foreigners. Hatsumi wondered what outfit these men belonged to and why the Americans had decided to send them to Japan.

"A samurai sword is an unusual weapon for terrorists," Bolan commented. "Wasn't there a member of the Japanese Red Army who was known to use a *katana*?"

"Arashi," Hatsumi said with a nod. "You have a good memory, Mr. Belasko. Arashi is still wanted for a series of terrorist acts in the late 1970s and early 1980s, but he is probably dead or at some training camp in the Middle East. The last reliable report on Arashi placed him in South Korea two years ago. He disappeared and hasn't been seen since."

"Not by anyone who could identify him at least," James commented. "Nobody was alive after the hit on the chemical plant to say shit. Has Kompei done a rundown on present and former employees to see if any of them smell funny?"

"Smell funny?" The Kompei man was puzzled by the expression.

"*Shokko to rekishi-warui,*" Trent explained.

"Yes," Hatsumi said with another short nod. "We have checked the backgrounds and whereabouts of plant employees. Two former chemists and technicians appeared to be suspicious. They had been members of rather radical political groups a few years ago. However, both men moved to Saudi Arabia last year to work at chemical-processing companies in that country."

"Saudi Arabia," Bolan said with a frown. "Did you contact the Saudi outfit to make certain it checked out?"

"No," the Japanese Intelligence officer admitted, "but they told everyone that was where they were going. We also know that they purchased airplane tickets to Saudi Arabia and left Japan on a flight there eight months ago. There is no record that they returned to Japan since."

"Check out the story in more detail," the Executioner suggested. "If those two went to the Middle East, they could have easily moved on to Iraq, Libya, Syria or somewhere else where terrorist camps are located. Maybe they even teamed up with Arashi."

"And then they secretly returned to Japan to carry out the attack on the Hagiwara Company?" Hatsumi asked. "That doesn't seem likely. I believe you call the expression 'grasping for a straw'?"

"We don't know anything for certain yet," Bolan replied. "Until we do, we need to check every possibility. Even if they do seem unlikely. Do you have a car ready for us?"

"Yes, and we have a driver who knows the city and speaks English. He'll drive you to the hotel. I'm sure you must be tired after such a long flight."

"Slept on the plane," Bolan told him. "Grissum needs some rest because he flew the C-130 half the distance from the United States to Japan."

"I just flew from California to Hawaii, and another pilot took us to Wake Island so I could get some rest before flying the final leg of the journey here," Grimaldi said with a shrug.

"That's still a lot of work," Bolan insisted. "I want you to get some rest. How about you two?"

"I took a couple of naps during the flight," James assured him. "If we're going somewhere tonight, I'm ready."

"So am I," Trent added. "Besides, it will be best if we meet with certain people at night. They are men who don't spend much time in the daylight."

"Sounds like you're going hunting for vampires," Grimaldi muttered.

"Not that far off," James commented. "Real vampires might be less dangerous than the dudes we're going to see."

"We'll assign some men to accompany you," Hatsumi told them. "The police can supply some officers and an escort if you desire."

"Absolutely not," Bolan said firmly. "We don't want to take a caravan where we're going. In fact, we won't need your driver and you don't need to know where we're going."

Hatsumi leaned back in his chair and studied the tall, dark American. The stranger's behavior would have seemed rude to Hatsumi if the warrior's manner was less direct. Bolan had entered Hatsumi's office and taken command. The idea of a foreigner doing this in a high-ranking Kompei official's own office would have been offensive, but Bolan displayed no ego or conceit. He was a man with a job to do, and this seemed to be the way to get it accomplished.

"Mr. Belasko," Hatsumi began, "I understood that your people and Kompei would be working together. We are doing our best to cooperate with you and supply whatever you might need while in Japan. Keeping information from us and refusing to tell us what you are doing is not a display of equal cooperation and consideration on your part."

"We're not trying to be uncooperative," Bolan assured him. "But the people we need to see tonight conduct business outside the law. Obviously they won't talk to us if we show up with a dozen cops and squad cars."

"It is unlikely they will talk to foreigners," Hatsumi commented.

"That depends on who the foreigners are," Trent replied.

"I hope you know what you are doing," the Kompei officer said with a sigh. "If you're planning to meet with Yakuza, that can be extremely dangerous. If you get in trouble and we don't know where you are, we will not be able to help you. That means you will be on your own. If the Yakuza choose to kill you, we probably won't know about it until your bodies are fished out of the bay."

"Well," James remarked with a shrug, "if we don't come back, you'll just have to guess where to send flowers."

OSAKA IS ONE of the largest and most heavily populated cities in Japan. It was very much alive and active as the black sedan made its way through the dense traffic. Cars, motorbikes and buses filled the streets. Neon lit up the night in every direction. Signs bore writing in English, as well as Japanese ideograms. Many signs advertised American products, and others carried the names of Japanese manufacturers well-known in the United States and most of the rest of the world.

Skyscrapers and office buildings towered above the smaller shops that displayed colorful barrel-shaped lanterns and various types of merchandise. Japan was a fascinating blend of cultures. Western influence had been embraced by Eastern traditions and developed into a hybrid uniquely Japanese.

"I hope you know where we're going 'cause I don't," James commented as he sat behind the steering wheel, eyes fixed on the crowded road beyond the windshield.

"We turn at Makimono Street," Trent replied. "You'll find the nightclub easily enough. It's hard to miss."

"When was the last time you spoke with Otsubo?" Bolan inquired. He sat in the back seat of the car, an aluminum briefcase beside him.

"Two years ago," Trent answered. "He's a family friend. Actually a business associate. I assume your organization has a file on me and knows that some of my relatives were formerly members of a Yakuza clan."

"Yeah," Bolan admitted. "Your uncle was involved in minor criminal activities. Mostly bootleg videotapes and counterfeit wristwatches, clothing and such with fake labels claiming to be expensive brand names. Nothing that casts doubt on your credibility, John."

"But this Otsubo dude isn't minor league," James remarked. "You say he's a big shot, John? Sort of the Yakuza version of a Mafia capo?"

"An *oyabun*," Trent confirmed. "Otsubo is a powerful man. I know Calvin has encountered Yakuza in the past. Are you familiar with them, Mike?"

"I've come up against them once or twice," Bolan answered. "They're different from American mobsters because there isn't much of a market for drugs in Japan. Nobody buys the stuff, so the Yakuza doesn't peddle it here. The small outfits mostly deal in gambling, prostitution and protection rackets in small neighborhoods. Big Yakuza clans are involved in some smuggling, major gambling operations and other business, but they make most of their profits through legitimate businesses. Of course, that also helps them get away with so-called white-collar crimes and supplies them with respectable fronts for other trade. Easier to run smuggling operations when you own a genuine import-export business."

"Exactly," Trent said with a nod. "*Oyabun* like Otsubo consider themselves to be businessmen. They are not apt to use violence except as a last resort. It isn't good for business. It upsets the police and the public. Yakuza rarely kill anyone who isn't also Yakuza."

"Yakuza have tried to kill me on a couple occasions," Bolan commented. "You and Cal have been Yakuza targets, too. That rule isn't exactly ironclad."

"No," Trent admitted, "but none of us has clashed with Otsubo's clan. He'll probably talk to me, but he might be suspicious of you two. This might work better if I went in alone."

"If we sit in the car in the parking lot, he'll know we're with you," Bolan stated. "Even if we drop you off and circle the block for an hour or two, Otsubo will know you're not alone. He might have people watching this car ever since we left the Kompei office and started heading toward his club. He's going to know you're connected with some sort of enforcement agency, and he knows you live in America so he'll probably figure you're working for CIA or Interpol. If he's as smart, influential and well-informed as you say he is Otsubo's people may have made us within minutes after we arrived in Japan."

"And that means we ought to meet the man," James declared, following Bolan's logic. "Otherwise, he'll figure we're chicken-shit."

"No shrewd businessman considers another man his equal if he thinks the guy is scared of him," Bolan added. "Does Otsubo speak English?"

"Fluently," Trent answered. "If he doesn't want to talk to you, he'll pretend he doesn't understand. That would mean he won't cooperate with us at all."

They approached the nightclub. Trent was right. The place was hard to miss. It was a large, gaudy building with an exaggerated pagoda-style roof. Japanese characters flashed in neon above the twin oak doors. Other signs in English and French announced that the establishment had music, fine food, dancing, lovely ladies and fun.

Posters of scantily clad women and samurai warriors in wooden armor revealed the confusing attitude of the establishment. The place was sleazy in the unique manner displayed by the bizarre taste of a hood with tons of cash. Bolan wasn't surprised to discover this was the sort of place the *oyabun* favored. A gangster could call himself a businessman, don three-piece suits and spend money like an oil sheik, but he would still be a gutter savage in disguise.

James parked the sedan. They emerged from the car and locked three metal cases in the trunk. The aluminum luggage held pistols, knives, garrotes and other tools of war. None of the men felt comfortable without their weapons, but they couldn't expect to meet with Otsubo while armed.

A group of hardcases moved into the parking lot and made their way to the Stony Man commandos and John Trent. Although well dressed in dark suits with color-coordinated shirts and ties, they were obviously thugs. Young and tough, the hardmen looked at the foreigners as if they were invaders from a hostile planet.

"What do you guys want here?" a thin-faced youth demanded. His accent revealed he was originally from the United States, and English was his original language.

"*Otsubo-san-wa uchi-ni irasshai masuka?*" Trent inquired, addressing the question to an older man among the Yakuza hoods.

"So you speak Japanese," the youth snorted. "So do I. Big deal. You guys are all Yankee foreigners and you smell like cops to me."

"Is Mr. Otsubo here?" Trent repeated his question in English.

"You know him?" the snotty youth asked.

"Yes, I do," Trent replied. "And I was born in Japan. That probably makes me less a foreigner than you are. I was also raised with some decent manners."

The youth looked at Bolan and James. "You two pretending to be Japanese, too?"

"We came here to speak with Mr. Otsubo," the Executioner explained. "If you keep wasting our time we'll leave, but Otsubo won't be very happy with you when he finds out we came here to meet with him in an amiable manner."

The two other hardmen addressed the youth in rapid Japanese. Bolan and James didn't understand a word. Trent's expression didn't change, but the cocky youngster seemed disappointed by whatever his companions said.

"Okay. We'll take you inside. This half-breed had better not be lying to us about knowing Mr. Otsubo."

"There's an easy way to find out," Trent told him.

The hardmen escorted them to a side door of the nightclub, frisking the trio before allowing them to enter.

They walked a corridor beyond the center of the club. Loud music, whistles and laughing voices floated from the entertainment elsewhere in the building. John Trent gave the hardmen his name, and one left to relay the message to Otsubo. The others, including the surly youth, remained with the strangers.

A short, gray-haired man appeared in the corridor, flanked by bodyguards. Dressed in an Italian suit with a turtleneck shirt, he seemed almost casually dressed compared to the other Yakuza. Light reflected along the lens and gold trim of his glasses as he turned his gaze from the American trio to his young subordinate.

"You threaten my guests?" the elder man demanded. "Such rude behavior is a disgrace to me and my clan."

"I am sorry, Otsubo-san," he said quickly as he bowed deeply and extended one arm, palm upright to express the extent of his apology.

"I will deal with you later." Otsubo turned to Trent and bowed. *"Nagai koto omeni kakari massen desthitane."*

Trent bowed in return. "Yes. It has been a long time since we saw each other," he replied in English. "May I introduce my friends?"

"We'll talk in my office," Otsubo stated. He gestured at the drab corridor and added, "This is no place to discuss business or converse in a friendly manner. Let us speak in comfort, as well as security."

Accompanied by his bodyguards, the *oyabun* led the three visitors through the hallway to his office. The room was spacious, with lush carpets, and silk-screen paintings on the walls. Outsubo didn't move to his massive teak desk, but took a seat in a black leather wing-back chair. Bolan and James waited for Trent to sit in another chair before doing likewise.

Hardmen stood by the bar, near a myriad of glasses and bottles in case their boss or his guests wanted a drink. Two others closed the door and stood guard at the threshold.

"I apologize that you were treated with such suspicion by that young fool," Otsubo began. "He is related to a family that has served this clan for many decades. When he got in trouble in America, I agreed to take him under my wing. I thought it would be good to have a Japanese-American because he would be able to meet with certain clients from the United States and make them feel more at home in a strange land. However, he lacks good manners. Etiquette."

"His behavior is his own, and we don't feel it reflects the hospitality of you and your clan," Bolan assured the *oyabun*, playing along with the man's illusion of civility. "You knew we were coming?"

"When John arrived, I thought he might visit me," Otsubo answered. "There is very little that happens in Osaka I don't know about. The city is my turf. That is how you say it in America?"

"Yeah," James agreed with a nod. "Do you also know why we're here?"

"I know you spoke with someone in Kompei," Otsubo answered. "I don't know what connection that may have with me, but I assume you are not fools. If you threaten my operations here, you would not be so bold as to come to me like this. May I offer you a drink? Perhaps cigarettes or cigars? We have an international selection of tobaccos that include American and Turkish blends."

"No, thank you," Bolan answered. "You are familiar with the incident at the Hagiwara Chemical Company?"

"I know only what I have heard on the news," Otsubo said with a frown. "Surely you don't believe I would have anything to do with such a terrible and wasteful action. What would I have to gain by something like that?"

"If we did suspect you, we wouldn't have come to meet you like this. You have connections throughout the city and Japan. We hoped that you could help us find those responsible."

"The police and Kompei haven't been able to do so. Why would I be more successful than they?"

"Because you have eyes and ears in places the police don't even know about," James explained. "Because you have an Intelligence network within the Japanese underworld that Kompei can't begin to equal. Because this is your turf."

Otsubo smiled. "Perhaps I could help. However, I am a businessman. One does not do favors without a reason. What would I get in return for assisting you?"

"What would you want?" Bolan asked.

"You are CIA," Otsubo stated. "Correct? You could arrange for a few of my men to enter Hawaii without interference. We'd like to extend certain business transactions to the States. If you could arrange to have the authorities look the other way, it would make matters easier for us."

"We're not CIA and we're not making any deals like that," the Executioner said firmly. "We're not here to stop your business, but we're not going to help you with it, either."

"This conversation seems to be at an end," the *oyabun* said, his tone soft, but with an added edge.

"You're not interested in protecting your own business interests?" Bolan inquired. "Aren't you part owner of one of the largest shipyards in Osaka? You make a fortune every year from importing oil from the Middle East and Indonesia. You're also involved in the manufacture of plastic products and electronic equipment sold abroad."

"Those are legitimate businesses," Otsubo replied. "None of them have been questioned by the police or Interpol. You cannot frighten me with hollow threats. In fact, that is not a very wise thing to do under the circumstances."

The bodyguards noticed the stern expression on the face of their boss and unbuttoned jackets in case he signaled them to draw their weapons to deal with the strangers.

"Nobody is threatening you. Not yet. We aren't your problem—the terrorists are. They attacked the chemical plant because they were carrying out environmental terrorism. The terrorists are connected with the same outfit that attacked other targets in America, Scotland and France."

"I heard of those incidents," Otsubo said with a frown. "It is odd all these things occurred so close together. Are you certain they are related?"

"Positive," Bolan confirmed. "The terrorists are attempting international blackmail. If they don't get their way, they say they'll launch more environmental attacks. Your shipyards and plants could be next."

"They wouldn't dare evoke my anger. My Yakuza would hunt them down and make them pay with their lives."

"No offense," James began, "but these terrorists are thumbing their collective nose at the governments of three or four countries and trying to make demands of the United Nations, as well as the countries already victimized. You really think they won't attack your businesses because they're scared of Yakuza revenge?"

"If they attack us," Otsubo said, "we'll deal with them."

"But the damage to your businesses will already be done," Bolan reminded him. "It would be better to stop them before your operations suffer."

The *oyabun* considered this logic. "You have a point," he decided. "Any idea how we should start working on this?"

"There is a possibility Tao Arashi was involved in the terrorist attack," Trent suggested. "He may have surreptitiously returned to Japan. It is also possible a pair of Japanese chemists who formerly worked for the Hagiwara plant may have also entered the country by stealth. Perhaps other Red Army fanatics may have accompanied Arashi. They may have been in the Middle East before coming here."

"Arashi," Otsubo said with contempt, as if the word tasted bad. "I thought we had heard the last of that beast years ago. It is said he is a superb swordsman and carries an eighteenth-century *katana*."

"Maybe we'll find out after we catch the son of a bitch," James commented. "Figure you guys can find out if these dudes sneaked into the country?"

"We'll have an answer for you by tomorrow," Otsubo assured him. "What hotel are you staying at?"

"Hotel New Hanku," Bolan answered. "You can leave a message for me, Mike Belasko."

"Very good," Otsubo said with a nod.

CHAPTER TEN

"So Locke isn't our man?" Yakov Katzenelenbogen asked with a sigh as he held the telephone receiver to his ear with his single hand.

"Unfortunately," came the voice of Rafael Encizo. "He certainly acted suspicious when we confronted him in the pub. Locke and some of his friends started the fight with us when we tried to just talk with him."

"How well did your companion behave?" Katz inquired, familiar with McCarter's sharp tongue and short temper.

"Pretty good," Encizo assured him. "Locke just panicked because he's an ex-con and his buddies were bullies who jumped at a chance to beat up a couple strangers."

"Xenophobia on the moors," Katz remarked. "You two have other possible candidates to investigate?"

"A couple. Are you having any better luck in France?"

"Too soon to tell," the Phoenix Force commander replied. "You two see if you can get a decent lead at your end. We'll do the same here. Whoever gets something first will let the others know."

"Okay," Encizo agreed. "So far, it doesn't look too promising, but there must be some sort of trail. The bastards didn't just pop up out of the ground and disappear after they did their deed."

"Be careful what you say on the phone," Katz urged. "There's no such thing as a completely secure telephone line. One never knows who might be listening."

"I know. So far, there isn't much to say that would be of interest to any eavesdroppers anyway."

"Hopefully that will change soon," the Israeli replied. "Take care and we'll be in touch."

Katz hung up and reached for a pack of cigarettes in his pocket. Inspector Henri Richet looked at the one-armed man from the United States. The Sûreté officer had been told to cooperate with the foreigner who called himself Jacob Silverman. Richet had expected this to be a weary task designed to appease the Americans rather than deal with the sabotage. However, Silverman surprised the Sûreté officer. The man spoke French fluently, with a proper Parisian accent, and he was well mannered, as well as highly professional.

"Not good news from your friends in Scotland?" Richet inquired. He had a working vocabulary in English, but was still uncertain about the conversation Katz and Encizo had conducted on the phone.

"Not yet," Katz replied. "The man they encountered in the pub seemed promising. He was an ex-convict and had been fired from the oil derricks where he had formerly been employed as a pipe fitter. However, he couldn't be involved with the terrorists. The man was arrested for assault with a deadly weapon the day after he was fired. Tried to carve his initials in someone with a broken bottle. He was in jail until three days ago."

"Perhaps he gave information to someone while he was in jail," Richet suggested.

"Scotland Yard already checked that possibility. Locke didn't have any visitors. There's a vague possibility he may have met someone in prison and they relayed information to conspirators on the outside, but this seems very unlikely."

Gary Manning opened the office door and entered. The big Canadian was built like a lumberjack, but his massive chest and brawny shoulders belied a near-genius IQ and mental determination even greater than his physical endurance. Manning, like many Canadians, spoke French as well as English. He had no trouble conversing with Richet and the other Sûreté personnel.

"I finished examining the reports on the explosion at the nuclear power plant," Manning announced. "It wasn't a homemade pipe bomb prepared by some amateur zealot. A grenade launcher was used to deliver the explosive, and the grenade was expertly aimed to go off a safe distance from the silos to the reactors and control room. Whoever did it wanted to send a message, not cause a nuclear disaster. Not this time, at least."

"They're letting us know they could have blasted the silos and spewed radioactive pollution all over southern France," Katz commented. "These people aren't bloodthirsty fanatics. They're cold-blooded manipulators, shrewd and ruthless. That may be worse than a gang of extremists."

"Whoever fired that grenade launcher was no stranger to small arms," Manning stated. "It was fired from more than two hundred yards and landed precisely where intended. That suggests someone with military training and recent practice with a grenade launcher. You don't assign a man to a job like this who hasn't touched a launcher in the last ten years."

"Since this is an international conspiracy, the terrorists could be of virtually any nationality," Richet commented. "Trying to find the person responsible for firing that grenade launcher is going to be almost impossible if he isn't a Frenchman."

"Let's not concentrate on finding that person at this time," Katz suggested. He tapped the hooks of his prosthesis on a folder on the desk. "However, this individual may be worth looking for. He's a former security officer for the nuclear power plant. The name he used was Charles Carrel. Highly qualified. Ex-paratrooper, police officer and a security adviser for a company in Nice."

"With those qualifications I'm surprised he was working as a rent-a-cop at a power plant," Manning remarked. "Unless he was in charge of the security there."

"He wasn't," Katz explained. "That may be why he quit after only working at the place for two months, but I think we should find out where Carrel is now and check out his past. His background seems suspiciously professional for a man working as a security guard, even briefly."

"Maybe," Manning commented, "but I've seen some people work at some pretty lousy jobs that didn't pay very well, although they were certainly qualified to do much more. When times get hard, a person will take any kind of work they can get."

"I know," Katz agreed. "I'm not saying this Carrel character is a terrorist, but I still think we should check on him."

"We can do that," Richet told the Phoenix Force commander.

Two hours later Sûreté had finished a detailed computer investigation of Charles Carrel. They discovered most of the story was true. A man named Charles Carrel had been a paratrooper in the French armed forces and became a policeman after he left the service. However, Carrel had been involved in a traffic accident that left him with a broken neck and a fractured skull. He'd been transferred to a Swiss hospital for therapy and was still a patient. The man had suffered brain and spinal damage and had lost most of his memory and was being retrained to walk, feed himself and read again.

Whoever claimed to be Carrel had used a blend of fiction and fact. The records he gave to the nuclear plant mentioned the accident, but claimed Carrel had recovered with only a slight limp. The story about being a security adviser for another company was a total fabrication. The outfit he listed was a front. The company had been formed less than a week before "Carrel" applied for a job at the plant. It existed long enough for a fake employer to verify Carrel had been in charge of security when the plant ran their background check on the man. Then the bogus outfit shut down and disappeared.

"They should have made a more careful security check," Richet commented as Katz and Manning finished reading the reports. "They would have known Carrel was a fraud before this could happen."

"His story had enough truth to convince them he was genuine," Katz remarked. "They had no reason to suspect he was lying about the rest or that the previous company listed on his records was a front. Someone went to a great deal of trouble to convince them Carrel was who he claimed to be. I agree they should have investigated more deeply, but unfortunately security checks on personnel for many companies that deal with sensitive and potentially serious materials tend to be less than satisfactory. Especially if they've never been victims of internal sabotage."

"Few businesses take security seriously until something goes wrong," Manning added. "Well, we have the address left by the fake Carrel. Unless he's an idiot—and we already know he isn't—he won't be there now."

"Let's visit the place anyway," Katz suggested. "I don't think we have any other leads to look into right now. One uses what one can find."

"So far, we haven't found much except the terrorists have remained several moves ahead of us," Richet said glumly.

"That just means we have to catch up with them," Manning replied, trying to sound more optimistic than he felt.

THE MANAGER of the apartments seemed distrustful of the two strangers who arrived with Inspector Richet to see the room of one of the guests. The manager was a local man, born and raised in Toulouse. He recognized Katz's Parisian accent, but this didn't score in the one-armed man's favor. The man hated Paris and those who lived in the capital city. He felt they were conceited, greedy and selfish people. Manning's Quebec accent was foreign to the man, and he was even more distrustful of the big, tawny-haired stranger.

"Charles Carrel has been a good tenant," the manager declared with a frown. "He is quiet and keeps to himself. He paid in cash for the room. Six months in advance. This cannot be said about anyone else staying here."

"Is he in his room now?" Richet asked.

"As far as I know," the manager replied with an exaggerated sigh. He raised his palms with fingers spread wide in a gesture of helplessness. "I don't pry into the business of my tenants. Unless they tell me they are going away and ask me to look after the room or unless someone complains about them, I don't bother my guests."

"This is a serious matter," Katz said. "We will have to enter Carrel's quarters whether he is home or not."

"I understand," the manager said, and took a key ring from his pocket. "Follow me."

He led the three men upstairs to Carrel's quarters. The manager knocked and announced himself. Manning stepped to the side of the doorway, one hand inside his jacket on the grips of the Walther P-88 in shoulder leather and the other hand near the manager's jacket collar in case he needed to pull the man away from the door. Katz also stood clear of the doorway, his left hand by his holstered pistol.

No one answered the door. The manager used his passkey to unlock it and pushed open the door. The place was unoccupied. The bed was unmade, a closet door stood open with only a few bare coat hangers inside and a layer of dust had formed on the furniture.

"No one has been here for at least a week," Manning commented. He moved to the bathroom to check the shower stall and medicine cabinet.

"We'll have the place dusted for prints," Richet said as he glanced about the room. "The man couldn't have worn gloves the entire time he was here."

"What?" the manager asked, confused by the conversation. "I don't understand."

"This is a confidential matter," Katz said. "I'm afraid we have to ask you to wait downstairs until we've finished looking at the room."

"There is nothing to see," the manager said with a sigh, shaking his head. "Mr. Carrel must have left. He seems to have taken everything with him. I didn't know he left...."

He continued to mutter about the situation as he shuffled from the room. Manning emerged from the bathroom, a small magnifying glass in his hand. Katz moved to the nightstand by the bed and checked the drawers. Both were empty.

"I found some hairs in the sink," Manning explained. "It looks like the sink was wiped down and washed out, but a few hairs remained. Looked at them with the magnifying glass. The ends appear to be clipped."

"So he trimmed his beard," Richet suggested. "He has a beard in the photograph in his file."

"Or he may have clipped it down to make it easier to shave it off," Manning replied. "Might see about an artist's conception of what the man might look like without a beard. Also found some black stains on the floor in there. I might be wrong, but I think it's hair dye, not ink. Our man may have black hair instead of brown with a little gray at the temples as he appeared in the photograph."

"We'll do that," Richet said with a nod. "I mentioned to Silverman that we'll have the place dusted for fingerprints."

"I don't know what good it will do," Manning said with a shrug. "In the file Carrel's prints were 'incomplete' due to scar tissue at the tips of his fingers. Supposedly they were burned in the car accident. Probably surgically altered prints to prevent the imposter from being identified in a background check."

"These people don't make many mistakes," the Sûreté man muttered.

"They might make one or two," Katz remarked as he knelt on the floor by the bed. The Israeli held a small notepad in his hand. "Apparently our mystery man left here in a hurry. It looks like he dropped his notepad and kicked it under the bed. Hopefully by accident."

He gave the pad to Richet. The Frenchman leafed through the small sheets and frowned. "All the pages are blank," he said with disappointment.

"Let me try something," Katz urged as he placed the pad on the nightstand and took a pencil from his pocket. "This is an old trick, but once in a while it works."

He lightly scribbled the pencil over the top sheet. The imprints of four numbers appeared in the middle of the gray pencil marks, 358 clearly visible. Katz showed it to Richet.

"When the numbers were written on the missing page at the top, they were traced onto the next piece of paper," he explained. "Too bad it doesn't explain what 358 refers to."

"It doesn't help us much," Richet commented. "He's probably fled the country. Certainly he already left Toulouse. However, all we can do at this point is contact Sûreté headquarters and Interpol with what information we have."

THE PHOENIX FORCE PAIR had dinner at the hotel restaurant. They didn't say much about the mission during the meal. They had accomplished more than Sûreté and the French police had previously done, but that was small comfort since they were still not even close to locating the terrorists.

Inspector Richet entered the dining room and approached their table. The Phoenix commandos were surprised to see the French Intel man and hoped he brought them good news. Katz offered Richet a seat.

"Thank you," Richet said as he accepted the invitation. "I have some information that may be of interest.

The police were checking all the regular routes a fugitive might take. Airports, trains, buses and roads. Remarkably a clerk at a local bus station here in Toulouse said he recognized the man from our artist conception with black hair and no beard. The clerk said she remembered him because his hair seemed too black, too dark for his complexion. She even remembered he was carrying a large army duffel bag, as well as a suitcase."

"Does she remember what ticket he purchased?" Manning asked. "What his destination was?"

"Yes," Richet replied. "He was headed for Paris. This was yesterday. The man left Toulouse within hours of the attack on the nuclear power plant."

"Any word from Paris?" Katz inquired.

"No one remembered seeing the fugitive," Richet answered. "Paris is a much larger city and full of busy people going to and fro. We are still looking for him in Paris, but he might have already left France on a flight to God knows where."

"Maybe we can find out, too," Manning remarked.

"At least we have no doubt we are after the right man," the Sûreté officer added. "At the bus station in Paris, the police discovered a locker numbered 358."

Richet chose to be melodramatic and waited a moment before telling them what was in the locker.

"The police opened it to find a German-made Heckler & Koch Model 69 grenade launcher inside, along with a 9 mm pistol."

"The locker was selected by the man's comrades in Paris," Katz remarked. "They must have told him the number and probably had it unlocked, with the key inside, when he arrived. Then he got rid of the weapons, stored them in the locker and possibly picked up an envelope with instructions inside before he left the station."

"That's what we suspect, as well," Richet stated. "You were right, gentlemen. This is the man responsible for the attack on the power plant. Unfortunately it looks like he got away."

"Only temporarily," Katz replied. "We'll find him. We'll find all of them. We have to."

CHAPTER ELEVEN

Greg Harrimon spilled his guts. He didn't think the three Able Team commandos had called on him at his fleabag dump in the Lower East Side of Manhattan because they wanted to be his new good buddies, but Harrimon also realized the gun-toting hoods who arrived at the same time hadn't come to rescue him. The hired guns had been sent to take him out because he was a loose end and expendable.

The big man seemed relaxed as he sat in an interrogation room with Carl Lyons and Lieutenant Perry. The Able Team captain even agreed to let Harrimon have a sandwich, coffee and a pack of cigarettes to feel more comfortable. The guy wanted to talk, and there was no need to play hardball with him if he would respond better to a more cordial approach.

"So you were contacted by some guys you met in the joint back in Ohio?" Perry inquired. The NYPD cop was less willing to handle Harrimon with kid gloves.

"Naw," the guy replied. "I didn't serve any time with these guys. They knew I'd served some time and knew I was on the run from that charge in Cleveland. I'm not sure how they found out, but they knew everything about me except what brand of toothpaste I use."

"And they knew you'd worked at the docks?" Lyons inquired.

"I was still working there when they first talked to me," Harrimon explained. "They said they wanted a little information about how things worked at the docks and the schedule of the different boats. I figured they were planning a rip-off. Hell, I didn't owe the company nothin'."

"You were working for them, you punk," Perry snorted. "You got a paycheck for doing an honest job."

"Working on the docks is tough, Lieutenant," Harrimon complained. "They don't pay all that much considering how hard the job is."

"You knew how much the job paid...." Perry insisted. "Never mind. I'm expecting too much if I think a petty crook should have any sense of loyalty toward a legal employer. How come guys like you feel loyal toward your asshole hood buddies but you don't give a shit about decent people who are trying to help you or give you an honest regular job?"

"I don't feel loyal toward those scum bags because they were gonna waste me," Harrimon replied. "You need me, cop. So get off my back or I'm gonna dummy up until I speak to a lawyer."

"You want to make a deal?" Lyons asked. "Then you'd better tell us something useful, Harrimon. Right now we can nail you for at least half a dozen crimes, including conspiracy to commit murder and an act of sabotage that caused several million dollars in damages. That means you could spend the rest of your life in prison, pal."

"Hey, I didn't know what those crazy bastards would do."

"You'd better tell us what you know, Harrimon," Lyons warned. "We don't have time to play games. We'll cut a deal with you because you're a little fish and we're after a school of great whites, but you'd better cooperate or your ass will be on line."

"Okay," Harrimon agreed, nervously lighting a cigarette. "First time they contacted me I just sold them some information about the docks. Seemed like an easy way to pick up a couple hundred bucks. Then they got real interested in the garbage scow. Guess they already knew about it because I was already a crew hand for Captain Lampert. They paid me five thousand bucks to tell them everything I could about the big garbage haul. They wanted to know the size of the scow, the exact route it would take and how fast it would be going. Everything."

"You didn't ask why they wanted to know?" Perry asked.

"They paid me five grand. I didn't ask nothin'. Figured they were up to something big, so I quit my job after I gave them the info. After the scow was attacked, I figured I'd better get out of town. That's what happened."

"Uh-huh," Lyons grunted. "You refer to the guys who hired you as 'them.' Who are they?"

"A couple dudes from Jersey and a bunch of Hispanics," Harrimon answered. "You ever heard of Ace Leonard? Deals coke in Newark. Ace and these taco benders are up to somethin'. I don't know what, but they didn't do that garbage scow for kicks."

"Bullshit," Perry muttered with disgust. "Why the hell would a coke dealer have any reason to blast a boat in the bay? You're blowing smoke up our asses, Harrimon."

"I'm telling you the truth," the man insisted. "They didn't tell me what they were up to, let alone why they were doin' it. I figured they were Colombians, but maybe they were Cuban terrorists or something."

"And maybe you're telling us a bullshit story," the cop replied.

"Hold on, Lieutenant," Lyons began. "The gunmen who came for Harrimon appeared to be Hispanic. They were carrying fake ID that claimed they were Puerto Ricans. Maybe Harrimon's telling the truth."

"Damn right I am," Harrimon declared. "Go find Ace Leonard and his buddies."

"So where do we find them?"

"Leonard hangs in Newark," Harrimon explained. "The Jersey cops know about him. Hell, he didn't introduce himself to me as Ace Leonard. I knew who he was 'cause a street buddy of mine recognized him when we first met."

"So you're not sure this guy was Ace Leonard?" Perry inquired, still unconvinced Harrimon was telling the truth.

"Let's test him," Lyons suggested. "The Newark police should be able to give us a photo of the guy. We'll put it with some pictures of other crooks in a lineup of mug shots and see if Harrimon can pick the right one out of the collection."

"Go ahead," Harrimon agreed. "I'm not jerking your chain."

"Okay. We'll find you a nice cozy cell to meditate in peace and see what we can find out from the Newark police," Lyons said.

"What about our deal?" Harrimon asked. "I help you and you keep me out of the joint."

"How much we help you will depend on how useful you turn out to be," the Able warrior replied. "If you don't like those rules, that's tough because that's the way we're playing it."

"And I just have to take what you'll give me?" Harrimon inquired, clearly unhappy with the arrangement.

"Considering the people you've been making deals with and the way they were going to give you your final payoff with a bullet, I wouldn't say you've got too much to complain about."

ABLE TEAM DROVE through the streets of Newark as twilight descended. They had traveled the Holland Tunnel, connecting New York and New Jersey. Leo Turrin, still using his "Leonard Justice" alias, flew directly to Newark to meet with the local police and arrange surveillance of Ace Leonard. Thanks to Turrin's connections with the Justice Department and White House authority via Stony Man, he was able to coordinate federal officers and police on short notice for the operation.

Newark wouldn't win any awards for being one of the most beautiful cities in America. Pollution hung in the air like a brown-and-gray cloud. Numerous factories were located in the city, producing machinery, leather goods and electrical appliances. It was also the center of New Jersey's financial, trade and transportation businesses, but manufacturing remained the most important and largest enterprise in the city.

"Hard to believe this place was originally a Puritan settlement back in 1666," Gadgets Schwarz commented as he glanced over a brochure about New Jersey. "Wonder what they'd think if they could see it now."

"Maybe they wouldn't be too thrilled," Rosario Blancanales remarked. "We passed one Presbyterian church and two cathedrals, but I haven't spotted a Puritan church so far."

"Could you guys concentrate on looking for the Larabye Electronics Company instead of counting churches or reading stuff on Jersey history?" Lyons complained. He was driving the car, and his nerves were strained with the stress of driving in the heavy, hectic traffic. He found himself in the middle of rush hour, and the drivers all seemed to be kamikaze pilots.

At last they located the Larabye Company and pulled into the parking lot. The trio left the car and headed for a door at the side of the building. Leo Turrin, several police officers and two FBI agents waited inside for the Able Team commandos. The cops were dressed in riot gear, complete with helmets, flak vests and M-16 rifles. Things were definitely getting serious.

"So what came down?" Lyons inquired as he glanced at the police and turned to face Turrin.

"We used a laser mike to eavesdrop on the warehouse where Ace is known to do business," the little Fed explained. "You know how it works. Fix the laser beam on a window and it bounces back to the microphone and amplifier with sounds vibrated on the glass, including voices."

"An improved version of the old rifle mike," Schwarz, the electronics expert, said with a nod. "So what did you hear?"

"Ace was having a conversation with his guest in Spanish," Turrin explained. "Officer Lopez translated for us. They're planning to hit a chemical plant here in Newark. They say they have explosives to use on tanks in the plant loaded with toxic waste. If they carry it out, they'll dump hundreds of gallons of poison slush into Newark Bay."

"Are they still in there?"

"They're being monitored," one of the FBI agents answered. "If any of them leave the building, we would have been told."

"Okay," Lyons said, rapidly assimilating the information. "Did you get a judge to authorize the surveillance and use of eavesdropping devices?"

"That's covered," Turrin assured him. "Hell, we had a New Jersey State Supreme Court judge filling out the paperwork before we landed at the Newark International Airport. No problem making this bust stick because we violated anybody's civil rights."

"Good," Lyons replied. "That means we can go in after those bastards. We got search warrants and all that legal shit ready?"

"Yeah," an agent answered. "That's not the problem. What we have to worry about is there are at least ten armed men in that warehouse, and they apparently have a cache of explosives, as well as firearms."

"If we raid the place, they might just blow up the building and all of us with it," a cop declared. "Hard to say how much explosives and firepower they have in there. A lot of people could get killed."

Schwarz whistled softly. "Do you have blueprints or details on the warehouse?"

"Sure," a police sergeant confirmed. "We've tried to nail Ace Leonard before, and we've staked out his warehouse more than a dozen times over the years. Never had much luck, but we know a lot of useless information about the building."

"Maybe not so useless," Gadgets replied.

"Looks like we do this the hard way," Blancanales remarked. "Best way to handle a situation like this is for a small unit of experienced professionals to go in and neutralize the threat. Lucky us. We just happen to fit those qualifications."

"What are you saying?" an FBI agent asked. "How many of us do you suggest go in there?"

"Just three," Lyons answered. "The police should form roadblocks and clear out people from the area. Try to be subtle. We don't want to tip the enemy that we're moving in on them."

"You guys have seen too many John Wayne movies. You three go in there, you're as good as dead."

"Look," Lyons began, "nobody wants to play hero. Especially when so many lives are at stake. But if we don't go in after them, we'll have to wait for them to come out and head for the chemical plant. That situation would be even more risky and difficult to control. The terrorists may not have explosives ready to use right now, but they will when they hit the street to go to their target site."

"How do you plan to go in?" a senior Newark cop inquired.

"We'll figure that out after we know more about the warehouse," Schwarz explained. "Every building has strong points and weaknesses. We'll have radio contact with you guys, but you don't call us. We'll call you when it's time to move in."

"Three against ten are pretty bad odds," another policeman remarked. "Might be even worse than that. Sure you shouldn't take some volunteers when you go in?"

"You'd have to be crazy to volunteer for a job like this," Blancanales replied with a grin. "Three lunatics are enough. Besides, if it doesn't work out, we won't get anyone killed but ourselves."

"You have a funny way of looking at the bright side, man," Schwarz commented, shaking his head slightly.

"Doesn't seem so funny to me," Lyons remarked. "Let's get our gear and figure out how we're going to do this. Time to earn our paycheck for this month."

CHAPTER TWELVE

Able Team was ready for combat. The three commandos had donned black camouflage uniform and boots for the night mission. Their faces were smeared with dark camouflage paint. They carried Heckler & Koch MP-5 submachine guns with extra magazines in ammo pouches. They were also armed with concussion grenades, knives and garrotes as well as their .357 Magnum Colt revolvers.

They had studied blueprints of the warehouse and listened to additional information from Newark police officers who had been involved in previous stakeouts of the building. The structure was located by the bay, one of many storage centers at the harbor. Although it was three stories high, there were only two levels inside the warehouse. The ceilings were high, and the place was designed to contain crates and boxes rather than people.

There were two doors and several windows. Most of the latter were located upstairs. One wall of the building was blank, without a door or a single window. However, two guys were posted at the doors. They didn't carry weapons openly, but the men of Able Team knew the lookouts were probably armed. Ace Leonard was no fool. He wouldn't have sentries hanging around the place with weapons on display that might draw the interest of the police, but they would be carrying. If the guards didn't have criminal records, they most likely had gun permits to legally pack heat.

Able Team approached the warehouse from the blind side, Lyons taking the lead. He used available cover to draw closer. Stacks of crates, a forklift and the shadows helped conceal his movement. Lyons held the MP-5 close to his chest to reduce noise and prevent banging metal against other objects in the dark. He was a veteran at stealth, and the guards didn't appear to be expecting trouble. One of them even fired up a cigarette and sat on a coil of rope, his back resting against a wall.

Lyons reached the warehouse undetected. He slipped the Magnum from shoulder leather and moved to the edge of the corner. The bored guard was calmly chatting with his companion at the front entrance to the building. Neither man was prepared for the Able Team leader when he made his move.

He swung around the corner and slashed the barrel of his Colt Python across the mastoid bone behind the seated man's left ear. The unexpected blow knocked the guy from the rope coil and dumped him unconscious on the ground. The second sentry's eyes opened wide in astonishment as he suddenly found himself face-to-face with Carl Lyons, only two feet away.

Lyons's empty left fist swung a punch to the startled sentry's face. The man staggered from the blow and reached inside his jacket for a gun in his belt. The big ex-cop lashed a boot to the guard's abdomen. The guy doubled up with a groan, and Lyons quickly chopped the butt of his revolver at the nape of his opponent's neck. The guard collapsed across his equally senseless companion.

"Hey!" a voice said from the opposite side of the building. "Did you hear somethin'?"

"I'm not sure," another man replied. "We should call Ace. It's better to bother him for nothin' than let it ride and turn out we screwed up."

"Don't do that, guys!" Lyons called out in a raspy whisper. He hoped his voice would be too distorted for the backdoor sentries to realize it belonged to a stranger. "This asshole bad-mouthed my old lady so I punched him out. No big deal."

"What is this shit?" one of the guards complained. "You guys actin' like you're still in junior high? You're on guard duty for God's sake."

The sentry marched to the front of the building, angered by the adolescent behavior of his comrades. He turned the corner to find Lyons waiting for him. The big blond warrior swung a brawny forearm and clotheslined the guy under the chin. The blow lifted the sentry off his feet and dumped him on his back. Stunned by the unexpected attack, the man looked up and saw Lyons towering above him. The Able Team leader bent a knee and dropped it into the fallen man's stomach with all his weight behind it. The guy gasped as the breath was knocked from his body. Lyons hit him on the point of the chin with a rock-hard fist to put the guy in dreamland.

The remaining sentry at the rear of the warehouse was confused and worried. He thought he heard yet another struggle at the opposite end of the building. He drew a 9 mm Smith & Wesson autoloader from his belt as he tried to see what had happened without moving from his post at the back door.

He was so distracted he didn't notice Rosario Blancanales creeping from the shadows until the Able Team commando jammed the muzzle of a Colt Python in the small of his back. The guy stiffened and moved his hands to shoulder level, pistol still in one fist.

"Don't be stupid," Blancanales whispered. "Drop the piece."

The sentry released the gun. He heard it clatter on the planks of the pier and hoped it distracted his stealthful adversary. The guy whirled and slashed an arm at Pol's gun hand in a desperate effort to disarm him.

The trick might have worked against a less experienced man. Blancanales stepped back and moved his revolver clear of the other man's arm. He quickly swung the Colt and slammed the barrel across the sentry's skull. The blow drove the man to his knees, and Blancanales kicked him in the temple, rendering him unconscious.

"Now, that was stupid," Blancanales muttered.

Schwarz appeared and joined the Hispanic warrior. He glanced down at the defeated sentry as Blancanales bound the guy's wrists with unbreakable plastic riot cuffs. Schwarz stood watch while Pol gagged the guy. Lyons would have to frisk and secure the other three sentries on his own and watch out for himself.

Blancanales completed his task and stepped to a steel pipe that extended from the ground to the top story. The pipe protected underground cables that fed electricity to the building, and looked sturdy enough to support Blancanales's weight. He sure hoped so as he gripped the pipe with both hands, placed a boot on the wall and climbed hand over hand, walking up the wall to the top of the pipe.

Schwarz placed a packet of plastic explosives into the doorjamb by the lock and inserted a special blasting cap and detonator. It was a tiny charge of C-4, but the plastique packed an extremely powerful punch. Gadgets waited for Blancanales to get into position and to allow Lyons to set a similar charge at the front door.

"Knock, knock," Schwarz whispered as he triggered the electrical squib attached to the detonator.

The explosion erupted with a roar and brilliant bright light. The door burst open and dangled on broken hinges. Schwarz immediately yanked the pin from a concussion grenade and lobbed the minibomb through the opening. A second explosion at the front of the building announced that Lyons had performed the same maneuver and no doubt lobbed a second grenade into the warehouse.

Blancanales slipped the crook of an elbow through the pipe to brace himself as the wall trembled. The metal pole seemed to sway, as if jarred loose from its foundation. He heard glass shatter and the cries of pain and surprise from the lower portion of the warehouse. The shouts of anger and alarm from men upstairs sounded far more threatening.

Blancanales held on to the pipe with his arm hooked around the pole as he pulled the pin from a concussion grenade. He hurled the bomb at a window as hard as possible from his awkward position. The grenade shattered glass and fell into the room within. Blancanales scrambled down the pipe as the enemy responded with pistol shots. Glass burst from the pane above him as he clung to the pole and pressed himself to the wall, head bowed low.

The grenade exploded. Windows on the top level burst apart, and broken glass showered on the Able warrior's hair and shoulders. The pole vibrated and seemed about to snap loose from its base, but he held on, his heart performing a brief rumba as he was in danger of falling and completely vulnerable to enemy gunfire, as well.

Blancanales clenched his teeth and began to stubbornly climb up the pole once again. He leaned on the pipe harder than before and moved his hands and feet faster to reach the top before the pole broke or the enemies within the building could recover from the blast and organize a counterattack.

He scaled the wall to the summit and reached high to grab the eaves of the roof. Blancanales released the pipe and grasped the lip of the roof with both hands. He swung his body forward, aimed his feet at the broken windowpanes and let go of the eaves. The commando hurled forward and plunged through the opening.

CARL LYONS DIVED through the front entrance of the warehouse. He hit the floor and rolled to a pile of crates that had been toppled to the floor by the concussion blasts. The Able Team leader assumed a kneeling stance behind a pair of large wooden boxes. He braced his MP-5 across a crate and pointed it at the dazed hardmen still on their feet after the unexpected grenade attack.

"Raise your hands and surrender!" he shouted.

Nobody reacted to Lyons's order. He wasn't surprised. The concussion had probably ruptured the eardrums of most of the men, and the more fortunate terrorists would be temporarily deaf from the incessant ringing in their ears.

Several unconscious—or dead—figures littered the floor of the bay room. A variety of weapons were also scattered among the debris and motionless bodies. Assault rifles, shotguns and handguns had been dropped by dazed owners when the grenades went off. Furniture, papers, wood splinters from smashed crates and assorted merchandise added to the abundance of junk on the floor. This offered cover to Lyons and his opponents, but it also blocked access to or even pinned many of the weapons discarded on the floor.

However, some hardmen already had firearms in hand. Although they stumbled about on unsteady legs and blood oozed from their nostrils and ears, the terrorists still presented a genuine threat. Two gunmen swung their pistols in the direction of Lyons and opened fire. Their shots were wild due to blurred vision and hands that trembled from the aftershock of the punishing explosions.

Bullets punched into the crates Lyons used for cover. At least two rounds sizzled well above the commando's head. He retaliated with the Heckler & Koch gun. A 3-round burst struck the closest gunner in the chest, blowing him backward into a stack of cardboard boxes. Material inside the containers crunched under the literal deadweight of the man's body.

The second gunman aimed at the muzzle-flash of Lyons's chopper. He wasn't fast enough. The Able pro nailed him with another trio of 9 mm slugs, and the corpse crashed to the floor, falling across the back of a semiconscious comrade who lost all interest in trying to get to his feet.

Another opponent dived for cover behind an overturned card table, an Uzi machine pistol clutched in his fists. The guy wasn't thinking clearly due to the numbing effect of a ruptured eardrum. He might as well have ducked behind thin air and tried to form a bulletproof shield with his imagination. Lyons blasted another burst of MP-5 messengers through the flimsy tabletop. Parabellum rounds ripped into the guy's torso and dumped him to the floor in a rapidly dying heap.

ACE LEONARD CROUCHED behind a row of kegs and boxes only two yards from the body of the man Lyons had just taken out of action. The thirty-five-year-old hardcase had been in shootouts before. He had grown up in the street and had been a gang leader since he was fifteen. Leonard hadn't survived because he was a coward, but he wasn't stupid, either. His head was throbbing with pain; he couldn't hear and he could hardly see. The man was in no condition to kick anybody's ass, and he knew it.

What the hell had they used when they hit the place? The explosions had felt as if a giant had picked up the building, shook it violently until he bounced everybody off the walls and ceilings like a sadistic kid with a box full of hamsters.

José Verde lay on the floor unconscious. Leonard knew the name was a phony, but the guy was a big shot in a Colombian coke cartel.

Leonard had been trying to make a deal with the big boys from South America for the past six years. He had learned Spanish from Hispanic dealers in New York when he first got into the cocaine business when he was only twenty-three. Leonard knew one day he'd get a big break with the major dope dealers who dealt in huge shipments and billions of dollars every year. He didn't know what Verde and his people were up to or why they wanted to attack an oversize garbage scow or sabotage a chemical plant. Maybe the owners of the businesses had welshed on the Colombians. Whatever the reason, Ace saw his opportunity to climb up the ranks of the crime world.

Until this shit came down.

Ace Leonard held a .45-caliber Star PD in his fist, but he didn't intend to use it unless he had to. There was nothing he could do for Verde at the moment. Leonard had to concentrate on his own survival. He crawled to the canvas satchel bag that lay beneath an overturned chair and some newspapers and assorted litter, shoved the junk aside and gathered up the bag.

The satchel was loaded with more than twenty pounds of plastic explosives. Leonard was no expert in demolitions, and he wasn't even sure what sort of explosives were in the case, but he had seen Verde's people prepare the charges with blasting caps and detonators. Timers were rigged to the bombs. He figured they wouldn't be too hard to set for ten seconds or so to blast the hell out of one of the walls. He didn't know how powerful the explosion would be and realized he might blow himself up in the process. At least he'd take a few of the mysterious invaders with him when he died.

BLANCANALES SAILED through the broken windowpane and landed on his feet among the rubble on the floor of the second story. His knees were bent to absorb the impact, and he grabbed the MP-5 that hung from a shoulder strap. The warrior dropped to one knee as a volley of automatic fire erupted from the opposite end of the room.

Bullets hissed through air above Blancanales's crouched figure and raked the window and wall behind him. The Able Team fighter saw the muzzle-flash of an Ingram MAC-10 machine pistol in the hands of a man who stood among a cluttered mess of fallen bunk beds and torn mattresses. Blancanales snap-aimed his H&K subgun and returned fire before his enemy could reaim his weapon.

The triggerman caught three parabellum slugs in the chest. The impact pitched him backward as he fired the Ingram again, half a dozen rounds punching into the ceiling before he crashed to the floor. Blancanales glanced about the room. Most of the hardmen were already sprawled on the floor, unconscious or dead. He saw one large figure shuffle from the rubble with an unsteady gait. The guy wasn't armed, but another man worked the slide to a pump shotgun and swung the barrel toward Blancanales.

He wasn't fast enough. The Able Team commando triggered the Heckler & Koch chopper and nailed the shotgunner with a burst of 125-grain semijacketed hollowpoints. The hardman's head exploded when the high-velocity projectiles drilled into his skull.

Suddenly the big guy closed in. Blancanales tried to point his MP-5 at his adversary, but a boot slammed into his subgun and kicked it from his grasp. The larger attacker lashed another kick at Blancanales's head. He dodged the boot and grabbed the guy's pant cuff before he could attempt another attack. He wobbled off balance on his single foot, unsure what to do next.

Blancanales didn't suffer from indecision. He quickly drove a fist into the guy's legs, the man groaning in agony when knuckles mashed his manhood. Blancanales rose from the floor and threw an uppercut to the guy's jaw that snapped his head back. The hardman dropped to the floor, as if poleaxed.

GADGETS SCHWARZ had encountered little opposition when he charged through the back door to the warehouse. Two terrorists were on their feet, but only one man was armed. The other held his head in both hands and staggered about, moaning in agony. Schwarz responded according to the threat. He shot the armed man with a short burst of MP-5 rounds. The gunman hit the floor as Schwarz stepped forward and rammed the buttstock of the subgun into his opponent's gut. The second man doubled up with a gasp that expressed more surprise than pain.

"Take a nap," the Able Team warrior suggested as he slashed the gun barrel across the base of the man's skull.

Schwarz moved to cover behind a support post that extended to the ceiling. He saw several unconscious terrorists on the floor, rendered senseless by the detonated grenades. The sound of gunshots in other parts of the building revealed that Lyons and Blancanales had encountered more opposition, including some able to fight.

"At least ten, maybe more," Schwarz muttered, recalling the assessment made by the Feds who had run surveillance on Ace Leonard's warehouse as to the number of opponents in the building. "No shit. I'd say 'more than ten' was an understatement."

Sudden movement drew his attention to a hunched figure headed for the wall opposite Schwarz's position. He thrust the barrel of his MP-5 around the side of the post as he watched the shape carry a satchel in one hand and a pistol in the other. Gadgets realized shouting at the guy would be a waste of time. Even if the man's eardrums were still intact, he wouldn't be able to hear anything clearly for at least forty-eight hours. He had to stop the guy, and the only way to do that was with a bullet.

His finger began to squeeze the trigger as the targeted man turned slightly. Schwarz held his fire when he saw the man's face. He recognized Gerald "Ace" Leonard from mug shots supplied by the Newark police. The guy was one of the bigger fish. Not a major leader of the terrorist conspiracy, but he certainly knew more than little sardine-level dudes like Harrimon. Schwarz wanted to take Ace alive if possible.

Leonard was unaware he was in Schwarz's gun sights as he removed a bricklike packet from the bag. He placed it by the wall and pressed a red button above a small digital timer. Gadgets saw what the gangster was doing and sucked in a tense breath. Leonard had activated a bomb. The explosives were wrapped in brown paper and looked familiar to the Able Team warrior. The son of a bitch was using military explosives. Brown waxed paper suggested it was probably C-3 or C-4. Judging from the size of the charge, the explosion would pack enough punch to blow up the entire building.

"Stupid bastard seems to think he'll just blow a hole in the wall," Gadgets hissed through clenched teeth. "But he's gonna get us all killed."

Leonard turned and moved for cover by a row of crates. Schwarz lowered the aim of his H&K and fired a short burst. Parabellum rounds ripped into Ace's thighs and legs. He screamed and toppled forward to fall unceremoniously onto the floor. The Star PD was jarred from his hand when he hit the hard surface.

Schwarz bolted from cover and sprinted to the bomb. He realized he was exposed to enemy fire, but the explosive in the corner presented an immediate threat to the lives of his fellow Able Team members and the combined forces of the police and federal agents who were probably moving in to back up the commandos. No shots responded to Gadgets's move, and he reached the bomb without stopping a bullet.

He knelt beside the device and glanced at the timer, which had counted down to 0:03. Schwarz had only three seconds to deactivate the bomb. It appeared to be a simple timer wired to a detonator and blasting cap embedded in the explosives. Yet it could be rigged to go off if a person clipped the wires out of sequence or failed to cut the pressure-sensitive line first.

"No time," Schwarz muttered as he grabbed the wires at the base of the charge and yanked hard.

The timer buzzed loudly as Gadgets closed his eyes. No thunder erupted with extraordinary violence to tear him apart. No burst of killing light occurred to slice off skin, shatter bone and pop vital organs in an instant. He opened his eyes.

"Don't move!" a hard voice warned.

Gadgets released the wires and turned toward the sound. He saw Carl Lyons standing over the prone figure of Ace Leonard. The Able Team commander's boot pinned the man's hand to the floor, and Lyons's subgun was pointed at Leonard's head. The gangster's .45 pistol was on the floor, a few inches from Ace's groping fingers.

"This maggot looked like he was planning to shoot you in the back, partner," Lyons announced. "What the hell is that thing by the wall?"

"Tell you later," Schwarz replied, still too rattled to explain.

He took a deep breath. It felt good to still be able to breathe. To still be alive.

CHAPTER THIRTEEN

"I haven't heard from my people in the United States," Rico Gomez said as he entered the den. "Something has gone wrong. They should have launched the attack in New Jersey by now and reported back to us."

João Silva stood by a table, examining drawings of a new type of small, ultrafast fighter jet. The Brazilian arms merchant was still planning how to spend the blackmail money before the UN even agreed to their demands. He looked up from the charts and frowned at the Colombian.

"Perhaps they simply haven't been able to radio a message," he suggested. "They may have to hide from the authorities and wait until they can reach an international transceiver."

"I don't think so," Gomez answered with a shake of his head. "The escape route was well planned in advance. That American street trash Ace Leonard might have made a mistake, but my men should have corrected any error in judgment on his part. They are my best men."

Best men? Silva thought with contempt. Drug dealers who were accustomed to criminal enterprise, not paramilitary operations. The Brazilian had had doubts about working with these narcotics traffickers from the start. He would have preferred to use his own people. They were mercenaries and their loyalty had been bought and paid for, but they were trained for combat and most had experience in actual warfare. The Colombians and Bolivians were also interested only in financial gain. Silva trusted men to act in their own best interests. Greed was more reliable than patriotism, in his opinion, but the mercenaries had the skills the drug pushers lacked.

Silva had more faith in Ramon Cazazo than all the cocaine peddlers put together. The Knife might have started his career as a political extremist, but experience had given him a healthy dose of reality and his goals now seemed personal, rather than the abstract Marxist dogma dreams of Utopia following a monstrous bloodbath and international revolution.

The world would never be Utopia, Silva acknowledged. In fact, he believed it was destined to become even more dystopian in the future. That was fine with Silva. The more wretched and miserable the world became, the more demand for weapons of war. Tyrannical governments would need more military hardware to maintain their police-state rule. Revolutionaries of every type would want arms to fight against whatever regime they opposed. Silva would gladly supply any side, regardless of politics, as long as they could afford to do business with him.

He glanced at Cazazo. The Venezuelan master terrorist stood at the opposite side of the room. He'd been examining some of Silva's manuals to determine what weapons manufactured by the Brazilian's corporation might be practical for use by his people in the field. Cazazo had heard Gomez's grim announcement and immediately discarded the books.

"I should contact our comrades in Japan and Europe," he declared, a hand dropping to the knuckleduster hilt of his trench knife. It was an automatic response to danger, even to a distant threat.

Gomez was uncomfortable in the presence of Cazazo. The terrorist made him nervous. The Colombian fancied himself a businessman, albeit one involved in an illegal trade that frequently required violence. Yet he regarded Cazazo as a wild wolf on a leash. One could use the wolf to attack one's enemies, but a wise man never trusted a wild animal. When the current business was over, Gomez vowed, Cazazo would be history. Better to kill the beast than trust it not to turn on its masters.

"Let us not overreact," Silva urged. "The operatives in New Jersey might have decided to delay their attack on the chemical plant because something occurred that made them change their minds. A prudent man does not obey a schedule if doing so presents greater risk than necessary. It is also possible their radio is not working or the radio wavelength has been jammed by some sort of interference. Even conditions caused by sunspots could be responsible."

"I hope you're right," Gomez said, shaking his head slightly. "The Americans might not be as docile about obliging to our demands as we hoped. Perhaps the FBI and CIA succeeded in locating our people in New Jersey."

"*Your* people," Silva reminded him. "They are members of your cartel, Señor Gomez. You vouched for them and they, in turn, claimed the American gangster Leonard was reliable. If there has been a failure in New Jersey, your people are responsible."

Gomez bit his lip. He was tempted to reply to this accusation with angry words that would insult Silva by questioning his manhood, the legitimacy of his birth and the morality of his mother. The Colombian's temper rose, and his tongue was inclined to reveal his youth as a slum kid in Bogotá. He realized he wasn't in a good position to bad-mouth Silva. Not as long as he was at the Brazilian's stronghold, surrounded by Silva's hired gunmen with hostile jungle beyond the wall of the compound.

"My people in New Jersey have been operating within the United States for years," Gomez began, allowing his temper to cool a bit before he spoke. "The police never got close to them, and they told me the authorities had little interest in Leonard. Why would I not trust their judgment?"

"This argument does not tell us what to do next," Cazazo stated. "My contacts in Japan and Europe can strike as soon as we authorize it with the proper code words. Whether the operation in New Jersey has fallen or not, we should go ahead with the next phase of our mission."

"Our goal is to get the targeted nations to acquiesce to our demands," Silva reminded the terrorists, "not to cause as much destruction as possible. The public has a short memory. If we allow some time to pass and feed the authorities some scapegoats to blame for the actions already taken, we will be fairly safe from any retribution in the future. But if we conduct too many attacks too close together, the public will demand action and they won't be as apt to believe these attacks are not connected."

Gomez was somewhat relieved to hear Silva urge restraint. He had some doubts about the Brazilian, as well as Cazazo. The Knife looked at Silva with eyes as unemotional as two pieces of black stone.

"How long do we wait?" he inquired, apparently accepting the Brazilian's decision.

"Twelve hours," Silva replied. "If we have not heard from the Colombians in New Jersey by then, we'll assume it is because they have been apprehended or killed.

In that case, you will contact the Storm... What's his name in Japanese?"

"Arashi," Cazazo answered with a nod.

"Yes," Silva said, not bothering to try to pronounce the name in a language he was unfamiliar with. "Contact him and tell him to attack the next target."

"Very well, Señor Silva," Cazazo replied with a smile.

THE STRIDENT RINGING of the telephone woke Mack Bolan. He was a light sleeper, especially while in the field on a mission. The unexpected noise jarred him from his slumber, and he instinctively grabbed the Uzi submachine gun that lay beside him.

The Executioner was in the Hotel New Hanku in Osaka. The room was spacious and luxurious, not at all like what he was accustomed to. Often during a mission he was lucky to have a cot and blanket. The warrior rolled across the mattress to the nightstand and grabbed the telephone receiver from the cradle.

"Hello." Remembering he was in Japan, Bolan added, "*Moshi moshi*. I hope you speak English."

"I speak enough," a voice replied bluntly. "I work for a man you met recently. He tells me you're looking for a Mr. *A*. Okay if we call him that?"

"*A*" for Arashi, Bolan realized. Otsubo had promised to contact him at the hotel and the Yakuza *oyabun* had kept his word.

"That'll do," Bolan assured the caller. "What can you tell me about Mr. *A*?"

"There's a cement factory on Kame Street called Hinshitsu Semento," the caller explained. "It shut down a couple months ago because it was considered unsafe after a series of accidents. The factory is a dump and they're trying to decide whether to just fine the owners and allow them to make repairs or try to send them to prison. The owners will almost certainly have to sell the business either way. They're facing a number of big lawsuits. Not as big as they'd have back in the States, of course. We Japanese are not as fond of lawyers and courtrooms as you Americans seem to be."

"You're telling me about this cement factory for a reason aside from passing on some information about recent events in Osaka?"

"You're a bright fellow," the voice replied. "Do I have to spell it out for you, Mr. Belasko?"

"No. I get your drift. Pass on my thanks to your employer."

"And he wishes you good luck in return," the caller stated. "Bear in mind, the Hinshitsu Semento factory is considered unsafe. It might be a dangerous place to visit."

"Thanks for the advice."

"Have a nice day," the voice said, then hung up.

Bolan put the receiver in the cradle and climbed out of bed. Outsubo's Yakuza clan had apparently located Arashi's lair. Now it was up to the Executioner and his companions to deal with the terrorists. He'd have to wake Calvin James, Jack Grimaldi and Trent if they were still asleep.

They had a target, and it was time for action.

CHAPTER FOURTEEN

Arashi had once been known by the name of his birth, but he hadn't used it for many years. "The Storm" didn't like to think about that part of his past. His was a struggling, poor family in Kyoto, and his father was a factory worker who spent half his paycheck on plum wine and prostitutes. When he was home, the father tended to take out frustrations on his wife and son.

The boy learned to hate his father and everything the man stood for. His father was a drunkard and a weakling, a bully and a coward. The father didn't take pride in being Japanese and felt the emperor had led the country into destructive folly during World War II. Indeed, Japan was lucky the United States of America was willing to forgive them for Pearl Harbor and help the country rebuild.

The youth who would become Arashi turned against his father's philosophy. He embraced martial-arts training, finding solace in the traditions of samurai instruction that were so uniquely Japanese. Although he learned concentration and discipline of karate and kendo, his heart and mind remained poisoned by the experiences of his childhood. The martial-arts master taught that one didn't initiate violence, but defended oneself if necessary. A skilled martial artist had a responsibility not to abuse his knowledge, and he had to treat the arts with respect. That meant treating people with respect and dignity. An aggressor disgraced the arts and created bad karma that would eventually cause his destruction. Arashi didn't adopt these beliefs, but he was clever enough to conceal it from his teachers.

He also learned to despise Americans and the West in general because his father had admired them. He also felt these foreign influences were robbing Japan of its national identity. Eventually Arashi turned to Marxism because it was opposed to Western democracy. The Japanese Red Army was the most militant and violent sect of leftist activists, so he joined them.

Arashi created a fictional past for himself. He claimed to be descended from a samurai family and told others the *katana* he carried had been handed down father to son for generations. His background seemed mysterious and exotic. This was an illusion he reinforced so strongly that he believed it himself... unless he allowed his mind to wander to the painful and degrading days of his childhood.

Others watched as Arashi performed a series of *kata* with the long sword. He drew his blade from the scabbard and delivered a cross-body cut, his torso moving with the flow of the stroke. Arashi pivoted and gripped the sword handle with both hands to execute an overhead cut. Light flashed along the ribbon of steel as the *katana* sliced air in the hands of the terrorist swordsman.

Arashi's comrades admired their commander's ability. They were also students of *kenjutsu* and other martial arts. Many were quite skilled, but none equaled Arashi's prowess. Some had little faith in the swords, *sai* and stick weapons of traditional Japanese fighting arts. None of these could match a firearm if a gunman was beyond the reach of blade or club.

The terrorists had lots of time to practice martial arts in the abandoned Hinshitsu Semento factory. Most of them were getting bored with the constant training. Arashi insisted only men be used for the mission because he didn't believe women—even female veterans of the JRA—to have the physical strength or emotional stability for serious combat situations. This meant the young and overstimulated male followers didn't have female companionship while they remained cooped up in the cement factory.

There was no electricity. Battery-powered lanterns were placed throughout the building, and they had a number of small radios. Bottled water had to be used for bathing, washing clothes and dishes, as well as drinking and cooking. The meals were bland, consisting of boiled rice combined with prepackaged canned or freeze-dried foods. Arashi strictly forbade the use of alcohol or drugs by any of his people during the operation.

The terrorists were getting cabin fever. No one was allowed to leave the factory until Arashi received another coded message from Cazazo. The Asian fanatics didn't understand why so much relied on the decisions of a foreigner who was stationed on the other side of the world. In truth, most of them had only a vague idea why Arashi had agreed to the mission and why they were launching attacks on chemical plants. Yet they were violent young men who thrived on destruction. None of them would admit it, but they were all more eager to tear down the existing establishment and cause devastation and fear than try to build a new society to replace what they hoped to ruin.

Arashi completed his *kata* and bowed at the followers who formed a circle around the bay area of the factory. They bowed in return and applauded the demonstration with as much enthusiasm as they could display under the circumstances. Arashi assumed their reaction was sincere. He believed he gave them inspiration by such demonstrations. It was important to keep up the morale of the men.

Mitsuzuka, one of Arashi's top lieutenants, approached the terrorist commander. They exchanged formal bows before the henchman addressed his boss. "A message has finally been transmitted by the Venezuelan. It was 'green horse.' Obviously a code phrase. Do you understand it?"

"Yes," Arashi confirmed with a nod. "The term 'green horse' means we are to carry out the next phase of our mission. The horse is a symbol of charging forward, as a samurai horseman did in the past. Different colors would signal different actions and how long before these are to be taken. Green means we are to attack the next target without delay."

"I understand. We will prepare immediately. This will be a larger target, and the destruction will be far greater than last time, won't it?"

"Of course," Arashi replied as he stared at the long steel blade of his *katana*. "It will be a lesson to the Americans and the West and the traitors who would turn Japan into a pale image of those foreign societies."

MACK BOLAN CREPT along the wire fence that surrounded the Hinshitsu Semento factory. Dressed in night combat black, the Executioner blended with the shadows in spite of the arsenal he carried. A veteran night fighter, he moved quietly through the neglected tall grass outside the plant.

A sentry walked the perimeter of the property, unaware of the warrior hidden by the fence. The Executioner remained very still as the guard patrolled less than half a yard from his position.

He'd chosen this position after studying the factory through a pair of night-vision binoculars. The barrier wasn't electrified or rigged with any type of alarms, booby traps or sensors. Bolan had also been relieved to discover there were no surveillance cameras posted at the factory. Apparently the terrorists were relying solely on the sentries for security.

Bolan had picked a part of the fence with a gap at the bottom, wide enough so that he could wriggle through to the other side.

The Executioner eased the Beretta 93-R from shoulder leather. The holster had been specially designed to accommodate the silencer screwed to the threaded barrel of the machine pistol. Bolan preferred not to use the Beretta. Even with the sound-suppressor, there was a possibility the muffled report might be heard by the enemy or the guard might cry out when shot. However, he had to be prepared for the unexpected as he lay on his back and extended his arms through the hole, pistol held in his fist.

He wriggled on his back, digging in with his heels to push himself forward. The wire raked his chest. He shifted his body to prevent the metal from tearing or snagging fabric as he continued the reverse low-crawl.

Once clear, the warrior rolled onto his belly and scanned the area. The factory consisted of two large buildings, connected by catwalks. The machinery at the plant sat idle. Stacks of cement bags were placed on wooden pallets. He could only guess how many terrorists were hidden inside the buildings.

There was no point in dwelling on it. Bolan was already inside. He'd find out about the opposition soon enough. The warrior carefully got to his feet, watchful of possible danger. More than one guard patrolled the property, and there was no way to predict when one might spot the intruder. Bolan hurried to a stack of cement bags and crouched behind them.

As the sentry marched back toward the Executioner's position, Bolan saw him clearly by moonlight. The young Japanese was slender and moved with the grace and dignity of an athlete. Probably martial-arts training, Bolan concluded. The guy carried a short sword in his belt, as well as a Shin Chuo Kogyo submachine gun. The firearm was a blowback operated weapon, similar in design to a U.S. M-3A1 "greasegun."

Bolan figured the guy was well trained, though probably more familiar with karate and swordsmanship than gunplay. He didn't intend to give the sentry a chance to demonstrate his skill. The warrior waited for the guard to once again stroll past his place of concealment as he holstered the Beretta.

The Executioner held the handles of a garrote in his fists as he stepped from cover and crept behind the unsuspecting sentry. He quickly swung his arms and whirled the wire noose around the man's head, yanking hard to snap the steel cord tightly around the guy's neck. He slammed a knee to the small of the sentry's back and followed with a stomp to the back of his knee.

The terrorist's leg buckled, and he fell to his knees. With the garrote held taut, the man didn't have a chance to fight back or cry out. Within seconds he was dead. Bolan unwound the wire from the corpse's neck. The Executioner disliked taking out an enemy in such a manner. Face-to-face against an armed opponent was different. Yet there was too much at stake, too many lives in jeopardy. It was too important to neutralize the terrorists to stop to worry about fair play. This was war, and the rules were as brutal and simple as the law of the jungle. Kill or be killed.

Bolan dragged the corpse to the cement bags and crouched next to the body, which he briefly frisked. The warrior came up a small two-way radio, two spare magazines for the Shin Chuo Kogyo and a switchblade. No wallet, keys or coins. Not good news, Bolan realized. This meant the terrorists were probably on combat alert and ready to go on their next mission on short notice.

Taking out a nest of armed fanatics under those circumstances wasn't going to be easy. But the warrior hadn't expected it to be. Stony Man never took on easy assignments.

JOHN TRENT HAD SELECTED another entrance at a different section of the fence. Dressed in the black *gi*, hood and scarf mask of a ninja, Trent had slithered through the high grass to a tree outside the factory. He'd been a student of *ninjutsu* since childhood. Dark and silent, he was virtually invisible in the night.

He climbed the tree trunk with ease. His strong fingers and split-toe *tabi* footgear were well suited for the task. Trent stationed himself in a Y-shaped pair of branches, well concealed by the other limbs and the abundant leaves. The black sword handle of his ninja *ken* blended well among the branches. He carried the sword in a scabbard strapped to his back. A .45-caliber 1911A1 Government Issue Colt was holstered under his left arm, and he carried other traditional ninja weapons and tools concealed within his *gi*.

Trent waited, motionless and silent among the branches. A sentry walked along the fence near his position without even glancing up at the tree. He hadn't noticed that one large limb extended across the top of the fence to the interior of the factory property.

The ninja allowed the man to pass by the tree before he moved forward, grabbed the branch and swung down into the compound. Trent grabbed the sword handle while still in the air, drawing the long steel blade before his feet touched the ground. The guard heard movement and turned to see the flash of metal. Sharp steel struck the side of his neck before he could realize what happened. Trent's powerful stroke chopped through muscle and bone with a single blow, and the man was decapitated.

CALVIN JAMES SAW Trent take out the guard. His stomach knotted at the grisly sight, but the Phoenix Force veteran had witnessed far worse and realized the decapitation of the guard was an efficient method of taking the man out silently. The man's death was, in fact, mercifully swift.

The African-American warrior had remained hidden by some bushes at a knoll some distance from the plant. He covered the Executioner and Trent with an M-16 rifle held ready in case they needed backup. Fortunately it hadn't been necessary.

James moved forward. Burdened by a small black duffel bag, as well as his own weapons and gear, he jogged to the fence as quickly and as quietly as he could.

Trent waited for the Phoenix Force warrior at the fence, near the tree. The black commando hurled the bag over the barrier, which Trent caught. He sucked in a tense breath when metal rattled loudly inside the bag. But it didn't draw the attention of the patrolling sentries.

James climbed the tree and swung down from the overhanging branch inside the fence. The Phoenix pro and Trent moved to cover by a large metal bin. James unslung the M-16 from his shoulder as his companion opened the duffel bag. He removed a Remington pump shotgun with a cut-down barrel, and a combat pistol grip with a folding stock.

Firearms weren't generally regarded as ninja weapons, yet guns had been used by the ninja in Japan since the sixteenth century. They carried *futokoro-teppo,* pistols made of bronze, before the samurai appreciated the advantages of matchlock firearms in combat. Trent moved the ninja *ken* from his back and slid it into his *obi* belt at a cross-draw position. Then he slipped the sling to the shotgun over his right shoulder.

He removed an Uzi machine pistol from the bag and handed it to James. The commando nodded and accepted the weapon, which was standard for Phoenix Force. He also carried another Phoenix favorite, a Walther P-88 in shoulder leather under one arm. James also had a Blackmoor Dirk sheathed under the other arm and ammo pouches with spare magazines for his weapons on his belt. His medic's kit was in a case at the small of his back.

Trent took some more ninja weaponry from the duffel bag. He held up a *yumi* bow and a quiver of *ya* arrows. Shorter than the bow and arrows used in traditional *kyujutsu* archery, the *yumi* and *ya* were more compact and easier to conceal. He attached the quiver to his belt by the right hip.

A figure approached their position. Trent drew an arrow from the quiver and prepared to notch it to the bowstring. James reached for the hilt of his dirk, ready to draw the knife if a sentry moved close enough to take out with the blade.

The tall man in black gestured at the pair to relax. They recognized the Executioner. Bolan had retrieved his Uzi and carried it from a shoulder strap. The warrior had spotted the other two men and moved to their position. He barely glanced at the headless corpse of the slain sentry.

The Executioner checked his watch. Things were going according to schedule so far, more or less, as planned. There was still a lot to do, and the next ten minutes would be critical.

No words had to be spoken. Bolan tilted his head toward one building to indicate their target. He'd take the other one himself. James and Trent nodded in reply.

CHAPTER FIFTEEN

The guard was getting bored. He'd been on duty for the past four hours. The man was supposed to be patrolling along the catwalk to see the entire plant from the elevated position on the bridge, three stories high. However, he found the constant back-and-forth march along the catwalk tiresome and took frequent breaks inside a room by one end of the bridge, where he'd stashed a small flask of vodka. Some of the others had also violated Arashi's ban on alcohol, and at least one had smuggled in some hashish. The guard had blown a bowl with the guy the night before and hoped there was still enough left for another smoke after he got off watch.

Arashi was going too far with his "purity and sacrifice of the samurai" concept, in the sentry's opinion. None of them were children, and they had all picked up some vices of one kind or another. Arashi's followers were a mixed lot. Some were former Japanese Red Army zealots and political extremists with similar attitudes, but most were essentially strong-arm hoods who figured the terrorist's scheme had potential to net a lot of money in a short time. That was better than working as a bottom-of-the-barrel gunner for some minor-league Yakuza clan.

The sentry put away his bottle and walked from the room to the catwalk. He strolled with the warm ball in his stomach to comfort him. He was glad he had the vodka. If they earned as much money as they were supposed to with the operation, he figured he'd move to a South Pacific island and spend his time drinking Russian vodka and sleeping with beautiful, willing women.

The guard looked down from his perch. He didn't see the sentries on duty below. Maybe they got bored walking around and were sipping a bit of forbidden booze, as well. Suddenly he realized he hadn't noticed either of the men for the past four minutes. It was too unlikely both men would be goofing off at the same time. Especially since the watch commander checked on the sentries at irregular intervals to make certain they were alert.

He suddenly realized something had gone wrong. The sound of an object hissing through air confirmed this. The guard glimpsed the blur of a projectile a split second before a terrible pain stabbed into his chest. His hands instinctively grabbed the wooden shaft of the arrow. The metal tip and several inches of the shaft were buried in his flesh.

The guard's mouth fell open, but his tongue seemed welded to the bottom jaw. His muscles locked and he couldn't move. The man's heart stopped beating as the poison-tipped arrowhead constricted the life pump. The pain suddenly ceased as the curare robbed him of all feeling except for the stark terror of death. The end came quickly, and he collapsed to the catwalk, hands still clutching the arrow shaft.

John Trent lowered his bow. He knelt in the shadows by a building beneath the catwalk, satisfied that the sentry was dead. It seemed they had managed to dispatch all the guards without alerting the rest of the terrorists. The sound of door hinges creaking behind Trent abruptly drew his attention.

He turned to discover two men staring back at him. It was difficult to say who was more startled, Trent or the pair of terrorists who discovered the black-clad ninja lurking in the darkness. The first man, a short stocky Japanese with a drooping mustache, cursed under his breath and yanked a Nambu pistol from a hip holster.

Trent stepped forward and slashed the bow across the man's wrist. The hard bamboo struck the Nambu from the guy's numb fingers. Trent quickly thrust the heel of his other hand under his adversary's jaw. The terrorist fell backward into the wall as his taller comrade clawed at a revolver in shoulder leather.

The ninja warrior swung a kick to the second terrorist's arm. The edge of his foot chopped into the man's forearm to prevent him from drawing the gun. Trent snapped a back-fist to the side of the man's head and smashed a knuckle into his temple, taking him out of play. But Trent's first opponent whipped a switchblade from a pocket. He pressed the button, and a long blade snapped into place.

Trent's left hand grabbed the hilt of his sword in an unconventional draw as he turned slightly. The ninja *ken* cleared the scabbard, the blade jutting from the bottom of Trent's left fist. His right hand smacked the butt of the sword handle as he pivoted and drove the weapon into the knifeman's chest. The slanted tip pierced the man's solar plexus, and his mouth fell open as blood bubbled up into his throat.

The knife fell from the dying man's grasp as sharp steel bit into his aorta. He grabbed the sword blade in a desperate attempt to pull it out, but Trent shoved hard and drove the dying man to the ground. He didn't try to yank the sword from the guy's body. Instead, he turned to face his other enemy.

The second terrorist started to rise, still dazed by the temple blow. He once again reached for the revolver. Trent kicked him in the temple, driving him to the ground. The man in black quickly straddled his adversary's back and planted a knee between the guy's shoulder blades. He grabbed his opponent's hair with one hand and cupped the other under the fallen man's chin.

Trent pulled with one hand and pushed with the other. The force twisted the terrorist's head violently. Vertebrae cracked in the man's neck, and his body went limp. Trent released the motionless form, then moved to the other corpse and retrieved his sword.

He slid the sword into the scabbard with practiced ease as he glanced about for more signs of the enemy. He saw none. The pair he had encountered hadn't appeared to be stalking him. That meant they didn't know the factory was under siege. He took a deep breath to calm his racing heart as he carefully moved to the door.

MACK BOLAN LOCATED the motor pool. He knelt beside the corpse of a guard who had been stationed at the vehicles. The Executioner's garrote was still wound about the dead man's neck. He hid behind a pallet of cement bags as he watched two men haul a crate to the open tailgate of one of the three two-and-a-half-ton trucks parked in the pool.

They muttered something in Japanese. Bolan wished he understood the language because he was curious about what the terrorists were doing. The burden the men carried seemed quite heavy, as both were breathing heavily. The Executioner quietly advanced while the pair was busy loading the long box into the rig. One guy was inside the truck, pulling the crate, while the other stood at the end of the tailgate and pushed.

Bolan stepped behind the man at the rear of the rig. He held the Beretta in his fist and chopped the butt behind the hardman's ear. The man uttered a soft moan and crumpled to the ground. His companion stared down at Bolan with astonishment as the Executioner pointed the 93-R at his face. The terrorist clawed for hardware, and the warrior triggered the pistol. A single 9 mm parabellum round entered the man's open mouth and drilled upward to tunnel through his brain.

Boot leather behind Bolan warned him of danger. He turned swiftly as a wooden box hurtled toward his head. He dodged the crate, which smashed into the tailgate and split open. He heard metal clatter on the paved ground, but his attention was fixed on the terrorist.

The man launched a booted foot at the warrior, slamming into his hand and kicking the pistol from his grasp. The karate-trained terrorist shouted a *kiai* as he slashed a hand at Bolan's face. The Executioner ducked under the karate chop and thrust a hard left jab to his opponent's chin.

The punch drove the guy back two steps. The Executioner grabbed his slung Uzi and whipped the steel frame in a uppercut to the man's face. The guy's knees buckled and he fell to the ground.

The Executioner glanced down at the items that had spilled from the broken crate. Several magazines for assault rifles and submachine guns lay scattered on the ground. Bolan guessed what was in the larger crate. Guns. Maybe even mounted machine guns and rocket launchers. The terrorists were getting ready to move. They were either headed for a new base or about to carry out another attack.

Either way, Bolan vowed, they wouldn't be going anywhere. He climbed into the back of the truck, took a hand grenade from his belt and placed it on the floorboards by the long crate. The Executioner grabbed an end to the big box and lifted the heavy container. He was a strong man, but the task wasn't easy. He held the crate off the floorboards and used a boot to shove the grenade under it.

He lowered the crate onto the bomb, pinning it firmly. He checked for approaching terrorists as he opened a pouch that contained some emergency survival gear. He removed a length of fishing line and tied one end to the ring of the grenade pin. He loosened the pin to be certain the line would pull it out when desired. Then Bolan climbed from the truck and closed the tailgate. He tied the other end of the line to a stud at the center of the interior of the gate.

After preparing the booby trap, the warrior dragged one of the unconscious terrorists to the cement bags and used plastic riot cuffs to bind the guy's wrists behind his back. The hardman moaned as he began to regain consciousness. Bolan punched him on the chin to knock him back to dreamland.

Another figure emerged from the door to the storage section of the building. Bolan pressed his back against the wall and drew his Beretta. The new arrival carried another crate on a shoulder. It was about the same size as the one previously hurled at the Executioner. The guy hadn't noticed the still form of his battered comrade sprawled by the rear of the truck, but he'd certainly see him in another moment or two.

Bolan looked at the doorway. No one else was coming. He quickly moved behind the terrorist workman and kicked the back of his knee. The guy's leg buckled, and he started to fall. The warrior whipped the Beretta across the back of the man's skull. The crate hit the ground first, and the man fell across it.

He moved to the doorway and listened for sounds of more enemy laborers. Boot leather on concrete warned him someone was inside. Rock-and-roll music blared from a radio. It was a song popular in the United States in the mid-1970s, but sung in Japanese. Bolan carefully peered around the door frame.

Several crates were stacked in the storage room, some long enough to contain weapons and others the right size for magazines, ammunition or grenades. Bolan spotted two men. They were about to pick up another long crate, one at each end. The warrior ventured closer. Neither man noticed him.

Bolan pointed his Beretta at the pair and silently advanced. He held the pistol in one hand as he drew his Ka-bar combat knife from a belt sheath with the other. The Executioner stepped behind one terrorist as the pair lifted the crate, raised the gun butt and brought it crashing down onto the man's nape.

The other terrorist was stunned as he saw his comrade suddenly collapse and the tall foreigner appear behind the slain figure. Bolan lunged before the startled man could respond to the unexpected threat. He thrust the Ka-bar high and jammed the steel tip under the man's chin. The knife pierced the windpipe, and the warrior sliced it sideways to cut a carotid artery, as well. Blood spilled from the terrible wound as the terrorist uttered ugly gurgling sounds. Bolan slapped the Beretta against the guy's skull to knock him unconscious to allow him to die with as little pain as possible.

The Executioner checked his watch. Five and a half minutes remained before Grimaldi was due to arrive. He had to conceal the bodies and bind and gag the unconscious terrorists quickly.

CALVIN JAMES USED his dirk to jimmy a window. He slipped over the sill to enter a dark, unoccupied room, which turned out to be a men's rest room. The water supply to the plant had been cut off since the factory closed. Although the terrorists used buckets of water to flush the toilets, the smell of stale urine was unpleasant as James crossed the room to the door.

He carefully eased it open slightly to peer into the next room and discovered a bay section that had been converted into a barracks. Numerous sleeping mats were placed on the floor, but only one figure knelt by an impromptu bed. The lone man was busy packing a small duffel bag. Apparently the others had already gathered up their belongings and left.

The terrorists had to be getting ready to bug out, James thought. He considered capturing the man and interrogating him, but realized it would probably be a waste of time. Many Japanese spoke English to some degree, but the guy might not be one of them. Besides, experience had taught James that terrorists weren't easily intimidated into giving information. Some would gladly die rather than talk.

Maybe the guy wouldn't respond to questions asked at gunpoint, but James wasn't going to let him pack his bag and walk out to join his terrorist buddies, either. The African-American opened the door wider and emerged from the rest room. He pointed the silencer-equipped muzzle of the M-16 at the terrorist as he crept quietly toward the man's back.

The hardman didn't detect danger. James held his breath as he catfooted closer. The terrorist was still busy stuffing his gear into the bag and didn't turn to see the tall dark figure. The Phoenix pro judged the distance and swung the buttstock of his assault rifle to smash the guy in the base of the skull. The man groaned and fell across the sleeping mat.

James looked down at the unconscious figure and prepared to reach for a set of plastic riot cuffs. He heard the rustle of cloth and turned to discover another terrorist had appeared from the entrance to the bay section. The commando barely glimpsed the angry expression on the man's features and the flash of the long steel blade as he raised the M-16 instinctively, holding the rifle like a bar in his fists. The terrorist's sword clanged against the steel frame. James whipped a roundhouse kick to his opponent's rib cage before the guy could attempt another stroke with the samurai short sword.

The kick staggered the terrorist and knocked him backward almost two yards. Enraged, the swordsman raised his weapon. James quickly pointed the M-16 at the attacker and squeezed the trigger. A 3-round burst sputtered from the silencer. The 5.56 mm slugs tore into the man's chest, left of center. He charged and swung the sword in a wild overhead cut. James dodged the attack. The terrorist's body followed the motion of the sword and crashed to the floor in a lifeless heap.

James took a deep breath and turned toward the bay entrance. No more terrorists had materialized to threaten the Stony Man warrior. This was small comfort since he knew there were many enemies left to deal with. He didn't take time to count all the sleeping mats, but there were at least fifty. A hell of a lot of opposition for just three guys—even three very well trained and experienced fighting men—to take on. James also realized the mats in the bay area might only represent half or one third of the total number of terrorists at the factory.

"Oh, well," he muttered as he looked at his watch. "I volunteered for this, so I guess I shouldn't bitch."

CHAPTER SIXTEEN

Jack Grimaldi sat at the controls of the Bell gunship. A very nervous bilingual Kompei agent was in the copilot seat beside the Stony Man fly-boy. Grimaldi was pleased with the chopper. Kompei had made the modifications he required, and the helicopter was fit for duty—which meant it was ready for combat if necessary.

He had scanned the multilighted city of Osaka from the night sky, assisted by an aerial map of the area. Grimaldi concentrated on the controls while his companion consulted the map and assisted in directions. The Stony Man pro glanced at the digital clock on the panel. They had one minute to reach the Hinshitsu Semento.

The helicopter hovered near the cement factory. The dark aircraft circled the area to observe the setting below. Grimaldi didn't see any guards patrolling the factory, but he did see some vehicles parked in an improvised motor pool. Bolan, James and Trent were certainly inside. They would have contacted him if the place turned out to be a false lead. It had to be for real, and Bolan was maintaining radio silence. They had no way of knowing what frequencies the enemy might be monitoring or how sophisticated the electrical equipment at the enemy base might be.

Grimaldi concentrated on his role in the raid. He looked down at the uniformed figures that approached the factory. Japanese paratroopers and police officers had assembled in a horseshoe pattern. Kompei had called in backup. They were just waiting for the signal to move in. They might have to wait for a while longer. Grimaldi wasn't going to send in the cavalry unless he was sure it was necessary. If they hit too soon, they could alert the enemy to trouble. Apparently Bolan and his companions had been able to function inside the factory without being discovered by the majority of the terrorists. Otherwise there'd be a full-blown firefight going on.

The pilot was also concerned about sending in the Japanese soldiers and cops because they weren't experienced at this sort of operation. Grimaldi didn't question the courage or skill of these men, but that was no substitute for the hard edge acquired in actual combat.

"When should I make the announcement?" the Kompei agent inquired as he held the microphone to the loudspeaker installed under the chopper.

"As soon as we're over the factory," the pilot answered. "They'll hear these rotor blades anyway. This bird is a lot of things, but it ain't quiet."

The Intelligence officer nodded and looked down at the roof of the first building to the plant. He swallowed hard and began to talk into the mike. Grimaldi didn't understand the message that roared from the amplifier, but he knew the Kompei agent was warning Arashi and his people that the place was surrounded and they were to come out with their hands up. Not very original, but straight to the point.

Only trouble was, Grimaldi had never known terrorists to give up that easily.

THE BOOMING VOICE from the helicopter reached Arashi and the terrorists inside the building. They had congregated at a massive bay section for last-minute instructions by the leader. Thirteen of their number were missing, but the others assumed they were either standing guard or loading the trucks. However, no one had called out to announce the approach of the helicopter they heard overhead.

At the moment the absent personnel were of no consequence compared to the immediate threat presented by the announcement that the base was surrounded by the police and military. Most of their small arms, ammunition and explosives were being loaded onto trucks. Some of the terrorists still carried pistols, but most were armed only with swords, knives and stick weapons.

"You five men!" Arashi shouted. "Go to the storage room. Open any crates not already loaded onto the vehicles and bring what weapons and ammunition you can find. Hurry!"

The men dashed from the bay area to the storage sections, racing past a row of cement bags without noticing the crouching Executioner. Bolan allowed the enemy to jog by as he pulled the pin from an M-26 fragmentation grenade.

The warrior had observed the terrorists from his concealment. There were about fifty of them, but at least he didn't see any automatic weapons in their hands. Arashi was easily identified among his gray-clad followers. He still wore a *gi* with his fancy *katana* thrust in his sash. The terrorist boss was also barking orders at his henchmen. He sent two of them to a ladder that extended to the raised ceiling, no doubt to use the trapdoor to the roof to check on the location of the helicopter. The guy probably figured paratroopers might be sliding down cables to the roof.

They were about to find out the danger was even closer than Arashi feared. Bolan popped the spoon from the grenade and hurled the bomb into the storage room behind the five men who had entered it. As he moved along the stacks of bags to a more secure position beyond the mouth of the doorway, a startled cry revealed that one of the terrorists had spotted the grenade.

Too late. The blast sent dust and wooden splinters spewing from the room. In the confined area, there was no question the explosion had killed all five hardmen.

The blast sent terrorists scurrying for cover. The pair by the ladder froze in place. One had started to climb the iron rungs while the other ducked low at the bottom. The guy on the ladder glanced over his shoulder to see where the explosion came from. Something hit him in the side of the head as he fell, landing at the feet of his comrade. The second terrorist stared down at the lifeless, blank expression on the fallen figure. A metal throwing star was lodged in the corpse's left temple.

With a gasp of astonishment, the second man looked up to see a black shape suddenly appear from the shadows. John Trent swung his sword and struck the terrorist in the side of the neck. The blade sliced through the man's carotid artery, jugular and throat with a single stroke. The hardman staggered backward and clasped his hands around his throat. The effort to plug the wound failed, and the man slumped to the floor, bleeding to death.

Calvin James was hidden behind a huge cement-mixing machine, positioned opposite Bolan's station by the bags. He was ready when the explosion occurred. He'd been waiting for the Executioner to make the first move as a signal for the battle to begin. He didn't know Bolan would start things off with such a dramatic bang, but there was no doubt it was time for fireworks.

Taking advantage of the confusion and the fact the enemies' attention was turned toward the explosion in the storage room, James raised the M-16 to his shoulder and carefully aimed. He had a good view of most of the terrorists and selected his target based on which appeared to offer the biggest immediate threat.

He triggered a 3-round burst. The silenced assault rifle coughed harshly, the sound virtually lost in the roar of the grenade. A terrorist armed with a U.S. Army Colt .45 jerked violently as the 5.56 mm slugs slammed into his chest. James saw the guy go down and quickly swung his rifle toward a figure packing a North Korean Type-68 autoloader. His target reached cover by a forklift and sprawled on his belly. Unfortunately the guy was worried about an attack from the direction of the explosion and ducked behind the forklift accordingly. This kept him safe from Bolan, but presented James with a clear target. The Phoenix Force fighter fired another trio of rounds that drilled the terrorist through the heart.

"You can't win here," Trent shouted in Japanese. "Surrender while you still can!"

"Never!" an angry voice replied, and fired a pistol in the general direction of Trent's voice.

Trent had already moved to a solid concrete pillar two yards from his previous position. The enemy bullets didn't come close to the ninja. All the terrorist accomplished was to present himself as a clear target for the Executioner. Bolan fired his Beretta and nailed the man with two parabellum rounds in the back of the neck.

A few terrorists saw the muzzle-flash of the silenced 93-R. Pistols fired desperate rounds at the cement bags, but Bolan's cover was an ideal bunker. The bullets were absorbed by the thick sacks. The terrorists charged, some wielding handguns, others carrying swords or clubs.

The Executioner switched to the Uzi and thrust the barrel between two stacks of cement bags. He opened fire and sprayed four attackers with 9 mm missiles at torso level, punching them to the ground. The three survivors bolted away from the cement bags, unwilling to risk being gunned down like their comrades.

Two fanatics dared to continue and jumped to the stacks of bags, climbing to the top. Bolan raised the Uzi and fired a short burst into the belly of the closer man. Parabellum stingers ripped into the kamikaze and sent his body hurtling backward to crash to the floor.

The Executioner turned to aim the subgun at the second attacker. A *wakazashi* blade clanged along the barrel and frame of the Uzi to deflect the aim of the weapon. Bolan held his fire and jumped back as far as the cramped area allowed. The swordsman kept the flat of his short sword pressed against the Uzi to prevent Bolan from adjusting the aim.

The warrior shoved the gun upward, forcing his adversary to hold the subgun at bay with the blade. Bolan's other hand drew the Desert Eagle from shoulder leather. He rapidly pointed the big Magnum and blasted a .44 slug through the chest of his astonished attacker. The impact of the powerful projectile hurled the swordsman two yards and dropped him lifeless on the floor.

TERRORISTS ALSO CHARGED the positions held by James and Trent. The black American commando and ninja warrior opened fire. Full-auto 5.56 mm bullets and 12-gauge bursts of buckshot cut down several terrorists before they could get close to the fighting machines in black. Others quickly changed their minds and headed for cover, but a few continued the attack.

James blasted a sword-swinging terrorist with a trio of high-velocity slugs that tore into the guy's skull. Another hardman swung an unusual weapon that consisted of a long chain with a sickle blade at one end and an iron weight at the other. The *kusarigama* was an ancient samurai device. The terrorist unleashed the sickle end of the chain, and the deadly blade hurtled at James's head.

The Phoenix warrior reached swiftly and raised the M-16 to protect himself. Metal clanged on metal as the sickle met the steel frame of the rifle. The blade hooked the carrying handle, and part of the chain wound around the rifle barrel. The Japanese yanked hard, and the M-16 was suddenly ripped from James's grasp.

"Son of a bitch!" the black commando roared.

The second man was armed with a *bo,* or fighting stick. He screamed a *kiai* and slashed the stave in a vicious stroke intended to crack James's skull. The Phoenix pro dodged the attack, and the stick whistled through air, one end striking the concrete floor hard. The terrorist didn't have proper control of the *bo.* He not only missed his target, but he also stumbled from loss of balance.

James quickly grabbed the stick before his opponent could attack again. He launched a high roundhouse kick and slammed his boot into the side of the man's head. His adversary collapsed to the floor, unconscious, to join the increasing number of Arashi's slain followers.

TRENT WORKED THE PUMP to his Remington and fired another load of buckshot into the chest of a gunman who was about to pull the trigger of a Model-68 pistol. The force of the 12-gauge blast hurled him into the middle of the bay area.

The ninja jacked the slide action rapidly and ejected the spent shell casing. He pointed the shotgun at a trio of opponents armed with *wakazashi* short swords. Two of the terrorists lowered their blades and appeared to be ready to surrender, but the third raised his sword and charged. Trent squeezed the trigger.

A feeble click was the only response.

He had used up the shotgun shells from the tubular magazine of the riot gun. There was no time to reload as the swordsman closed in. Trent stepped backward and gripped the shotgun like a club as the terrorist screamed and advanced. The ninja swung the Remington while the attacker was still almost three yards away, releasing the shotgun. It slammed into the legs of the attacking figure, chopping him across the shins. He fell face-first to the floor, but the other two killers recovered and attacked Trent.

The ninja from the U.S. drew his sword as the enemy charged. He slashed a cross-body stroke, and the blade clashed with the one man's *wakazashi*. Trent suddenly stepped forward and passed his startled opponent. He delivered another stroke before the second man realized he was a target. The guy tried to parry the *ken* with his short sword, but he was a fraction of a second too late. Trent's blade bit into the man's neck.

Furious, the first swordsman raised his *wakazashi* and swung an overhead stroke at Trent's back, hoping to cleave his spine. Trent raised his right arm high, sword in his fist, and bent his elbow. The long blade of the ninja *ken* formed a bar to protect his back, and the enemy's blade met steel instead of flesh.

Trent pivoted before his dumbfounded adversary could attack again. His sword swooped with the motion of his body and slashed the terrorist across the stomach. Sharp steel cut cloth and slit flesh. The man gasped in surprise and pain, and sank to his knees, effectively out of the play.

Embarrassed that he had fallen on his face after being tricked by the ninja, the terrorist who had first challenged Trent was determined to take revenge in blood.

The ninja's arms rose, a sword in each fist. The terrorist's *wakazashi* descended, only to be blocked by the twin blades that formed a variation of an X-block. Trent pushed hard and shoved his opponent's blade to one side. He used the ninja *ken* to continue to press the enemy blade back and simultaneously swung the confiscated short sword in his other fist. The blade hacked into the side of his opponent's neck, and it was all over.

THE BATTLE WASN'T going well for Arashi's forces. Mitsuzuka, Arashi's lieutenant, decided he wasn't eager to join his ancestors or whatever happened when one died. That would happen soon enough. He didn't want to die and didn't want to see his comrades slaughtered. He knew Arashi wouldn't order them to surrender, so he elected to be the example for the others.

The terrorist removed a white handkerchief from his hip pocket and draped it over the tip of his sword. He held it up above the assembly-line conveyer belt he used for cover. Mitsuzuka hoped the other terrorists, as well as their opponents, noticed the white flag and appreciated what it meant.

"Stop this! We surrender!" he cried out.

Mitsuzuka slowly rose. The shooting abated on both sides. No shots were fired at him as he stood with the white banner held high. A few fellow terrorists reluctantly appeared, hands raised in surrender.

Arashi suddenly charged, his *katana* clenched in his fists. The terrorist commander reached Mitsuzuka in three rapid strides. The lieutenant turned to face his leader and saw a streak of light flash along the long blade. The *katana* struck with deadly speed and accuracy. Sharp steel sliced through the lieutenant's neck. His head hit the floor and rolled into clear view of the terrorists.

"Disgraceful," Arashi hissed with contempt. "If we are to die, let us do so as men, not cowards."

"Really?" Trent called out in a mocking tone. "Are you willing to show the others how this is done?"

"Yes," Arashi replied, brandishing the bloodstained *katana*. "Yes. Are you willing to face me in a duel of honor, or will you simply shoot me like the coward you no doubt are?"

"I will oblige you with a duel after I explain this to my friends."

Trent switched from Japanese to English and called out to Bolan and James. He told them he had agreed to fight Arashi in a duel and told them not to interfere.

The Executioner wasn't pleased. He had deliberately avoided shooting Arashi because he wanted to take the terrorist commander alive if possible. However, Arashi stood fully exposed to their line of fire. It was obvious the man was willing, maybe even eager, to die. He would probably commit suicide if he wasn't killed in combat, or might even cut himself open in the traditional manner of a samurai. Arashi was the type to choose *seppuku* if his plans failed.

"I don't like it," James called out from his position by the cement mixer, "but I figure John's taking the biggest risk, so it's his decision. Belasko?"

"Okay," the Executioner agreed reluctantly. "We won't interfere in the duel as long as Arashi's people do likewise."

Voices muttered in excited Japanese. Surviving terrorists rose from cover and eagerly nodded to express their willingness to abide by Bolan's rules. Arashi stepped forward, *katana* once again in the scabbard in his sash. He moved to the center of the bay section and waited for his opponent.

Trent emerged. He had removed his .45 and shoulder holster. The ninja carried his sword in his *obi*. Arashi was surprised to discover his opponent dressed in the black costume, hood and face scarf of an ancient ninja warrior. The terrorist smiled.

"You think you are ninja?" Arashi inquired with amusement. "I am samurai. Your ancestors were peasants and thieves. Mine were aristocrats, born to a ruling class that kept you rabble in your place. We were the finest warriors the world has ever known and you simply represent a tradition of cowards who could only fight at night. Was that so your people could hide in the shadows?"

"No one is hiding now," Trent replied simply. "Are you ready, or do you choose to fight with words instead of steel?"

Arashi stiffened his back and replied with a curt nod. Trent faced the terrorist. They squared off roughly three yards apart. The Japanese waited for Trent to bow first, acknowledging him as a samurai worthy of respect. Trent didn't oblige. He knew that angry men could be careless and perhaps forget their training in the heat of battle. He also hoped his adversary underestimated him in the duel. The ninja certainly wouldn't make the same mistake.

Since Trent refused to show him the gesture of respect by nodding first, Arashi decided to abandon all formalities and drew his *katana*. Trent's *ken* flashed from its scabbard as Arashi attacked. Blades clashed when Trent blocked the first enemy stroke.

Arashi continued the assault and forced the American to adopt defensive tactics. The terrorist's *katana* was longer than his opponent's sword, and the steel was better quality. Trent realized this and tried to strike at the flat of Arashi's blade while parrying attacks. A solid cut to his ninja *ken* by the edge of Arashi's weapon might break Trent's blade.

The terrorist swung a powerful blow that knocked Trent's sword aside, pivoting with the motion of the stroke. Trent was familiar with this move and also whirled, flowing with the movement of his blade when it was struck. Arashi completed the turn and slashed his sword in a diagonal cut. He had hoped to catch Trent off guard and with his sword unprepared for the cut. Instead, the ninja's blade once again met the terrorist's steel.

Trent hooked a kick under Arashi's ribs. The terrorist grunted and staggered from the blow. Trent tried to capitalize on this and attacked, but Arashi blocked the sword with a rising stroke of his *katana.* He held the sword handle with one hand to push Trent's blade and grabbed the ninja's wrist with his other hand.

The Japanese ducked under the blades, moved forward and suddenly dropped to one knee. He used the momentum and leverage to hurl Trent head over heels with an adroit aikido throw. The American crashed on his back hard. He managed to raise his head and absorb some of the impact with his feet, but the fall on the concrete was punishing nonetheless.

The terrorist swung his blade, aiming at Trent's neck. The ninja looked up from the floor and instinctively raised the ninja *ken*. Arashi's blade clanged along the sword. The terrorist shouted an angry *kiai* and kicked Trent's hand that clutched the ninja *ken* handle. The

American's fist popped open, and the sword flew from his numbed fingers.

Sensing victory, Arashi slashed a cross-body stroke, as Trent rolled and jumped to his feet. Trent ducked under the sword stroke, drawing his short blade. The *katana* slashed above his skull and tugged at the black hood to his ninja garb. Trent barely noticed how close he came to death as he moved closer and thrust his sword under Arashi's extended left arm.

The sharp edge cut deep into the sensitive nerve center at Arashi's armpit. The terrorist screamed in agony as blood oozed from the wound. Trent released his weapon and grabbed his adversary's wrists with both hands. The nerve damage tapped the strength from the terrorist and left him semiparalyzed. Trent easily wrenched the *katana* from Arashi's grasp. The terrorist sank to the floor.

The remaining terrorists raised their hands and stepped forward. Some bowed to Trent in honor of his victory. Bolan suspected Arashi might have been respected and feared by the followers, but they didn't appear to have liked him very much.

"John?" James inquired. "You okay, man?"

"A little out of breath," Trent replied as he pulled away the scarf mask and inhaled deeply.

"You'll have to catch your breath pretty quick," Bolan told him. "We need you to tell the prisoners to file outside. A lot of police officers and soldiers are waiting to meet them."

CHAPTER SEVENTEEN

Gary Manning and Henri Richet met David McCarter, Rafael Encizo and Inspector Alan Jenkins at the Paris international airport. Sûreté had waived customs for the Phoenix Force commandos, and no one had opened the aluminum cases carried by the British and Cuban members of the Stony Man operations group.

They said little until they were in a minibus supplied by French Intelligence. The rig was soundproof, the windows were tinted to ensure privacy and the driver was an agent of Sûreté who stayed with the bus to make sure no electrical eavesdropping devices had been planted in the vehicle. The rig lumbered from the airport parking lot and pulled into a road filled with traffic.

"This is Inspector Richet," Manning introduced the Sûreté officer. "He worked with us in Toulouse. Silverman and I had some strings pulled so he could help us here in Paris."

"Toulouse?" Rafael Encizo inquired with a frown.

"That's the closest city to the nuclear power plant the terrorists attacked," Manning explained. "We managed to figure out who launched a grenade shell into the plant, but he was using a fake ID and he may have already fled France."

"That's bloody lovely," McCarter complained as he fished a pack of Player's cigarettes from a pocket. "We got a pretty good lead on the bloke we're looking for connected with that attack on the North Sea oil derricks, but we tracked him here. Now he might have taken off with this other bastard, and God knows where those two are honeymooning now."

"I heard the guy you two hunted down in Scotland turned out to be the wrong one," the big Canadian remarked.

"Yeah," Encizo replied. "He looked suspicious for a while and sure acted like a guilty man when we caught up with him at a pub, but he's just a dumb hombre with a short temper."

"Where have I heard that before?" Manning said dryly as he stared at McCarter.

"Don't look at me," the Briton said with exaggerated offense at the implication. "I was a model of diplomacy in Scotland."

"That's a slight exaggeration," Encizo remarked. He recalled that they hadn't introduced Inspector Jenkins. The Cuban did so and added, "He's with Scotland Yard."

"Interpol section," Jenkins explained in a Cambridge accent that seemed too stuffy for a cop. "And we call it New Scotland Yard. Not that it's important."

So why was it brought up? McCarter thought, but he kept the remark from reaching his acerbic tongue.

Jenkins didn't look like a cop to Gary Manning. The man from Scotland Yard was slender and dapper, dressed in a neat blue double-breasted suit and a houndstooth tie. Jenkins hadn't made a good first impression with the Canadian, but Manning figured he could be jumping to conclusions. Besides, he didn't have to like the man in order to work with him.

"Sounds like you guys made some progress since that spot check yesterday," Manning said. "How about an update?"

"Sure," Encizo volunteered. "After we had that screwup with Locke, we went back to checking out personnel connected with the oil rigs. One of the suspects was a man who was on the payroll for a couple months as a security officer at the derricks."

"This sounds familiar," Richet commented.

"Well, this security bloke called himself McGregor," McCarter added. "Supposed to be a former army and ex-police constable. Turns out there was a real McGregor who fit that description, but he was killed in a house fire almost a year ago."

"Very similar to the cover story used by the man who assumed the identity of 'Charles Carrel,'" Manning said thoughtfully. "Of course, there's no reason why they shouldn't use similar tactics. How likely would it be for a French nuclear power plant and a British oil company to compare notes on the backgrounds of security personnel?"

"We're doing it now," Encizo stated. "The man we were after was pretty slick. Even his fingerprints were unidentifiable. He got away with it because he claimed his hands were burned in the fire."

"The same fire that killed the real McGregor," Jenkins added. "Those chaps with the oil company should have done their homework a bit better. Of course, the fire that killed McGregor happened in Greece, and he was hospitalized for some time before he died. I suppose the imposter convinced the oil people that reports of his death had been grossly exaggerated. Didn't Mark Twain say something like that?"

"I don't think Mark Twain ever met the bloke we're after," McCarter said dryly. "Anyway, we did have a description on the imposter and photos taken when he worked at the oil derricks. Luckily Aberdeen is a small city with a small population. Folks recalled seeing 'McGregor.' One even said he thought he had met the bloke when he was in the service, but the fellow wasn't known as McGregor back then."

"He didn't happen to remember the man's real name?" Encizo inquired hopefully.

"Said it was something like 'Nelson' or 'Nielson,'" Encizo answered. "So that's when we got Interpol involved."

"We were, in fact, involved on the case before," Jenkins insisted. "However, this was an intriguing possibility so our chaps ran the descriptions, photos and the probable names through those lovely computers at New Scotland Yard. They came up with a man named Roger Nielson. Our files tell us Nielson did serve in the British army and then joined a mercenary outfit. Did some work in Africa in the late 1970s. Probably did some smuggling and gunrunning after that. We have him listed as an undesirable, suspected of violations of various crimes in more than one country."

"How much do you know about his mercenary outfit?" Manning inquired.

"No better than a band of hired thugs," the British inspector answered. "International group that consisted of vermin from several European countries. Seems to have been formed by some villains who got the boot from the French foreign legion back in the seventies."

"Most soldiers in the foreign legion are not French," Richet stated. He sounded somewhat defensive, as if he felt the Scotland Yard officer was accusing his countrymen of being responsible for the situation they faced. "The legion is not regarded as a mercenary one. They have fought for the national interests of France in hundreds of campaigns throughout our history."

"The men who were expelled from the legion were kicked out because they were rotten apples," Enciso explained. "Crooked characters can be found in any army, and the legion has attracted misfits in the past. The legion was wise enough to get rid of these unprincipled thugs. They can't be blamed for what the bastards did after they left."

"And the commanding officers of the foreign legion are French," McCarter added, displaying a rare concern for diplomacy to ease Richet's ruffled pride.

"So you guys came to Paris to try to get a lead on the men who were in the foreign legion?" Manning inquired.

"Better than that," McCarter replied. "We checked with the airports in Scotland and England. McGregor— or Nielson or whatever his real name is—took a flight from Glasgow to Paris the morning after the attack on the oil rigs. So he wound up here. Same as the bloke calling himself Carrel."

"We might have a decent connection here," Richet remarked.

"It looks encouraging," Manning agreed. "Silverman is at Sûreté headquarters. We'll see what he says."

"Any word about how our mates are doing with their missions in certain other parts of the world?" McCarter asked.

"Not that I know of," Manning replied. "I hope they've made more progress than we have so far."

The minibus rolled into the heart of Paris. Although it was a city filled with history and an abundance of tourist sites, the men of Phoenix Force knew from experience they would only get to enjoy the places of interest from the windows of the moving vehicle. They had been to Paris on previous missions and never had much time to spare on sight-seeing.

The driver headed for the suburbs of St. Cloud, where the Interpol headquarters building was located. Since they were going to check both Interpol and Sûreté records, it was the best place to start, Sûreté being the French section of Interpol.

Yakov Katzenelenbogen was glad to see his teammates enter the conference room. Calvin James was still in Japan with Bolan, but the rest of the Phoenix team was now assembled in one room. They told Katz what they had learned so far.

"The French foreign legion is based on the island of Corsica," Katz announced. "Check with them and see what they know about Nielson. Also see if they know anything about an ex-member who fits the description of the man who claims to be Charles Carrel. Interpol is already looking into fugitives who fit the description."

"Makes sense," Jenkins agreed. "Any other suggestions?"

"The men we're looking for are professionals, and they're backed by an international network that obviously has a great deal of money behind it," Katz answered. "That means they can afford to use the best when they need things like forged papers, passports, previous work documents and letters of recommendation by former employers. The best forgers in France are probably in Paris. That's where they'd get the largest number of clients. Correct?"

"Yes," Richet confirmed with a nod. "And I am sure Sûreté knows about them even if we have not been able to arrest the forgers due to lack of evidence."

"This is the sort of thing you people do best," Katz told the inspectors. "We can count on the cooperation from New Scotland Yard to investigate forgers in Great Britain?"

"Of course," Jenkins assured him. "I'll make a phone call and they'll be working on it immediately."

"So we've got a lot of work to do, gentlemen," Katz declared. "Things are looking better than when we arrived. We'll find them. We just have to keep looking."

An hour later Katz's predictions seemed to be coming true. The combined efforts of consulting the foreign legion base and Interpol records produced the real name of "Charles Carrel." The description fit an ex-legionnaire named Louis Gounod. He had formed a mercenary group along with some other expelled members of the legion and a handful of Spanish military personnel who had left their homeland after the death of Franco figuring they wouldn't like living in Spain if it became a democracy.

The mercs had conducted several campaigns in Africa. They didn't appear to be concerned about which side they fought on and didn't show any favoritism toward politics. Despots and dictators tended to have more money than revolutionary organizations. Gounod's mercenary army was believed to have participated in numerous atrocities while serving tyrants in third world countries.

However, it was also believed the majority of soldiers of fortune were killed during these operations. Work available to mercenaries was also dwindling as the world began to change. Fewer nations were interested in hiring such men. Association with ruthless European soldiers for hire wasn't the sort of thing any third world leader wanted. Gounod and what remained of his outfit turned to smuggling and gunrunning as a new source of income.

The mercs, including Nielson, were reported to be dealing arms out of Singapore in the middle 1980s. They might have also assisted Triad heroin smugglers in Hong Kong in transporting drugs to Australia and New Zealand. Nobody seemed quite sure what had happened to the mercenaries.

But at least Phoenix Force and Interpol knew who two of the terrorists were. Sûreté also had a list of the most successful forgers known to be operating in Paris, Marseilles, Lyons and Nice. At the head of the list was François Le Porge, known as "the Napoleon of Paper."

Katz accompanied Richet to visit Le Porge, who had a printing shop on Rue Lafayette. It was an innocent-looking establishment, and the man who sat behind the counter didn't appear to be a master criminal. Short, heavyset and bald, Le Porge peered at his visitors through the thick lenses of wire-rim glasses.

"Good day, gentlemen," Le Porge greeted. "What may I do for you today?"

"Are you François Le Porge?" Richet inquired as he produced his identification card.

"Yes," the man replied wearily, "I am Le Porge. What do you police want with me this time? I am an honest businessman. This harassment will not be tolerated."

"No harassment," Katz replied with an exaggerated shrug. "We just want to ask you a few questions. First, would you like Sûreté and the Paris police to make you their pet project from now on? Would you like twenty-four-hour surveillance? Would you like photographs taken every time you meet with anyone? Recordings made of conversations on the telephone, in this shop or on the street?"

"And you do not consider this harassment?" Le Porge said with a frown. "I believe I will call my lawyer now."

"Go ahead," Katz invited. "You'll find he's busy talking with another Sûreté officer and a friend of mine. They're explaining that you appear to be associated with a network of international terrorists responsible for acts of destruction and murder in four countries. This includes the bombing incident at a nuclear power plant here in France. I'm sure you read about it in the newspapers."

"I am sure your lawyer knows about this incident, and he will not want to be associated with you in a case of such terrible magnitude," Richet added. "Defending a forger is one thing, but defending a man connected with an international conspiracy, mass murder and attempted blackmail is quite another."

"I have nothing to do with such things, and I do not know what you are talking about," the forger insisted.

Richet took some photographs from an inside pocket of his jacket. He placed pictures of Gounod and Nielson on the counter. Le Porge looked down at them without betraying any sign that the faces were familiar.

"Do you recognize him?" Katz demanded as he tapped the steel hooks of his prosthesis on the photos of Gounod.

The Israeli noticed the metal extremity made Le Porge nervous, and he took advantage of this. The forger trembled as if afraid the stranger might use the hooks on him at any moment.

"No," Le Porge replied. "I do not know him."

"Really?" Katz inquired. "Maybe you'd better reconsider your answer. We're not interested in arresting you. We want this man and his friend Roger Nielson."

Katz rapped the hooks on the photo of the Scot. Le Porge looked as if he were about to jump to the ceiling.

"You had better cooperate," Richet said. "I do not think you would like spending the rest of your life in prison. No one has been executed in France since the 1970s, but that does not mean it is beyond possibility that you might face the guillotine. This is a crime of considerable degree. National security is involved, and your role may well be regarded as treason."

"My role?" Le Porge stared at the Sûreté officer. "I have nothing to do with terrorists."

"That may be," Katz allowed, "but you have seen at least one of these men before. He needed a forged passport and other papers. Who better for the job than the Napoleon of Paper?"

Le Porge considered his plight for a moment and spoke softly. "You're not going to arrest me or accuse me in any way for the actions of the terrorists?" he asked.

"Not if you cooperate," Richet replied.

"One moment," Le Porge said, and turned to a beaded curtain.

He left the room and returned a few minutes later with several documents. The forger placed them on the counter. Pictures of Gounod and Nielson were displayed for the visitors, as were passports, drivers' licenses and other ID.

"I've kept copies of some of the work I've done for certain people in case of emergencies," Le Porge explained. "Of course, I haven't let them know this. They expect me to be discreet."

"I see," Katz remarked as he examined the papers. "You made passports for Gounod in three different names and two for Nielson. Any idea where they might be going after they leave France?"

"They did not share that information with me," Le Porge answered. "But they obviously plan to do a fair amount of travel or one passport would be enough."

"That makes sense," Katz agreed. "We appreciate your cooperation in this matter."

"Sûreté may be calling on you again in the near future," Richet added as he gathered up the documents. "I trust you'll continue to cooperate with us."

"But I thought you were only concerned with this one matter," Le Porge said, but he realized this was a naive remark.

"For now," Richet replied. "But there will be other matters in the future. I've no doubt of that. Goodbye. It has been a pleasure."

Le Porge didn't appreciate the Sûreté officer's sarcasm. He watched the two strangers leave the shop. Perhaps it was time for the Napoleon of Paper to retire and go on a long vacation. A very long vacation.

CHAPTER EIGHTEEN

"I've been wondering about something," Gadgets Schwarz began as he stared at a wall map of the United States. "What do you figure happened to the submarine after the terrorists launched that attack on the garbage scow in New York?"

"Don't ask me," Carl Lyons replied. "Those hoods we interrogated in Jersey didn't know anything about it."

"Nobody's complaining," Hal Brognola assured the big ex-cop. "You guys stopped the terrorists from attacking another target in New Jersey. It's the first big blow to the other side."

Able Team had returned to Stony Man Farm after completing their work in New York and New Jersey. Although they had succeeded with their part of the mission, Able Team hadn't been able to get much useful information from the American and Colombian terrorists captured during the Jersey raid.

The men gathered in the Stony Man War Room for a briefing. The news could have been better, but they all knew it could have been much worse. Nonetheless, the mission was still far from over.

A phone rang. Brognola turned to the trio of multicolored telephones and looked for a blinking light. It was the white phone, which meant it was a call from someone in the Stony Man complex. He picked up the receiver.

"Feel like some good news, Hal?" the voice of Aaron Kurtzman inquired.

"I could sure use some. What's up?"

"Got a coded message from Striker," the Bear explained. "Our guys in Japan had a successful raid on a terrorist base there. Fifty-eight enemies were either killed or captured. No good guys were hurt. That includes Japanese cops, soldiers and, of course, Grimaldi, James and Trent. They're interrogating prisoners and going through the terrorists' base for evidence. Then Striker and company will be headed home."

"Great," the Stony Man operations chief said, pleased with the message. "Has Katz checked in yet?"

"Not since the last report. The Phoenix guys haven't caught up with any terrorists in Europe yet, but the trail is getting hotter. The people they're after seem to be more elusive than the terrorists in the States and Japan. They've been playing hopscotch from country to country. Katz figures the sons of bitches probably aren't even in France or Scotland now."

"Katz is a veteran espionage agent," Brognola commented. "He's been doing spy versus spy since he was a teenager. If anybody can hunt these bastards down, Katz and Phoenix Force can."

"Just hope they do it before the terrorists nail another target," Lyons muttered as he heard Brognola's side of the conversation.

The Stony Man chief hung up and told the others about the progress made by the other Stony Man commandos in the field.

"I think Gadgets has a point," Kissinger remarked as he moved to the map. "The terrorists had to use a small submarine. That's already been established. It has to be designed to be fast and able to descend to considerable depth. That's a pretty sophisticated piece of equipment. They couldn't have gotten their hands on something like that from very many sources. If we could find the sub, we might be able to trace where they got it from. That's a lead worth looking into."

"Okay," Lyons said with a sigh. "But where the hell do we look? The Coast Guard didn't find anything, and neither has the ONI. The Navy radar didn't pick up a thing. Coast Guard must have stopped every boat within two hundred miles of the attack. They didn't find any trace of the sub or even anyone suspicious in the area."

"So the submarine didn't stay in the area," Gadgets insisted. "I think it headed down the coast. No one was looking for it off the coast of Delaware. Besides, it could remain deep enough to avoid detection by the Coast Guard and it would be small enough to be mistaken for a whale or a school of fish by radar unless the people knew exactly what they were looking for on the screen."

"Interesting theory," Blancanales said, "but if the submarine is so small it wouldn't be able to store much fuel in its tanks. How far could something like that go without refueling?"

"The terrorists obviously planned this in advance," Schwarz answered. "They would have refueling spots along the coast. Either by boat or by using platforms stationed along the path."

"Platforms would be more discreet," Kissinger said. "They could have part of it under water and refuel without surfacing by using frogmen to do it underwater."

"You keep saying down the coast, Gadgets," Brognola observed. "Why couldn't they have headed north? Toward Maine or even Canada?"

"That's possible," Schwarz admitted. "But I think it's more likely they'd go south. Apparently Colombian drug cartels are involved somehow. That would suggest they'd rather move south."

"Figure the sub went all the way back to South America?" Lyons asked, shaking his head. "That sounds awfully farfetched to me."

"I agree," Schwarz replied. "They probably traveled the coast some distance and parked the sub in an underwater cave or lodged it in a coral reef. Hell, maybe it just sank to the bottom of the ocean and they left it."

"A submarine like that must cost a fortune," Lyons remarked. "Maybe they wouldn't choose to abandon a million-dollar piece of equipment. Couldn't they have hauled it aboard a large boat or put it in tow somehow?"

"Not likely," Kissinger replied. "No matter where they did it, somebody might have seen them. Besides, there's always the chance a boat might be stopped by the Navy or Coast Guard. If they're caught with a minisub complete with torpedo tubes, that's going to be pretty hard to explain to the authorities. I think Gadgets might be right. They could park the sub, meet a boat at a prearranged site and head for shore."

Brognola considered what he heard. "Okay, it's worth a try. We'll contact the ONI and get some people looking for anything that could be used as platforms for refueling. Just in case, we'll have the coast checked north, as well as south. Leo is still at the Justice Department headquarters?"

"Yeah," Lyons answered. "I don't envy him having to play go-between with the brass. Of course, he's got to explain the 'official version' of what happened in Jersey to the Feds."

"I'm going to contact Turrin," Brognola told them. "I want Justice, FBI and anybody else we can get to start questioning people all along the coast to see if anyone recalls witnessing anything that might fit this theory. Strangers hanging around offshore water platforms, sand dunes, strange boats in the area, hydroplanes, whatever."

"Anything we can do?" Lyons asked hopefully.

"I want Gadgets here and ready to go check out the sub if we find it," Brognola answered. "Probably send Cowboy, as well. You and Rosario can either stay here or check with the police in Newark to see if they learned anything new from the terrorists captured there."

"No, thanks," the Able Team captain replied with a sigh. "I think I'd just as soon stay here and work out in the gym for a while. I haven't lifted weights for a couple days and I could do with a good run."

Blancanales and Schwarz exchanged glances and smiled thinly. They knew their teammate. Earlier they had agreed that if Lyons couldn't assume an active role as hunter, hot on the trail of his prey, he'd rather be working out all day than doing legwork or hanging around an office.

The other two Able Team pros would be glad to get some rest after the stressful and physically demanding ordeal in New Jersey. Lyons was a physical-fitness enthusiast and used exercise as a panacea for anything that bothered him. He worked out to deal with tension, emotional problems, ennui and just because he enjoyed it. He hadn't earned the nickname "Ironman" without good reason.

"Well, things are looking better than when this started," Brognola told his Stony Man personnel. "It looks like the enemy has been shut down in the United States and Japan. There might be other bases here and in the Land of the Rising Sun, but if we're lucky we've taken out the headquarters in both countries."

"Maybe," Blancanales stated. "But we're finding as many questions as answers. Why are Colombia dope dealers involved with an international blackmail scheme and environmental terrorism? Sure, they might plan a revolution in Colombia and they're doing this as a way of financing it, but the coke cartels rake in billions of dollars every year. They could probably carry out such a revolt without having to go to such extremes. The cartels virtually own Colombia and Bolivia anyway."

"Maybe they want more," Lyons suggested. "The cops and the Feds might be able to squeeze some information out of some of the Colombians."

"I think I'll go back to Newark and help interrogate them," Blancanales announced without enthusiasm. "Sometimes federal agencies and local police try to question foreigners without having someone on hand who speaks their native tongue."

"You can also make sure nobody tries to get information with brutality," Brognola added. "That's all we need at this point to get cases tossed out before these creeps can stand trial."

"Sounds like we've all got our work cut out for us," Schwarz remarked. "Hope we find that submarine."

"I hope we find the terrorists," the Stony Man chief replied. "It won't take them long to realize they've lost two of their main bases. That means they'll either pull back and adopt a low profile for a while or attempt another terrorist attack on an environmental target."

RAMON CAZAZO KNEW Arashi was dead. The Venezuelan had met the Japanese fanatic at a terrorist training camp in South Yemen almost a decade earlier. They developed a friendship based on mutual respect and similar philosophies. They were both violent, bitter killers who justified their actions by romantic fabrications that transformed them into warriors with honor, fighting incredible odds to liberate the masses.

They would have embraced any political or revolutionary attitude that would have allowed them to carry out destruction and murder. When the cold war appeared to dissolve and Soviet support of terrorism began to ebb, Cazazo and Arashi realized they would have to find another source to sponsor their deadly actions in the future. They hadn't become terrorists because they believed in a cause, but because they wanted to be terrorists.

João Silva supplied this need. The Brazilian was putting together an army for his plans of conquest. Mercenaries, cocaine barons and international terrorists were all welcome to join Silva's shadowy paramilitary force. Silva had been more than willing to recruit El Cuchillo, and Cazazo in turn brought Arashi into the conspiracy.

Now the Japanese extremist and self-styled samurai was dead. The terrorists in Japan were supposed to have carried out another attack, and Cazazo knew nothing would stop Arashi from this mission except death. There had been no messages from Japan to confirm that Arashi's unit had been crushed, but the Venezuelan had no doubt their operation in Japan was finished.

Cazazo stroked the double-edged blade of his trench knife along a sharpening stone. He wanted to kill someone. He wanted to bury the blade in human flesh and feel blood on his hands. He wanted the sensation of feeling a man's life leaving a body and flowing through his knife into his hand. Cazazo always felt stronger after he killed in this manner. He favored the blade for this reason.

Cazazo never got this sensation from firing a bullet into an opponent. The blade was more personal, like an extension of his fingers.

Of course, he had learned to handle a knife before he ever picked up any other type of weapon. He had been a slum kid in Caracas and learned at a very young age that he had to fight to hold on to anything in life. He didn't have the advantage of expensive schools, but his education came in other ways as he moved toward revolutionary youth groups as an outlet for rage born of poverty.

Highly intelligent, he learned fast, and at age fourteen he joined a Marxist rebel gang. Their hit-and-run strikes were clumsy and poorly planned. They were forced to flee to Guyana, where Cazazo learned strategy, small arms and English. His ability for language impressed the leaders of the terrorist outfit and led to instructions in French, Portuguese and German.

Yet assassination was Cazazo's specialty. His ability to plan and execute murders gained attention from international terrorist networks. Already known as El Cuchillo, Cazazo was in his midtwenties when he was assigned to Europe to carry out assassinations for other extremist outfits.

Like another famous Venezuelan terrorist, Illyavich Rameriz Sanchez, better known as Carlos the Jackal, Cazazo became associated with Palestinian terrorist outfits while in Europe. This eventually led to his visits to training camps in Libya, South Yemen and Syria. His connections with international terrorist forces increased, and he became one of the most feared and respected assassins in the bizarre underworld of terrorism.

Rico Gomez and Guillermo Aguilar seemed worried and depressed as Cazazo entered the den. They had good reason to feel that way. News from the United States was not encouraging. It was confirmed that the base in New Jersey had been raided and all the terrorists there were either dead or held by the authorities. This included many of Gomez's personnel.

The cartel heads in Colombia and Bolivia had also learned about this. They were concerned that their investments in Silva's scheme might be sponsoring a hopeless pipe dream. Gomez and Aguilar had convinced their superiors to support Silva's operation. If it failed, their heads would be on the chopping block by their own people even if the authorities didn't catch up with them.

"Señhor Silva," Cazazo spoke to the Brazilian. *"É importante—"*

"Your Portuguese is rusty, my friend," Silva replied as he rose from a seat at a worktable where he had been examining yet another drawing of a new weapon concept. "Besides, we should speak Spanish so Aguilar and Gomez understand."

"I wish to go to Europe to join the others in the next phase of our mission," Cazazo explained. "It is important that our next attack succeeds. We have lost too much. The entire operation will fall apart if we do not strike again and soon."

"What does that mean?" Gomez asked, concern in his tone.

"Arashi has not contacted us, and we have not heard of another strike in Japan. We must assume our operation there is finished."

"If Arashi was captured, they could interrogate him with drugs or even torture," Aguilar said, worried that they might be as good as ruined. "They will throw out the rule book if they have to to learn who is behind these sabotage attacks."

"Cazazo assured us Arashi would never talk," Gomez declared, trying to convince himself that they weren't in danger of being hunted down even in the jungles of Brazil.

"He would not be taken alive," Cazazo replied. "Arashi would rather take his own life than allow himself to be a prisoner. You don't need to worry that he betrayed us. Arashi would remain loyal to us to his death."

"How can you be sure of that?" Gomez demanded. "How much loyalty would a Japanese feel toward us?"

"Arashi regarded João Silva as a *daimyo*," Cazazo stated. "A warlord of ancient Japan. Arashi's code of honor would require him to die rather than surrender. That is the sort of man he was. A modern-day samurai to whom *bushido* meant more than breathing."

"Gounod and Nielson seem to be doing quite well in Europe," Silva announced. "I do not believe they are in any immediate danger. There are other things you must do, Cazazo."

"Then give me some work. I am of no value to you here. Send me into the field. Let me be a battlefield commander. That is what I do best."

"You will do so," Silva assured him. "We need to set up a new base of operations in the United States. We must force the Americans to give in to our demands. If they do not surrender to us, the other countries will never agree to do so."

"When do I leave?" Cazazo asked, eager to get to work.

"We'll see what sort of personnel we can assemble in the United States for a new center of operations," Silva explained. "That may take a day or two. Have faith, gentlemen. Even if we have had a few setbacks, this plan is still far from finished. There are literally thousands of targets for our agents to attack, and the Americans are especially vulnerable. We will strike again and deliver the worst disaster thus far in order to make it clear to them that they cannot stop us."

CHAPTER NINETEEN

Jack Grimaldi piloted the helicopter over the familiar forest of pine trees that surrounded Stony Man Farm. It didn't look like much from the air, but it wasn't supposed to. The main house, two other buldings and a tractor shack resembled some rich guy's version of a "mountain estate." Even the landing field for aircarft in the clearing wouldn't have attracted much attention from a casual observer.

The Stony Man pilot worked the controls to descend. The chopper touched down at the helipad, and Mack Bolan opened the sliding door, climbing from the aircraft while the great rotor blades were still spinning. Calvin James followed.

Barbara Price and Aaron Kurtzman waited on the porch to welcome the commandos. Lovely even dressed in a baggy blue jump suit, Price offered the Executioner a wide smile.

"Glad you made it back, Striker," Kurtzman declared as he rolled the wheelchair back to clear a path to the door. "Heard things went pretty well in Japan."

"Not bad," Bolan replied, "all things considered. Is Brognola here?"

"He's in his office," the Bear answered. "I think he's on the phone talking with Turrin or somebody from the Organization of Naval Intelligence."

"Did they locate the terrorists' submarine?"

"How did you know we were looking for it? Gadgets came up with the idea just yesterday."

"Makes sense," the Executioner explained. "They had to do something with the sub. I don't think they'd risk being caught with it aboard a larger boat because it has torpedo tubes and would be too suspicious. My guess is they ditched it somewhere. Probably some distance from New York."

"I should have figured you'd clue in to the sub. Come on in. I'll buy you a cup of coffee."

"Not if you made it," Bolan told him. The Bear's coffee was infamous and intolerable to most stomachs other than his own.

They entered the main house and within minutes were in the War Room downstairs. Hal Brognola joined them. His face was tired, and he hadn't shaved for at least eight hours, but the Stony Man chief smiled when he saw Bolan and James.

"Jack outside?" the big Fed inquired.

"Taking care of his chopper," Bolan answered.

"We'll brief him later. Let me fill you guys in for now. Able Team scored a big hit in Newark and put a gang of terrorists out of business for good. They were about to hit some toxic waste dump for another environmental attack. New Jersey is the nation's capital when it comes to toxic waste."

"I'm sure they'd appreciate that honor," James commented. "How about my pals in Phoenix Force? How are they doing without me?"

"I got a message from Katz," Price explained. "They haven't found a terrorist base yet, but they have a positive ID on several men who were using forged passports and identification papers. These characters were directly involved in the attacks on the nuclear power plant in

France and the North Sea oil wells. Now they're trying to find where the enemy is hidden."

"How did Trent do on the mission?" Brognola inquired.

"He did great," Bolan confirmed. "We might have been able to get the job done in Japan without Trent, but we wouldn't have gotten results nearly as fast. Since the terrorists appeared to be ready to bug out when we hit them, that's saying a lot."

"Cal and the other members of Phoenix have spoken well of him in the past," Kurtzman remarked. "I had some doubts about signing on a guy who plays ninja warrior, but I guess he's okay."

"Better than okay," Bolan declared. "*Ninjutsu* isn't a hobby for that guy. His skills came in pretty handy when we raided the terrorists. In fact, Trent took Arashi in a sword duel."

"The fight was close enough it had me holding my breath until it was over," James added. "John wanted to continue with us to carry out the mission to the end, but Mack told him he was only authorized for the job in Japan. John was disappointed when he had to go back to San Francisco."

"He might be good, but he's not Stony Man," Brognola stated. "We might be using him again in the future. Until then, Trent ought to take advantage of the fact he doesn't have to deal with this shit twenty-four hours a day like the rest of us have to. He doesn't have to worry about ulcers along with everything else."

"We learned something else while we were in Japan," Bolan began as he opened a side pocket to his duffel bag. "I found this in some gear that apparently belonged to Arashi."

He handed Brognola a photograph. Dog-eared and faded, it showed two men standing shoulder to shoulder, dressed in combat fatigues and armed to the teeth. The Asian figure had a *katana* sword in his gun belt. The dark, slender figure next to him wore a trench knife on his hip.

"The guy on the right is Arashi, of course," Bolan explained. "I might be wrong about this, but I think the other guy might be Ramon Cazazo. El Cuchillo himself."

"Holy shit," Kurtzman whispered. The Bear had a lot of knowledge about terrorists filed away in his memory, as well as in his computers. "Cazazo and Arashi together. Two of the most notorious international terrorists in the world. Looks like they were buddies from this picture."

"There's a desert in the background," Bolan stated. "The photo might have been taken in the Middle East somewhere. They might have met there."

"This photo doesn't prove Cazazo is involved with the current wave of terrorism," Price remarked. "It just means Arashi had a sentimental attachment to the picture. Even terrorists are human beings with all sorts of emotions."

"Most pretty twisted," James commented. "Maybe Cazazo is involved and maybe he isn't, but I seem to recall at least one of the men killed at the North Sea derricks was stabbed to death and hit with a blunt instrument that could have been brass knuckles. Take a look at that knife on Cazazo's belt. That sure fits the murder weapon."

"A trench knife is Cazazo's trademark," Bolan recalled. "They don't call him El Cuchillo without good reason. He's said to be a blade man and uses a knife whenever possible."

"I don't know how you can keep track of any details about these guys," Brognola said with a sigh. "There seem to be so many terrorists running around."

"Not many like Cazazo," Kurtzman said. "He kind of stands out in the crowd. I'll run a computer check on the sucker and see what they know about his present whereabouts."

"Okay," Brognola said with a nod. He turned to Bolan and James. "What did you learn from interrogating the terrorists taken prisoner?"

"They said Arashi and some of his lieutenants assembled the outfit from a collection of former JRA fanatics, gutter hoods and misfits," Bolan explained. "The motivation was greed. Somebody was going to pay them a lot of money to carry out attacks on chemical plants, oil tankers and whatever other target was available for environmental terrorism."

"Any of them know who was hiring them?" Price asked.

"Arashi probably knew," James answered. "The others just said there were foreigners involved. Arashi seemed to trust their main contact. Another reason to think Cazazo might be connected with this."

"I'm headed for my computers," Kurtzman declared as he rolled his chair toward the elevator.

"The terrorists were armed with an assortment of weapons," Bolan continued. "They had military hardware manufactured in Japan, the United States, North Korea and China. Black-market firearms and explosives. They had a lot of it, too. Whoever their source was, they seemed to be able to get their hands on anything short of tanks and surface-to-air missiles."

"And they obviously had the money to pay for it," Brognola commented as he chewed a cigar butt. "Or whoever hired the terrorists could afford to supply them with the hardware."

"Well, the terrorists we saw in Japan weren't living in luxury," James told Brognola. "They had a lot of cash in their knapsacks, but apparently they never got a chance to spend it."

"They won't get to spend it now, either," the Stony Man chief remarked. "Okay, let me bring you up to date. Gadgets figured it's possible the submarine that attacked the garbage scow in New York might be hidden somewhere along the coast. We got ONI to search for anything that might serve as refueling platforms for the sub."

"Any luck?" James asked.

"Kissinger and Gadgets are out checking a couple of sites the Navy thinks might be refueling posts," Brognola answered. "Leo has federal agents out questioning folks along the coast to see if anyone recalls seeing anything suspicious. We'll probably get a hundred false leads, but there is a chance somebody might have spotted the sub or terrorists leaving it, or something. I'm not even sure what we're looking for."

"If they find where the sub might be, I could go on a dive to search for it," James announced.

"You guys ought to take advantage of an opportunity to get some rest," Brognola advised. "I don't think it will be long before you'll be in action again."

JOHN KISSINGER SAT in the back seat of a long sedan, alongside Captain Andrew Edmonds. Kissinger had flown to Virginia Beach as soon as a radio message informed him that Navy divers had located something off the coast.

Edmonds met him at the helipad, and they immediately left Virginia Beach to head for the coast in an official Navy car. A tall, muscular black man in his midforties, Captain Edmonds was dressed in a white uniform and service cap. Kissinger recognized decorations on the officer's chest. Edmonds had served in Vietnam and earned medals for valor as well as the Purple Heart.

"You made good time, Mr. Kingsley," Edmonds said, using Kissinger's cover name.

The cowboy figured he could have used his real last name and the ONI officer would have figured it was fake anyway. Kissinger had been at Delaware Bay when the message arrived. Naval personnel had discovered a platform at the mouth of the bay, and an exhausted fuel tank was found under the surface of the platform.

Hopefully Edmonds's people had found something even more important than evidence of refueling stations. The captain glanced at a clipboard and scanned over information on a report form.

"We were looking for another platform off the coast," Edmonds explained. "A local resident who lives on the beach asked one of the divers what we were looking for. The sailor explained we were checking a sand dune off the coast. One might call it a miniature island. He asked if the civilian happened to notice anything odd at the island. The witness recalled seeing a helicopter at the dune one morning three or four days ago. The civilian also claimed the helicopter had flotation landing gear, which suggests it was a hydrocopter."

"And it flew from the island to the coast?" Kissinger asked.

"That's right," Edmonds confirmed. "It headed for Virginia Beach. The witness also said he saw a person in scuba gear climb into the helicopter before it left the island."

"Your divers checked the island?"

"The waters under the surface by the dune," Edmonds corrected. "They found a large object covered with camouflage nets with seaweed attached. We think it might be the submarine you're looking for."

The car reached the beach. Kissinger and Edmonds emerged from the back seat. A crowd had formed along the beach to watch as two boats lowered crane hooks into the water. Heads appeared from the surface, faces with diving masks. The frogmen grabbed the hooks and guided them downward as they descended once more into the ocean.

"Anybody know what's going on?" a curious spectator inquired. A line of white-helmeted shore patrol sailors kept the crowd at bay so the recovery crew could work undisturbed.

"We're looking for an experimental robot-controlled sea craft that might be in the area," Kissinger supplied an answer. "Nothing to worry about. It isn't armed and this is just a regular salvage operation."

"Oh," the spectator said with a shrug, satisfied with the explanation.

Kissinger and Edmonds walked through the crowd to the edge of the shore. Voices muttered among the civilians. Somebody voiced a theory that the "experimental sea craft" was probably nuclear-powered and the Navy was lying about there being no danger. Someone else complained that it sounded like another waste of taxpayers' money.

"A robot-controlled experimental sea craft?" Edmonds muttered to Kissinger. "How did you come up with that story?"

"Just made it up. Hell, they seem to have bought it."

"Yeah," the captain said, "and they're bitching about the Navy. Well, they do that all the time anyway. Last year we were still heroes because of Desert Storm, but things are getting back to normal now."

The pair boarded a small motorboat and rode to the island. The cranes began to tow an object from the ocean as they approached. Kissinger watched the hull of a yellow vessel break the surface. The submarine was shaped like a bloated fish with searchlights for eyes and propellers built into the tail section. Water poured from two barrels at the nose of the sub.

"Is this what you were looking for?" Edmonds asked as the small boat touched the sand dune.

"It sure looks like it."

The sub was lowered to the shore of the island. Two divers appeared from the water. They removed the mouthpiece gear from their breathing apparatus and pulled diving masks to forehead level.

"We found her on the bottom," the head diver explained. "The hatch was open, so she filled up with water. Whoever left the little sub must have done it deliberately. Sure weighted her down enough so she couldn't surface without those cranes."

"That was the idea," Kissinger replied. "You did a good job. All of you."

"This thing doesn't have any identification markings on it," Edmonds commented. "No letters or numbers that I can see."

"We didn't find any, either, sir," a diver added. "Damnedest thing I ever saw. Looks like torpedo tubes in front there."

"Yeah," Kissinger said. "That's sure what it looks like."

CHAPTER TWENTY

"I hate to say I told you so," Schwarz began with a grin.

"Shut up," Lyons replied gruffly. "So you were right. Don't be so smug about it."

"He's just jealous because he didn't think of it," Blancanales remarked. "So am I, for that matter."

"Well, Able Team shares alike in whatever any one of us does," Schwarz said. "That means you guys are lucky I'm part of the team."

"Let's get to it," Mack Bolan stated. "Cowboy's ready."

Kissinger sat at the War Room conference table and opened a notepad. He skipped the information about the precise size of the submarine, estimated top speed and other data he figured was less important.

"Unfortunately I couldn't haul the sub here to go over it personally," he began. "The Navy has it, and they're doing a good job. There's no doubt this is the vessel we were looking for. It's well made to stand up to deep pressures. There's only one seat in the sub, and it has two torpedo tubes."

"Sounds good so far," Brognola remarked. "Any idea where it came from?"

"It has no identification, serial numbers or much of anything else," Kissinger said. "All we did find was some labels on the controls. This isn't English, so I'll probably mispronounce these words—*em cima, em baixo*. And the firing trigger buttons for the torpedoes were marked *primeira* and *segunda*."

"Sounds like Spanish," Brognola commented, and turned to the three men of Able Team and James, all of whom spoke Spanish. The Stony Man chief didn't.

"*Segunda* means 'second,'" James answered. "'First' in Spanish is pronounced *primera*. Let me see how it's spelled."

"With two *i*'s instead of one?" Blancanales inquired.

"Yeah," Kissinger replied. "And I copied it the way it was spelled, too."

"It's not Spanish," Blancanales told him. "It's Portuguese. The labels *em cima* and *em baixo* mean 'up' and 'down.' Might be for the periscope."

"Portuguese?" Brognola said with a frown. "This is driving me nuts. Colombians, Japanese, a notorious Venezuelan terrorist and now a Portuguese submarine. Who the hell are we up against?"

"Portuguese doesn't mean the submarine is from Portugal," Bolan said. "Portuguese is also the official language of Brazil, and Macao is still Portuguese territory."

"Go on," Brognola said.

"Macao is a peninsula in southeast China. I guess that may not be much help."

"No kidding, Striker."

"Yeah," Bolan went on, unruffled by the big Fed's ill temper. "But, both Portugal and Brazil produce military arms and both have been known to sell weaponry to foreign clients."

"Striker is right," Kissinger declared. "There are some real big arms dealers operating in Brazil. Some of them aren't too particular about whom they do business with, either. Of course, some arms dealers in the United States and Great Britain fit that category, too."

"Unless they supplied the terrorists with that submarine, I don't care about them at this time," Brognola said. "Take those notes and see the Bear. See what you and Aaron can come up with when you run a check on Portuguese and Brazilian arms dealers. That includes ones who work for the state. Until we have some answers, just about everybody is a suspect."

"Gotcha, Hal," Kissinger assured him, and rose from his seat.

"Not just arms merchants," Bolan added. "Check on manufacturers, as well. A submarine with no serial numbers sounds like it was assembled deliberately that way to avoid being traced. If you can find someone who manufactures military weapons, deals in selling them abroad and has projects on experimental devices like miniature submarines...I'd say you've got a pretty good candidate."

"I'll see what I can come up with," Kissinger replied, heading for the elevator.

BOLAN HAD RESTED enough. He needed to keep his edge, and he couldn't do that by sitting around the War Room or the den, waiting to hear from the Stony Man personnel who specialized in gathering data. Hal Brognola, Cowboy Kissinger, Aaron Kurtzman and Barbara Price spent most of their time at the Farm. Bolan didn't envy them. He was a man of war and couldn't remain inactive for long.

The Executioner decided to spend a couple of hours in the gym. Lyons was already there. The Able Team captain lay on a bench, pumping iron with nearly three hundred pounds on a barbell. Calvin James was also present.

He had donned a *gi* with a black belt knotted around his narrow waist. The African-American tough guy worked out by hammering a heavy bag with karate kicks and punches.

Bolan started his workout with fundamentals. Push-ups and sit-ups, the same tiresome calisthenics he had had to do in the Army for basic combat training. He was still doing them.

He did some stretching exercises and moved to a sturdy rope attached to the ceiling. Bolan grabbed it and climbed the rope, hand over hand to the top. He descended in the same manner until his feet touched the mat. He was about to continue, but noticed Kissinger had entered the gym.

"We got a name," the weapons expert declared. "Want to see?"

"You bet," the Executioner confirmed.

James was also too busy practicing a series of *kata* exercises to realize Kissinger had arrived. Bolan figured it was just as well to let the two other warriors burn off some tension. He and Kissinger headed for the main house and found Kurtzman waiting for them at the entrance.

"You guys are too much," the Bear complained. "I'm still trying to dig up something on Cazazo, then I'm supposed to bust my butt to get information on Portuguese and Brazilians who might have built a baby submarine."

"Ain't it awful," Bolan said, aware Kurtzman was bitching because it was part of his personality. "So what did you come up with?"

"This," the computer whiz stated as he handed Bolan a printout. "There's an arms dealer and manufacturer in Brazil named João Silva. Three years ago he tried to sell a couple of his experimental projects to the Pentagon. Guess what one of them was?"

"A miniature submarine equipped with torpedoes?" Bolan asked.

"You got it," the Bear confirmed. "Just like the one used by the terrorists."

"Not really," Kissinger stated. "I've seen the draw ups on the one Silva tried to sell to the Pentagon. It would have been bigger and slower, equipped with four torpedo tubes and could have carried two men—"

"So you mentioned," Kurtzman cut him off, annoyed by what he considered nit-picking. "You also said the drawings strongly resembled the construction of the terrorist sub."

"Modified some," Kissinger said with a nod. "Looks like Silva made a smaller, faster model that could be used by a single man."

"I get the idea," Bolan told him. "What else do you have on Silva?"

"Basic stuff," Kurtzman answered. "His age, marital status, address and so on. He's somewhere between the ninth to thirteenth richest man in Brazil, depending on which source you check. Needless to say, the guy is well heeled. He sells lots of military hardware to various countries. Maybe does some crooked deals, as well, but anybody that rich has friends in high places. A guy like that can get away with a lot."

"The good old double standard for the rich and the poor," Bolan said. "Pretty much the same everywhere. Did you check the CIA and NSA files?"

"Yeah," the Bear confirmed. "The Company used Silva a couple of times in the past. You know how some of those guys in the CIA operate. They wanted to get guns for the Contras and other anti-Communist groups in Central and South America, so they used every source they could. Silva could supply them and seemed to have his own covert sources, as well."

"How about contacts in Europe, Japan, the Middle East and maybe the Pacific?" Bolan asked.

"Definitely the Middle East," Kurtzman confirmed. "Everybody sells weapons and goods to the Middle East. Of course, the U.S. usually gives that stuff away."

"After the taxpayers pay for it," Kissinger muttered.

"Where do you think your paycheck comes from?" the Bear reminded him. "Silva does have connections in Europe, but I don't know about Japan. His inventories include cargo shipped to Singapore and Pakistan. The stuff was labeled as 'machinery,' but it was probably weapons. Odds are it wound up on the black market."

"So Silva was supplying arms to gunrunners," Bolan mused. "This guy is beginning to look like a very solid suspect."

"He's already rich and influential," Kissinger remarked. "Why would he want to risk everything in a crazy scheme involving international terrorism and blackmail?"

"Some people never have enough," the Executioner replied. "I've seen this more than once in the past. Drug kingpins who already have more money than they could ever spend. Gangsters and crooked industrialists with millions. Third-world dictators who had fortunes while their people suffered in dire poverty. Those types always want more money and more power."

"We still don't know for sure that Silva is responsible," Kurtzman insisted. "Even if we can prove he sold the submarine to the terrorists, that doesn't mean he's directly connected with them."

"Too many other things fit," Bolan stated. "The terrorists in Japan were being very well paid and well armed with black-market military hardware. From what I've heard about the American hardmen involved, they were all motivated by big bucks, as well. The Colombians could be connected with this because they're backing Silva."

"What do they hope to gain?" Kissinger asked with a shrug. "Blancanales already mentioned that the cocaine cartels virtually run Colombia and Bolivia already."

"But they can't demand billions of dollars in aid from the United States, Western Europe and Japan," the Executioner replied. "Remember the videotapes with the demands by the terrorists? They plan a coup in the future, then foreign aid support after that. Silva and the cartels could set up any kind of government they want under those conditions. They could become strong enough to rule all of South America."

"That's the fourth-largest continent in the world," the Bear remarked. "There are twelve or thirteen countries in South America, and it covers an area close to seven million square miles."

"More territory than Europe and Australia put together," Bolan said with a nod. "Almost as much as the United States and Canada combined. South America is filled with natural resources. Gold, diamonds, coal, petroleum, enormous forest regions are all found there. Not to mention cash crops such as coffee, cotton, bananas and sugarcane."

"You left out cocaine," Kissinger said.

"Not because I forgot it," the Executioner assured him. "Imagine how the cartels would operate if they could grow coca plants anywhere they want in South America and harvest as much as they please. No worries about the authorities because they'd be the authorities. They could process it in government-operated chemical plants and ship out deliveries of cocaine to embassies in diplomatic pouches."

"That's a pretty scary scenario, Mack," Kurtzman said as he mentally digested what he heard. "It could also lead to the worst environmental terrorism of all. If it came to that extreme, you can bet men like that wouldn't give a hoot in hell about how much ecological damage they caused by mining minerals and chopping down trees for lumber. You know how much of the world's oxygen is believed to come from the tropical rain forests in South America?"

"I've heard those stories, too," Kissinger said. "They say the massive amount of forest being destroyed by the lumber companies currently in charge in South America is causing the ozone layer to dissolve."

"Have you noticed how odd the weather has gotten in the past couple of years?" Kurtzman inquired. "Notice how the number of cases of skin cancer have increased? The ozone layer is in trouble, and I sure as hell wouldn't gamble on doing anything that could screw up this planet's ecology any worse than it already is. If Striker is right, those sons of bitches could get us all killed or mess up the world beyond repair for the next generation."

"If it isn't already too late," Kissinger said. "That might happen even if terrorists don't take over in South America."

"Let's take care of stopping the enemy we're in a position to stop first," Bolan declared. "Evidence seems to suggest there's good possibility João Silva is among those enemies."

"Oh, Aaron forgot to mention the miniature tank Silva tried to sell to the Pentagon at the same time he tried to peddle the submarine," Kissinger said with sudden amusement. "Why don't you tell him what Silva called that tank?"

"Because I know you'll get far more pleasure from telling him yourself," Kurtzman said dryly.

"Okay," the Cowboy agreed. "Silva calls the tank 'the Bear.'"

"Very funny," the computer expert growled. "If that son of a bitch turns out to be a bad guy, maybe I'll sue him for defamation of character."

"You won't have to worry about taking him to court," the Executioner promised.

CHAPTER TWENTY-ONE

Gunter Holdern had thought the days of intrigue, espionage and terrorism were over. He realized such things still existed, of course, but he had hoped they were finished in his country. Born in the Federal Republic of Germany, he had grown up in a land burdened by the sinister image of a Nazi nightmare of the recent past and a cold war that had produced a massive wall dividing Germany into two parts.

East German agents of the SSD and their KGB coordinators had constantly attempted to infiltrate West Germany to subvert the FRG. The Baader-Meinhof Gang, 2nd June Movement and German Red Army Faction conducted hundreds of acts of terrorism. Holdern remembered those days all too well. When the Berlin Wall finally fell and Germany was reunited, he thought the whole world had changed. The communists had relinquished their hold on the East. The Marxist-oriented terrorists would surely realize their ideology had failed with the end of the cold war.

Germany was now one nation. The people had come together. There would be no more reason for espionage or subversive activities. The problems of the past were over, and Europe was no longer a chessboard for the superpowers of the West and the East.

However, Holdern stood in the foggy, damp evening as a plane arrived from France. Four men emerged from the craft. They had special authority from the White

House, and the American President had influenced the chancellor to grant these visitors extraordinary power. They were agents of some sort, sent by the superpower of the United States.

It seemed the cold war hadn't ended after all, or perhaps it had simply changed. This worried Holdern as he watched the men approach. At least in the past he had had some idea who the other side was supposed to be. Who were the enemies now?

"Good evening, sir," Yakov Katzenelenbogen said in German as he and the other three Phoenix Force members drew closer. "Where is the toilet and the opera?"

Katz smiled as he spoke the recognition phrase. Holdern returned the gesture. It was possible a stranger might ask him where the toilet was or the opera, but not both jammed into one sentence. Holdern knew these were the men he was supposed to meet at the Frankfurt airport.

"I had expected you to ask that question in English," Holdern commented. "In fact, I didn't even know you spoke German."

"Actually I was given the recognition phrase in French at Interpol headquarters, and they didn't tell me what language to use when we arrived," Katz explained. "By the way, two of my men don't understand German."

"My English is pretty good," Holdern stated, switching languages to prove his point. "I'm not quite sure what this is about, Mr. . . . ?"

"Silverman." Katz gave his cover name. "We'll explain everything in a more secure environment."

Holdern led the Phoenix commandos to a Volkswagen minibus in the parking lot. Katz joined the German officer in the front seat. The others got in the back. Encizo and Manning opened their aluminum suitcases and removed two black plastic boxes, roughly twice the size of a pack of cigarettes. They pressed buttons on the boxes and slowly ran the contraptions along the interior of the rig.

"What are they doing?" Holdern inquired, puzzled by their actions.

"We're checking for hidden microphones," Manning answered. "These gizmos detect the presence of electronic listening devices."

"That isn't necessary," Holdern assured them.

"Yeah," Encizo replied. "We've heard that before and turned up bugs in the past. Just humor us, okay?"

The Cuban and Canadian announced that the minibus was secure.

"Do you work for the Bundesnachrichtendienst or Interpol?" Katz inquired as they traveled the foggy streets of Frankfurt.

"I used to be with BND," Holdern replied, using the abbreviated name for the German Federal Intelligence service. "After the wall came down, I left and joined Interpol. It seemed the Communists were no longer a problem, so it was better to concentrate on conventional criminals."

"The men we're after are not conventional in any way," Katz stated. "Have you been following the news? I'm sure you heard or read about the terrorist attacks in Scotland and France."

"But none have occurred here in Germany," Holdern replied.

"That could change any day now, mate," McCarter told him.

"I don't understand."

"We've been tracking the terrorists in Scotland and France," Katz explained. "We managed to get positive identification on two of the terrorists. They are using forged passports made by a man in Paris. These two used different identities when they worked at an oil company and a nuclear power plant. However, they assumed other names and different passports to fly to Germany after completing the terrorist attacks."

"How do you know this?" Holdern asked.

"The terrorists made a mistake." Gary Manning supplied the answer. "They didn't think anyone would find out what names they'd assume after carrying out the sabotage incidents. They used those names to order plane tickets in advance so they could flee from Paris to Germany."

"And they didn't know we'd learn their real names as well," Encizo added. "Gounod and Nielson were members of a mercenary army. We got a list of other known members. Names include Heinrich Rilke and Theodor Hesse. Both men are currently living in Nuremberg."

"We call it Nürnberg here," Holdern corrected. "And you believe these terrorists have joined forces with their former mercenary comrades?"

"Almost positive," McCarter replied. "Several of the other former mercs are currently in Bavaria."

"How many?" Holdern asked with a frown. "Are they all German?"

"Eleven that we know of," Katz answered. "Most of them aren't German. Some are French, two are Belgian, a couple are Spanish and the rest are German and British."

"These guys are in Germany as tourists," Manning added. "All of them are using false ID because they're wanted for gunrunning and war crimes while carrying out mercenary campaigns in Africa. The others managed to avoid being directly connected with such activities. They still would be pretty stupid to use their real names."

"You are certain of these facts?" Holdern inquired, a bit suspicious of how accurate their information could be.

"Ninety-five percent," Katz replied. "A couple of the identifications of the ex-mercs are less than positive, but the other information is solid."

"Why would former soldiers for hire become terrorists?" the Interpol agent demanded. "Mercenaries are motivated by greed. I know some of them are supposed to be political, as well, but that breed tends to be anti-Communist. Terrorists are fanatics. I encountered quite a few when I was with the BND in the 1980s. Every one I met was a Marxist lunatic with the exception of a few Turkish Grey Wolves."

"There are right-wing terrorists, as well as left-wing," Katz assured him. "But the men we're hunting are different. Just as some people in positions of national security have betrayed their country for financial gain, some commit acts of terrorism for profit. These terrorists are cut from that bolt of cloth. We can't give you more details than to say this is an international conspiracy that threatens your country, as well as others."

"Which explains why the United States is involved," Holdern remarked. "My superiors told me to cooperate with you men in every way possible. Apparently you're in charge until I'm told otherwise. What do we do first?"

"We need to find the terrorists," Katz told him. "The logical place to start is to check out Rilke and Hesse. We know where to find them and what names they are using these days. It seems very unlikely all the other ex-mercenaries would be in Bavaria at this time unless they were planning something big."

"If nothing else," Manning added, "it's the most probable place for Gounod and Nielson to head for."

"I'm sure we can get the cooperation of the Nürnberg police and the BND," Holdern declared. He glanced at his wristwatch. "We have plenty of time to reach the train station and travel to Nürnberg by rail."

TRAINS IN MOST EUROPEAN countries are still a pleasant and efficient method of transportation. The trip was comfortable, though Phoenix Force couldn't see much of the countryside or towns the train passed through on the way to Nürnberg. The fog seemed to follow the railroad, and the gloom of night concealed their view, as well. Besides, the Stony Man commandos hadn't embarked on a sight-seeing tour.

The train station at Nürnberg was as big and well-supplied with shops and restaurants as many international airports. The halls were crowded with people moving to and fro. Phoenix Force and the Interpol officer were ignored among the herds of busy folk at the station. Holdern led them from the station to the street, then onto a bicycle shop on Durerstrasse. The place was closed for business, and the shades were drawn, but someone inside the shop opened the door when Holdern knocked twice.

They entered a dimly lit room and were surrounded by bicycles and parts. A stout figure dressed in work clothes shut the door and locked it. Holdern introduced the man to Phoenix Force as simply "Klaus." The guy nodded as if uninterested in carrying on a conversation until it became necessary.

Two other men were waiting for Phoenix Force to arrive. Both wore gray single-breasted suits and striped ties.

The commandos recognized them as federal agents of some kind before either man spoke.

"I am Captain Brecht of the BND," one man announced with a curt nod. "And this is Herr Smith of the American CIA."

"Yeah," the Company man said as he stepped forward and glared at Phoenix Force. "And 'Herr Smith' wants to know what the hell you think you're doing!"

"Bloody hell," McCarter muttered, and shook his head. "What's this bloke's problem? His wife put him in dry dock?"

"Hey," Smith began, "I'm assigned to this post. I'm the case officer in charge of this assignment. You people aren't CIA, so what the hell are you doing here?"

"We're doing our job," Encizo replied with a sigh. "If you're smarter than you seem to be—and if you're able to feed yourself, you must be—you won't interfere with us."

"Excuse me, Herr Smith," Holdern began, "but I understand these men have authority directly from your own President, and they most certainly have it from the head of our own government, as well."

"That was also the understanding of the BND," Brecht added. "We assumed the Central Intelligence agency was part of this because you contacted us to participate in this meeting."

"If the CIA office here wasn't informed, it means there was a failure in communications somewhere along the line," Manning explained. "That means Smith and his superiors found out some other way."

"In other words," Encizo declared, "somebody's office or phone at BND headquarters has been bugged or wiretapped by the Company."

Brecht turned to look at Smith. "You're spying on us?" he asked. "We are, after all, on the same side."

"Don't get sensitive, Captain," Smith replied. "Intelligence work doesn't consist of mutual trust. It's gathering information, and you get it any way you can. That's what bothers me about these four guys. I don't have shit when it comes to them."

"If you're looking for some, you might try between your ears," McCarter suggested.

"You're not even an American!" Smith exclaimed. "Don't smart talk me, you limey bastard!"

The other members of Phoenix Force knew what was about to happen, but McCarter acted before they could stop him. The short-tempered Briton suddenly bolted forward and swung a fist to Smith's jaw. The blow caught the Company man completely off guard, and he staggered backward into a trio of bikes. The clatter of metal and the sound of Smith's body hitting the floor filled the room.

"David," Gary Manning rasped as he grabbed McCarter by the back of the jacket and held him at bay, "will you calm down?"

"I could do it easier if you'd let me hit that silly sod again," the Briton hissed through clenched teeth, but he didn't struggle with Manning.

"This is not the sort of behavior I expected from men who are supposed to be top-level professionals," Captain Brecht remarked, an astonished tone in his voice.

"You're right," McCarter agreed as he pointed at Smith. "That son of a bitch hasn't acted at all like a professional."

"Just shut up," Encizo urged. "Things are bad enough."

Smith sat up and moaned as he gingerly touched his swollen jaw. A ribbon of blood trickled from the corner of his mouth. He was too dazed to realize what had happened, but everything would come back to him after his head cleared.

"I see we're off to a fine start," Katz said with an exasperated sigh.

CHAPTER TWENTY-TWO

Leo Turrin sauntered into the Stony Man den. Jack Grimaldi followed the little Fed and closed the coded access door. Brognola was relieved to see Turrin. The Justice Department go-between officer had been out of touch with Stony Man Farm for more than forty-eight hours. He had finally called less than an hour ago and told Brognola to send Grimaldi to Richmond to pick him up.

"Where the hell have you been?" the Stony Man boss demanded. Now that he was sure Turrin was all right, Brognola could afford to be his usual gruff self.

"I've been interrogated by the FBI as if they thought I was an enemy spy working for the KGB, Khaddafi and Saddam Hussein all at the same time. Those FBI dudes stuffed me into a car and drove me to a cabin outside of Richmond. Guess it was a safe house. Hell, I thought they were gonna give me the third degree. You know, what happened to me a couple of times when I was a kid. This one cop used to wrap a billy club in a towel so it wouldn't leave marks—"

"Spare me the stories of your misspent youth," Brognola told him. "The FBI didn't give you the rubber-hose routine or any other droll variation?"

"Naw," Turrin said with a shrug. "They questioned me about who I was working for, where my authority came from and what I knew about ONI, CIA, NSA and I don't know what else. I was getting tired of trying to answer all their questions. They asked a bunch of stuff at once. Two or three questions to try to get me confused and break down my 'cover story' so they could get what they figured was the truth... whatever they figured that might be."

"Sounds to me like they were trying to find out who you work for," Grimaldi commented. "The FBI obviously figured you weren't just a special officer in the Justice Department. They must have decided you belong to some outfit they don't know about and they wanted to find out. An outfit that is directly linked to the White House and has top-level authority."

"Great," Brognola muttered. "That's all we need right now. Terrorists are trying to blackmail the industrial nations of the world and might be planning a major coup in South America that could lead to even bigger problems in the near future. The bastards could strike again any time, and nobody knows how much environmental damage or loss of life will occur if this happens. Now we've got the federal law-enforcement agencies and Intelligence outfits spending their time trying to mess with us instead of helping us catch the goddamn terrorists."

"What's this about a South American coup?" Turrin asked, confused by the remark.

"It's a theory Striker came up with based on information we've been putting together," the big Fed explained. "I'm going to talk to the President and tell him to contact the Bureau director. This crap is going to end right now before it can create more obstacles for us."

"Well," Turrin said wearily, "I didn't get much sleep during that question-and-answer session. If it's okay with you, I'm going to crash for a few hours."

"Good idea," Brognola replied. "You should get as much rest as possible because I want you to go to Brazil."

"Brazil? Why?"

"I want you to meet with a man there," the Stony Man chief explained. "We might need his help if the mission leads to Brazil."

Kurtzman's voice boomed from the intercom speaker in the den.

"Hey, Hal. You'd better get on the red phone. I don't think you can hear it ringing in there, but believe me, it is."

The red phone was the "hot line" to the President. Brognola headed for the computer room. Kurtzman already had the coded-access door open. The big Fed entered, glancing at the lights to the phone line indicators on a wall above the Bear's infamous coffeemaker. The red light blinked repeatedly.

"I need an extension phone for this line," Brognola muttered as he moved to the elevator.

He rode to the next floor and impatiently slipped between the elevator doors as soon as they opened. Brognola galloped for the phone banks, but the ringing ceased before he could reach it. He picked up the phone anyway, aware it would automatically ring at the Oval Office.

"I'm here," the President's voice announced as soon as Brognola raised the receiver to his ear.

"This is Brognola. You want to talk to me, Mr. President?"

"Not on the phone. Come to the White House."

MOST PEOPLE would consider a trip to the White House to be a special occasion and a private meeting with the

President of the United States to be an extraordinary honor. To Brognola, it was just part of the job.

"You haven't been in touch much since taking on this current mission," the President began as Brognola settled into a chair opposite the Man's desk in the Oval Office. "My sources tell me you've had some success. Your people raided terrorist bases in New Jersey and Japan. Correct?"

"That's right. I figured you'd hear about it from FBI, CIA, NSA and whoever else is involved. Not much sense in me filling in the details until we wrap up the mission."

"You think you're close to finishing it?"

"We're getting there, Mr. President," Brognola replied. "We're closer than we were when this started."

The President was familiar with the big Fed's personality. Brognola wasn't a sycophant. He was a straight shooter and not inclined toward bullshit. The President wasn't sure if he liked this about Brognola or not, but he knew he could trust the Stony Man chief to be honest about how a case was progressing.

"I'm hearing some distressing news about your people in the field," the President began. "One of them is accused of ordering hundreds of agents of the FBI and Justice Department to participate in a pointless series of questioning civilians about whether they saw 'anything strange' along a coastline."

"That's their version," Brognola replied. "The questions weren't pointless, and we had the agents asking them because we were trying to locate the submarine used by the terrorists."

"In fact, the Navy located it," the President said. "I assume you know that already?"

"Yeah," Brognola answered. "We got the ONI on the case, and one of my people was there when they fished the sub out of the water. We're doing our job, Mr. President. I got a complaint about how some of the agents have been acting since this mission began. One of my guys was tied up by three FBI men for interrogation when I needed him in the field."

"Tied up?" The President frowned. "You mean that figuratively, I trust. Why would they do that?"

"Hell, you were CIA once. You know what sort of rivalry goes on between law-enforcement and Intelligence outfits. Those clowns were trying to find out what connections my guy has. They're supposed to be on our side, and they're getting in our way."

"Is CIA getting in your people's way in Europe, as well?" the President asked. "Four of them are currently in Germany. Isn't that right?"

"Yeah," Brognola said with a sigh. "What happened?"

"The district deputy of CIA operations in Germany has faxed a complaint about their conduct. He says they ignored CIA jurisdiction and didn't even bother to contact the Company. Of course, CIA found out, and a case officer confronted them. He reports that they were not only uncooperative, but one of them actually struck him, too."

"Geez," Brognola muttered. He wondered what had set off David McCarter. The Briton was almost certainly the one who slugged the Company man.

"I'm beginning to wonder if you should keep your troops on a shorter rein, Hal," the President said wryly. "They do have to obey *some* rules..."

"Don't worry about my guys. Tempers flare. You know they're the best. My people get results. Has anybody else?"

The President couldn't argue with the success of Stony Man. They had never failed in the past, and they had succeeded with their present mission while everyone else had failed.

"NSA and the Company have a theory that there might be a Middle East connection," the President began. "Saddam and some others have a history of bellicose actions and state-sponsored terrorism."

"Some of the terrorists were probably in the Middle East at one time, and some of the weapons may have come from gunrunners who've done business in that part of the world," Brognola told him. "No Arab terrorists are involved. No Arab or Iranian leader is behind this. Some of your advisers might be influenced by their own racism when it comes to those ethnic groups."

"That's a strong accusation," the President remarked.

"I'm not accusing them of anything except jumping to conclusions," the big Fed replied. "We're looking into some leads. When we have something definite, I'll let you know."

"Keep in touch, Hal. Your men are good. I'm counting on them."

"They're the best, Mr. President," Brognola corrected. "They've proved that time and time again in the past, and they've been proving it on this mission as well. If they didn't contact CIA, it was because they decided it was either unnecessary or risky. The Company hasn't been helpful since they arrived on the scene in Germany. Interpol has cooperated, and they made progress for that reason. CIA can either be part of the solution or part of the problem."

"I'm sure this has just been a misunderstanding."

"And I don't want any more crap from anybody in FBI or any other outfit," Brognola added. "Can you see that it doesn't happen again?"

"I can guarantee it."

CHAPTER TWENTY-THREE

"I thought El Cuchillo would come in person," Louis Gounod commented. The French mercenary frowned as he looked at the two strangers. "I don't even know you two."

"Does it matter?" Miguel Sanchez replied with a shrug. "You have your money. Isn't that what is important?"

Sanchez was uncomfortable and nervous. He and another Bolivian, named Quevedo, had been given the job of bagmen to deliver six million dollars in cash to Gounod and the other mercenaries assembled at the building in Nürnberg.

Veteran soldiers of fortune and gunrunners surrounded the Bolivians. They were a nasty-looking gang of cutthroats, most of whom carried pistols. A few kept assault rifles and submachine guns within easy reach. Sanchez and Quevedo weren't armed. It would have been too risky to travel to Europe with any sort of weapon concealed in their luggage.

Getting the money hadn't been difficult. The Bolivian cartel had more than a billion dollars in a Swiss bank account. The visitors had authorization to sign for the money, and Swiss bankers had a reputation for being discreet. The size of the large sum of cash presented the biggest problem. Sanchez and Quevedo had had to transport it in large steamer trunks.

The money was a temptation, but the Bolivians knew they could not hope to rip off the cartel and live. Wherever they went, Aguilar and the syndicate would eventually find them. Better to prove to the cartel they could be trusted. Both men would be richly rewarded when they returned home. The reward would be considerably less than six million dollars, but at least they would be alive to enjoy it.

Roger Nielson and some of the other mercs still stared at the open trunks with amazement. They had been promised the biggest payday of their careers, and João Silva had kept his word. Nielson was tempted to try to count the money, but there was simply too much of it. Theodor Hesse worked a calculator to try to determine how much each man would receive. No one would have anything to complain about.

"I just don't like dealing with strangers," Gounod explained. "Cazazo was with us at the North Sea oil incident. I trust a man more after serving with him on a combat mission."

Sanchez almost laughed out loud. "Combat mission"? The Frenchman and his fellow soldiers had murdered some oil-company employees and blown up a couple of wells. To call that "combat" seemed a gross exaggeration.

"I believe Silva has other plans for Cazazo," Sanchez answered, "but I don't know for certain. They tell me what I need to know and little else."

"That's as it should be," Gounod stated with approval. "Commanding officers should tell their troops just enough to accomplish their mission."

The former mercenaries still preferred to think of themselves as soldiers. They still wore uniforms when possible and addressed one another by ranks that had no real meaning. In reality, they had been criminals for years.

"Of course, you will carry out the next phase of your mission," Sanchez reminded the Frenchman. "That was the agreement."

"We got our pay and we'll do our job," Gounod assured him.

"You know what target will be next?"

"If we didn't have another target already selected," Nielson stated, his Scottish brogue lingering on each vowel as he spoke, "you'd probably have been told to give us one."

"Good," the Bolivian replied. "Aguilar did state that there have been some problems in America and the Orient."

"Which America?" Gounod demanded, concern in his voice. "North America, which includes the United States, or the South American continent?"

"North America," Sanchez explained. "I assume that would be the United States, because we haven't carried out any operations in Canada or Mexico yet. I believe some are planned in the future."

"That means there have been some raids on groups in the U.S., or Silva's people there haven't been able to carry out their mission for some other reason," Gounod guessed. "Probably the same thing happened in Japan. Not exactly good news, but it could be worse. At least the base in South America still sounds secure."

"Maybe not for long," Nielson said grimly. "If the others are being taken out, it might be just a matter of time before Silva's headquarters is discovered."

"We can't change that," Gounod declared. "We can just do our job and collect our money. We'll carry out our assault on the next target. After that, we'll expect our next payment. Agreed?"

"We'll remain in Europe until that is done," Sanchez promised.

"Twelve milliion dollars," Nielson said with pleasure. The idea of such a large sum thrilled the Scot. Each of the mercenaries would receive more than five hundred thousand dollars for the mission.

"After we get that payment, we're gone," Gounod told the Bolivians. "If Silva is still in operation in two or three months, we might establish contact again for more work. It sounds like his plan might be in trouble. We'll disappear until we know one way or the other. Don't ask where we're going."

"I wasn't going to," Sanchez assured him.

"YOU'RE GOING to a jail cell or a cemetery," Gary Manning whispered as he listened to the conversation through the earphones strapped to his head.

The set was wired to a laser microphone. The Canadian had fixed a laser beam on a window to the building at the outskirts of Nürnberg. Manning had been chosen to eavesdrop on the terrorists because he understood French and German, but the terrorists had discussed their illegal business in English. Apparently it was a language both Gounod and the Bolivian spokesman had mastered.

Phoenix Force had set up surveillance at an ideal time. Thanks to Gunter Holdern, Captain Brecht and the Nürnberg police, they had discovered the base of the ex-mercenaries. The two German members of Gounod's band living in the city—Heinrich Rilke and Theodor Hesse—had rented the building. It had formerly been a toy factory, one of many in Nürnberg. The city was the site of the annual Toy Trade Fair. However, this particular factory had gone out of business months earlier, and the mercenaries were hardly interested in the manufacture of toys in the future.

The laser microphone was hooked up to a tape recorder. Phoenix Force had the necessary information to confirm the terrorists were involved in the conspiracy, had already participated in terrorist actions and planned to do so again. They had accepted pay for their criminal acts, and the bagmen had even mentioned other names associated with the plot. "Silva" and "Aguilar" were unknown to the commandos, but another name was familiar to them.

"Cazazo?" Rafael Encizo repeated when Manning gave the others an abridged version of the conversation he had heard. "El Cuchillo?"

"Who is this person?" Brecht asked, unfamiliar with the terrorist career of the Venezuelan renegade.

"Someone who has been getting away with a hell of a lot for a very long time," Manning explained. "And somebody we've wanted to find for quite a while."

"El Cuchillo can wait," David McCarter announced as he checked his Uzi machine pistol. The Briton didn't have to inspect the Browning Hi-Power in shoulder leather. He knew it was ready for combat. "Let's take care of the gang of bastards we've got right now."

"Perhaps we should contact Mr. Smith at the embassy and see if CIA wants to take charge here," Captain Brecht suggested.

"I don't care what Smith and the Company want," Yakov Katzenelenbogen declared bluntly. "This is your country, Captain. These terrorists are here in a major German city, and they're about to carry out sabotage at an environmental target somewhere in Germany. That means the lives lost will be German lives."

"There is no need to wait," Gunter Holdern agreed as he gathered up a Heckler & Koch MP-5 submachine gun. "We have the necessary evidence. It was obtained by court order, and the Antiterrorist Act, passed when this was still West Germany, grants us authority to raid the building without a search warrant."

"I think we should get more people," Brecht urged, trying to find some reason for delay. He obviously wanted to pass the responsibility for the raid to someone else. Or perhaps he was simply afraid. "There are more than a dozen terrorists in there."

"There are six of us and fifteen Nürnberg police officers," Katz replied. "That's better than fair odds. We can't afford to wait to bring in more police and military to outnumber them ten to one. If we give them time to prepare for their strike on the next target, they'll be heavily armed and possibly have explosives readily at hand."

"How do you know they don't already?" Brecht demanded. "They'll be more apt to surrender if faced by unbeatable odds that make it clear they cannot possibly win."

"That would work if we were dealing with conventional criminals," Manning said. "I've listened to these people. Gounod and his men don't think of themselves as criminals. They believe they're an elite fighting unit. Men like that aren't going to be inclined to surrender regardless of what odds they face. They'll go down fighting."

"And we want to take as many of them alive as possible," Katz added. "Even more important is the protection of innocent people in the area. Captain, I want you to assist the police in setting up roadblocks and moving people to cover so they'll be reasonably safe during this operation."

"How many police officers should I use for this?" Brecht asked. He seemed eager to accept the task that would also move him from immediate danger...even if there was no real place of safety in such situations.

"Take half," Katz replied. He also wanted Brecht in the background. The Israeli wasn't apt to accuse any man of being a coward, but Brecht was obviously not up to participating in the raid in an actual combat capacity.

"Seven or eight officers?" Brecht inquired.

"Take eight," Katz answered. "I want Herr Holdern to use the others to form a backup unit in case we need to call them in after we begin the raid."

"What does that mean?" Holdern asked with surprise. "You're going into that nest of killers alone?"

"My people are trained and experienced in this sort of operation," the one-armed Israeli explained. "Frankly neither you nor the Nürnberg police can say the same. Best you work as backup. If any of the terrorists try to escape, you might have to stop them."

"But I've been in law enforcement for nearly twenty years," Holdern insisted. "I've dealt with terrorists before..."

"I've seen your file," Katz stated. "It is very impressive, but you've never been in a real firefight and your training hasn't included special combat skills such as those taught to GSG-9 antiterrorist commandos."

"So I was never in GSG-9," Holdern replied. "I still know how to use a gun, and I've been in some dangerous situations in the past."

"I admire your courage, Herr Holdern," Katz assured him. "But this isn't a matter of being brave enough to go with us. We've worked together as a unit for a number of years. We know what to do without instructions. We trust one another to do what is necessary in such a situation."

"We also try to reduce the risk to others' lives when we carry out a mission," Manning added. "We don't want you or any of the policemen killed if we can avoid it."

"But you'll be outnumbered," Holdern warned. "They'll have at least a three-to-one advantage."

"We're aware of that," Encizo stated as he patted a canvas case on his left hip. "That's why we're taking these M-17 gas masks and tear-gas grenades. The enemy will be teary eyed, coughing and choking, and damn near blind. We'll also have the element of surprise in our favor. That ought to compensate for the superior number of opponents we'll be facing."

"It still sounds like quite a risk," Captain Brecht remarked. The BND officer was beginning to feel ashamed of himself.

"No doubt about that," McCarter said with a smile. "It wouldn't be any fun otherwise."

The German Interpol and BND officers were startled by the Briton's remark. The other members of Phoenix Force were accustomed to McCarter's behavior. He was an unabashed thrill seeker and admitted he thrived on action. Yet he wasn't capricious and handled himself in a highly professional manner in actual combat.

"Aren't you glad he's going with us instead of staying with you guys?" Manning asked the Germans.

"All right," Katz began as he glanced up at the sky. Night was fading, and the predawn sky would soon become light in preamble to sunrise. "This will be a good time to hit them. Some of the terrorists are probably asleep, and the others are probably fatigued from lack of sleep. People also tend to become more relaxed just before dawn and at twilight."

"Why is that?" Brecht asked, puzzled by this claim.

"Perhaps it's because if people expect trouble, they think it will happen in the daytime or at night. The few moments between the two seem like some sort of safe zone," Encizo explained. "Or maybe it's because a guy standing guard duty for hours sees the predawn or twilight as a signal that his watch is almost over and nothing has happened, so it makes a subliminal impression that he'll be able to complete his watch without incident and get some sleep soon."

"Whatever the reason," Katz continued, "experience has shown us this is true. Now, there are two doors to the building. One front and one back. No sentries posted outside, but we know men are watching from the windows. Hopefully they're now tired and bored and more interested in those steamer trunks loaded with millions of dollars than standing guard."

"They don't have any reason to think we've caught up with them," McCarter said. "Aside from the fact a couple of the other operations in the United States and Japan seem to be in trouble."

"That would be enough to make me extra cautious," Encizo stated. "Of course, money isn't my top priority in life and it must be for those mercs. Having all that cash on hand would probably make it hard for them to think about anything else."

"Maybe we'll get real lucky and they'll start fighting over the money," Manning said with a shrug. "I guess that's not too likely to happen. At least, not right away."

"Don't expect infighting when they know they can collect another six million by carrying out another terrorist strike," McCarter reminded the Canadian. "Of course, that's one payment none of them will ever get to lay eyes on."

"We'll see to that," Katz agreed. "Is everybody ready?"

The Phoenix professionals were armed to the teeth. Each of them carried micro-Uzis with extra 32-round magazines in ammo pouches. Tear-gas grenades and masks were attached to their belts. They carried combat knives for emergencies. Encizo, the supreme knife artist, had his Cold Steel Tanto in a cross-draw position and a Gerber Mark I dagger in a boot sheath. Every man except McCarter carried a Walther P-88 in shoulder leather. The double-action 9 mm pistols had ambidextrous features that made the handgun easy to use left-handed, as well as right. This fact was appreciated by Katz, who had only one hand, and Manning, who was almost fully ambidextrous and could use either hand with equal ease.

McCarter still refused to carry the Walther because he didn't trust double-action autoloaders. To the Briton, this was just something else that could go wrong with a gun. He continued to carry his Browning Hi-Power. The single-action autoloader was designed in a manner first developed in 1935, but it was still a reliable and durable weapon. Since McCarter was a superb pistol marksman, the others didn't argue with his decision.

In addition the men carried backup guns. Katz had a Beretta pistol at the small of his back, while Encizo packed a Walther PPK. McCarter carried a Smith & Wesson .38 Special snub-nosed revolver, and Manning, who favored larger calibers, had a .357 Magnum stainless-steel Ruger.

They were ready. Katz nodded. It was time to get to work.

CHAPTER TWENTY-FOUR

There was adequate cover surrounding the defunct toy factory. Phoenix Force approached from all sides, using trees, trash bins and a large Dumpster to conceal their movements. As they hoped, the terrorists didn't seem to pay much attention to what was going on outside the building.

Yakov Katzenelenbogen knelt by a trash barrel about ten yards from the front of the factory. He took a tear-gas grenade from his belt and slid a hook into the ring to the pin. The Israeli waited for the others to make the first move. He realized his limitations. Although he was in his fifties, Katz was still in very good physical condition. He was strong and he could move quickly when necessary, but his endurance wasn't as good as that of the younger members of the team.

Katz couldn't throw as well as the others. He had adjusted to the loss of his right arm and could do almost anything a man with two flesh-and-blood limbs could do. However, pitching grenades was no longer one of his greater abilities. Katz would have to get closer, and that would require waiting for a good distraction. He had no doubt his fellow commandos would supply that before the sun rose in the pale sky above. Katz watched as Gary Manning moved into position at the rear of the building.

The Canadian demolitions expert and rifle marksman would have preferred to use an FAL rifle or a packet of

C-4 plastic explosives, but the situation didn't require his primary skills. He pulled the pin from a tear-gas canister and judged the distance to the closest window. It was about five yards, and he had no doubt he could lob the grenade through the glass pane.

He hurled the canister, which hit the window forcibly. Glass shattered, and the grenade landed inside. Voices shouted alarm in several languages.

McCarter and Encizo took their cue and threw stun grenades through other windows. Explosions bellowed within the factory. More glass shattered, and tear-gas fumes began to flow from already shattered windows.

Katz jogged to the front of the building, yanked the pin to his tear-gas grenade as he ran and hurled it at the nearest window. The front door burst open even as the grenade smashed glass and fell inside the factory. Two figures charged from the threshold, one man carrying a French-made MAT-49 submachine gun, the other an H&K pistol.

Both men were already stunned and coughing from the effects of the gas attack, but they were also armed and presented an immediate threat. Katz grabbed the micro-Uzi that hung from a shoulder strap near his left hip. Teary eyed, the terrorist gunmen saw the blur of Katz's form and swung their weapons toward the Israeli, who opened fire, spraying the enemy with a long slash of 9 mm slugs.

One man stopped three bullets with his chest, the MAT-49 chopper falling from his fingers as he toppled to the ground. The second gunman was struck in the upper torso, but the bullets didn't connect with any vital organs. A slug smashed a rib and shattered the guy's collarbone. The impact drove the opponent back toward the doorway.

A salvo of automatic fire erupted from within the building. Projectiles ripped into the wounded man and split his backbone. He fell forward, spinal cord severed and both lungs punctured. Katz leaped to the wall and pressed his back against it. The terrorists inside were shooting blindly, confused and dazed by the grenades. The Phoenix commander stayed clear of the doorway and waited for the gunfire to subside.

ENCIZO RACED to the factory as the shooting blazed from the front and rear entrance. Manning had fired a volley of Uzi rounds at the door and windows at the back of the building to draw attention from the terrorists long enough for the Cuban and McCarter to hit the enemy from a less likely direction.

The Cuban reached the factory and shoved a rain barrel from a drainage pipe. It rolled next to a window. Most of the glass had already been shattered by the grenade explosions, and no bullets seemed to be sizzling through the broken panes as Encizo placed a boot on the barrel. He didn't hesitate.

Encizo used the keg for a springboard. He jumped from the barrel and threw himself into the window. The Phoenix warrior wore an M-17 gas mask with a plastic hood and gloves. These protected him from glass fragments as he plunged through the window. Framework gave way, and he heard glass break. It harmlessly struck the thick rubber and Plexiglas lenses of the mask.

The Cuban landed surefootedly inside the factory. His boots touched the floor, and his bent knees absorbed most of the impact. He found himself next to a man who was trying to mop his eyes and nose with a damp cloth in an effort to combat the effects of tear gas. Encizo slammed the frame of his Uzi into the side of the guy's skull and knocked him unconscious.

The place was pandemonium. Dazed figures staggered about the factory. Some held guns in one hand and pawed at their faces with the other. A few terrorists had kept their wits despite the bedlam conditions. They broke open a crate to remove gas masks stored among their emergency gear. The former mercenaries were well prepared. That wasn't going to make the job for Phoenix Force any easier.

Right behind Encizo, McCarter crashed through another window in the same manner employed by his Cuban partner. The Briton literally landed on a terrorist. Feetfirst he slammed into the gunman. The guy hit the floor with McCarter on his chest. The Phoenix fighter slugged his opponent and left the senseless figure on the floor. A gas mask concealed his features, but Encizo was certain McCarter was grinning as he moved to cover by a row of shelves.

A half-blind gunman had heard McCarter crash through the window and tried to aim his pistol at the Briton. He didn't see the Phoenix pro until it was too late. McCarter fired a short burst of Uzi rounds and ripped the guy open from breastbone to throat. Another terrorist glimpsed the glare of the Uzi and swung his Skorpion machine pistol toward the Briton's position.

Encizo saw the threat to his partner and snap-aimed his Uzi. He triggered a 3-round burst and blasted the enemy's head and neck with parabellum devastation.

Weapons opened fire and spit rounds in the general direction of McCarter and Encizo. They stayed low as slugs splintered the shelves they used for cover and punched holes in walls above the commandos. The Phoenix fighters returned fire. One opponent was caught in the path of both Uzi streams. The cross fire tore into the masked man's torso, the high-velocity projectiles chopping him into lifeless pulp.

Katz charged from the front entrance and fired on a trio of terrorists preoccupied with trying to take out Encizo and McCarter. An Uzi burst sent one gunman hurtling into a card table, which collapsed under his weight and crashed to the floor. The man's corpse sprawled across the wrecked furniture as the others dived for cover.

"Surrender!" Katz called out, his voice muffled by the rubber and plastic of his gas mask. "You're surrounded! Even if you get past us, the police will stop you outside!"

He shouted this warning in German, French and English to make certain the enemy understood. The terrorists weren't impressed and responded with more gunfire. However, the ex-mercs also retreated farther to the rear of the building as they exchanged fire with the three Phoenix warriors. Several of their comrades had already been taken out during the battle, and they realized they were pitted against experienced and well-armed opponents.

McCarter charged forward to pursue the fleeing terrorists. Something grabbed his ankle and threw the Briton off balance. He crashed to the floor. The unexpected fall caught him off guard, but he managed to slip his finger free from the trigger guard to prevent firing the Uzi by accident when he hit the floor.

Miguel Sanchez had seized McCarter's ankle. Sanchez and Quevedo had dropped to the floor when the first grenade smashed through a window. Unarmed, the Bolivians stayed down while the battle erupted all around them. The mercenaries seemed to have enough trouble keeping themselves alive. It seemed obvious they weren't going to protect the two bagmen from South America. They'd have to take care of themselves.

Sanchez and Quevedo had covered their mouths and noses with handkerchiefs for protection from the tear gas and donned sunglasses to reduce the effect of the fumes on their eyes. It was successful to a degree, but the Bolivians were still struggling to keep from betraying their position due to coughing on the gas. When McCarter passed their hiding place, Sanchez and Quevedo saw an opportunity to take out an invader and steal the man's weapons. Neither of the Bolivians was in a very good mood when they finally had a chance to fight back.

McCarter rolled onto his side as Quevedo rose from the floor to a crouched position and dived for the fallen Briton. Sanchez still held McCarter's ankle. The Phoenix commando raised his Uzi as Quevedo pounced. The steel frame struck the Bolivian in the upper arm, but he managed to grab the weapon and push the barrel away from his chest.

"Sod off!" McCarter hissed through clenched teeth.

The Bolivians had him pinned, with Quevedo on his chest and Sanchez holding an ankle. McCarter realized the guy who held one leg would try to grab the other. He lashed out with his free boot, unable to see Sanchez, but guessing where the man's head would be. McCarter also pushed the Uzi into Quevedo to try to ease the burden on his chest.

A boot struck Sanchez in the shoulder when McCarter's first kick missed its target. The Bolivian drew back to avoid another kick and grabbed for McCarter's flailing leg while holding on to the captive ankle with one hand. The boot hit Sanchez's groping fingers. The bagman cried out as a finger was snapped back and bone cracked at a knuckle.

Quevedo continued to play tug-of-war for possession of the Uzi, but also released one hand to swing a fist at McCarter's masked face. The Briton raised a forearm to block the attack, then jabbed his fist into Quevedo's face. The punch caused the Bolivian's head to bounce, and McCarter quickly grabbed the guy's necktie and yanked forcibly.

The bagman was pulled forward as McCarter moved his head away from his opponent and continued to shove with the Uzi. The combined effect propelled Quevedo face-first into the floor. McCarter also caught a glimpse of Sanchez, who was still looking at his injured hand. The Briton thrust another kick and slammed the boot heel into the center of the handkerchief wrapped around the guy's mouth.

Sanchez moaned and collapsed on the floor. His fingers slipped from McCarter's ankle. The Briton took advantage of this to bend a knee and whip it upward to slam into Quevedo's kidney. The blow stunned the already battered Bolivian, but Quevedo turned suddenly and wrenched the Uzi from McCarter's grip. However, to do this, he also shifted his weight from the Briton's chest.

McCarter quickly pushed himself up with one arm and hooked his left fist to the side of Quevedo's jaw. A bloodstain on the hood's handkerchief mask already revealed his nose had been mashed when he slammed into the floor with his face. The punch rocked the Bolivian and knocked him onto his back. Yet he still held the confiscated Uzi machine pistol and rolled away from McCarter, weapon in his grasp.

The Briton reached for the Browning under his left arm. Quevedo completed his roll and pointed the Uzi at the Phoenix commando. He had moved away from McCarter's hands and feet. At last he seemed to have an opportunity to use the micro-Uzi to blast this troublesome and mysterious opponent.

McCarter drew the Browning, aimed and fired in a single fast and fluid motion. He relied on years of combat pistol training and battlefield instinct. Quevedo's head recoiled violently as a 9 mm round drilled into the frontal bone. The Bolivian fell to the floor. The impact jarred his fist, and the Uzi snarled. Several rounds shot up to the ceiling as the dead man flopped on his back. The gun fell silent, and Quevedo's limp arm dropped across his chest.

Sanchez groaned and started to stir. McCarter swatted him behind the ear with the steel frame of the Browning to render the man senseless. He knelt and glanced about, pistol in a two-handed Weaver's combat grip. There were no terrorists in sight, except for those either killed or beaten unconscious. Katz and Encizo had also vanished.

"Where the bloody hell did everybody go?" McCarter complained.

KATZ AND ENCIZO had continued to chase the fleeing gunners into the next room. The Phoenix fighters discovered Roger Nielson by one of the steamer trunks loaded with money. The Scottish terrorist had donned a gas mask, but he was more interested in scooping out bundles of money and shoving them into a duffel bag than participating in the battle.

"What are you doing?" Heinrich Rilke exclaimed as he took cover by a support pillar that extended to the ceiling. "Money is no good to a dead man!"

Nielson didn't respond. One of his eardrums had been ruptured when a grenade exploded. He was deaf and couldn't hear the German. And he was too concerned with grabbing as much cash as possible to even look around. Nielson had risked his life for the money, and he intended to take as much as he could before he made a run for it. The Scot didn't realize how critical the situation had become.

"Ignore that fool!" Theodor Hesse told his fellow German terrorist. "We have enough problems."

A grenade landed on the floor and rolled from the doorway. Hesse abruptly rushed forward to kick the grenade back where it came. In his haste he failed to notice the pin was still in the miniexplosive. Rilke stayed behind his cover and ducked. Nielson continued to stuff his bag with money, impervious to anything except his own greed.

Hesse presented a clear target when he exposed himself to kick the grenade. Katz immediately opened fire from the doorway and drilled the German with a trio of parabellums in the center of his chest. Hesse's sternum exploded. Bone shards pierced his lungs, and the force of the 9 mm punch kicked him off his feet to land heavily on the floor.

Katz plunged through the doorway, Uzi braced along his prosthesis. He hit the floor and slid to cover behind a stack of crates. Hilke saw the movement as he finally looked up. The grenade had been a trick to draw them out, the terrorist realized. Hesse lay on his back, pink froth bubbling from his open mouth. Nielson still wasn't paying attention to anything except the money.

Rilke considered firing at Katz's position, but he guessed one or more opponents were also stationed by the doorway. They could easily keep him pinned down until he exhausted his ammunition. Rilke was only armed with a pistol, and his opponents had automatic weapons. He decided there was only one thing left to do. Rilke tossed his H&K autoloader into the open and raised his hands.

"I've had enough!" he declared. "Don't shoot!"

"Keep your hands raised and walk to the doorway," Katz instructed. He repeated the order in German to make sure the guy understood.

Rilke obeyed and marched dutifully to the threshold. Encizo was ready for him and told the terrorist to face the wall and assume a spread-eagle position. Rilke wasn't certain what this meant, but he guessed correctly and didn't attempt to resist as Encizo handcuffed his wrists together at the small of his back.

Katz saw there was no one in the room aside from the obsessed Nielson. The Israeli stepped forward, Uzi pointed at the Scot's head. He was amazed the beefy terrorist still didn't pay attention. Nielson gripped the mouth of the duffel bag and shook it to try to make more room inside for even more money. Finally he noticed the barrel of the machine pistol less than a yard from his nose.

Blood from the man's ear explained why he hadn't heard the battle raging around him, but even a deaf man would have realized he was in danger if he hadn't been so consumed with collecting some ill-gotten gains.

Suddenly the Scot swung the duffel bag and batted it across the Israeli's weapon. Katz triggered the Uzi, and a burst of 9 mm rounds tore canvas, ripped through wads of paper and came to rest somewhere inside the bundles of money. Nielson snarled with rage and chopped a hand across Katz's wrist. The Uzi fell from the Phoenix commander's grasp.

Nielson swung his other fist toward Katz's face. The prosthesis rose swiftly, and the terrorist's forearm connected with the hard plastic shell of Katz's artificial limb. The Israeli thrust the steel hooks forward like a striking cobra. Metal talons struck an eyepiece in Nielson's mask. Plexiglas cracked and burst as Katz drove the hooks deeper. Sharp metal pierced Nielson's eyeball and burrowed into the socket to his brain.

A scream of agony turned to a whimper that barely escaped the filters of the gas mask. Nielson's body sagged to the floor as Encizo and McCarter moved through the doorway to join Katz.

"You okay, Yakov?" Encizo asked, barely glancing at the corpse of Roger Nielson.

"I'm fine," the Phoenix commander replied. "And I'm still Silverman until this mission is over. Don't forget that."

"Next time you blokes take off somewhere, you might at least let me know where you're going," McCarter chided.

"We thought you were right behind us," Katz replied. "When we noticed you weren't, we assumed you were busy cuffing prisoners and would be along presently."

"I had two bastards trying to kill me back there," the Briton stated. "Wouldn't you have felt pretty bad if they'd succeeded?"

"I guess we'll never know," Encizo said with a shrug.

LOUIS GOUNOD had retreated to the rear of the building. It was a small storage room, already filled with tear gas and riddled with bullets. The corpse of a fellow terrorist lay sprawled on the floor. The green fog from the tear gas canisters obscured his vision even with the protective lenses of his mask. Gounod wasn't certain which one of his comrades had been slain by a burst of automatic fire at the beginning of the battle.

The corpse appeared to have been one of the senior members of his former mercenary forces. Probably one of two Spanish mercs in the outfit. The Franco fascists had been with him since he left the legion years earlier. Gounod didn't bother to take a better look at the dead man. It didn't really matter who the slain merc had been. They would all be killed or captured... if they weren't already.

The sounds of battle had ceased within the building. Gounod knew there was no point in trying to run. The police or the military would block any route he might take. Hiding would be equally useless. They would search the factory diligently. There was no place to hide and too many of them to fight. Gounod didn't intend to surrender. He would rather die than spend the rest of his life in prison. That left only one option.

The French terrorist had managed to grab three kilo blocks of C-4 plastique from the supplies before he'd retreated to the storage room. He also had some primacord and detonators. If Gounod was going to die, he'd take a hell of a lot of the opposition with him. The mercenary placed his MAB pistol on a tabletop and unloaded the explosives from a knapsack. He set up the C-4 and primacord on the table and began to prepare one enormous bomb.

Gary Manning rose from a corner of the room. He had hidden among the dense green gas fumes that sputtered from a canister and patiently waited for the terrorist to put down his pistol. The Phoenix Force demolitions pro guessed what the guy was up to when he saw the shape of the objects in the knapsack. Gounod wanted to go out with a bang, but Manning wasn't going to allow that.

The big Canadian advanced quickly. Due to the gas mask, Gounod's peripheral vision was cut off by the lenses and rubber. He didn't see Manning until the Phoenix pro was next to the table. Gounod glimpsed the figure and automatically reached for the pistol he had placed next to the explosives. Manning slammed a boot into the table and kicked it hard enough to tip the furniture over. C-4, primacord and the handgun hit the floor, followed by the table itself.

Gounod didn't react by surrendering or trying to dive after the fallen pistol. He swung a roundhouse kick to Manning's Uzi. The boot struck the subgun from the Canadian's hand. The Frenchman whirled with the motion of the kick. His foot touched the floor, and he instantly launched a fast side kick with the other leg. The boot caught Manning in the abdomen hard enough to knock the Phoenix fighter across the room.

Manning hit the wall. The breath had been driven from him, and he had been stunned by the unexpected kicks. He had encountered the French style of kick-boxing in the past. Gounod was obviously an expert and determined to stomp the life from the Canadian warrior.

The French merc launched himself across the room and leaped into the air, one leg extended, boot aimed at Manning's head. The Phoenix fighter dodged the attack. Gounod's boot slammed into the wall. Manning quickly scooped an arm under Gounod's thigh before the guy could retract his leg and shoved hard.

Gounod was thrown off balance and fell to the floor. His back hit the surface, and Manning twisted the guy's captive leg to try to force him over on his belly. Then he could mount the merc's back and control him long enough to cuff him. Manning also figured he ought to bind the bastard's ankles with another set of plastic riot cuffs.

The mercenary braced himself on his shoulders and swung his free leg. He smashed a boot to the side of Mamning's head, the kick staggering the big Canadian. He lost the grip on Gounod's leg and fell into another wall. The protective mask had spared Manning some of the impact of the kick, but the blow still filled his head with stunning white pain. He tried to shake it off, but Gounod was already back on his feet and rammed a hard fist to the Canadian's gut.

The terrorist swung his other fist at Manning's head. The commando ducked and avoided the second punch, driving his own fist under the man's ribs and grabbing his arm. He yanked Gounod forward and pumped a knee to the enemy's belly. Manning was rewarded by the sound of a muffled groan. He shoved Gounod into the wall and hammered a fist between the merc's shoulder blades.

Gounod thrust a back-kick at Manning's groin. The Canadian expected something like this tactic. He dodged the boot and adroitly swung his own kick to Gounod's other leg. The merc was once again thrown off balance and crashed to the floor. This time Manning stomped a boot heel into the fallen opponent's stomach. Gounod sat up with a gagging sound, as if he might throw up.

Manning grabbed the Frenchman's gas mask and pulled hard, yanking the protective face gear off Gounod's head. Tear gas immediately assaulted the man's umprotected nostrils and eyes. He wiped his face with one hand as he violently coughed and spit. His other hand began groping for the discarded pistol on the floor. Manning terminated this effort by stomping on Gounod's fingers.

The terrorist yelped in pain and swallowed a mouthful of tear gas. Nearly choking on the fumes, he got to his knees and clutched trampled fingers in his good hand. Manning decided the best way to cuff the guy was to make sure he didn't have any fight left in him. He hit Gounod with all his weight behind the punch. The terrorist dropped to the floor.

The Canadian reached for some riot cuffs in his gear when a figure appeared at a doorway. Manning reached for the Walther P-88 in shoulder leather, but he recognized the figure's prosthesis and Uzi machine pistol, even if Katz's face was concealed by a gas mask.

"Is that the last one?" the Israeli inquired.

"If you guys got the rest of them," Manning replied. "How'd we do? Anybody hurt?"

"Just some men who would have hurt a lot of innocent people if we hadn't stopped them," Katz stated. "Actually most of the terrorists are dead. We did manage to take a few prisoners."

"I've got another live one here," Manning declared. "As a matter of fact, I think I just decked Louis Gounod himself."

"Well, well," Katz remarked. "The man we've been looking for since we arrived in France. I'm looking forward to having a nice long chat with him."

CHAPTER TWENTY-FIVE

Calvin James was delighted to see the other four members of Phoenix Force arrive at the airfield at Stony Man Farm. They appeared to be a little tired, but no more than one would expect after taking a long flight back from Europe. Aside from a bruise just above Manning's right temple, they all appeared to be in fine shape.

"Well, it sure took you guys long enough," James declared. "I guess that's what happens when you don't have me with you in the field."

"Guess so," McCarter replied, unable to repress a smile. "Glad to see you made it back from Japan. Didn't eat any of that *fugu* blowfish, did you?"

"No, but we took out a shitload of terrorists," James replied proudly. "Do any of you ever recall hearing about a former JRA loonie known as Arashi?"

"Is that the one whose name means 'the Wind' or 'the Storm'?" Katz inquired. "Something like that. Japanese isn't one of my languages."

"But your memory is still good," the African-American warrior assured him. "We caught up with Arashi in Japan. The sucker is history now, but you'll never guess who we think might be involved with the terrorists. Somebody even bigger than Arashi. Give you a hint—he's from Venezuela, and I ain't talking about Carlos the Jackal."

"El Cuchillo," Encizo replied.

"Yeah," James said with surprise. "How the hell...?"

"We met some name-droppers in Germany," Gary Manning said. "We might as well explain this to Hal and whoever else is here."

"You picked a good time," James stated. "Just about everybody is here except Leo and Barbara. Hal sent them to Brazil."

"Brazil?" Katz asked with interest. "Maybe we don't have much to add to what the rest of you already put together."

"Every bit helps," James replied. "Right now Hal's sort of running on a theory Mack came up with. He figures a Brazilian arms dealer and manufacturer may have formed some sort of conspiracy with a Colombian coke cartel."

"Colombian?" Encizo said with surprise. "Are you sure you don't mean Bolivian?"

"The guys in New York and Newark were Colombians," James told him. "Able Team nailed them. They're here, too. So is Bolan."

"That's rare," Katz remarked. "Let's get inside. I think we all need to ruminate about current events."

A few minutes later Phoenix Force was seated at the conference table in the Stony Man War Room. The Executioner and Able Team were also present. Hal Brognola listened to the four commandos who had just returned from Europe. The news they brought was welcome music to the big Fed's ears. Not only had the terrorists responsible for the North Sea oil sabotage and the attack on the French nuclear plant been dealt with, but Phoenix Force had also discovered information that supported previous evidence about the source of the terrorist network.

"We first got suspicious of Silva when we located that miniature submarine," Brognola explained. "Actually Striker was the one who put the pieces together."

"Gadgets figured out how to find the sub, Kissinger was there to investigate the sub, the Bear found the information on Silva and you coordinated the Feds and Navy involved in the search," Bolan stated. "We all have to work together if we're going to solve this mess."

"None of us figured a Bolivian cartel was involved with this, as well as a Colombian outfit," Lyons remarked. "No wonder the terrorists have been able to pay millions of dollars for fancy minisubs and high-priced mercenaries and terrorists."

"Not to mention the fact Silva himself is very wealthy and has a lot of influence in Brazil," Blancanales added. "You know, it may not be easy to go after a man like that. He's certainly got contacts in the government and the military. Maybe even in our own CIA."

"Records show he did some business with the Company back in the eighties," Brognola explained. "Speaking of CIA, the President got some complaints from the Company office in Germany."

"That makes it even," Encizo said. "We've got some complaints about them, too."

"Did you punch out that CIA case officer or did McCarter do it?" Brognola asked. "I forgot that CIA aren't your favorite people, Rafael. Until now, I assumed David slugged the guy."

"You guessed right," the Briton admitted. "I hit the bastard. With a mouth like his, he ought to expect to get a fist in it once in a while."

"You can't punch out every CIA operative who rubs you the wrong way."

"We'll try to be good boys in the future, Hal," Katz remarked, firing up a cigarette. "Let's get back to the subject of the mission itself. We interrogated one of the Bolivians. The only one still alive, naturally. His name is supposedly Sanchez. He wouldn't say much else, and we didn't have Cal on hand to administer scopolamine."

"Told you, you guys just aren't the same without me," James commented with an exaggerated shrug.

"Uh-huh," Manning said dryly. "Well, even without truth serum, we did hear Sanchez and Gounod mention somebody named 'Aguilar,' as well as Silva and El Cuchillo."

"No one referred to him as Ramon Cazazo," Katz explained. "There is probably more than one Latin American blade artist known as 'the Knife,' but Gounod did mention that El Cuchillo took part in the North Sea oil-well sabotage."

"The photograph of Cazazo with Arashi and the type of knife, as well as the skill employed, supports the probability the man is indeed the real El Cuchillo," Bolan stated. "According to what little we have on record about Cazazo, he speaks English and French, probably at least a working vocabulary in Portuguese, and possibly German and Arabic, as well."

"I used to hear stories about that guy all over Central America when we used to concentrate operations in that part of the world," Blancanales stated. "Usually spoken in whispers. Cazazo was becoming some sort of boogeyman down there. There were even stories that he was some kind of phantom or a *brujo*, a male witch, with magic that helped him kill and protected him from the police."

"Well, it will be a pleasure to put an end to that myth," Lyons remarked. "Now all we have to do is go to Brazil and find these bastards. Piece of cake. Of course, Brazil is the fifth-largest country in the world so it might take awhile."

"One thing we know for certain is we don't have much time before the terrorists strike again," Bolan reminded the others. "Every base we hit was preparing to carry out another attack. If we had been a day or two late, or even a few hours in at least one case, another strike on an environmental target would have occurred. They've got too much riding on this lunatic operation. They can't stop now, and they know the authorities will never stop looking for them if their plan fails. They'll try to launch another attack as soon as possible. They don't have any other choices."

"Yeah," Gadgets Schwarz agreed, "but if we go down to Brazil and start looking for terrorists, we'd better have some idea where to start. We're also going to have a problem because we can't be sure who we can trust. It's hard to say who Silva has in his pocket. Police, politicians, military commanders and God knows who else might be on Silva's payroll."

"That's why I sent Leo and Barbara ahead to establish a reliable contact," Brognola explained. "We found somebody who looks promising, but I wanted them to scout him out first before I send you guys in."

"We might have some trouble getting weapons and other equipment into Brazil," Katz commented. "Best way to get them into a foreign country when one doesn't have cooperation from the host nation's government is to send it to the U.S. Embassy in diplomatic pouches. Providing no one decides to violate the rules of diplomatic immunity, the pouches can't be opened by the authorities."

"Yeah," Brognola said with a nod, "we've used that before, of course. The United States doesn't have diplomatic relations with a few countries, but that won't be a problem with Brazil. Relations between the U.S. and Brazil are still okay. Of course, that also means we'll have to ship the pouches to NSA or CIA operatives at the embassy."

"And we're on such good terms with the Company right now," Manning commented with an exasperated sigh. "Is that going to be a problem, Hal?"

"The CIA in Brazil doesn't know you guys had friction with the Company in Germany," Brognola replied. "However, the Bear suggested we might do better to deal with the NSA stationed in Brazil anyway. National Security Agency has some listening posts there and receiver units for spy satellites. They have at least one radio station positioned somewhere in the Andes or some mountain range."

"The Andes extend along the western portion of South America and are found in five or six countries," Blancanales said, trying to recall exact geography. "But I don't think Brazil is included."

"Okay," the big Fed agreed with a weary nod. "So the Andes aren't in Brazil and the NSA has stuff set up at some other mountains. What's important is the NSA is pretty well established in Brazil, and we can use them to get weapons and gear through the embassy. We'll get the pouches loaded and send them out pronto."

"The NSA might be a better choice for another reason," Lyons added. "According to our records, there's a chance Silva has done some deal with CIA. NSA might not have a conflict of interest when it comes to Silva."

"The NSA operates in a manner very similar to CIA," Katz reminded the Able Team captain. "If anything,

NSA is even more secretive than the Company and manages to maintain a much lower profile. Of course, the NSA is the largest of all American Intelligence networks. Bigger than CIA or FBI, but not nearly as well-known to the general public."

"You mean Silva may have done business with NSA personnel and we don't have anything on file about it?" Gadgets Schwarz inquired with a soft whistle. "Who the hell do you trust these days?"

"No one outside the immediate members of Stony Man," the Executioner answered. "We have to work with other people, but the only ones we can really trust are within our own organization. That might sound a little paranoid, but that's just the way things are for us."

"I don't think most people can really trust a hell of a lot of folks out there," James commented. "Maybe we're just more aware of how treacherous people can be."

"That's a cheerful observation," Brognola said. "Probably true, but sort of beside the point as far as we're concerned. We have to deal with covert outfits, which by their nature tend to be distrusting and less than trustworthy at times. Goes without saying that international terrorists are about as treacherous as human beings get."

"But we know how to cure them of those nasty traits," McCarter said with a thin smile. "So let's get back to the hunt."

CHAPTER TWENTY-SIX

Commodore José Guimarães didn't like going to the slums, located along hillsides in Rio de Janeiro. This was a part of Rio the tourists didn't see, far from the expensive homes and apartment complexes at the Copacabana and Ipanema beaches.

Guimarães had been born to poverty. He might have remained in the slums if he hadn't found a new home in the military. He was very intelligent and hadn't been afraid of hard work. He continued his education while still an enlisted man and qualified for officer candidate schooling. Guimarães became a commissioned officer in the Brazilian navy, and had risen to a high field-grade rank in the service.

His last promotion had occurred in 1990, five years after the elections that established a civilian government in Brazil after decades of oppressive military regimes. Guimarães was proud of this because it meant he wasn't associated with the human rights violations of the past. The military had lost much of its authority, but it had had too much in the past. Guimarães was glad Brazil was now a federal republic and, more or less, a democracy.

However, all the ills of society hadn't vanished with those changes. The shabby houses and poor conditions of the slums remained. Guimarães found the slums to be a place of memories he tried to repress. He was also realistic and knew the neighborhoods could be dangerous. The commodore dressed in old chinos, a T-shirt and jacket that concealed the .45-caliber pistol in shoulder leather.

Antonio Durao had arranged the meeting. The thin, nervous NSA agent looked as if he wished he had chosen a different rendezvous spot. Like most members of the National Security Agency, Durao was more at home with computers than cloak-and-dagger operations. This wasn't the sort of thing the young intellectual was comfortable with, and the setting was less than reassuring.

The NSA officer had arrived in a Jeep with two passengers. One was a man, short and approaching middle age, but still tough with keen senses and a sharp mind. The other was a lovely blond woman. She wore a white pants suit and boots, not the type of clothing Guimarães thought appropriate for women. A lady with such a superb figure, prominent breasts and long legs ought to wear tight-fitting dresses with plunging necklines and slits up to the thigh, in the commodore's opinion.

He openly cast an admiring gaze at the woman as he climbed into the vehicle. Guimarães tried not to be salacious, aware that the lady wasn't there for romance. The other man stayed in the back with the female, so the commodore was forced to sit next to Durao. The vehicle rolled forward to a dirt road and began to circle Rio de Janeiro. The view steadily improved as they moved from the slum area. Towering office buildings and apartment houses revealed that most of the city was beautiful and modern. This was the Rio people recognized, a vacation spot for parties and night life.

"These are the people I told you about, Commodore," Durao said in English, signaling that Guimarães should also speak in this language.

"Good afternoon," the Brazilian said, smiling at the blonde. "And that it is when one has the opportunity to meet such a beautiful lady from the United States."

Barbara Price didn't reply. She knew enough about Brazil to realize women's lib wasn't a thriving success in the largest country of South America. Men had very chauvinistic attitudes toward women, and they didn't regard females as equals. The fact Guimarães found her attractive could be a problem, and she wasn't about to encourage him with a smile.

"We understand that you've been doing some work for the NSA for quite a few years now," Leo Turrin said. He came straight to the point. "You're a very reliable source, and they tell me you're trustworthy."

"I have been happy to help the United States of America as long as your country's interests do not conflict with those of Brazil," the commodore replied.

Turrin knew the guy had also been receiving pay from NSA for his cooperation, but he didn't mention this. Guimarães hadn't betrayed his country and he did seem to genuinely support democratic reforms in Brazil. He was still a patriot, more or less, but simply took advantage of a chance to make some extra money from Uncle Sam. This wasn't really ethical, and the navy would have court-martialed him if they found out, but the arrangement made him an ideal contact for Stony Man.

"What do you know about João Silva?" Price asked, meeting the Brazilian's eyes. "He's a big industrialist here in Brazil."

"Weapons manufacturer," Guimarães replied with a nod. "He also sells arms to other countries. Sometimes sells to so-called revolutionaries. The Brazilian military hasn't purchased much from Silva because his plans for innovations in weapons designs would simply be too expensive to develop in mass quantities needed for use by the army or the navy. If you want to do business with him, I strongly advise you to find someone else."

"Just the opposite," Turrin replied. "We think he's been involved with something pretty bad, Commodore. Evidence suggests he's connected with international terrorism."

"That really would not surprise me," Guimarães said mildly. "Silva is a ruthless, ambitious and potentially very dangerous man. I should warn you—if you don't know already—Silva has many powerful friends. If you plan to arrest him, you may have a great deal of trouble."

"Brazil doesn't generally extradite foreign criminals who come here to hide out," Durao added. "The odds of getting the government to hand over Silva to stand trial in the States are just about nil."

"Yeah," Turrin stated. "We figured that already. Still, if we can prove this guy is involved with an international conspiracy that would threaten the national security of Brazil, as well as thousands of lives throughout the world, I don't think Silva is going to have too many people willing to admit they ever knew him, let alone friends willing to stick their necks out for him."

"Are you certain this is true?" Guimarães asked, startled by the claim.

"We got a coded message from our headquarters in Washington confirming it," Price confirmed. "We also have to stop him quickly. In fact, a special unit of topnotch experts is being sent to take care of Silva. We could sure use your help."

"The best-trained commandos in the Brazilian military are probably the Amphibious Reconnaissance Marines," the Commodore stated. "They're qualified as frogmen, paratroopers and trained to deal with special operations. However, I can't dispatch a company or more of these men without some sort of explanation."

"Why do you figure we'd need that many troops?" Turrin asked.

"Silva has an army of security personnel. I understand they're really mercenaries. It's also said he built a secret base somewhere in Amazonas. If that's true, you'll have a very difficult time even finding him there. Amazonas is a very large state and much of it is jungle. Thousands of miles have not really been explored or mapped. You'll need an army to locate him and probably an army to take him out."

"Man," Durao commented, "I don't know how you people think you're going to do this. There's no way you can bring in enough personnel to handle a situation like this and still maintain security."

"You might be surprised," Price commented.

Guimarães looked at her and tried another smile. "Perhaps we could discuss this over dinner, Miss . . . ?"

"I'd just give you a fake name, and I don't care to have dinner with you, Commodore," Price told him.

"You sound as if you're prejudiced against Brazilian men or perhaps Hispanics in general," Guimarães said with a frown.

"Neither one, Commodore," she assured him. "There are a couple of points, however. First, I'm here on business and I have no time for a social life. Second, I read a file on you and I know you're married."

"Actually," Guimarães began with a shrug, "my wife is married."

"Too bad for her," Price said dryly.

"Ease up," Turrin whispered. "We're on the same side."

"All right," Guimarães began, apparently willing to let the matter drop. "Exactly what do these supermen from the United States plan to do when they arrive?"

"Some of them will try to establish contact with Silva at his plant in São Paulo," Turrin answered. "Others will try to get a lead on him through his family. We know he's been separated from his wife and kids for years, but Silva never bothered to get divorced. It's a long shot, but his old lady might know something about her dear hubby."

"And what will you need from me?" the commodore asked.

"Any information you can find through your sources in the military," the little Fed explained. "We'll also need some equipment. The United States sold Brazil some Bell helicopter gunships more than ten years ago. We know that you have several ships under your command with at least seven choppers. Can you get us two of them?"

"You want to just borrow two navy aircraft worth millions of dollars?" The commodore stared at Turrin in amazement. "How do you suggest I explain that? Tell the navy they were misplaced?"

"How about stolen?" Turrin said in a matter-of-fact tone. "Look, Commodore. If we find Silva, prove he's mixed up with terrorists and kick his ass, you can come in and claim lots of glory for your role in this. If we fail, then you can head to the U.S. Embassy for asylum."

"That's not something I'd care to do," Guimarães told him. "I'm afraid I'll have to think about this before I agree to taking on such risks."

"You really don't have a choice," Turrin said reluctantly. "We don't want to reveal to the Brazilian government that you've been selling information to agents of the United States for the last ten years."

"Wait a minute!" Durao exclaimed. "You guys can't use that information. NSA benefited from the commodore's help. You'll embarrass the United States government, as well as betray him for his cooperation."

"Tough shit," Turrin replied. "Maybe you guys haven't been listening. There are thousands, maybe even millions of lives in jeopardy unless we stop this son of a bitch and his terrorist cronies. I don't want to put the screws to Commodore Guimarães or cause a scandal for the U.S. government—although, it would really be more a scandal for NSA. Still in my book that's small potatoes compared to the lives of countless innocent people, massive destruction of the environment and a power play that could turn the entire continent of South America into Silva's own empire."

Guimaraães stiffened in his seat. He felt the weight of the .45 autoloader under his arm. The idea of drawing the pistol flashed through his mind, but he dismissed it as an impulse of desperation. The commodore wasn't a murderer and he didn't want to become one. Besides, he realized killing these people wouldn't solve anything. The organization they worked for already knew all about him. If Turrin, Price and Durao never returned from the Jeep ride, two and two would be put together.

"You know this is a form of blackmail," Guimarães stated.

"If that's what you want to call it," Turrin replied. "At least you can go to the U.S. Embassy and defect or whatever to the United States. They'll set you up with something nice. Better than going to prison. Of course, you will be in disgrace here, but you can't have everything."

"Hey, I don't want to be in the middle of this," Durao said. His hands were sweating so badly he had trouble holding the steering wheel.

"You're NSA," Price said sharply. "That means you serve the interests of American national security. Terrorism and mass murder is a worse threat to national security than a possible embarrassment to the government. If you don't see it that way, your morality is really twisted. You don't like risks? Get out of Intelligence operations and join the Peace Corps."

"You two aren't afraid of taking risks," Guimarães remarked with a bitter laugh, "are you?"

"Oh," Turrin said, "you mean because you're packing heat? Hell, you're not stupid, Commodore. This isn't a problem you solve by pulling your gun. Like it or not, the smart thing is to cooperate with us."

"I couldn't bring myself to shoot a woman as beautiful as you anyway," Guimarães told Price with a smile. "Even if you do think I'm a cad. Don't tell anyone, but I've always had a weakness for women who talk back to me. You should hear my wife. And my mistress."

Price rolled her eyes and shook her head. The commodore laughed with genuine amusement, and the tension finally melted. They suddenly realized they were overlooking a massive collection of luxury apartment buildings and hotels along Copacabana Beach. A long, wide mosaic sidewalk with colorful designs separated the beach from a parking lot. Tourists headed for the sand and sea, unaware that a discussion about the fate of the world was in progress less than a half a mile from the beach.

"I will cooperate in any way possible," Guimarães announced with a sigh. "Can we agree that the gunships won't be used unless you first locate Silva?"

"Agreed," Turrin said with a nod. "Maybe we won't need them at all. Just make sure they're ready just in case. Fully fueled and armed. That includes infrared night-vision gear, as well."

"I don't have to supply pilots?" the commodore asked.

"We got a couple of real aces to handle the choppers," Turrin replied. "Maybe we'll get really lucky and catch up with Silva at his plant or at his wife's home. The guy might stop by to pick up his mail or drop off some gifts to the kids. You never know how things like this work out."

"One never knows how anything is going to work out," Guimarães commented, "but I guess we're all going to find out. One way or the other."

CHAPTER TWENTY-SEVEN

"There has been no word from Europe," Guillermo Aguilar announced as he entered the quarters assigned to Rico Gomez. "My people sent to deliver the money to the mercenaries have not contacted the cartel in Bolivia or Silva."

"So the soldiers of fortune led by Gounod have certainly been captured or killed," the Colombian said grimly. Gomez reached for a vial of cocaine, but reluctantly grabbed a pack of cigarettes instead.

"There is another possibility," Aguilar said, trying to calm his companion. "Gounod and his mercs might have decided to take the six million dollars and run rather than risk another terrorist operation. They could have killed Sanchez and Quevedo when they took the money."

"I doubt that," Gomez replied. "The mercenaries must know the cartels would hunt them down. Everyone knows our syndicates never stop seeking revenge. At least they know better than to cross the Colombian cartels. You Bolivians have a softer public image. Maybe those damn mercenaries don't realize they'll have to deal with us, as well."

"Gounod was aware of that," Aguilar said in a weary tone. He didn't relish having to listen to the Colombian boast of his cartel's reputation for being ruthless killers. "The mercenary knew about Silva and El Cuchillo. Gounod and his fellow mercenaries have been wanted by the authorities for years, and they realized carrying out the sabotage missions in Scotland and France would intensify the search for them. Do you really think they would be afraid of our cartels, even your mighty and fierce Colombian outfit?"

Gomez puffed a cigarette nervously and said, "You really think that's what happened?"

"Possibly," Aguilar replied. "They may have learned that the missions in the United States and Japan failed. If that happened, it would seem quite logical to grab what money they could get and flee for their lives."

"Or their base could have been raided by police or international Intelligence organizations." Gomez stabbed his cigarette into an ashtray and picked up the coke vial. "You know that's more likely what has happened, Guillermo."

"Yes," the Bolivian reluctantly admitted. "Considering what has already happened, that does seem probable."

Gomez shook out a line of white powder on a small mirror and used a razor blade to even out the streak. He cut the line and formed three thin trails of cocaine. Aguilar resisted the urge to cuff the Colombian across the head. They needed to think clearly and decide what to do next. This was no time to be snorting nose candy and getting high.

Aguilar didn't use coke. He sold it to idiots foolish enough to waste hundreds and thousands of dollars on the white powder. The Bolivian didn't think much of any dealer stupid enough to use his own supply. Cocaine created instant euphoria, but it didn't solve problems. It just made a new one of drug dependency.

"We have to accept the fact that this entire operation is in danger of coming apart," Aguilar stated. "And we have to try to convince Silva that the plan is going down the drain."

Gomez fitted a silver tube in a nostril and snorted a line of cocaine through the fancy straw. Aguilar was exasperated with the Colombian, but waited until he finished inhaling the dope.

"We'll tell this Brazilian pig that he'd better listen to us," Gomez announced with a smile. The cocaine had filled him with a false sense of well-being and invincibility. "We put too much money into this to tolerate any more of his nonsense. He either does what we tell him or he's a dead man."

"Threatening him won't work," Aguilar insisted. "This is Silva's base. The men here work for him. I don't think Silva is as afraid of death as he is of failure. He won't hesitate to have us killed if he thinks we're turning against him."

Gomez used his finger to wipe the remaining traces of cocaine from the mirror and rubbed it over his upper gums. "The cartels will cut off his finances now anyway. We'll have enough trouble convincing them not to cut off our heads, as well."

"They'll want someone to blame," Aguilar agreed. "In fact, I don't believe we'll be able to convince them not to execute us. We need to get out of here, Rico. Perhaps head for Australia or the Fiji Islands."

"How much money have you got?" Gomez inquired. "We'll need to set ourselves up somehow for years. Perhaps even for the rest of our lives."

"I have about two hundred thousand," Aguilar replied. He was understating how much money he really had. The Bolivian actually had more than eight hundred thousand dollars hidden in his room, but he didn't intend to tell Gomez the truth.

"That's all? I have four hundred thousand dollars in American currency and gold coins. That won't last long if we have a lot of expenses."

"It'll have to do," Aguilar said with a shrug. He was already adding up the total of his stash combined with Gomez's minifortune. Twelve hundred thousand dollars would be enough for Aguilar. He could also sell Gomez's cocaine and make a few thousand more.

The Bolivian had no intention of going on the run with the ill-tempered, dope-snorting Colombian. After they got clear of Silva, Aguilar figured he'd take care of Gomez with his little .25 Raven, shoot the Colombian twice in the back of the skull and take the fool's belongings. The idea didn't bother him. After spending long months at Silva's jungle base, he was ready to kill every one of the bastards to save his own neck.

They found Silva in his office. Ramon Cazazo was already there, and he didn't look happy. The master terrorist was certainly aware of what was happening, but seemed to think he could turn the tide around if he were allowed to go into the field and personally command the terrorist strike operations.

"You told me you would be sending me to the United States to command the next mission," Cazazo complained as he stalked the floor in front of Silva's desk. "You said I would be leaving today."

"We haven't been able to establish a functioning network in the United States," Silva explained. He glanced at the doorway and saw Aguilar and Gomez. "You may as well come in unless you're fond of eavesdropping."

"We did not mean to interrupt," Aguilar apologized, "but we need to talk to you about the progress—or lack of it—in Europe."

"Apparently something happened to Gounod and the mercenaries," the Brazilian said in a solemn tone. "They haven't reported back or carried out their mission."

"This sounds familiar," Gomez said sourly. "I suppose you still intend to continue the operation the same as you have so far?"

"I just told Mr. Cazazo that we're trying to put together enough people in the United States to resume operations there." Silva's face was lined as the strain was finally beginning to show. "Besides, having problems assembling an adequate number of personnel, we still haven't been able to find out what happened to the original group in New York and Newark."

"Didn't you learn they were killed or arrested?" Aguilar asked.

"I seem to recall some of your cartel contacts with informers within the federal government and the New York City police acquired that data," Silva answered, aware the Colombian was rubbing his figurative nose in this fact. "We know many of them were killed and the survivors were arrested by either the federal or local authorities. However, no one seems to know who actually conducted the raids. They were not local police, FBI, Justice Department or any other organization we have any taps into."

"Information on who carried out the raid in Japan suggests they were not police or Kompei," Cazazo added. "The same may be true about what happened in Europe."

"We don't have adequate information about Japan or Europe to draw any conclusions," Silva declared. "What are you suggesting? There's some secret organization that's more effective than all the combined forces of law enforcement and Intelligence networks of the Western world?"

"A number of revolutionary groups I knew in the past were crushed in the process of carrying out operations against the United States and the interests of the Americans in other lands," Cazazo insisted. "It was said they were defeated, not by the conventional authorities or military, but by an elite commando unit."

"You mean Delta Force?" Silva inquired. "They're the antiterrorist unit for the United States. Supposedly they're very well trained and professional, but I doubt they could be responsible for our present problems."

"Not Delta Force," Cazazo corrected. "This is something else. Apparently they can operate like espionage agents or perhaps use Intelligence networks to help them accomplish their goals."

"There have been similar stories about mysterious covert warriors who have struck at cartel operations both in Colombia and the United States," Gomez added, his drug-fogged memory suddenly jarred by Cazazo's remarks. "Those cells were taken out by someone who struck with miltitary efficiency."

"The military isn't always that efficient," the Brazilian remarked. They were all beginning to sound like old women gossiping and exchanging horror stories. Silva was annoyed with the lot of them.

"I've known of Bolivian-based operations to fall, as well," Aguilar added, "and I've heard similar stories. Some even say..."

He hesitated before he completed the statement. "They say it reminds them of the way the Executioner used to deal with Mafia operations."

Gomez looked at Aguilar as if the Bolivian had just uttered some terrible obscenity. In the criminal world the mention of the Executioner was still regarded as a major faux pas. Ramon Cazazo also recognized the name, but he nodded as if welcoming a confrontation with the one-man army who had successfully taken on the Mob years earlier.

"The Executioner is supposed to be dead," Silva declared bluntly. "Those stories about him were probably exaggerated anyway. Besides, no one man could threaten us or defeat even one of our bases."

"You can't be certain he's dead," Cazazo said, his voice almost hopeful. "Any man who survived campaigns against the Five Families would certainly be clever and resourceful enough to fake his own death. The Executioner must have had allies during his war against the Mafia. Perhaps they've joined forces and organized. They might be working for the U.S. government now."

"That's the most absurd thing I've ever heard," Silva said. He glared at Aguilar and Gomez. "You're all getting nervous because we've had some major setbacks. The fear is making you conjure up images of dead warriors coming back from the grave like some sort of zombies with military weapons."

"I'm not saying the Executioner is still alive or involved in this," Aguilar stated. "But we've had more than setbacks. Since the first successful campaigns, every operation has been destroyed. We have to assume the authorities know about you and probably Rico and myself. Gounod may have even told them about Cazazo."

"That's assuming far too much," Silva replied with a shrug. "Perhaps we should stay here for a while. We'll keep a low profile until we know exactly what we're dealing with. No one can find us here. This base is the safest place in the world. The Amazon region is one of the least-explored areas on the planet, and this base is not located on any map."

"I think Gomez and I should return to Colombia and Bolivia to discuss this with our superiors," Aguilar urged. "They'll cut off finances if we can't convince them that this is a situation that will blow over."

"You'll stay here," Silva said in a hard voice. "I don't trust you two not to tell them tales of doom that will ensure we don't receive further payments."

"There won't be any at this rate," Gomez said. "The cartels know things aren't going well. They've lost millions on this business. Six million dollars alone was lost when the Bolivians tried to deliver payment to those mercenaries in Germany. The only chance you have to stay on decent terms with them is if you let us go back, plead your case and see if we can salvage the relationship."

"You'll stay here," Silva insisted. "Perhaps I'll have some prostitutes flown out here. I have that done occasionally so the men can enjoy themselves with female companionship. Of course, they also help themselves to an occasional girl from the Indian villages, but that sort of thing may not be to your taste."

"Why are you talking about sex at a time like this?" Aguilar asked, amazed by the suggestion.

"Because it does a man good to have a woman," Silva replied. "We've all gone too long without one. Maybe you'll act more like men than frightened children after you've been reminded you have balls."

"I could go to the United States alone and carry out a simple act of sabotage," Cazazo stated. "They have a nuclear power plant near San Diego, located on an earthquake fault line. A perfect target and I could do the job with a hundred kilos of explosives."

"I'll consider it," Silva said thoughtfully. He smiled as he considered the possibility that the operation was far from over. There were still lots of targets left, and as long as he could find men like Cazazo, there was still a chance his plan could succeed.

CHAPTER TWENTY-EIGHT

The huge statue of Christ stood atop Corcovado Mountain, arms extended wide in welcome, the stone face peaceful. Mack Bolan stared out the window of the plane as it passed the statue known as Christ the Redeemer. The enormous carving was breathtaking.

Rio de Janeiro seemed very appealing as the plane approached the airport. Too bad the Executioner and the five other Stony Man warriors aboard the airliner weren't on vacation. The plane touched down on the runway and taxied to a halt. The passengers deplaned and headed for the terminals.

Bolan and Carl Lyons strolled past Rafael Encizo and Rosario Blancanales without even glancing at the two Hispanic commandos. Their cover stories didn't have the four men traveling together. The Executioner and the Able Team captain were supposed to be a pair of American sales representatives from Chicago. Encizo's and Blancanales's passports claimed they were from Mexico City. Jack Grimaldi and David McCarter were also passengers. The Stony Man pilots had ID claiming they were helicopter maintenance engineers hired by Varig, the government-owned air-transport system of Brazil.

Leo Turrin, Barbara Price and Antonio Durao waited for Bolan and Lyons. They moved into a cocktail lounge and sat at a booth. Turrin introduced the Stony Man personnel to Durao. Bolan wasn't surprised by the NSA man's appearance, but he had hoped the guy wouldn't be what he expected. Durao looked as if he was halfway to a nervous breakdown.

They had read the National Security Agency file on the man. The encouraging facts were Durao's high IQ and ability with computers and SIGINT—signal intelligence—electronic surveillance and spy satellite equipment. He had been born in Brazil, but his parents had taken him to the United States in 1967. Durao spoke Portuguese, Spanish, English and French.

Unfortunately Durao was also a pencil pusher who really had no business being part of a mission in the field. He had joined the NSA virtually out of college and had no military background. Durao hadn't been trained in the use of firearms, martial arts or basic strategy aside from the push-button mentality of the SIGINT corps. Bolan preferred to work with soldiers or at least ex-soldiers. This guy's idea of war was a computerized chess game.

"A couple of packages arrived for you guys in diplomatic pouches at the embassy," Turrin explained. "Durao has them in the trunk of his car."

"Glad to hear it," Bolan stated. He was uncomfortable being unarmed and would be relieved to get his hands on the weapons those pouches contained. "How did things go with the commodore?"

"Commodore Guimarães has agreed to the demands made by you people," Durao said, glancing down at the table, "but I can't say I think much of your methods."

"Oh?" Lyons replied with a raised eyebrow. "NSA has been paying the commodore for confidential information and basically bribing him to use his influence to help you guys set up listening posts in Brazil. Isn't that right? But you question our ethics?"

"We already had a discussion on this," Turrin said sharply. "I got a couple of locker keys for our two fly-boys so they can pick up some suitcases with their gear. I'll give the keys to them before Ms. Jones and I fly back to the States."

"Sorry we can't stay and help," Price told Bolan. "Orders are to go back after getting things set up here."

"What about the gear for our friends from south of the border?" Lyons asked, referring to Blancanales and Encizo.

"That's been taken care of," Turrin said with a grin. "In fact, they're in for a pleasant surprise. I think we'll be able to see it from here."

"What do you mean?" Lyons inquired as he looked at a window by the passengers' baggage claim area.

Blancanales and Encizo waited for their luggage to descend the ramp to the baggage carousel. Their suitcases were easy to recognize because prominent stickers—the Mexican flag—were pasted on each article of luggage.

The flags weren't only part of their cover. The marked luggage would help them be recognized by the Venezuelan Interpol agents assigned to assist them while in Brazil. Because Interpol had already assisted Stony Man in Europe and Venezuela had a special interest in nailing Ramon Cazazo, Stony Man Farm had arranged for Venezuelan operatives to serve as contacts to the commandos.

Blancanales and Encizo were less than certain this was a good idea. They had been assured that the Interpol personnel were familiar with Brazil in general and Rio in particular. Due to Brazil's unwillingness to extradite criminals, Interpol tried to keep tabs on fugitives staying there. Apparently the Venezuelan agents were veterans of such surveillance operations. The Stony Man commandos figured the Interpol agents might get in their way more than benefit their efforts to find Silva and the terrorists.

To help the Venezuelans recognize them, Blancanales wore a Panama hat with a low crown and Encizo wore a straw Stetson. They also carried alligator briefcases. Although they didn't look suspicious, both men felt awkward because they knew these were all items to make them recognizable.

A feminine voice inquired. "Are you waiting for someone?"

The Stony Man pair turned and saw two stunningly lovely women. Both were Hispanics. The taller of the ladies stepped close to Blancanales, placed a hand on his shoulder and smiled. She was slender, her torso and limbs long and well-shaped. The other woman drew close to Encizo. Her features seemed to reveal more Indian heritage than those of her companion. She was more muscular, as well. A denim miniskirt displayed her strong, beautifully shaped legs.

"You'd better be waiting for us, Carlos," she said in soft-spoken Spanish.

Encizo's cover name was "Carlos Ruiz." He was startled that this attractive stranger knew him by this name. She wrapped her arms around his neck, and Encizo embraced her in turn. The woman whispered close to his ear.

"Call me Lucia," she instructed. "I'm your contact from Venezuela. Now kiss me and act like you're glad to see me."

"That won't be hard," Encizo assured her.

He pressed his mouth to hers and drew her close. Blancanales pulled the other woman to him. She kissed him lightly on the lips and stroked his hair. The Able Team pro whispered, "What's my name?"

"Luis is the name you are using," she replied softly. "I'm Maribel. Interpol sent us to help you. I hope you don't object to working with a woman."

She suddenly kissed him and thrust her tongue deep into his mouth. He figured he wouldn't mind working with her. Their assignment was looking more promising by the minute.

"HOW COME THEY GET two gorgeous females to play kissy-face with?" Lyons muttered as he watched Lucia and Maribel welcome Encizo and Blancanales to Brazil.

"Jealous?" Price asked. She looked at Bolan, hoping he didn't share Lyons's attitude.

The Executioner smiled with mild amusement. The Hispanic commandos left the luggage area with the Venezuelan women. Turrin chuckled and sipped his beer. Durao was too nervous to find any humor in the situation.

"Their cover story claims they're visiting from Mexico City," Turrin explained. "Since they're Spanish, the Venezuelan Interpol section figured they wouldn't draw as much attention with a pair of ladies pretending to be their wives or girlfriends. Don't let the appearance of those two women fool you. They're both experienced agents, and they didn't get the assignment because of their looks."

"But I bet our two buddies don't object to the way they look," Lyons commented. "Well, I guess they got lucky. We all agreed that Interpol would be kept in an investigative role and not involved in military preparations or combat. Carlos and Luis thought they were getting stuck with the boring part because they were getting saddled with Interpol. Yeah, I bet they'll be bored."

"They'll be trying to get information about Silva through former plant employees and the arms merchant's family," Turrin reminded the others. "It's well-known that Silva has been separated from his wife and kids for a long time. She probably doesn't have much sense of loyalty toward her hubby, but it's also doubtful she knows much about his current activities."

"We have to cover every possibility," Bolan said. "The other members of our unit will be arriving on a later flight. Did their equipment arrive at the embassy?"

"Yeah," Turrin assured him. "You guys will be able to contact the others and get their weapons and other gear to them. Meantime, NSA will watch after the stuff and Durao will be your go-between with the agency and the embassy."

"Okay," Bolan said, "I assume you've already checked for Silva in the obvious places."

"Yes," Durao answered. "The commodore mentioned that Silva supposedly has a secret base somewhere in the Amazon region. Trying to find him there won't be easy. Frankly I question the truth to this story. It could just be a rumor."

"Let's not dismiss the possibility," the Executioner told him. "Silva and his coconspirators have been able to carry out international terrorism, hire lots of expensive operatives and they've got almost limitless funds thanks to support from the Colombian and Bolivian cocaine cartels. They're capable of doing just about anything."

"NSA has listening posts in the Amazonas state," Durao explained. "Only two, and they use them occasionally when requested to do so by Washington or some other government agency. Actually the posts are located along the borders of Colombia and Bolivia. Sometimes DEA runs operations in the two big coke-producing nations. They may ask us to monitor radio broadcasts and use satellite laser photography to search the jungles for hidden bases."

"Laser photography?" Lyons asked with surprise.

"Part of LASINT," Durao explained, using another abbreviation common to NSA surveillance personnel. "Lasers are used by the satellite to increase knowledge of an area targeted for surveillance. It's high-tech stuff, but to simplify how it works, the satellite sends out a laser beam. It bounces off the targeted area and returns to the satellite receiver unit. It relays data on the shapes, heat level and dimensions of objects within a two-square-mile area. Dot-matrix computer printouts create a sort of photo based on the information transferred by the satellite to the listening post below."

"How well does this technology work?" Bolan inquired.

"Depends on the area being covered," Durao replied. "Jungles are difficult because the foliage covers so much area. Trees, plants, even animals can cause confused readings. If the jungle is dense enough, it will even block the laser scan."

"Do the satellites pass over Amazonas?" Bolan asked. "Can they also scan radio frequencies? Especially VHF frequencies, which are most likely to be used by a base that doesn't want to be picked up by radio stations in the area."

"I see you know a little about electronic surveillance," Durao said with surprise. "Yeah, that can be done. It helps if we know what frequency we're looking for and whether we're talking about long or shortwave radio broadcasts."

"If you know where the broadcast is being sent or received," the Executioner continued, "will that help pinpoint the location of a hidden base in the jungle?"

"Sure. But how the hell do you plan to arrange that? If you knew how to make a radiophone call to Silva, you'd already have a pretty good idea where he's located anyway."

"Maybe we can convince somebody else to make that call," Bolan stated. He noticed McCarter and Grimaldi had entered the lounge. "We'd better be going."

"Yeah," Turrin replied. "Watch your ass, man."

"We always try to," Lyons assured him.

Bolan, Lyons and Durao rose from their seats and left the lounge. Turrin and Price remained at the booth and watched the trio depart. They would have to remain until McCarter and Grimaldi made their way to the booth and struck up a conversation. The Stony Man pilots would ask if they were Americans or British. Turrin would invite them to have a seat, pass the locker keys to the pilots and tell them where to meet the contact arranged by Commodore Guimarães.

"When this is finished, we'd better be ready to catch our flight," Turrin reminded Price. "We've got to be out of here by one o'clock and headed back home to report our progress to Hal."

Price nodded. She watched Bolan's head and shoulders above the heads of the shorter members of the crowd in the hallway. As he moved beyond her view, she wondered if this would be the last time she would ever see the man known as the Executioner.

CHAPTER TWENTY-NINE

Pedro de Souza was a busy man. The vice president of Silva Industries Inc. had been left in charge of running the corporation while João Silva was gone. It was a tough situation for de Souza. People didn't want to deal with him. They wanted to speak directly with Silva. He didn't even know where the head of the organization was, so he could hardly tell anyone when Silva would be able to get in touch with them.

De Souza resented the attitude of these people. He actually handled most of the business deals for Silva anyway. He had to deal with the labor unions and employees. He carried most of the management responsibilities even when Silva was at the plant. Sure, Silva had built the company, but de Souza kept it going. Silva was an idea man, a dreamer who conjured up concepts and schemes, but it was up to others to accomplish these ideas and make them reality.

Most of his ideas were shit anyway, de Souza thought with resentment. For every idea Silva came up with that turned a multimillion-dollar profit, there were fifty that never got off the drawing board. Silva had become obsessed with notions about superweapons, miniature versions of fighter jets, combat submarines, tanks and armored cars. He believed these could make small fighting forces superior to large armies.

That could be true, de Souza admitted, but Silva's concepts were expensive and impractical. The prototypes for the minisubs and minitanks had cost millions, and no military force was interested in a contract for these one-man weapons. Silva's company would have gone down the drain if it hadn't been for de Souza's efforts to continue production of more conventional military hardware.

Of course, Silva did manage to get profits from selling arms to certain questionable contacts. A lot of their income came from shipping arms to gunrunners overseas. De Souza was aware of this, but tried to remain out of those deals as much as possible. He figured one day those deals would catch up with Silva. The boss had friends in high places, but they wouldn't remain friends if they found out he was supplying arms to terrorists.

Silva Industries was in financial trouble. Expenses outnumbered profits. Fewer sources were contracting with Silva, and the company had been in the red for more than a year. Silva seemed to take this in stride, certain that somehow business would improve. Now, when the company was in dire straits and close to bankruptcy, Silva decided to head for his mysterious base in the Amazon.

What was he doing in the jungles? Probably something illegal, de Souza guessed. He knew Silva had contacts with Colombian and Bolivian gangsters. He sold weapons to them and transported arms to criminal cells located throughout South and Central America. Whatever wild scheme Silva had to save his business probably involved something illegal. De Souza wished he could get out, but he earned a fat paycheck as vice president and it was never easy to walk away from large sums of money.

His ulcer began to act up as de Souza sat at his desk at the plant headquarters in São Paulo. His secretary called to say Mr. Mueller and Mr. Bohler were waiting outside. De Souza didn't recognize the names, but recalled two representatives of a German arms manufacturer had arranged an appointment with Silva. The call had come just yesterday. Short notice, but the possibility of a contract with the Germans seemed too promising to postpone. There were plenty of other sources they could turn to, especially in South America, and de Souza didn't want this one to slip away. He told his secretary to show them in.

The visitors were well dressed. The elder man wore a gray suit and pearl gray gloves. His right arm seemed stiff, and the fingers never moved. De Souza suspected the arm was a prosthesis. The other man was larger and muscular with the light complexion and hair usually associated with Germanic people.

"Good day," de Souza greeted in German as he stepped from his desk. "Welcome to Silva Industries."

"Your German is exceptionally good," Katz replied.

"I am from Pôrto Alegre, in Rio Grande, a state to the south. German and Italian are common languages there."

"I apologize that neither of us speak Portuguese."

De Souza waved away the apology. "Please be seated and we can discuss business."

Katz and Gary Manning sat across from the vice president's desk. De Souza offered them coffee and cigars. They accepted the former, and de Souza called his secretary and instructed her to bring in coffee and three cups.

"Unfortunately Mr. Silva isn't here today," de Souza began. "We spoke to your contact on the phone, and you said you'd be in São Paulo and come here anyway in hope that he might be here. I am his executive in charge during his absence."

"Of course," Katz replied. "Herr Silva will have to confirm any arrangement we can make. My corporation in Bonn, Germany, is interested in forming a partnership with Silva Industries. Basically we'd like to have our firm become an extension of your company."

"We're not in a position to buy your company," de Souza said with a frown.

"That's not what we're suggesting," Manning explained. "We want to buy into your organization. Let's say forty-five million deutsche marks?"

The sum certainly appealed to de Souza. The secretary arrived with coffee. She served the men and left the room. De Souza took advantage of the lull to consider the offer and mentally warned himself not to jump at an offer that sounded too good to be true.

"What exactly would you want for this investment?" he asked, trying not to look as eager as he felt.

"You are aware that uniting East and West Germany has caused a financial hardship for my country," Katz stated. "Germany is increasing income tax. That means our corporation will have to pay considerably more to remain in business in Germany. By closing down and moving here, we will avoid that expense and be able to reestablish operations with Silva Industries."

"Buying into your company will be an advantage to us and to you, as well, because we'll share contacts and contracts with buyers," Manning added. "I don't believe Silva has many contracts with West European buyers. We do, and we'll be able to maintain those deals even with the change. We've already been in touch with them, and they know we're going to relocate in South America."

"We also have exports to the United States," Katz said. "Sporting goods. Hunting rifles and shotguns. The ban on semiautomatic rifles being imported into the U.S. cut off that market, but we still ship some handguns. Mostly 9 mm pistols and some smaller calibers."

"Americans like guns," de Souza said with a smile. "This offer sounds very agreeable to both sides. I can safely guarantee Mr. Silva will gladly accept your terms. In fact, we can start the contracts for this partnership immediately."

"That would be fine," Katz replied. "However, our superiors will want official acknowledgment to that fact. I realize Mr. Silva isn't here, but we do need his personal approval. When can we meet him?"

"I'm afraid I don't know," de Souza said. "He's working on a project that's out of the country and takes up a great deal of his time."

"Leaving you to run the business," Manning said, shaking his head. "Sounds to me like Silva is taking a vacation, claiming it to be a 'project' so he can write it off as a deduction on taxes. Mr. de Souza is the real leader here. Silva is just a figurehead."

De Souza was pleased to hear this recognition of how important he was to the company, which was exactly why Manning had made the remark.

"That may or may not be the case, Erich," Katz told Manning. "But we'll still need confirmation that Silva agrees to our arrangement. We do have copies of previous contracts made with other buyers with whom Silva has done business. That will allow us to identify him accurately by his handwriting. If you can contact Mr. Silva and get him to give us a written and signed statement testifying that he agrees to our merger, that will be satisfactory for all concerned."

"I'm certain that can be arranged," de Souza stated. "I'll try to get the papers to you tomorrow morning. Tonight, if possible."

"That sounds excellent," Katz replied. He took a business card from his pocket. "Let me give you the address of the hotel we're staying at in Rio, as well as our room number. Please call us when you have the papers ready."

Katz placed the card on the desk and used a pen to write the information on the back of the card.

"I'm looking forward to our partnership," de Souza declared, and offered his left hand to Katz.

The Israeli shook hands, noting that de Souza had been observant enough to notice his prosthesis, although Katz wore the less-obvious model with five metal fingers concealed with a glove. Manning shook hands with de Souza. The Brazilian seemed delighted with the meeting as he walked them to the door.

"I hope we'll hear from you soon, Mr. de Souza," Katz said. "I've enjoyed our discussion. It sounds most promising."

Pedro de Souza wouldn't argue with that. As soon as his visitors left the building, the company vice president hurried to a communications center in the plant. Telephones and radio transceivers were located in the room and attended by operators. Since Silva Industries did business all over the world, and some of their clients found radio communication more practical than telephones, the commo section was open twenty-four hours a day.

"I need to make a confidential call," de Souza announced. "I have to ask you all to leave for the next five minutes or so."

The operators obeyed and left de Souza alone. He sat by a transceiver and adjusted the frequency level before keying the signal code used by Silva in the field. A strange voice responded.

"Please identify," the man demanded.

"This is de Souza," the vice president explained. "I have to speak to Mr. Silva immediately. It's urgent."

"Don't use names on the radio," the voice snapped.

"Security isn't going to matter if this company goes out of business," de Souza insisted. "And that's what will happen if he doesn't get back in touch with me as quickly as possible."

"Shut up and don't say another word."

"Who do you think you're talking to?" de Souza demanded. "I'll have your job for this disrespectful and rude behavior."

He realized the man had cut off communications. De Souza tried to establish contact again. Five minutes passed. An operator opened the door, looked in and saw de Souza wasn't finished. The vice president was left alone to struggle with the radio for two more minutes before he finally got a reply.

"This is de Souza!" he announced when he heard the voice once more. "Look, I won't fire you and I'll forget about your rudeness if you'll just—"

"Stop right there!" a familiar voice cut him off. "You know who this is? Don't use my name. Just say yes or no!"

"Yes," de Souza replied. Of course he knew it was Silva's voice. "We have a chance to make a merger worth forty-five million deutsche marks up front. That can get us out of debt and put us in a position to become one of the top arms dealers in the world."

"I should have changed this frequency," Silva commented. "I forgot you had it."

"Didn't you hear what I said?" de Souza asked. "This is our salvation, João. Don't you understand?"

"You're fired, Pedro," Silva snapped. "Don't try to contact me again, you idiot. You have no idea what you may have done."

"What are you talking about?" de Souza demanded, but he realized Silva had cut off contact with him once again.

GADGETS SCHWARZ STUDIED a series of white blips on a board. It resembled a radar screen and white dots extended to a central point. The Able Team pro smiled as he turned to look at Antonio Durao. The NSA man wore a set of earphones, wired to a special radio receiver unit. A tape recorder was positioned next to Durao's surveillance gear.

"We got it, Tony," Schwarz announced cheerfully. "Let's run a dot-matrix map of the area and see what sort of terrain we have to cover to find the source of the radio waves."

"Too bad you don't understand Portuguese," Durao declared. "I was listening to the conversation while the LASINT and RADINT data was locked on the P-Double 0. The infinity amplifiers worked great here. Those new fibers for clear reception worked slicker than a mouse in an IBM."

"Do you understand what he's saying?" Calvin James asked as he stood at the back of the room, confused by the jargon used by the other men.

"All you need to know is we've got a fix on the enemy base and a clear recording of the conversation, which includes de Souza talking to Silva," Schwarz assured him.

"The trick worked. Tell Mr. Mueller and Mr. Bohler they get an *A* for acting. They sure convinced de Souza they were for real."

Durao was glad Schwarz was among the four Stony Man commandos who'd arrived on the evening flight after the first six men hit Brazil. Gadgets was the only one of the group who appreciated high-tech electronics and satellite surveillance. The guy had even helped Durao work the equipment at the NSA listening post near Porto Velho, a small city located in the Rondônia territory, not far from the Amazonia border.

The Stony Man professionals had done some research on Silva Industries Inc. They knew the business was in bad shape financially, and Pedro de Souza was the manager in charge during Silva's absence. Information on de Souza suggested he wasn't a criminal or directly involved with Silva's sleazy operations. It was unlikely he was connected with the terrorists, but he probably knew how to contact Silva in an emergency. The arms merchant would have wanted to be able to contact his plant or be informed if something important occurred.

Stony Man had given de Souza something important... or at least a deal that appeared to be important. The vice president had taken the bait and tried to get his boss to listen to the deal. The radio contact allowed Durao and Schwarz to locate the hidden base in Amazonas thanks to the use of the NSA spy satellite and radio detection gear.

"So we know where to find the sons of bitches," James said, looking at the printout of the map based on information accumulated from the NSA study. "We're talking about some pretty dense rain forest, aren't we?"

"And lots of it," Durao replied. "There's no way you'll be able to get through it to reach the base."

"Silva managed to get in there and apparently built himself a fortress with lots of people and probably plenty of weapons and lots of other neat shit," Schwarz stated. "Hell, they would have had to haul truckloads of stuff into the jungle. If they could do that, we can get through the rain forest to the base, as well."

"Do you have any idea what that territory is like?" Durao asked, shaking his head. "Guimarães said Silva has a small army of professional mercenaries working as his so-called security force. That's probably how he managed to establish a base area in the jungle."

"What do you mean?" James asked. "How would a gang of hired killers help him construct a base? These guys all carpenters, brick masons, electricians and building engineers?"

"I don't know about that," the NSA officer admitted, "but I know that area is crawling with Cutai Indians. You know anything about the Cutai?"

"I don't recall ever hearing about them before," Schwarz admitted. "What are they? Headhunters? Cannibals? Astrologists?"

"They're a tribe of hunters," Durao explained. "I don't think they collect heads or eat people, but they're extremely fierce and hostile toward outsiders. Can't say I blame them. They were persecuted by early European settlers in the past, slaughtered by government troops under some of the more repressive regimes in this century and even raided and kidnapped to serve as slaves for rubber plantations. The Cutai will consider you guys enemy invaders. If you're lucky, they'll kill you outright. Otherwise, they may take you back to camp to entertain themselves by torturing you all night."

"I guess that's what happens when people don't have cable TV," James said dryly. "We've come too far, gone through too much crap and the job is too important to stop now."

"We'll just have to put together the best defenses possible and go for it," Schwarz commented.

"Commodore Guimarães can't give you backup troops," Durao reminded them. "What are there? Ten of you guys put together? Even if the Indians don't get you, you'll be up against Silva's army if you find the base."

"Yeah," James said wtih a nod. "They won't know what hit them."

CHAPTER THIRTY

Casa da Lisbon was one of many fine restaurants in Rio de Janeiro. White china and crystal glasses were set on the bright scarlet tablecloths. Mack Bolan was surprised by the weight of the silverware. It was sterling silver, with some gold inlaid designs of flowers and parrots. He recalled that the average income of most Brazilians was the equivalent of two thousand dollars a year. Bolan figured an enterprising thief could make that much from a fence after lifting the silverware from two or three tables.

The Executioner rarely wore a suit and tie, but he wasn't particularly uncomfortable. A man who had mastered the way of a chameleon learns to adjust to different social settings. David McCarter looked as if he had slept in his clothes. His black jacket was wrinkled, and his tie resembled a tangled vine. Bolan wondered if McCarter had an aversion to hanging clothes in a closet, using an ironing board or visiting a dry cleaner's. He certainly did not fit the popular image of a dapper Englishman with impeccable manners.

Carl Lyons wasn't much for dress up. He had loosened his necktie and opened his jacket as much as possible without revealing the .357 Magnum under his arm. Gadgets Schwarz and Gary Manning also favored casual attire, but they rarely got to enjoy a good restaurant and accepted the regulation about a jacket and tie as being a small sacrifice. Calvin James enjoyed an opportunity to put on some nice threads for a semiformal evening.

Yakov Katzenelenbogen appreciated artistic settings and fine food. Casa da Lisbon offered both. The fish was superb, although he would have preferred a little less salt. He also found the *caldo verde* delicious, although the others were less enthusiastic about potatoes and shredded cabbage in soup with a lot of olive oil.

Jack Grimaldi didn't even want to look at the soup. He didn't like fish much, either, and it seemed half the choices on the menu consisted of seafood. He was reasonably happy with the steak he ordered, but it seemed odd to the American pilot that it would be served in a pottery dish. Durao had picked the restaurant because he figured these guys were probably having their last meal and wanted them to enjoy it.

"None of you guys want to try this Vinho Verde?" the NSA man inquired as he poured himself another glass of wine.

"Green wine?" McCarter said with distaste. "No thanks, mate. Sounds like it already passed through somebody."

"Where are Carlos and Luis?" James asked, using the cover names for Encizo and Blancanales. "I thought they were going to join us."

"They're having dinner at the hotel with the Interpol agents from Venezuela," Lyons replied. "Probably had it delivered by room service."

"You said you were glad you wouldn't have to work with Interpol," Schwarz reminded the Able Team captain.

"Shut up," Lyons said gruffly. "Do you think they even tried to get in touch with Silva's wife?"

"Yeah," Bolan replied with a shrug. "It doesn't matter now. We know where the base is, and tomorrow morning we'll start our trek through the Amazon. You found that guide who helped NSA in the past?"

"We got him," Durao replied. "He calls himself Alfredo now. He's a Cutai Indian and knows the jungles about as well as any man you'll find anywhere outside the heart of the Amazon itself. He must be crazy because he's agreed to guide you."

"Good," Bolan said. "We don't have any quarrel with the Cutai and we'll try to avoid them. Hopefully Alfredo can explain that to his people if we encounter them in the bush."

"Did I ever tell you I hate jungles?" Calvin James remarked. "Hated them in Nam and I hated the ones we had to go into on previous missions."

"Sorry," Bolan told him. "You're a trained medic. We may need you. Besides the Cutai, there are a variety of poisonous snakes, including the fer-de-lance and bushmaster, in the Amazonas rain forest. There are also some species of spiders and scorpions that can be deadly."

"Yeah," Manning remarked. "I looked it up. There are black widows—usually bigger than what you find in the States—and a very venomous 'wandering spider' often called a banana spider. Pretty big spider, too. Scorpions include the *tityus*, which is very poisonous. There are also some very aggressive bees, wasps, army ants and of course, jaguars, peccary, piranha, electric eels and crocodiles in the Amazon. There's even a species of giant catfish, almost three yards long, which is said to attack people...although zoologists say they haven't found an authenticated case of a fatality connected with this big fish."

"Thanks for the encouragement," Schwarz said, rolling his eyes. "What the hell. The Amazon can't be any tougher to survive in than New York or Washington, D.C."

"I wouldn't bet on that," Durao said grimly. "You hear a lot of strange stories about things happening in the Amazon and the Mato Grosso. Most are probably bullshit, but some of them could be true. Stories about anacondas nine yards long and cattle found dead with their tongues ripped out, supposedly killed by a Mapinguary. Sort of the Brazilian version of a sasquatch or Bigfoot."

"We have enough real hazards to worry about without fretting over make-believe monsters," Schwarz stated. "Unless the jungle yeti packs a machine gun, I'm not impressed."

"Speaking of weapons," Katz began, eager to change the subject. "What can Guimarães supply besides the gunships?"

"He can give us plenty of extra ammunition in every caliber we'll need except for .44 Magnum shells for my Desert Eagle," Bolan answered. "The commodore can also supply us with a NATO M-971 MAG, basically the same as the FN MAG made in Belgium. Belt-fed machine gun operates similar to a BAR with a bipod mount."

"Sounds pretty good," Lyons remarked with interest. "How about the choppers? You guys got everything you need?"

"Yeah," Grimaldi answered. "Bell helicopters. No problem operating those babies, and they're equipped with lots of firepower. Guimarães isn't too crazy about letting us borrow them, but he was fairly cooperative."

"We've both logged hundreds of hours in similar copters," McCarter added. "Wish we had a better idea what sort of defenses Silva has at that stronghold. Guess we'd better assume he has antiaircraft weapons."

"The LASINT reading of the area is unclear," Durao admitted. "Pretty sure he has aircraft and vehicles down there. Photos were real grainy, even for dot-matrix, but heat registers and general shapes suggest he's got some trucks and maybe Jeeps. There seems to be an airfield with at least two helicopters. No planes that I could tell."

"Choppers would make more sense than planes in a jungle," McCarter told him. "This must be a pretty good-sized compound."

"Yeah," Schwarz confirmed. "Big enough for Silva to have as many as five hundred troops on hand. I know we've all taken on some pretty impressive odds in the past, but that's one hell of a stacked deck any way you look at it, man."

"Well, we have our strategy planned," Bolan announced. "Mueller and Sims will go in the gunships along with the pilots."

"Oh, no," Katz groaned. "I hate flying. I'd rather be on the ground marching through the jungle."

"Hey, Mueller and I can keep up," Schwarz stated. He realized he and Katz were the eldest team members of the Stony Man commandos.

"I still want you two in the copters," Bolan insisted. "It will require a lot of stamina to make decent time in the jungle. You guys can probably keep up, but we also need gunners in the choppers in case they fire on the birds and the pilots need more firepower than what they handle while flying the gunships. So you two get the job."

"Okay," Schwarz reluctantly agreed. "But that just leaves six of you to travel through hostile territory to assault the base."

"Seven including Alfredo, the Cutai guide," Bolan corrected. "Besides, we want to approach the compound with as little attention as possible. A smaller number of men can do that more effectively than a larger group."

"Providing you get there alive," Durao commented grimly.

"Yeah," the Executioner stated. "That's part of the plan."

ROSARIO BLANCANALES and Rafael Encizo reluctantly said farewell to Lucia and Maribel. They left the hotel and headed for Avenida Rio Branco at the commercial core of Rio de Janeiro. The district was usually crowded with people on their way to and from work, or on shopping trips, or banking and other activities.

However, there was little traffic two hours before dawn. The Stony Man pair had no trouble driving to Avenida Rio Branco in their airport rental. Durao was waiting for them at a parking lot to an insurance company headquarters building. Blancanales and Encizo climbed into the rear of the NSA man's minibus, joining James and Schwarz.

"I hear you guys got the best deal on this mission," James remarked. "Have a good time with those two Venezuelan ladies?"

"A gentlemen doesn't discuss certain things," Encizo replied with a sly smile. "Sorry we missed dinner. What did you guys talk about?"

"Oh, just the mission," Schwarz answered. "You know we're going into the Amazon jungle today? Hope you managed to get some rest."

"I used my bed to sleep in," Blancanales stated. "Part of the time, at least. So this is the big one, right? We found the head of the octopus and we're going in for the kill?"

"That's right," James confirmed. "We'll brief you on the way to the heliport. Everybody else is already there."

They arrived at the heliport outside Rio. Located on a hilltop, it was a lonely spot, generally used by the military for transport operations. Two Bell helicopters waited on the landing field. Jack Grimaldi and David McCarter were already in the pilots' seats. Mack Bolan and Gary Manning would act as copilots for the flight to Amazonas.

"Better suit up for jungle combat," Lyons announced. "We're not going on a picnic, fellas."

Encizo and Blancanales were the only Stony Man operatives dressed in civilian clothes. The others had donned tiger-striped jungle combat fatigues, the camouflage uniform favored by the U.S. Special Forces and Marine recon teams. Lyons and Schwarz carried the standard weapons of Able Team—Heckler & Koch 9 mm submachine guns and .357 Magnum Colt Pythons in shoulder leather. Phoenix Force members were equipped with their usual Uzi machine pistols and Walther P-88 pistols.

Bolan carried his Beretta 93-R and .44 Magnum Desert Eagle. The Executioner, James and Manning also had M-16 assault rifles with M-203 grenade launchers attached to the underside of the barrels. An extra M-16 was ready for Blancanales, as well. The warriors were all equipped with grenades, knives, garrotes, and other weapons of war. Lyons hauled a big NATO M-971 machine gun by a carrying handle and loaded it into the nearest gunship.

Blancanales and Encizo changed clothes rapidly. They pulled on the tiger fatigues, paratrooper boots and headgear supplied for the occasion. Investigation of Silva's expenses had revealed that he produced military uniforms, as well as weapons. The styles included the olive-drab fatigues worn by the Brazilian army, and a type of brown-and-green camouflage uniform with a random pattern. Tiger stripes weren't among the Silva wardrobe, so Stony Man went with that design to avoid confusion in combat.

"Commodore Guimarães says he'd appreciate it if you try to keep the choppers from being shot up too badly," Durao remarked. "He's going to report them as stolen. That's going to be a big embarrassment, but it will be lessened a bit if they can recover the copters later."

"If we can avoid getting ourselves shot up," Katz commented, "we'll see what we can do about getting the gunships back in relatively good condition."

"He also said if you can find definite proof Silva is involved in terrorism," Durao added, "he'll dispatch at least three companies of Amphibious Recon Marines to head for the site."

"I thought we already had definite proof," Encizo said as he made certain his Cold Steel Tanto knife was in a cross-draw position on his belt. "How much more does the man need?"

"Enough to justify military action against one of the richest and most powerful men in Brazil," Durao replied. "More than tape-recorded conversations, confessions by terrorists or even surveillance photographs. He needs files, records, actual terrorists located at the base. If you can prove El Cuchillo is there, for example, that would be enough."

"That's great," Blancanales said, slipping on a boonie-style camouflage hat. "The only way we can do that is by raiding the base and finding that sort of evidence. That's when we can call for the cavalry? Tell Guimarães thanks a lot."

They climbed into the helicopters and closed the sliding doors. The big rotor blades came alive and cut the air with a sound of metallic thunder. Dust rose from the ground in a dense cloud as the gunships prepared for liftoff. McCarter's craft leaped into the sky first. Grimaldi allowed the first chopper to rise higher and take the lead, before lifting off.

CHAPTER THIRTY-ONE

The Amazon jungle is a different world, one that seems to have been untouched by the passing of time. Although hundreds of acres of rain forest are cut down almost daily, the Amazon region of Brazil covers approximately one million square miles. The area Stony Man was concerned with had remained almost unmolested by modern technology—except for the portion where João Silva had constructed his base of operations.

Trees and other plants grew everywhere. Myrtles, palms and various hardwood trees formed a close-knit ceiling with leaves and branches. Alfredo, the Cutai guide, wielded a machete to hack through a tangled wall of vines and bushes. The small, wiry man with nut brown skin and long black hair was impressed by the six foreigners. They handled themselves well in the jungle. Most outsiders would be exhausted after two hours of trudging through the rain forest, but these men didn't show the slightest sign of fatigue.

The guide came across some pineapples and decided to call a break to collect some. Alfredo and the Stony Man commandos used machetes to cut loose some pineapples and chopped the fruit into pieces. They checked a fallen log for snakes and scorpions before sitting on it. The pineapple was sweet and filled with refreshing juice. The temperature was around eighty-five degrees, but the humidity in the jungle increased the effects the heat had on the men.

"This is about as fresh as it comes," Blancanales commented as he bit into a wedge of fruit and savored the taste.

"You'll never starve in the Amazon," Alfredo declared with a grin. He cocked back a straw hat high on his head and added, "Not if you know what to look for. There is food everywhere here. Grapes, bananas, mangoes and other fruit are here for the taking."

He listened to the calls of birds among the trees. A macaw watched them from a branch of a nearby tree. The big parrot cocked its head and stared down at the intruders, more curious than frightened. Alfredo pointed at the bird with the barrel of his lever-action Marlin rifle.

"That fella up there would be good for a meal," Alfredo stated. "Roast parrot is better than chicken. Want a real feast? Kill yourself a peccary or even a tapir. You can feed a hundred people with a tapir. Meat is a little tough, but if you beat it enough before you cook it, the food is fairly tender."

"Wonder if *The Frugal Gourmet* has a recipe for it," James commented as he checked a compass. "How much farther you figure we have to go?"

"About twenty-five miles," Carl Lyons replied, gladly setting down the big MG to carve into a pineapple. "Give or take five or ten miles."

"Think we could contact the guys at the choppers?" Encizo inquired.

"Maintain radio silence until we have to call them in," Bolan replied. "We don't know what sort of radio-scanning equipment Silva might have or what kind of range it covers. No sense taking a chance of alerting the enemy until we're right on top of them."

"We'll be in the Cutai region soon," Alfredo told them. "My people do not welcome intruders. If we come across them, I'll explain that we won't be doing any hunting with our guns. They don't like the noise. Frightens game out of the area."

"How welcome will you be by your people?" Blancanales inquired. "Would they resent the fact you left the tribe to live in so-called civilization?"

"I'm not the only one," Alfredo explained. "My people can't continue to live in the old way. That's probably too bad for them, but it's a fact. The jungles are being consumed by industry bit by bit. Civilization is closing in. The Cutai will either become part of it or die out.

"I think it wise that we continue on," the guide said abruptly. "We have a long way to travel."

THEY CONTINUED to make steady progress as they chopped their way through the jungle foliage. Blancanales and Manning took point, hacking aside vines with jungle knives to give Alfredo's "machete arm" a break. The others followed as the rain forest became even more dense and difficult to penetrate. They accepted the challenge with determination and continued to work their way closer to the objective.

Suddenly Bolan noticed something was wrong. The chirping of insects and tree frogs had ceased. The creatures had heard something and fell silent. The Executioner wasn't the only one to realize they might be in danger. The others were also aware that the sounds of the rain forest had changed and what this could mean.

Blancanales saw something move among the ferns and tree trunks. Leaves rose as an arrow appeared. The Able Team warrior threw himself to the ground and shouted, "Ambush!"

The others dived for cover as arrows and blowgun darts streaked from the bush. Something struck the ground near Bolan's left hand. He glanced at the wooden shaft of an arrow, the head buried in the soft moist soil. A dart hit the radio transceiver unit strapped to Encizo's back. Another arrow bounced against the frame of the M-971 machine gun, the shaft brushing Lyons's hair before dropping to the ground.

Alfredo shouted in his native language, but the hail of arrows and darts continued. The Stony Man warriors couldn't stay put or they would be literally sitting targets for the Cutai attackers. They returned fire with assault rifles and submachine guns. Operating like men carrying out a well-rehearsed drill, they fired in all directions simultaneously.

The Cutai weren't the enemy, and they didn't want to kill any of the Indians. The commandos deliberately aimed high and fired for effect. They hoped the tumultuous noise and multiple muzzle-flashes of the weapons would frighten the Cutai into retreat. Bullets slashed leaves and splintered branches. The bush moved as Indians shuffled from position to position. Two or three hastily aimed arrows shot from the foliage, but none came within a yard of the defenders' position.

They hurried to the best available cover, taking advantage of the lull in the Indian projectiles to dash for tree trunks, fallen logs and large rocks. The cessation of arrows and darts was temporary, and the warriors knew it. More primitive missiles were launched even before they succeeded in finding shelter.

"They're doing a good job at staying concealed," Encizo said, stating the obvious. "They know the area, and they've had years of stalking prey in the jungles to become experts at moving silently and hidden in this environment."

"Tell us something we don't know," Lyons growled. He scanned the jungle, but couldn't detect movement in the bush. "We could burn up ammo all day without hitting anyone, and I don't think these guys are going to cut and run."

"They don't seem to scare too easy," Blancanales agreed.

Arrows sailed from all directions and forced the Stony men and Alfredo to stay low and cling to cover. Arrowheads bit into wood and struck stone. Some lost velocity and fell across the heads and shoulders of the defenders. Bolan determined the general direction of at least one opponent's projectiles. He pointed his M-16 and opened fire.

A stream of 5.56 mm slugs raked the bush. A voice screamed in response. Others followed Bolan's example. Automatic fire blazed and ripped into the jungle. Sprays of bullets claimed more targets as screams of pain echoed through the rain forest.

"Tell them to back off!" Bolan ordered, raising his voice because he knew Alfredo's ears would be ringing after the eruption of gunfire. "We don't want to fight them! Let us go and they won't lose any more of their people! Keep fighting and they'll be slaughtered."

Before the guide could translate the instructions, another salvo of arrows bolted from the bush. The warriors were forced to duck once more. While some Cutai archers fired arrows, other Indians broke cover and charged. The commandos finally saw their attackers. Small, slender, dark figures, clad only in loincloths and decorative necklaces and arm bands, rushed for the defenders' position. Some carried bows or blowguns. Most wielded machetes or spears.

A bold Indian advanced and hurled his lance at Manning. The Canadian raised his rifle and slammed the barrel into the airborne weapon. The spear dropped harmlessly to the ground. Another lance sailed at Carl Lyons. The Able Team commander barely glimpsed the projectile, but rolled clear in time to avoid the chipped-stone warhead.

The Cutai weapons might have been antediluvian technology, but they could be just as lethal as bullets. The commandos fired from prone positions and blasted four attackers with 5.56 mm and 9 mm rounds. Indians fell, torsos streaming crimson. The surviving Cutai remained committed to the charge and lunged at the Stony Man forces, unmindful of the storm of high-velocity slugs.

Blancanales's M-16 ran out of ammo as a spear-wielding opponent closed in. There was no time to reload the rifle. The Able commando dropped the assault rifle and rolled to avoid the thrust of the attacker's lance. The spear stabbed ground near Blancanales as he sprawled on his back and drew the Colt Python from shoulder leather. The Cutai yanked the spear from the earth. Politician pointed his revolver at the Indian and squeezed the trigger. A .357 Magnum round punched through the Cutai's solar plexus and burned upward to blast the man's heart.

Alfredo was reluctant to shoot his fellow Cutai. The guide fired his Marlin, but shot above the heads of the other Indians. The effort convinced a couple attackers to retreat, but two others kept coming. Encizo saw their ally was in trouble and quickly sprayed the Cutai with a volley of slugs from his Uzi.

The aggressors' bodies fell to join the mounting number of corpses on the earth floor of the jungle. Encizo ejected the spent magazine from his micro-Uzi and reached for a fresh magazine. A Cutai suddenly dashed forward, his machete raised high. The Cuban warrior discarded the empty Uzi and grabbed the handle of the Tanto sheathed on his belt. He drew the Cold Steel knife with one hand and seized the handle of a machete strapped to his back with the other hand.

Encizo drew the jungle knife and swung it at the attacker. Steel clashed as the machetes met. The Cuban lunged before his opponent could attempt another attack. He thrust the slanted point of the Tanto between the Cutai's ribs. The Indian screamed and staggered as the hot pain filled his torso. Encizo grabbed the machete with both fists and delivered a killing blow.

Carl Lyons sliced open a charging Cutai tribesman with a burst of 9 mm rounds from his MP-5. Something sharp pierced his left triceps, and the Able Team captain glanced at his upper arm to see a needle-shaped object jutting from the sleeve of his shirt. He sprayed a salvo in the general direction he guessed the dart had come from and ducked behind the log he used for cover.

"Stay calm," Ironman whispered, aware that any action that increased the tempo of the blood flow would accelerate the poison to his heart or brain.

This was no easy task, since his heart was hammering like a drum played by a madman. Lyons pulled the dart from his flesh and tossed it aside. He reached for a knife on his belt, but James suddenly appeared beside him. The African-American warrior's Blackmoor Dirk was already in his fist.

"Lie still, man," James instructed. "Don't do nothing. Leave everything up to me."

Lyons obeyed and sprawled on the ground. James slit open the shirtsleeve and examined the tiny droplet of blood caused by the dart. He opened the medic's kit on his belt and removed a scalpel and a small suction device with a rubber ball attached to a short tube. James made an incision with the sterile blade and placed the suction device over the wound. He squeezed the ball to draw out blood and poison.

"Carl was hit?" Blancanales asked as he moved next to them.

"Ask Alfredo what kind of poison they use for these darts," James demanded, not bothering to answer a question whose answer seemed obvious. "Plants, animals, whatever."

"Could be curare," Lyons commented, trying to sound more calm than he felt.

"I don't need your opinion," James replied. "You just lay still until I tell you to do otherwise."

The Phoenix Force medic suddenly realized the fighting had ceased. The Cutai had finally had enough and retreated into the jungle. He figured they would be back, and there was little time to treat Lyons before the battle would begin again. James took several vials from his pack and unwrapped a syringe.

Alfredo approached them and knelt beside James. He glanced at Lyons's arm and frowned. "I'm not certain what poison they might have used," the guide stated. "Lately I understand the tribesmen in this area have favored snake venom because it can be largely pumped out when bleeding a game animal killed with darts or arrows."

"What kind of snakes?" James asked. "*Crotalidate* or *elapidae?*"

"I...I don't know what those are," Alfredo admitted. "Fer-de-lance, bushmaster, maybe a rattlesnake."

"Pit vipers," James said with a nod. "That's *crotalidate*. Hemotoxic poison. Sounds like that would be it from your description of bleeding game animals."

He inserted the needle of the syringe into a vial of polyvalent antivenin. James injected the serum at Lyons's wound. The medic glanced up at the worried expression on Blancanales's face and the solemn features of Alfredo.

"Hemotoxic poison is the lightweight division of snake venom," he explained. "I think our pal will be okay, but I want him to rest as much as possible."

"The poison dose probably wasn't very large," Alfredo said. "When the Cutai hunt with blowguns, they usually shoot as many darts as possible into an animal because one generally doesn't kill it. You probably sucked out all the poison already."

"Let's not take any chances," Blancanales replied.

"Alfredo!" Bolan called. "We managed to take a few of the Cutai alive. They're beginning to regain consciousness. I want you to talk to them."

The guide returned to Bolan's position. Four survivors of the battle had been collected by the Stony Man warriors. Two had been knocked senseless in hand-to-hand combat. The other two had been wounded. One had stopped a bullet with his thigh, but the other had only been grazed by a ricochet and appeared to be otherwise unharmed.

"Okay," the Executioner began, "explain to these men that we didn't come here to harm the Cutai. We have no quarrel with them. We regret the loss of life in this battle, but we didn't start the fight. Ask them why they attacked us when we did them no harm and fired no guns."

Alfredo spoke with the Cutai in their native language. The Indians seemed confused, but stared defiantly at Bolan and the other Stony Man commandos. One of the Cutai said something in an angry tone and spit at the warriors.

"He says you know why they attacked you," Alfredo translated. "He claims you are soldiers from the evil place. These soldiers have killed many of the Cutai. Raided villages and occasionally stolen women. Young, pretty women. Sometimes they return after being beaten and raped. Others are found murdered in the jungle near the evil place."

"Sounds like Silva's mercenaries have been working overtime at being scum," Gary Manning remarked. "The evil place might be Silva's base in the jungle."

"Tell them we're not from the evil place," Bolan instructed. "We're hunting for an evil place to destroy it. Their enemies may be the men we came to put an end to. Ask them to describe the evil place."

Alfredo and the Cutai conversed once more. The guide told Bolan that the Indians described the evil place as a big village with the sort of magic wagons found in the outside world. They had large huts, lodges and many guns. The men wore clothes spotted like a jaguar, but the colors weren't as beautiful as the big cat. The clothes were colored like dull parts of the rain forest.

"All right," Bolan declared. "Tell them that is the place we're looking for. Tell them we intend to destroy the evil place because its evil extends beyond the jungle to the outside world, as well. Might point out that our uniforms aren't like the green-and-brown-spotted clothes of their enemies."

Alfredo translated. The Cutai captives seemed baffled, but their attitude became slightly more relaxed. Calvin James approached and looked at the man with the wounded leg.

"I'd better take care of that or this guy will die from infection," James stated. "At the very least, they'll have to amputate that leg if I don't treat him now."

"Just a minute," Bolan replied. "Alfredo, explain that this man knows medicine. He'll treat their wounds and make them much better. When this is done, we'll allow the Cutai to leave and return to their people."

Bolan turned to James. "See what you can do to make these guys think we're not such bad guys after all. Since we just had to kill more than a dozen of their people, that might not be easy to do."

Alfredo explained the situation to the prisoners. They seemed amazed by the statement. James got to work on the wounds as Bolan concentrated on the problems facing the commandos. The other Cutai might return at any moment, and he had to prepare for another attack.

"Make sure your weapons are fully loaded and stay close to cover," the Executioner ordered. "We have to stay put for a couple of hours until we're sure Carl is going to be all right."

"It was just a pinprick," Lyons complained, but he didn't attempt to get up.

"Hopefully the Cutai won't attack before we can send these fellows back to the tribe and explain this was a tragic misunderstanding," Bolan continued. "If the Indians don't believe us, we might have a hell of a time making our way through the jungle to Silva's base. And there might not be many of us left to destroy it."

CHAPTER THIRTY-TWO

Carl Lyons was permitted to sit up. Calvin James checked his heartbeat and found no irregular rhythm. The Phoenix Force medic told Lyons to flex his fingers, close his eyes and touch his nose with index fingers, one at a time. He held up three fingers and asked his patient to count them.

"You feel any dizziness, chills or nausea?"

"No," Ironman replied, bored with the examination. "I feel fine, Cal. No trouble hearing, no blurred vision or trouble breathing. In short, I don't feel like I got poison running around inside me."

"Okay, but I want you to tell me if you feel ill, confused, fatigued or notice any symptoms or poisoning. No macho bullshit, man. Tell me if anything is wrong. Now, I'm going to give you some more antibiotics and water. When you take a leak, let me know if the urine is reddish brown. Okay?"

"Talk about prying into a man's personal life," Lyons muttered.

Bolan glanced at his wristwatch. They had remained at the site of the Cutai battle for almost an hour and a half. The Indian captives had already been released. James had removed the bullet from the wounded man's leg, stitched him up and set him on a stretcher. The guy with the dislocated kneecap was supplied with a pair of improvised crutches. He limped into the jungle, accompanied by the two healthiest members of the group, dragging the stretcher with the wounded Cutai.

The Executioner had also allowed the Cutai to take their weapons with them. This served as further evidence of the Stony Man team's goodwill and sincerity toward the Indians. Also, Bolan understood hunters and warriors. Such men valued their weapons as much as their limbs and senses. To deny them their weapons would be like destroying their manhood.

"You're sure he's fit to travel?" Bolan inquired as James finished examining Lyons.

"Yeah. I'd rather he didn't, but I can't detect any signs of poison. Ironman is tough. The poison probably never had a chance."

"I'm still glad you were here, Cal," Blancanales stated. "How much longer do we wait?"

"We can't afford to stay longer," Bolan replied. "Just to be sure, I want somebody else to carry that machine gun. Carl shouldn't exert himself too much until there's no doubt about his condition."

"I can handle it," Lyons insisted as he got to his feet.

"Let Manning carry the machine gun. You can operate the weapon when we reach the enemy base. Until then, you'll take it easy."

"The Cutai may set up another ambush," Encizo reminded the others. "They'll probably plan something more clever next time. I bet they know lots of nasty mantraps they can prepare if they know which way we're headed."

"Alfredo told them we're going to that evil place to destroy it," Manning stated. "Why would they want to stop us?"

"Because they may not believe us," Encizo replied. He gestured at the corpses that still littered the ground. "Can you blame them if they don't trust us?"

"They didn't leave us with much choice," Blancanales said. "If we hadn't fought back, all seven of us would have had Cutai arrows, darts and spears sticking out of our bodies."

"We have to go on," Bolan announced. "If the Indians try to stop us again, we'll have to deal with it."

"I can't fight my people again," Alfredo declared. "I can't stand to watch them getting gunned down."

"What the hell got into you?" Lyons demanded. "You knew there was a chance we'd clash with your people. You also know Silva and his mercenaries have been victimizing the Cutai deliberately. That's going to continue if we don't stop him."

"Men with fancy weapons and machines," Alfredo said with contempt. "Modern men like Silva and you six heroes have always come into the jungles and killed or enslaved the Cutai. And I have become one of those modern men, too. I actually thought it would be best for the Cutai to join the outside world—"

"You want to make a speech?" Bolan cut him off. "Do it while we're walking, but keep your voice low because we have to stay alert to danger."

Movement in the bush drew their attention. The Stony Man warriors swung weapons toward the figures that appeared from the foliage. Manning, Encizo and James covered the backs of the others and scanned the jungle for other dangers still hidden in the walls of trees and plants.

Several Cutai tribesmen stepped into the open. All but one carried bows and spears, but they didn't aim the weapons at the commandos. The unarmed man was elderly. It was difficult to guess his age. His skin was wrinkled, and he had no teeth. His shoulder-length hair was snow white, and his eyes squinted as if he could barely see. Yet the senior Cutai spoke in a firm, clear voice.

"He's the chief," Alfredo translated. "He has come to personally praise you as warriors and apologize for the attack by his men. He says that was very rude and no way to treat visitors."

The chief clasped his hands together and nodded his head. Bolan realized this was a gesture of greeting or apology or a sign of respect. The Executioner had worked with the primitive hill tribes of the Montagnards when he was in Vietnam. Fierce warriors with a strong code of honor, the Montagnards appreciated strangers who showed consideration for their customs. Bolan figured this would apply to the Cutai, as well. He clasped his hands together and nodded at the chief.

"Tell the chief it is an honor to meet him and we accept his apology," Bolan said. "We're sorry his men died, but they were brave and should be buried—or whatever the Cutai do with their dead—with honor."

Alfredo translated the message. The chief seemed satisfied with this. He spoke again, sweeping an arm toward his armed escort.

"The chief says he knows you have come to destroy the evil place," Alfredo told Bolan. "That is a good thing. The men with him have volunteered to help us. They are the best bowmen and... the best translation I can come up with is 'fighters with spears.' They want to go with us."

"They know the way to Silva's base?" Manning inquired.

"They know where it is. And they're eager to take us there."

"Thank the chief and tell him his warriors will be welcomed," Bolan stated. "But they have to understand that they must follow orders from us."

"I'll tell him," Alfredo agreed with a nod. "I also want to apologize for that outburst a few minutes ago. I was out of line...."

"Forget it," the Executioner assured him. "A battlefield always stirs a man's emotions, especially when he sees his own people among the dead."

"I... I never saw anything like this before," Alfredo explained.

"You never get used to it. No man *should* get used to it. Sometimes war is necessary, but never forget what it means and never take it lightly."

HUGE WALLS SURROUNDED João Silva's jungle base. The thick brick was painted brown and green for camouflage from a distance. Nets hung with fake foliage had been strung between posts to create a type of camou ceiling. Some palm trees inside the compound provided further concealment from the air.

Bolan observed the base through binoculars. He couldn't see much above the walls, but a pair of radar dishes were visible atop a building. The heavy wooden doors of the gate were big enough to allow vehicles to pass through, and a crude road extended for several miles into the jungle.

"That's a pretty impressive accomplishment in the middle of the Amazon jungle," Lyons commented as he studied the site. "Too bad Silva didn't choose to put his energy and ingenuity into a more worthwhile ambition."

"A little late now," Encizo said. He noticed that uniformed figures patrolled the top of the walls. "Wonder what defenses they have besides the guards?"

"Wouldn't make much sense to use motion detectors or heat sensors in a jungle," Manning stated. "Too many large animals and plants that sway in the breeze. They'd be checking alarms every five minutes. The walls would be pretty good protection against most threats. At night they'd probably use floodlights or maybe infrared."

"We can only guess what sort of weaponry they have inside," Blancanales mused thoughtfully. "Silva's an arms manufacturer. You can bet he supplied his base defenses with the best he could come up with."

"We'll find out fairly soon." Bolan turned to Alfredo and the Cutai Indians. "Time for you fellas to head back. This is as far as you come."

Alfredo blinked with surprise. "I thought we'd help you storm the fortress."

"You're not trained for this sort of operation," The Executioner replied. "Explain to the Cutai warriors that this isn't a matter of courage. If we could draw the enemy into the jungle, they could help us fight. However, we have to go into the evil place where guns and bombs will be used. We can fight such battles better on our own."

The guide translated. The Cutai were obviously upset that they had been ordered to return to their tribe without doing battle with the enemy. Yet they had vowed to follow orders, and they reluctantly headed for the bush. Alfredo hesitated.

"Will we know how this turns out?" he inquired.

"You'll hear about it one way or the other," Lyons assured him. "If everything works out the way we plan,

Durao will give you a somewhat edited version of what happens. If we fail, well, let's not think about that."

"Good luck," Alfredo said, aware that the expression seemed terribly lame under the circumstances, but he could think of nothing else to say.

Alfredo followed the Cutai into the bush. Bolan waited ten minutes to give them time to get clear of the fortress before he told Encizo to switch on the transceiver radio. Just sending a radio broadcast on any frequency might alert the enemy if they were monitoring wavelengths with sophisticated equipment. Blancanales was the only member of the group who had a working vocabulary in Portuguese. An English transmission might seem suspicious. He knelt by the radio and keyed the mike.

"Queria uma cerveja," Blancanales announced. He repeated the expression three times and waited for a reply.

"O meu nome é Moreira," a voice replied. They knew it had to be Yakov Katzenelenbogen, but they didn't recognize it because he had effectively mastered a convincing Brazilian accent for the brief sentence. *"Saùde!"*

They left the radio on. The signal would help Grimaldi and McCarter locate the area. If anyone had monitored the brief conversation, they would have heard one voice say he wanted a beer and another guy introduce himself as "Moreira" and tell the thirsty fellow the Portuguese equivalent of "Cheers." An odd conversation, but they hoped no one would suspect these were passwords and signals.

"Okay," Bolan began. "Let's get ready. The gunships will arrive in approximately thirty minutes, and we'd better be ready to move when they get here."

The Stony man soldiers planned their strategy and moved into position. They broke into two-man teams. The Able Team and Phoenix Force members had considerable experience working together, so Lyons and Blancanales moved to the rim of the jungle near the west wall of the fortress. Encizo and James covered the east wall. Bolan and Manning took their positions by the north side of the base.

They waited. Minutes seemed to crawl by.

Activity burst into life within the fortress. The nets above the compound were hastily pulled away. The camouflage covers had been set up like giant curtains and parted by guidelines and pulleys. Thunder rumbled within the base. Bolan and the other veterans of Vietnam immediately recognized the sound of helicopter rotor blades. The memories associated with choppers in Nam were too vivid to be forgotten, and the sound would be with them the rest of their lives.

The choppers rose from the base, small and sleek aircraft with pointed snouts, resembling flying sharks. Bolan thought the helicopters looked vaguely familiar. Then it struck him—the choppers were smaller versions of a HueyCobra. Another Silva invention. The guy seemed to think smaller was better.

Two craft headed south. Another pair rose as soon as the first cleared the area. All four moved in the same direction. Although small, the choppers were equipped with machine-gun mounts and aerial rockets. Probably similar to the arsenal of a Cobra, Bolan guessed, but the smaller craft would only be able to carry less than half the number of rockets hauled by the larger craft. Still, it was a lot of firepower.

"They must have picked up McCarter and Grimaldi on radar," Bolan whispered as he watched the helicopters vanish beyond the treetops.

"Can we warn them with the radio?" Manning asked tensely.

"They'll know in a matter of seconds anyway. Our guys in the sky are on their own. So are we if they can't get past those four flying killers."

CHAPTER THIRTY-THREE

"Holy shit," Jack Grimaldi rasped when he saw the enemy choppers. "They've sent a welcoming committee!"

"Wonderful," Gadgets Schwarz moaned as he peered over the pilot's shoulder and gazed through the windscreen. "Can we take them?"

"Do we have a choice? Get strapped in and prepare for a real roller-coaster ride."

Grimaldi realized they were in trouble. His gunship was a Bell UH-1D, bigger and heavier than the enemy copters. The smaller craft would be faster and able to maneuver better than the Bell. The only advantage Grimaldi had was the fact he was armed with machine guns and rockets, as well, and the Bell had a larger arsenal than any single Silva chopper. The superior numbers of the enemy made that advantage questionable.

Of course, David McCarter piloted another Bell UH-1D. The odds were two against one. Both the British ace and Grimaldi were superb chopper jockeys. It was doubtful the mercenaries flying the other rigs had a fragment of their skill or experience. Grimaldi decided to find out. The enemy was still out of range, but he triggered a short burst of machine guns mounted at the nose of the Bell.

The smaller helicopters scattered and returned fire, the bullets falling far short of their mark. One merc pilot launched a rocket. It streaked through the sky, exhausted energy and plunged to the jungle below. Whoever they were, they had little if any actual combat experience. That was another plus on the side of the Stony Man warriors.

One enemy pilot decided on the bold approach. He hit the throttle and charged, firing his machine gun as he attacked Grimaldi's craft. The Stony Man fly-boy turned the Bell swiftly to present the side of his chopper to the opponent. Bullets raked the fuselage. Grimaldi hoped the Bell was more sturdy than the enemy's lightweight craft. He quickly completed the turn and opened fire with his own guns.

Bullets smashed the windscreen of the aggressive copter. The pilot was cut to ribbons at his controls, and the aircraft spun out of control, performing an awkward series of circles before it smashed into the rain forest. The fuel tank exploded on impact, and the blast erupted beneath the battling choppers still in the sky.

Grimaldi gambled that the fallen copter would startle and distract the remaining opponents. He immediately rushed the nearest chopper, firing his guns. Slugs hammered the body of the smaller craft, but the pilot swung the nose around and returned fire. Grimaldi had already climbed higher into the sky, anticipating the enemy's response, and locked on target before firing a rocket.

The projectile slashed a white line across the sky and slammed into the upper carriage of its target. Flaming debris descended to the treetops like some ghastly rain from Hell.

McCARTER CONTINUED to head north as if trying to slip past the enemy. One aircraft gave chase, confident he could outrun the slower, heavier Bell. The enemy pilot fired a salvo of machine-gun rounds and struck the fuselage of the Briton's Bell.

"My God!" Yakov Katzenelenbogen exclaimed as he huddled as low as his seat belt and harness strap permitted. "I hate flying, and I hate being shot at when I'm flying even more."

"Try not to think about it!" McCarter shouted back his advice as he raised the Bell and turned in the air sharply.

The Briton executed this maneuver because he guessed the enemy would launch a rocket in an effort to finish off the Bell. His assumption proved correct. The pilot fired a missile too soon. The projectile sizzled beneath the landing gear of McCarter's helicopter. The Briton was glad the enemy wasn't armed with heat-seeking missiles, or the trick wouldn't have worked.

He turned to point the nose of his Bell at the aggressor and fired his machine guns. Slugs shattered the window by the pilot and tore into his face. More bullets struck the controls and ricocheted within the copter. The pilot didn't have a chance. Wounded and unconscious from massive shock, he slumped in his seat as the helicopter tumbled out of control to crash to the earth.

Machine-gun fire rattled out a metallic tune of destruction. The remaining enemy aircraft blasted McCarter's gunship with a long burst. Bullets raked the tail pylon, broke the horizontal stabilizer and damaged the tail rotor. McCarter worked the controls, but the gunship began to whirl in wild circles.

Grimaldi launched another rocket and scored a hit broadside before the copter could attempt to finish off McCarter's chopper. Silva's warbird exploded in a shower of metal parts and burning fuel. However,

Grimaldi watched McCarter's gunship swirl in an uncontrolled pattern, unable to assist the fellow Stony Man pilot.

"Brace yourself!" McCarter called out to Katz. "We're going down, mate!"

"Going down?" the Israeli repeated.

"Rather fast," the Briton explained through clenched teeth as he fought to adopt a hover.

The gunship fell. The rotor blade helped slow the descent, but the helicopter increased speed as it plunged to the treetops. It hit the branches, limbs cracking under the massive weight. The helicopter crashed through the branches to land heavily on the ground.

"There," McCarter began with a sigh of relief, "we landed."

GRIMALDI HEADED for Silva's stronghold. From his position in the sky, the pilot clearly saw the compound. Without the nets to block his view, he scoped the buildings, motor pool and airfield within the brick walls. He was astonished by the size of the base and the amount of equipment below. The motor pool contained three trucks, four Land Rovers and two odd-looking armored vehicles. Two helicopters remained at the airfield, Boeing-Vertol CH-47 choppers, better known as Chinooks.

The workhorse of helicopters, the Chinook could carry in excess of seven thousand pounds more than one hundred miles without refueling. So large it required two rotor blades, a Chinook could serve as a transport craft and carry forty-four passengers. Grimaldi had a pretty good idea how Silva had managed to haul in the manpower and construction materials for the base.

The enemy had been busy. The main house was a mansion, two stories high and made of brick with a comou-painted roof. Four billets were also located at the base. Each was large enough to house thirty to fifty troops. Sandbags formed bunkers near the barracks. Dozens of uniformed figures raced about the parade field below, many swinging assault rifles toward the Bell chopper. Other mercs were positioned along a catwalk at the top of the protective walls.

"This is it, fellas," Grimaldi said as a hard, cold ball formed in his stomach. "Time to rock 'n' roll."

He triggered the machine guns and sprayed the mercenaries with twin streams of .30-caliber rounds. Bodies toppled, torn by high-velocity slugs. Survivors of the first run dashed for cover. Some returned fire, but Grimaldi kept the chopper beyond effective range. It was easier to fire down at a target than to shoot at one two thousand feet in the air.

Grimaldi picked his targets with care. The Chinooks wouldn't be able to present a threat without announcing they were about to lift off. The rotor blades were motionless, so Grimaldi didn't have to worry about the big helicopters at the moment. Instead, he launched rockets into one of the barracks. Two missiles exploded and blasted the wooden structure to pieces.

Another volley of rounds slashed more mercenary gunmen and sent corpses sprawling across the parade field. Grimaldi was creating a superb distraction for Bolan's unit to launch their attack on foot.

THE EXECUTIONER and Manning jogged from the jungle. The Canadian sharpshooter raised his M-16 and squeezed off a short burst. The silencer-equipped assault rifle coughed three muffled rounds and nailed a sentry in the chest. The guard convulsed from the impacts of the trio of 5.56 mm slugs and fell from the top of the wall.

Bolan stood watch as Manning moved to the gate and placed a prepared charge of C-4 plastique by the thick wooden doors. The demolitions expert set the timer and moved away from the gate. A sentry peered down at the Stony Man duo and the Executioner's Beretta responded with a blast of muffled 9 mm projectiles. The sentry's head recoiled as parabellums knifed through it.

Bolan and Manning hustled from the gate and took cover along the wall. The C-4 exploded and blew the doors apart as if they were made of cardboard.

Moments later they heard Grimaldi fire another rocket and score a hit with one of the Chinooks. The big chopper exploded in a shower of flying metal, and sprayed flaming fuel across the airfield. Bolan and Manning watched the Bell gunship swing in a semicircle to launch two more rockets at the motor pool. The three trucks and four Land Rovers burst apart into fiery wreckage.

Bolan and Manning took advantage of the distraction and dashed through the gates. They sprinted for the main house as mercenaries emerged, assault rifles in hand. The Executioner and the Canadian opened fire before the enemy could take aim. Uniformed mercs collapsed as the commandos continued on. Bolan holstered his 93-R and unslung his M-16. He pulled back the charging handle and chambered the first round.

MERCENARIES AT THE east wing of the fortress were startled to discover Rafael Encizo and Calvin James. The Phoenix Force pair charged through a crudely made opening in the wall and fired on a trio of unprepared mercs, who had thought the explosions were caused by rockets launched by the gunship. They didn't expect a breach in the wall.

The opposition fell to the dust in a twitching, drying heap as the Phoenix warriors moved to cover by a stack of bricks kept for the purpose of repairing walls. They scanned the area, taking in the scene. Fires burned from Grimaldi's rocket attacks. Many dead mercs already lay on the grounds, and others scrambled in panic.

However, not all hired troops were responding in a mindless manner. Three mercenaries emerged from a barracks and hauled an antiaircraft gun to a bunker for shelter. The big 20 mm cannon was designed to launch shells far distances with great accuracy. The mercs with assault rifles might not be able to score an accurate strike against the Bell chopper, but the antiaircraft gun was a genuine threat to Grimaldi.

James quickly judged the distance, aimed his M-16 and triggered the M-203 attached to the underside of the barrel. The 40 mm shell sailed from the muzzle of the launcher and landed in the center of the sandbag bunker. The explosion took out the antiaircraft crew and transformed their weapon into a twisted piece of useless junk.

LYONS AND BLANCANALES entered the compound from the west wall. Three mercenaries still had their backs turned to the gap in the barrier, their attention fixed on the invading helicopter. One of them held a rocket launcher similar to a Soviet RPG. The guy braced it across a shoulder and knelt, weapon aimed at the gunship.

Lyons rushed forward and smashed the heavy barrel of his M-971 into the guy with the rocket launcher. Bone cracked and the man slumped to the ground, the unfired launcher landing beside him. Another merc whirled, startled by the sudden appearance of the commandos. Blancanales quickly whipped a rifle buttstroke to the second trooper's temple, rendering him unconscious.

The third hardman pivoted, a submachine gun in his fists. Lyons slapped the MG across the barrel of the merc's weapon, deflecting the aim of the subgun as the mercenary opened fire. Bullets tore harmlessly into the ground, and Lyons slashed the toughened end of his hand across the gunman's throat. The guy dropped his weapon and staggered backward, hands clutched to his throat, eyes wide open in terror. The karate stroke had crushed the merc's windpipe. He was choking as he lost consciousness and slumped to the ground.

Blancanales scooped up the discarded rocket launcher and braced it across his shoulder. He peered through the elevated sights and drew a bead on the nearest barracks. The Able Team pro fired the weapon and watched the projectile streak across the parade field. The warhead exploded, blasting out a wall and knocking down the roof on the mercs inside.

Surviving soldiers of Silva's private army decided it would be suicide to remain in the shattered building. They swarmed from the billets, weapons blasting in all directions. Lyons hastily unfolded the bipod to the M-971 and dropped to a prone position, the butt of the machine gun braced against his shoulder. Blancanales helped feed the ammunition chain into the breech of the weapon.

Lyons opened fire. The machine gun snarled a continuous volley of 7.62 rounds, and bodies fell so fast that the Able Team captain wasn't sure how many opponents he took out. Blancanales added bursts of 5.56 mm to the deadly hail of bullets. A few mercs managed to retreat back to the billets. Apparently they figured even a wrecked building was better cover than none at all.

However, there was no place to hide. Blancanales triggered the M-203 attachment to his M-16 and fired a 40 mm grenade into the smashed barracks. The shell exploded and destroyed what remained of the structure. The Able Team pair looked at the destruction. It was a shocking sight, even for veteran warriors.

Suddenly two men climbed from a window of the main house. Lyons and Blancanales didn't recognize Rico Gomez and Guillermo Aguilar. The representatives of the cocaine cartels had decided the best chance of survival was to slip out of the house, find a hiding place and escape while the raiders and Silva's mercenaries were busy fighting with each other.

The Able Team commandos spotted the two men. They didn't appear to be regular grunts because they were dressed in suit trousers and dress shirts. Blancanales fired a salvo of M-16 rounds at their feet. The pair stopped abruptly. Gomez whirled and pointed his Glock 9 mm pistol at the Able Team pair.

Another burst of 5.56 mm slugs ripped into the Colombian's chest. He landed on his back, a diagonal line of bullet holes stitched across his shirtfront. Aguilar dropped on his belly next to his slain companion. He realized he was pitted against men far better armed than he. Aguilar tossed away his SIG-Sauer autoloader and shoved the briefcase he carried across the ground toward the warriors.

"Keep your hands in view!" Lyons warned as he advanced.

"English?" Aguilar looked up with surprise. "I speak your language, mister. I'm glad you are here. Silva kidnapped me—"

"Uh-huh," Lyons snorted. "I bet. Get up. Slowly."

Aguilar started to rise. His foot seemed to slip, and he fell to one knee. The Bolivian dropped his hands to his leg as if trying to rub the bruised knee. Blancanales closed in and warned Aguilar to keep his hands raised.

"Look," the Bolivian said through clenched teeth, his face screwed into an expression of pain, "I'm not part of this. Look in that briefcase. You'll find proof that I am innocent."

"Check it," Lyons told Blancanales, but kept his MP-5 subgun pointed at Aguilar. "And you, get up!"

"Sure," Aguilar said, nodding nervously as he slid his hand down to the .25-caliber Raven in an ankle holster.

He suddenly threw himself sideways and thrust his arm at Lyons, the tiny pistol in his fist. He hoped the tactic would catch the man off guard and allow him to pump two or three slugs into the big gringo's face before the mysterious gunman could adjust the aim of his weapon.

The trick didn't even come close to working. Lyons fired the Heckler & Koch subgun the instant Aguilar made his move. Parabellums slammed into the Bolivian's upper chest, and two 9 mm rounds smashed through his upper teeth and the bridge of his nose. Aguilar flopped onto his back, pistol still clenched in his fist.

"Dumb ass," Lyons muttered and shook his head.

"Money," Blancanales announced as he jimmied open the briefcase. Bills of different currencies were stacked inside the valise, as well as a few gold coins. "It's just a case full of money. What should I do with it?" Blancanales asked.

"Leave it with these two," Lyons replied. "Money was probably the reason they threw in with Silva. In a sense they died for it, so let them have it until somebody else comes along."

Blancanales nodded and shoved the valise next to Aguilar's corpse.

CHAPTER THIRTY-FOUR

"Venha aqui!" João Silva shouted to a pair of mercenaries as he stood outside the mansion surveying the devastation.

The mercs obeyed the order and hurried to their boss. The arms merchant felt as if he were staring at Hell itself. The barracks and airfield were destroyed. Every vehicle in the motor pool was crushed except for the two miniature tanks. Fires raged throughout the base, and the majority of his mercenary force was already dead or otherwise taken out by the invaders.

Who was attacking the base? Silva glimpsed the gunship circling the compound, picking targets and firing machine guns and rockets. Gunshots and explosions elsewhere within the base revealed that enemy ground forces were also at work. Silva scanned the parade field, hoping to see slain invaders among the corpses. Everybody seemed to be clad in the uniform of his security forces.

"We're being cut to pieces, Mr. Silva," one of the mercs declared. His face was pale, and he was obviously close to panic.

"Get the fire extinguishers and put out the blaze so I can get to a tank," Silva commanded. "Do either of you have experience with the vehicle?"

They shook their heads. He clucked his tongue with disgust. Silva would have to handle the tank himself. The arms merchant didn't know what had happened to Gomez, Aguilar or Cazazo. And he didn't care. The cartel representatives weren't fighting men, and he didn't expect them to be much use in combat. Cazazo talked as if he were a courageous fighter and a master strategist, but Silva no longer had any faith in the terrorist.

They had all failed him, Silva thought bitterly. His hired mercenaries didn't seem to be faring any better than his forces abroad had. Damn cowards and idiots. Silva pulled on a pair of gloves as he watched the mercs spray the motor pool fire with white foam. There was no one he could rely on now but himself.

He marched through dense smoke to the nearest minitank, covering his nose and mouth with a sleeve as he opened the hatch. He climbed into the seat and locked himself in. Surrounded by the steel armor and bulletproof plastic shields, the Brazilian felt protected. He also had fearsome firepower at his command. The tank had recently been equipped with a short-range cannon, as well as twin machine guns in the turret.

"If I'm going to die, I'll take some of these bastards with me," Silva vowed as he started the engine.

Explosions erupted within the mansion, windows blowing apart at both ends of the building. The enemy had invaded Silva's head shed. The place was more his home than the ultraexpensive ranch house he owned in São Paulo.

"Damn you!" Silva exclaimed as he punched the trigger button for the cannon.

A 30 mm shell burst from the stubby barrel, drilling into the second story at the front of the house. The explosion blew off part of the roof and took out a corner of the brick building. Silva fired another round and blasted a wall beneath the first explosion, laughing as he watched brick tumble from the structure.

"That ought to give them something to think about at that part of the house," Silva muttered as he pushed the tank into drive position. "Now let's deal with the other scum."

The mercenaries at the motor pool fled the area. They decided Silva had lost his mind—the crazy man was attacking his own house.

The tank rolled toward the mansion, Silva guiding the vehicle toward the French doors to his den.

"WHAT THE HELL was that?" James wondered aloud when he heard the monstrous crash of glass and the rumble of machinery in the next room.

"I'm not sure I want to know," Encizo replied as he clutched the micro-Uzi tighter in his fists.

The Phoenix Force pair had hit the rear of the house as Bolan and Manning entered from the front. Grenades were used to clear the way before crossing thresholds. James and Encizo had encountered a few mercenary soldiers in the house, but the enemy had been stunned by the concussion grenades and presented little resistance.

However, something else awaited them in the room next door. The pair crept closer to the entrance of the den. The growl of engines and smell of gasoline surprised them. Encizo guessed one of the Land Rovers had gone out of control and crashed into the mansion. James ventured forward and peered inside to see a small tank barreling through the room.

"Oh, shit!"

James jumped back and fired his Uzi at the tank. Bullets sparked on metal and ricocheted against the shatter-proof plastic dome. Encizo also fired at the mechanical monster, concentrating his fire on the dome, aware that the term *bulletproof* was relative. Any surface could be penetrated by a projectile if the material was subjected to enough molecular stress by repeated pounding.

The 9 mm parabellum rounds didn't seem to be troubling the odd little tank. James had left his M-16 outside because the rifle was awkward in close quarters. The Uzi had seemed a better choice for inside the house. But the 5.56 mm ammunition wouldn't be any more successful against a tank than 9 mm, and James couldn't use the grenade launcher when they were so close to the armored vehicle.

The tank continued to advance. The smiling face of João Silva stared from the transparent dome. He squeezed the triggers to the machine guns, and a steady stream of rounds blazed from the barrels. James and Encizo leaped away from the vehicle and dived to the floor. Bullets punched two dozen holes in the walls in a matter of seconds. Silva's smile faded as he worked the turret to adjust the aim. His quarry were too low and beneath the line of fire.

Encizo rolled to a corner and reached for a grenade on his belt. His hand froze in place. Maybe an M-26 fragmentation device would damage the tank, but it would just roll off the metal and plastic curves of the machine. The Cuban would be more apt to blow himself up than stop the tank.

James jogged backward down the corridor, firing his Uzi machine pistol on the run. Silva swung the guns of his turret toward the African-American. James leaped for shelter behind a long leather sofa an instant before another salvo of machine-gun fire ripped across the den.

Bullets smashed into walls and burrowed into the thick cushions of the furniture.

Silva wasn't certain if he hit his prey or not, but it didn't matter. He could run the tank right over the sofa and crush it along with the gunman using the couch for cover.

Encizo quickly stripped off his fatigue field jacket and ran to the rear of the miniature tank. He had stuck two M-26 grenades in the cargo pockets of the jacket. The Cuban had a plan, and he would only have one chance to see if it worked. He jumped onto the back plate of the tank and quickly slung the jacket over the plastic dome.

Silva shouted something as the cloth suddenly blocked his view. Encizo barely heard the voice through the shatter-proof dome. With the jacket temporarily secured in place, the Phoenix fighter reached into a pocket and yanked the pins from the grenades inside, then leaped from the back of the tank.

"What the hell did you...?" James began as he rose, unharmed from behind the sofa.

"Run!" Encizo shouted, and bolted for the archway that had formerly held the French doors.

Both men dashed outside, threw themselves to the ground and covered their heads a split second before the first grenade exploded. The second went off a moment later. Debris spewed from the archway and pelted the commandos.

Encizo got to his feet first. He stared at the den. The tank had run into a wall and was still rolling, gradually pushing its way into the plaster and foundation. Dust swirled within the room, but the Cuban saw that the dome was missing from the vehicle. The grenades had blasted it to bits... along with João Silva's head.

BOLAN PUSHED BACK the rubble and spit out a mouthful of dust. A wall had crashed down on the Executioner and Gary Manning. The unexpected cannon shell fired by Silva had knocked plaster and brick onto the Stony Man warriors.

Bolan grit his teeth as the pain in his left arm commanded more attention than the assorted bruises suffered in the incident. He flexed his fingers, and was relieved to discover that his hand wasn't broken. Then he noticed the inert figure of Gary Manning.

The warrior knelt beside the big Canadian and placed two fingers to Manning's neck. He found a pulse, which was strong. A lump on the Phoenix pro's skull revealed he had been hit by a brick when the wall caved in. It was hard to tell if the man had sustained serious injury.

The Executioner glanced about the hall. Debris littered the area, and sunlight streaked in through gaps in the walls. He wondered what had happened. Someone must have set off a bomb. He would find out later. For now he had to stay alive and complete the mission.

A figure appeared at the end of the hallway. Bolan's hand reached for the 93-R in shoulder leather, but a voice ordered him to freeze. The shape moved closer, and Bolan saw a pistol in the man's fist. He also recognized a lean, cruel face and the trademark trench knife sheathed on the guy's hip.

"El Cuchillo," Bolan remarked. "I thought you would have left before we could hit this place."

Ramon Cazazo smiled as he approached, his Browning automatic still pointed at Bolan. "You knew about my involvement?" the terrorist asked in flawless English.

"You left an impression on a couple of your victims. Your friend Arashi had a photo of you two, as well."

Cazazo's face seemed to become stiff. "Arashi is dead?"

"Killed in a sword duel. He had enough guts to fight with cold steel. I thought you were supposed to be a blade man, too."

"I have my moments. Who are you? You're American, and you're carrying an interesting choice of weapons. Looks like a Beretta and one of those big .44 Magnum pistols. Perhaps the Executioner isn't dead after all."

"Perhaps not. You want to go for it?" Bolan asked, trying to sound casual in a situation that was filled with tension. "Squeeze the trigger. It'll be all over. Of course, you wouldn't be talking if that was what you wanted."

"I always wondered how good you really were, Executioner. Everyone knows you're an expert with firearms and explosives, but I always suspected a man like you wouldn't be much without his guns and grenades."

"I've got a knife. Interested in putting your reputation on the line instead of running off at the mouth?"

"Get rid of the guns," the terrorist ordered. "Very slowly. Use the thumb and forefinger to draw the gun by the butt. No tricks. I'd rather kill you with my blade, but I'll use a bullet if I have to."

Bolan followed instructions and drew the pistols, one at a time, and dropped them to the floor. Cazazo nodded and gestured for the warrior to move closer. He backed up as he led the Executioner away from the weapons. The spacious hall left ample room for an arena. Cazazo drew his trench knife. Sunlight gleamed along the double-edged blade. The brass-knuckle hilt formed a cestus around the terrorist's fist.

The Executioner unsheathed his Ka-bar. The combat Bowie knife wasn't as fancy as El Cuchillo's weapon. The blade was a few inches shorter and the handle wasn't equipped with knuckle dusters.

Cazazo was amused. The knife was standard for U.S. military personnel, he realized, which probably meant the Executioner was an amateur with a blade.

"I guess we're both legends," Cazazo remarked as he thrust the Browning pistol into his belt. "One of those legends ends to—"

Bolan wasn't going to waste time letting his enemy complete his cute little speech. The gun was no longer a threat, so the Executioner attacked. Cazazo hissed and delivered a thrust to meet the warrior's lunge. The Executioner anticipated the move, and hoped to draw out his opponent. He dodged the knife thrust and delivered a karate snap-kick to the terrorist's gut.

El Cuchillo doubled up with a groan. Bolan slashed his combat knife at the side of the guy's neck, hoping to cut the carotid artery. Cazazo suddenly whirled and struck out with his own blade. The sharp steel sliced the warrior's sleeve and bit into his forearm.

Bolan retreated. Cazazo followed his attack with a roundhouse kick to the Executioner's left side, nearly knocking the warrior off balance. El Cuchillo swung his trench-knife fist and punched Bolan in the left triceps with the brass knuckles.

The terrorist knew he had him. He feinted with the trench knife and hooked another kick to the warrior's belly. Bolan doubled up and gasped as his breath seemed to freeze inside his lungs. El Cuchillo was almost disappointed. He had hoped the famous Executioner would be more of a challenge. The terrorist prepared to plunge his knife into his opponent's kidney.

The warrior suddenly braced himself on his right fist, Ka-bar still firmly in his grasp, and lashed out with his left leg. The "iron broom" technique clipped El Cuchillo across the ankles. The terrorist was literally swept off his feet and crashed to the floor. He rolled away from Bolan, no longer underestimating his opponent. Both men got to their feet.

"Not bad, Executioner," Cazazo admitted as they squared off once more.

El Cuchillo attacked. His style was similar to fencing techniques, Bolan noticed as he danced away from the trench knife. Cazazo's double-edged blade was designed for thrusts more than cuts. Bolan avoided the short stabbing motions and slashed his Bowie at the guy's wrist to try to disarm him. The blades clashed together, and El Cuchillo shot a right hook to Bolan's jaw.

The Executioner staggered from the punch. Cazazo lunged toward the warrior's heart with the trench knife. He sidestepped the attack, and Cazazo's momentum carried him past his adversary. The Executioner swung a hook kick to the small of Cazazo's back and sent the terrorist hurtling face-first into a wall.

El Cuchillo whirled and slashed wildly to keep Bolan at bay. His other hand grabbed the Browning in his belt. So much for a fair fight. Cazazo drew the pistol, but Bolan's boot slammed into the terrorist's wrist. Bone popped, and the gun fell from numb fingers. Cazazo immediately lunged and tried to stab his blade in the warrior's throat.

Bolan weaved and ducked under the attack. He drove his own knife into Cazazo's solar plexus. The force of the lunge drove the terrorist back into the wall. Bolan's right shoulder shoved under Cazazo's extended arm as he jammed his Ka-bar deeper. Bolan heard an ugly death rattle and the sound of the trench knife clattering on the floor.

The Executioner left the knife in the corpse and pushed away from Cazazo. He looked at the infamous terrorist as he slid to the floor. Death of a legend? Bolan knew better. The Executioner and El Cuchillo were just men. The terrorist was dead. That put an end to a bloody and vicious career. Cazazo had paid for lives taken in the past, and he would take no more in the future. That was good enough for Bolan.

DAVID MCCARTER and Yakov Katzenelenbogen had some trouble finding their way to the fortress. When they arrived, the battle was over. A handful of surviving mercenaries had been rounded up and secured with riot cuffs. Manning had regained consciousness and suffered nothing worse than a headache and mild scalp wound.

"I wondered what happened to you two," Grimaldi said. He had landed his gunship on the parade field and stood near the craft. "Saw you go down. You both okay?"

"Aside from nearly having a heart attack," Katz said sourly. "Looks like you've got everything taken care of here."

"And we bloody well missed it," McCarter complained bitterly. "Where's Silva? Manage to take him alive?"

"What's left of him is still inside his toy tank," Encizo answered. "Bet it takes out another wall before it runs out of fuel."

"That's okay," James said. "We found some records of Silva's involvement with the terrorist conspiracy. That tank can bring down the whole house. We got all the evidence we need to make the President and the Brazilian authorities happy."

"What do we do with them?" Blancanales inquired as he tilted his head toward the prisoners.

"Leave them," Mack Bolan replied. "We'll call Guimarães and tell him to come pick them up. He can consider it compensation for losing one of the choppers he lent us."

"The commodore will take credit for this," Lyons said with disgust. "He'll come across as a hero before this is over, and they'll probably promote him to admiral."

"Cheer up," Schwarz urged with a grin. "We know what really happened. That's what counts."

"What counts is we completed the mission and put an end to the conspiracy of international environmental terrorism," the Executioner told them. "We're all still alive and none of us got any injuries that won't heal. That, my friends, is worth more than ticker-tape parades and medals."

"Well, I got the taxi ready," Grimaldi announced. "Let's go home."

They climbed into the Bell UH-1D. The chopper was large enough to carry fourteen passengers, more than enough room for the ten Stony Man commandos. Grimaldi fired up the aircraft, lifting his companions from the earth once more.

They knew Bolan was right. Success and survival was better than parades and medals. Besides, no medals were given for carrying out justice.

**America's most classified
weapon is back in**

**DON PENDLETON'S
MACK BOLAN**

The hellfire warriors of Stony Man—Mack Bolan, Able Team and Phoenix Force—comprise an ultrasecret, superelite operations force dispatched when crisis calls for a lightning strike against enemies of society.

This time their mission is to shut down a South American drug pipeline. The President wants a scorched earth operation: destroy the pipeline end to end. Fast. The stakes are life and death. Stony Man wouldn't have it any other way.

Available in July at your favorite retail outlet.

Or order your copy now by sending your name, address, zip or postal code, along with a check or money order for $4.99 (please do not send cash), plus 75¢ postage and handling ($1.00 in Canada), payable to Gold Eagle Books, to:

In the U.S.
Gold Eagle Books
3010 Walden Avenue
P.O. Box 1325
Buffalo, NY 14269-1325

In Canada
Gold Eagle Books
P.O. Box 609
Fort Erie, Ontario
L2A 5X3

Please specify book title with your order.
Canadian residents add applicable federal and provincial taxes.

SM7

A Western crime alliance threatens Russia's new freedom

DON PENDLETON's MACK BOLAN®

ONSLAUGHT

The Brotherhood—an alliance between a North American Mafia family and a South American drug cartel—could spell doom for a newly free Russia. Fearing that a sudden crime wave might shift the balance of power back to Communism, the U.S. President sends in the man who represents ultimate justice, within or beyond the law. Only the Executioner can deliver.

Available in May at your favorite retail outlet, or order your copy now by sending your name, address, zip or postal code, along with a check or money order (please do not send cash) for $4.99, plus 75¢ postage and handling ($1.00 in Canada), payable to Gold Eagle Books to:

In the U.S.	In Canada
Gold Eagle Books	Gold Eagle Books
3010 Walden Avenue	P.O. Box 609
P.O. Box 1325	Fort Erie, Ontario
Buffalo, NY 14269-1325	L2A 5X3

Please specify book title with your order.
Canadian residents add applicable federal and provincial taxes.

SB31

**A new age of terrorism
calls for a new breed of hero**

NOMAD

SMART BOMB
DAVID ALEXANDER

**Code name: Nomad. He is the supreme fighting
machine, a new breed of elite commando
whose specialty is battling 21st-century
techno-terrorism with bare-knuckle combat
skills and state-of-the-art weapons.**

**Desperately racing against a lethal countdown,
Nomad tracks a rogue weapons expert but runs
into a trap. He comes face-to-face with his
hated nemesis in a deadly contest—a contest in
which the odds are stacked against him.**

Available in April at your favorite retail outlet, or order your copy now by sending your name, address, zip or postal code, along with a check or money order (please do not send cash) for $4.99, plus 75¢ postage and handling ($1.00 in Canada), payable to Gold Eagle Books, to:

In the U.S.	In Canada
Gold Eagle Books	Gold Eagle Books
3010 Walden Avenue	P.O. Box 609
P.O. Box 1325	Fort Erie, Ontario
Buffalo, NY 14269-1325	L2A 5X3

Please specify book title with your order.
Canadian residents add applicable federal and provincial taxes.

NOMAD3

Omega Force is caught dead center in a brutal Middle East war in the next episode of

by PATRICK F. ROGERS

In Book 2: **ZERO HOUR**, the Omega Force is dispatched on a search-and-destroy mission to eliminate enemies of the U.S. seeking revenge for Iraq's defeat in the Gulf—enemies who will use any means necessary to trigger a full-scale war.

With capabilities unmatched by any other paramilitary organization in the world, Omega Force is a special ready-reaction antiterrorist strike force composed of the best commandos and equipment the military has to offer.

Available in **June** at your favorite retail outlet. To order your copy now of Book 2: **ZERO HOUR** or Book 1: **WAR MACHINE**, please send your name, address, zip or postal code, along with a check or money order (please do not send cash) for $3.50 for each book ordered, plus 75¢ postage and handling ($1.00 in Canada), payable to Gold Eagle Books, to:

In the U.S.
Gold Eagle Books
3010 Walden Avenue
P.O. Box 1325
Buffalo, NY 14269-1325

In Canada
Gold Eagle Books
P.O. Box 609
Fort Erie, Ontario
L2A 5X3

Please specify book title(s) with your order.
Canadian residents add applicable federal and provincial taxes.

Meet Jake Strait—a modern-day bounty hunter in the ruthless, anything-goes world of 2031.

JAKE STRAIT
BOGEYMAN

by FRANK RICH

Jake Strait is a licensed enforcer in a world gone mad—a world where suburbs are guarded and farmlands are garrisoned around a city of evil.

In Book 1: **AVENGING ANGEL,** Jake Strait is caught in a maze of political deceit that will drench the city in a shower of spilled blood.

AVENGING ANGEL, Book 1 of this four-volume miniseries, hits the retail stands in May, or order your copy now by sending your name, address, zip or postal code, along with a check or money order (please do not send cash) for $3.50, plus 75¢ postage and handling ($1.00 in Canada), payable to Gold Eagle Books, to:

In the U.S.	In Canada
Gold Eagle Books	Gold Eagle Books
3010 Walden Avenue	P.O. Box 609
P.O. Box 1325	Fort Erie, Ontario
Buffalo, NY 14269-1325	L2A 5X3

Please specify book title with your order.
Canadian residents add applicable federal and provincial taxes.

JS1

The year is 2030 and the world is in a state of political and territorial unrest. The Peacekeepers, an elite military force, will not negotiate for peace—they're ready to impose it with the ultimate in 21st-century weaponry.

2030
by MICHAEL KASNER

Introducing the follow-up miniseries to the WARKEEP 2030 title published in November 1992.

In Book 1: **KILLING FIELDS**, the Peacekeepers join forces with spear-throwing Zulus as violence erupts in black-ruled South Africa—violence backed by money, fanaticism and four neutron bombs.

KILLING FIELDS, Book 1 of this three-volume miniseries, hits the retail stands in March, or order your copy now by sending your name, address, zip or postal code, along with a check or money order (please do not send cash) for $3.50, plus 75¢ postage and handling ($1.00 in Canada), payable to Gold Eagle Books, to:

In the U.S.	In Canada
Gold Eagle Books	Gold Eagle Books
3010 Walden Avenue	P.O. Box 609
P.O. Box 1325	Fort Erie, Ontario
Buffalo, NY 14269-1325	L2A 5X3

Please specify book title with your order.
Canadian residents add applicable federal and provincial taxes.

WK2